THE WRONG HUSBAND

HILARY KINGSLEY

WP
Wrate's Publishing

First published in 2025 by Wrate's Publishing

ISBN 978-1-0686952-9-2

Typeset and Edited by Wrate's Editing Services

www.wrateseditingservices.co.uk

Cover design by Rachel Middleton

A CIP catalogue record for this book is available from the British Library.

For Anna, Dan and Hatty

'Just, if the Lord send me no husband, for the which blessing I am at Him upon my knees every morning and evening.'

Beatrice, Much Ado About Nothing, Act II, scene I.

1

WHY THE HELL had she thought this would be a good idea?

She bloody hated giving parties. The planning, the lists, the checking, the worrying. This one would be the last, she decided, then grabbed her sleeping husband's shoulder and shook him to stop him snoring.

'This time tomorrow, it'll be over,' Pen consoled herself, as she turned on one side, then the other.

By early morning, old, cold Batts Farm was warming up. Caterer John Hardwick had already arrived in his van and had been met by Mrs Gibbs, the house's doughty chatelaine, in the grassy area next to the house. Years ago, the family called it their tennis court and Tom and Bella used to bat balls about there. No white lines, no net, lots of shouting and giggling. As they grew up, Tom switched to proper courts and Bella decided she had better things to do. Like shopping and seeing friends. Now it was the Batts Farm car park.

Today a January frost covered the ground and, Pen thought, when a glint of sun caught it, it was as if handfuls of diamonds had been sprinkled on it. Car tyres would soon be churning it black. Mrs Gibbs – or 'Mrs G' as she was known – was to be a *guest,* not a helper. Pen had emphasised this when telling her about the 'Knighthood Party'. Guest or not, Mrs G clearly felt it her duty to supervise guest arrivals. She'd come early from her bungalow in wellington boots and an ancient green duffle coat, its hood up. Puffs of wire wool hair were escaping and flapping in the breeze. She pulled off a knitted glove to tuck them back. Later, she would almost certainly be popping in and out of the kitchen to check there were no problems with the food or drinks, annoying John Hardwick – he was never just John – and amusing the waiters.

In the house, John Hardwick slipped the straps of his blue-and-white-striped apron around his waist and tied them carefully at the front while surveying the kitchen work tops, familiarising himself with the Aga cooker and the general lay out. He always did this. He spooned Colombian coffee into the filter of the percolator and switched it on. Then he pulled a list from his pocket and checked that the ordered glasses, plates, cutlery, serving trays and starched tablecloths were present and correct. His two hefty helpers, big Doug and fairly big Joe, appeared on cue, lit log fires and arranged the hired pedestal tables and gold-painted dining chairs in the two adjoining reception rooms.

They brought in food from John's van, helped by a couple of the waiters who'd strolled in, bleary-eyed, after guessing rightly they'd be welcomed with a mug of decent coffee and a roll. After that they could concentrate on the job before collecting £100 and tips at the end of the shift. John learned long ago that he must cater for his staff as well as the clients' guests. Bacon was now cooking in the top lefthand oven and rolls were warming in the righthand one.

Puffed with pride at the prospect of being able to talk

about the surprise of his knighthood, Dietrich Olson stepped on to the bedroom carpet, narrowly avoiding the open laptop on which he'd been fiddling with his speech the night before. He knew he'd wing the speech anyway, so he pushed it aside with one foot.

Padding downstairs in a dressing gown and old slippers, he spotted Doug and Joe wandering around the ground-floor rooms, making snarky remarks about a painting of an Edwardian woman in a large hat – someone he falsely claimed to have been a titled ancestor – and sneering and laughing. He stood in the doorway, watching them. And smelling them. Unwashed clothes, beer, cigarettes. What were they doing? Delivering chairs and tables? Surely nothing to do with the food?

Were they memorising the layout and the position of each valuable item for their return to collect the hired things? Or for a future visit, to help themselves to things that weren't hired? Clocks, rugs, crystal vases, glasses and silverware in mahogany cabinets? Dietrich said nothing. Bit of a risk, perhaps, but he didn't want anything to spoil his day.

The helpers went back into the hall and outside to collect more chairs. Dietrich headed to the kitchen, took a mug of coffee and returned to his bedroom.

Already in her green silk dress, her shoulder-length hair shining, Pen sipped coffee and bit into a slice of buttered toast. She smiled at the waiters, students probably, noticing that most had longish hair pulled back into ponytails or knots. A look she liked. She'd have urged Tom to try it, but he couldn't be bothered. Someone once said of Dietrich that he knew the location of every mirror in the Houses of Parliament and most of London's restaurants. He was proud of his blond mane. Tom combed his mousey brown hair with his fingers after showering and had a haircut only when he couldn't see where he was going.

Out of their coats and scarves, the waiters were all good-looking boys, as you'd expect of John Hardwick, who told people he valued standards in all things, including his waiters. Never waitresses. His niece Alison had begged him to let her do shifts because she needed pocket money. He'd told her to take out her nose stud and get the tattoos on her arms and neck lasered off, or at least covered with concealer. *Then* they'd talk. As a concession, he'd said at a family gathering at Christmas, mainly to please his sister, that Alison could help in the kitchen for the Olson do. So long as she didn't get in the way or mingle with the guests.

John Hardwick's preference for young men didn't surprise Mrs G, who liked to whisper that he was 'a bit, *you know*'. Most people did know and didn't care. She knew Alison from the village and waved as the teenager cycled into the car park. Inside, Pen approached a couple of the boys and asked them to be especially patient with the guests' children, and to offer them fruit juice and show them where baskets of paper and crayons had been left on side tables.

Mid-morning, a young man with flopping black hair and a sweaty face came into the kitchen, rubbing his aching legs with gloved hands, having cycled from Godalming station, up and down hills. John Hardwick had been warned about him but still pushed him away from the trays of food as if he might contaminate them.

Because he was Ed George, Bella's boyfriend, he was shown to the upstairs' shower room. He emerged almost unrecognisable in crisp black shirt and ironed trousers, his wet hair tucked behind his ears. He tested the piano, adjusted the piano stool and began playing, looking around with an expression that seemed to say, 'So, this is how Middle England celebrates!'

At the door, someone with a shrill voice with a touch of cockney. 'Hello! Anyone home?'

It was Karen Peters, Dietrich's constituency secretary, with Don, her quiet insurance broker husband. Don wandered around the two adjoining sitting rooms and out into the gardens, which seemed to stretch over half of Surrey. He normally wore an expression of blankness and today was no exception. Pen thought of him as plain dull.

Then, as instructed by Karen earlier, Don returned to congratulate Dietrich. Then he paused and turned away from the noisy knot of people around the new knight. Pen watched him and concluded that he must have felt shy. Karen was busy topping up the water in the flower bowls and vases and didn't notice.

Bella had slept until after 10, after too much Prosecco with a pal in Guildford the night before. Her brother's thumping on the bedroom door to tell her he was about to bag the shower woke her. The door had a broken lock, and he didn't want his sister to barge in and moan about using her shower gel.

'Get on with it!' she grunted, remembering that she'd showered before bed partly to avoid his wet towels and underwear on the floor the next morning. She got up, dressed quickly and grabbed her toothbrush, hairbrush, tube of foundation and mascara from her bag. She used the downstairs loo to brush her teeth and put on make-up, then it was straight to the kitchen for what looked like the last bacon roll.

Karen walked towards her and was struck again by Bella's close resemblance to her mother. Same long legs and bouncy, chestnut-brown hair. Slim and elegant. Both women could stop traffic but didn't know it.

'Ooh! Gorgeous dress,' Bella cooed, admiring Karen's navy taffeta number, with its stiffened full skirt and elbow-length sleeves.

'Lovely, isn't it?' She did a twirl and laughed girlishly. 'My Christmas present from your dad. I spent about four hours choosing it in Selfridges! A great way to spend an afternoon. He told me to get something special as a reward for finding gifts for loyal constituency supporters.' She didn't add that she'd also chosen and wrapped the Olson family's presents. As she always did.

Guests in party clothes trickled, then streamed, in. Small girls dressed as fairies, boys in buttoned shirts and new trainers, older children tethered to their mobile phones. Pen talked to each of them, remembering names and doting over tiny tots for whom she'd filled party bags with small toys and sweets. Within minutes, the house was humming with conversation. Already Pen could feel her reservations draining away. Perhaps Dietrich – alias Mr Wonderful to so many – was worth it, after all.

Dietrich's old school friend Michael Wilson-Green arrived early and greeted her with theatrical gasps, sighs and kisses on each cheek. He called her Penny, despite her having told everyone that she preferred the shortened, less twee and girly form. She laughed lightly. She knew he was a lonely man and that he hated working as a sales assistant in a kitchen appliance shop. He asked her quietly if he might use a bathroom to change his shirt as he'd come straight from work on the train and felt a bit grubby.

Poor Michael, she thought.

'You know where the bathroom is, up the stairs and first on the left.'

The house filled up rapidly. In his newest Savile Row blue suit, Dietrich sought out the important people to thank them for coming and to wish them a happy New Year. The leader and deputy leader of Camden Council, two parliamentary private secretaries, a couple of tame journalists, all with partners in tow, received warm smiles and hearty handshakes. A businessman with whom Dietrich had worked on property projects, and then Michael, were grabbed for breath-stopping man hugs and back slaps. Each was slightly surprised and winded by it.

Once Michael had regained his composure and accepted a glass of Champagne, he cornered Dietrich, bending slightly so they were nose to nose. 'I've a great new idea for us. Setting up an online wine business—' he began.

Dietrich raised a hand in front of his pal's face. 'Let's meet one afternoon in the tearoom at the House for tea and a sticky cake, eh?'

Big smile. No actual invitation, no date. Effectively a brush-off. Like the last time and the one before. Once again, Dietrich was telling Michael in headlines that he was no longer interested in his schemes – or in him.

Waiters circulated with trays of canapés. Soon guests were filing into the dining room and helping themselves to a venison casserole, or grilled fish on a bed of tiny tomatoes, or a vegetable curry with rice. A few greedy children spooned all three on to their plates. On another table were platters of fruit kebabs and small pastries.

Then the waiters returned with trays of cups, small silver pots of tea and coffee, and jugs of milk.

Pen glanced at her watch. Nearly three o'clock already.

Time for the toast to Sir Dietrich. Can't have guests slipping away before that, she thought.

Dietrich had been standing near her, laughing with a pair of civil servants she recognised from a recent parliamentary drinks do. But just at that moment, he must have moved to talk to others. She scanned the room but annoyingly couldn't see him.

Running a hand through her hair, then patting down her dress and forcing a big, bright smile, she grabbed a teaspoon from a table to tap against a wine glass. At that, children were shushed and conversations paused. Soon she had everyone's attention. She looked around for her new knight, so he could make his fussed-over speech.

Still no sign of him.

'Don't tell me he's got stage fright!' she joked to guests who had pulled up chairs. Inwardly she was seething.

Where the fuck is the man? she thought. *He knew this was coming.*

A few fruitless moments later, Pen told the audience, who were already growing restless, to hold on a minute. Then she rushed into the kitchen.

'Dietrich? Anyone seen him? I want to make the announcement, do the toast, the speech and cut the cake before people start to leave... the bloody man's disappeared.'

Blank looks.

Out in the hall, Tom broke off from talking to Bella's boyfriend Ed after spotting his mother coming from the kitchen. He couldn't read her face as he rushed towards her.

'What?'

'Can't find your pa. Look in our bedroom, will you? Perhaps he's changing his shirt. Find Bella and get her to look in the garage and the summer house. You never know.'

Tom was back in a few minutes, shaking his head. He'd undone his top shirt buttons, his tie hung loose.

'No luck. No one remembers seeing him in the last half hour.' He shrugged.

Pen dashed away to look in the boot room and the guest cloakroom. She called up the stairs again and again.

Bella came in. 'I spoke to two blokes in the car park waiting to collect the hired stuff later – they haven't seen Dad.'

Tom began checking with the people seated on high-backed sofas and armchairs, weaving around the guests, asking them if they'd seen Dietrich. An eerie panic was creeping up his tall body like a rash.

Back in the kitchen, Pen dabbed the beads of sweat on her forehead with a napkin. It occurred to her that he might have gone into what the family called the back kitchen, a semi-basement accessed through a narrow door in the main kitchen. Inside, through a wooden door that few ever opened, was a smaller, cobwebby room. It was here that wines and beers had been stored for decades. Perhaps Dietrich was looking for bottles of vintage Champagne for the toast, she thought. They'd discussed the idea only a few days earlier, then decided that their guests would have drunk so much by then they wouldn't tell the difference.

She walked towards it quickly, pushed the unlatched door then used her left hand to search for the light switch on a wall that felt cold and clammy as she made circles on it. When she finally found the switch, two fluorescent ceiling strips bleeped and hissed before flooding the darkness with blue-tinged light. Racks of dusty bottles on each side were suddenly illuminated.

Tripping her, just inside the door, was a pile of what could have been rolled-up dust sheets, maybe bits of cardboard wine boxes and the old coats people used for trudging around the garden. She tried to push the stuff aside with her foot. It locked with something solid, and she bent down to look.

She pulled back a blanket, releasing a musty smell. In the shadow, to the side, a man's body lay still and silent, legs bent, a clump of hair over his eyes. She stood up, took a breath then touched it gently with the toe of her shoe. No movement, no sound.

Gently, she moved the arm covering the lower half of his face. Apart from a small graze on his forehead, probably from the sharp edge of one of the wine racks, there was no blood, no bruises, no sign of an injury or a struggle.

Neither was there a pulse when she bent down and put two fingers to the cold neck.

Nor a mystery about who he was.

2

'WHAT SHALL WE DO WITH THAT?' asked Mrs G, to no one in particular, looking at a huge, untouched chocolate cake decorated with the word congratulations. It was sitting on the kitchen counter like a sticky, brown Buddha. There was no answer.

After a few moments, she opened a drawer, pulled out one of her aprons, shook it and tied it over her best dress. She signalled to Alison to help, then busied herself collecting Batts Farm glasses, plates and coffee mugs, so they wouldn't get mixed up with the hired ones, and loading the dishwasher. She inspected the space in the fridge and freezer before deciding to leave the caterer to organise the dispatch of any uneaten food. No one spoke.

In the wine store earlier, Pen had felt sick. The walls moved back and forth, the ceiling swirled, and the sounds of chatter and laughter became a drone. She'd stumbled into the kitchen and sat on a chair by the table. Tom was puzzled as she got up and walked unsteadily towards him. She pulled him down to her level and whispered the news. He rushed to the wine store to see for himself.

Tom thought about calling the police. But why? There was no sign of an attack. So, he summoned an ambulance, then watched as two paramedics photographed, then swiftly lifted and stretchered the man's body into their vehicle to take it to the Royal Surrey Hospital. He followed in his car.

There, in the Accident and Emergency department, Jonas Christos, a serious-looking junior doctor, carried out a quick examination, called over a nurse and asked her to arrange blood tests.

He spoke to Tom, checking Dietrich's name and address and telling him that in all probability, sudden cardiac arrest would be recorded as the cause of death.

Bella had led her mother upstairs, helped her on to the bed and given her a glass of water. But soon afterwards, as if sleepwalking, Pen had gone back down to the kitchen, where Mrs G was busy. She looked around without seeing. Eventually, she gestured to the older woman.

'Why don't you leave everything till tomorrow? Take whatever you want back home with you, of course. Don't forget the flowers. Such a shame...' her voice trailed off.

Mrs G – she preferred to be called this because no one had ever managed to pronounce properly, let alone spell, Saoirse, her Irish Christian name – patted her employer's arm.

Pen clasped the hand. 'Take some of this food to your boys at the club? Whatever you think they'd like.'

She meant the youth club in Godalming that Dietrich had founded and supported and where Mrs Gibbs volunteered. Pen turned and climbed back up the stairs.

On her way, she looked at all the strangers still in the

house and mumbled, as if in prayer, 'Please let them soon be gone,' noticing only then, as she took the last steps, that she was barefoot. She remembered kicking off her shoes outside the wine store.

Now, as she climbed the stairs again, she looked down over the banister to the small hall by the front door, at the array of packed food ready to go out and the prettily bagged gifts that guests had brought. What was supposed to happen?

Mrs G had been looking through the kitchen window watching her three hens prancing through the cold grass and remembering the shock when her own husband, Gordon, died after weeks in hospital from a relentless cancer. She grabbed a sheet of kitchen towel to wipe her eyes then rushed up the stairs to embrace her employer and then back down to Bella, before resuming the tidying and wiping.

Meanwhile, John Hardwick gathered his papers and files and began covering plastic boxes of food in clingfilm to store in the Batts Farm freezer, boxes which would probably never be defrosted.

Hearing people talking loudly and moving things, Pen forced herself to get up from the bed and return to the back kitchen to collect her shoes. She looked at the rough, stained wood door to the wine store. They'd meant to have it painted and fitted with a functioning lock of some kind but had never got around to doing it. The door had now been wedged closed and she never wanted to open it again.

Buoyed by the unreality of it all, Bella interrupted guests by now concerned conversations.

'Dad's had a serious accident. An ambulance has taken him off to hospital. Awfully sorry, but I think it'd be better if you left early. It was so kind of you to have come out on this cold day. I know Dietrich was thrilled when he heard you could make it... he was so pleased about the knighthood.'

'You'll let us know the news?' the guests asked.

Bella nodded, biting her lip, knowing the family wouldn't have to. The media would do the job soon enough.

She watched as they found their coats and filed out.

Ed caught her arm as she was making her way back to the kitchen. She whispered the news. He looked as if he didn't quite understand. When it had sunk in, he hugged her, asked if there was anything he could do. She shook her head, and he left quietly on his bike.

Bella handed John Harding the envelope of cash her mother had left for him to tip his team. A teary Mrs Gibbs grabbed her coat to be the traffic warden for guests driving out into the road.

An hour or so later, Bella eased her mother, still in the green dress, off the bed, helped her to lace up some trainers and stuffed some other items into a couple of bags. She grabbed their coats, and the two women stepped carefully downstairs. She pulled a large bunch of lilies and pink roses from a vase and, as she walked towards the front door, noticed just by the side the basket of undistributed party bags for the departing children. A dozen or so tiny disappointments adding to the larger, more painful ones.

John Hardwick and his helpers had swiftly collected their equipment and some of the buffet food they'd put into containers before letting themselves out.

'Bell, I'm leaving the hospital now and going back to the house to make sure all the hired things are collected tomorrow. Then I'll close everything up,' Tom's message on his sister's phone said. He could have added, but didn't, that he'd also look around the house to try to make sense of what had happened.

With a Lang Lang CD playing Chopin softly on the radio, Bella drove her father's car, her silent mother in the passenger seat, to Colt Court, the family's main home in a corner of Bloomsbury. She managed to squeeze the big car into one of the five resident parking bays at the back of the block, next to Dietrich's sit-up-and-beg bike. Looking at it, Bella hazily thought her dad must be waiting upstairs for them after a cycle ride, one trouser bottom still tucked into a sock. Then she realised he wouldn't ever be there again.

Later in the week, Bella spoke to a Godalming undertaker. The burial would be an affair for the immediate family only, in a cemetery behind a small church between Godalming and Guildford, in ten days' time. She chose an available corner plot and spoke to a masonry firm about a granite headstone, to be erected when the earth settled. The usual inscription, 'In loving memory' above his name and dates of birth and death, seemed adequate.

On the day, grey and misty, the funeral director, a man whose jowly face had set in the solemn expression necessary for the job, arrived early, and with three assistants lowered the oak coffin from wooden slats into a muddy grave. Pen stared at it, almost unable to believe that her noisy husband was remaining quiet inside, not knocking and shouting. Part of her wanted to cry 'stop!', prise open the coffin lid and help Dietrich to climb out so she could reprimand him for his bad-taste joke. Instead, she silently watched, wishing she believed in a God who would keep him in a paradise – a sort of spa-hotel, perhaps – while he waited for her to show him the way home.

Bella buried her face in Tom's coat as he pulled up the

collar, pushed hair out of his eyes and wiped away his tears with a tweedy sleeve.

Later, back at the flat, the three began to arrange a memorial service – Bella's idea – to be held in the Hawksmoor-designed St George's Church, Bloomsbury, four weeks after the party. It involved very little planning because it was to be the simplest of ceremonies with only a couple of eulogies, two readings and a pair of hymns whose music was familiar and pleasing.

Dietrich had been an atheist, although he kept quiet about it – it wouldn't have won him many votes, even among the liberal-minded constituents of Camden. He used to joke that he was a 'lapsed atheist' because he couldn't be bothered to think about religion, the afterlife and all that stuff.

He said he would be happy to be wrapped in a black plastic bag and put out for the binmen. No funeral. No fuss. Pen and the children knew he was lying about that. He was a man with an ego and had been proud of what he'd achieved after a less-than-promising start. He would have wanted people to know about it, to have it recorded somewhere, if only on his Wikipedia page.

How long is the shock of finding the corpse of a husband supposed to last? Pen kept thinking. Weeks? Months? When do the sharp stabs of pain stop? Is there such a thing as closure, or is that just psychobabble they put in the scripts of American television shows?

In bed, she thought about her future without Dietrich. Life would be simpler. No doubt about that. Goodbye to Conservative Party events. No more openings. No more fêtes. No more ghastly gala dinners. Bliss! No more pretending she supported the party's policies while she often agreed with the Labour Party's alternatives.

There'd be more time to help Bella with her legal practice course and make sure Tom wasn't overwhelmed by his medical studies. It'd seemed to both his parents that he'd made the decision to go for medicine at university too suddenly. He'd been a clever boy at school but had shown no curiosity or aptitude when it came to biology, psychology, or the workings of the human body.

There'd be more time for herself, too. She imagined relaxed breakfasts with Radio Four before walking out to her job lecturing blank-faced students in family law in the law school of the London School of Economics at the bottom of Kingsway. No more having to listen to Dietrich's catalogue of complaints about Camden Council's dustmen, or the need to change the one-way system around Holborn Underground Station, or his suspicions of behind-the-scenes plots in the parliamentary party, when she wanted only to check notes for her lectures, skim-read *The Times*, drink coffee and eat toast. She could devote more time to her students and see more of her lawyer friends. And take her time deciding what was next for her.

Those were small benefits, she knew. There was plenty of money. Everyone knew a deceased spouse's assets were automatically transferred to the surviving partner. She could spend or not spend, without thought or discussion.

But she'd be lonely. The children lived together in a flat in Bankside. Evenings alone in Bloomsbury would be – what? Strange. She'd hear neighbours come home in the evenings and chatter, laugh, go out again and call to each other. She'd be staring at Dietrich's books, the photographs of him standing with Big Ben and the Houses of Parliament behind him, his victorious election nights, his graduation ceremony at Oxford and the traditional paintings he'd picked up in antiques shops and exhibitions that she thought were dull. She remembered the arguments they'd had over if and where to hang them. Arguments he always won.

She'd have no one to walk with over to the Royal Opera House in Covent Garden for a night of music or ballet. No one to talk to about things she'd seen in magazines: shoes, coats or handbags she liked but thought too expensive or too 'young' for a woman pushing fifty-five.

'If you like it, buy it, woman!' he'd bark. 'It's not as if we'd have to sell one of the polo ponies to raise the cash!' He'd laugh at that line. Every time. He'd never grasped that she didn't want to look like Mrs Moneybags, even if she *was* a banker's daughter and a rich man's wife. Anyway, of course, he wasn't really interested.

There were a few jobs Dietrich *did* tackle without having to be nagged, such as travelling across France in the summer, driving like Mr Toad at the wheel and loudly singing Gilbert and Sullivan songs, all the way to the villa in Provence. One of his companies paid for it, and they'd spent many holidays there eating and drinking too much while the children and their friends splashed around in the swimming pool and shouted for Dad to judge the diving contests.

Would she ever enjoy weekends at Batts Farm again? She doubted it. She might visit Mrs Gibbs, who'd come as part of the package when they bought the place as a weekend retreat.

She'd miss his body too, of course. There'd be no more sleepy, married lovemaking. She'd be able to occupy the centre of the bed, answering emails on her laptop or reading with the bedside light or radio on, without his moans about how late it was. But those things wouldn't outweigh the absence of a foot or an arm always ready to pull her towards him for a warm hug or for sex.

That thought, more than anything, made her sigh.

She'd often asked herself why she'd stayed with Dietrich. Did she really love him? Had she ever? She'd often disliked him. Each time he'd persuaded her to settle disputes for him – disputes with constituents and local councillors that he'd ignored for months – or remained resolute and uncaring when she'd sympathised with the complainants, she'd felt unhappy that she was condoning his behaviour.

He, on the other hand, took no interest in her work, her conflicts with colleagues or with troublesome students. When she wanted to moan about this or that at the college, he'd just shrug and say, 'Hand in your notice, then. For God's sake, you don't *have* to work.'

But they'd rarely had shouting rows and never reached the plate-throwing stage. There'd never been a good enough reason to split up. Quite a few men let her know they were drawn to her, but she never felt a strong enough pull towards another man.

And each time she looked at Tom, Dietrich's questionable ethics mattered a little less. In the early days, Dietrich was the most caring parent, painstaking with toys, helping with homework and volunteering for school events and museum outings. Pen had shown Dietrich a photograph of her baby son when they first met at a party at the investment bank where her father was a partner. He'd smiled at the photo, and from then on, it was as though he'd deleted the knowledge that Tom was the accidental son of Pen's one-time law tutor, a baby the tutor had badgered her to abort.

Tonight, she poured herself a glass of Merlot and sipped

it slowly while stretched out on the sofa. She didn't need to say anything, explain anything. That was a relief.

Back to business, she told herself the next morning. The Order of Service leaflets had to be printed in good time for the memorial. She rang the church organist, and they agreed on a Mozart piano concerto to be followed by a Bach sinfonia. They'd need to find a good pianist and violinist, or perhaps a cellist, for those. Bella would have chosen Ed, who'd played piano so beautifully at the party, but she sensed that her mother had reservations about him. She was right. Romanian Ed needed to sort out his right to remain in Britain and sometimes seemed to think he was entitled to free legal advice. Pen felt guilty for thinking that. It probably wasn't fair.

Bella had sorted through Dietrich's collection of CDs and picked Nina Simone singing 'Lilac Wine' to be played as people filed from the church. The words were probably inappropriate, but so what?

Pen rang Karen and asked her to let the Tory chief whip know about the memorial service so that political friends could organise their diaries. The Press Association also needed to be alerted, and a brief announcement posted on Dietrich's social media accounts.

Ah, Karen, Pen mused, as she put down the phone. The sympathetic secretary in the blue taffeta dress. Little Miss Efficiency. The thought had occasionally crossed her mind that Karen's duties might have been more than just secretarial. Yet nothing she'd seen or heard had ever provided evidence for it. Karen had a pretty face, and big breasts hoisted on bras whose straps dug into her shoulders. Had the straps ever given way, Tom once joked, the crash would have caused tremblings all over Camden.

Pen liked Karen because she got on with the job, passed on the important messages and seemed to understand her boss's strengths and weaknesses. But she knew the secretary was... what? Not quite posh enough for Dietrich. When she ate using a knife and fork, she held the knife like a pen, and said lay when she meant lie. She ate white bread sandwiches for lunch and took sugar in her tea. She and Don enjoyed ballroom dancing and got into it long before *Strictly Come Dancing* became a hit on TV. Hardly hanging offences, even judged by a snob. And Pen knew she was a snob. As Dietrich had been. But still.

So, on the balance of probabilities, as a family lawyer like Pen would say, an affair seemed unlikely. But still.

When Pen and Dietrich were first together, she'd quickly decided that he'd had few sexual encounters in the past. He wasn't an imaginative lover, and she'd had to train him. He'd responded well. She had to give him that. And his enthusiasm never waned.

When she went through pockets in his suits due for dry cleaning, she never found packets of Durex Extra Sensitive or receipts from restaurant dinners he'd slyly enjoyed without her. She'd never caught him staring at other women. He'd faithfully loved *her*, his practical, clever wife. In her heart she *knew* that. It calmed her.

The day of the memorial service arrived. Looking straight ahead to keep his voice from wavering, Tom gave the eulogy and spoke of Dietrich as a hands-on, devoted, homework-helping father to him and Bella and a supportive, loving husband to Pen. Karen had provided him with a few anecdotes about his father's early years as an MP, his occasional faux pas and his rapid learning of Westminster dos and don'ts. There were a couple of jokes about his lack of proficiency as a cyclist and his ability to get lost on even a short journey.

Pen, the teacher, used to addressing large audiences in lecture rooms, was composed enough to read out a short tribute that Bella had prepared. It included a touch of irony – 'You all remember how bashful Dietrich was!'

A former Tory Prime Minister followed her with an even shorter tribute including a statement that Dietrich had been earmarked as a future member of the cabinet.

Oh really, Pen thought bitterly. *Easy to say now, you creep.*

Another former leader recited the six-line Joyce Grenfell poem, 'If I Should Go', without fluffing the lines. A string quartet at the front of the church played Bach's 'Air on the G String'. Karen and Mrs Gibbs each soaked pocketsful of Kleenex tissues.

Pen walked slowly along with about half of the mourners to the restaurant near the British Museum they'd hired for the 'wake', where waiters served English 'Champagne', Chablis, a decent red and fruit juice accompanied by small, neat sandwiches and cheesy tartlets. At the restaurant door, Bella and Tom stood at either side of their mother so that she needed only nod as they shook hands with guests who paused to express their condolences. Most of the people who filed in were what Bella, whispering to Tom, called 'the usual suspects'. Dietrich's fellow Tory politicians and Camden councillors, a couple of civil servants, Colt Court neighbours, two of Pen's cousins and a rarely seen cousin of his from Tring, where Dietrich had grown up.

There were also a few unfamiliar faces belonging possibly to people from Dietrich's past in business, nosy locals and a few of his constituents who were intent on helping themselves to free drinks and food.

Among the unfamiliar faces were those of a woman probably in her mid-to-late fifties. She was holding a tweed coat and was accompanied by a man in his late twenties or early thirties wearing tortoiseshell-framed spectacles and carrying a black padded jacket. While the woman's dark hair was twisted and clipped into a loose pleat with tendrils over her forehead, his curtain of fair hair was swingy fresh, as though he'd just washed it. He turned to her as they stood to pull on their coats and asked, 'OK, Ma?'

She nodded.

None of the Olsons recognised them, yet something about the woman's serious demeanour signalled that she hadn't come just for a free sandwich. Conversations were muted. Pen couldn't help but contrast it with the loud voices and the laughter at the start of the knighthood party.

Then, as mourners lifted their last full glasses from the waiters' trays and put empty ones on tables before heading to the door while buttoning up their respectful dark coats, Pen noticed the uninvited woman studying the line of photographs of Dietrich that Bella and Tom had picked out from boxes of albums stored in cupboards at Batts Farm. They'd put them in black frames and arranged them on a table near the coat racks.

The woman was looking at photos of Dietrich as a schoolboy and young man. Then she picked up one of his wedding to Pen thirty years earlier in a restaurant in Gigaro, in the South of France. Pen noticed the woman's unvarnished short nails and intense dark eyes.

She approached her, held out a hand and said in a soft voice, 'Hello, there. I'm Pen Bryant-Olson. I don't believe we've met.'

'Jane. Jane Page-Smith. No, we haven't. Dietrich looks so young and so happy here.'

'He was generally a happy person,' Pen replied. 'But yes, it was a perfect wedding. Lots of guests.'

'Ours was far more modest.'

'Ours?'

'I was Jane Olson then, married to the man you believe was your husband.'

'Didn't know Dietrich had a first wife,' Pen stuttered, still smiling, certain this was a joke, and she should play along.

Jane looked her squarely in the face. 'First and only. That's Charlie over there. Charles William Olson, our son.'

Pen realised it wasn't a joke, yet she couldn't process what she was being told. It felt as though her heart was thumping so hard it would soon burst through her rib cage.

'Dietrich and I were not divorced,' the stranger said.

She stared hard at Pen, then slowly put the photograph back on the side table.

'Come on, Ma,' the young man said, stepping back to take her arm and propel her into the street. His voice was low, the accent public school. Pen watched the pair as they disappeared into the small crowd gathered outside the restaurant.

She found a chair and dropped on to it. Had that conversation really happened?

Bella and Tom arrived to find their mother staring ahead, trancelike.

'Sit down and listen. That woman – the one we didn't recognise – has just told me she was your father's wife. And that they were never divorced.'

She would repeat this brief conversation with Jane Page-Smith many times to them, and to herself.

Bella gulped, looked at her shocked mother and then said, 'Oh, you hear about these delusional people. Stalkers, nutjobs. Alastair Campbell had one, I think. Pop stars and glamour models get them. Maybe she was a discarded girlfriend who could never accept it or really let go.' She was trying hard to believe what she was saying.

'Fucking hell!' Tom muttered. 'The mad, twisted bitch!'

The three of them looked out of the restaurant's doors, biding their time for a chance to escape unnoticed by the waiting reporters and photographers.

A light rain didn't deter many of those leaving the restaurant from clustering, shaking hands and exchanging business cards or phone numbers. Large cars with chauffeurs in black caps pulled up and drove away with businessmen or politicians in the back seats. Heads of charities, of which Dietrich had been a patron, hailed taxis. Younger people dashed for Warren Street or Tottenham Court Road tube stations.

A couple of reporters and photographers had walked from St George's church, drunk coffee from paper cups and eaten sandwiches in the street as they waited for a famous face, preferably a television 'celebrity', to leave the restaurant, hoping to nab them and collect a publishable tribute or a soundbite to appease their news editors. Alas, no actors or sports stars, not even a newsreader, let alone a stand-up comedian, emerged. The well-known politicians had already dashed back on to the green benches of the House.

'This is going to make all of three pars,' moaned a young reporter, pushing a notebook into his coat pocket and stomping off to find his car.

As Jane and Charles walked out and looked for a taxi, a young woman from the *Daily Mail* stuck a tape recorder in front of them while a colleague snapped pictures. Jane scowled and shook her head when asked how she would best remember Sir Dietrich. Then she stopped, took a few steps back and said, 'Generous, even when he had very little, and always inventive and exciting. He should have been knighted years ago. He was my husband, so I should know.'

The puzzled journo pushed on. 'May I have your name? You and Sir Dietrich were married? When was that exactly?'

'Soon after leaving Oxford in the early seventies. Register office, no fuss. We went hitchhiking in France for our honeymoon. Had about twenty quid between us when we got back. But that changed, as you know.'

'And you divorced when?'

'We didn't divorce.'

Journalists were checking their tape recorders and scribbling for their lives. The woman seemed aware of the bombshell she was dropping but kept her tone light. 'We were still married when he died.'

'It'll make the splash,' muttered a hugely cheered-up reporter.

Pen continued to watch from the doorway, then she went back inside the restaurant, found a different chair and sat staring up at a chandelier. She took the glass of water that Bella had put in her hand and lifted it to her mouth.

She kept in control of her body while her mind flitted from the wine store to the chocolate cake, to the politicians at the service, and finally, to the woman looking at the wedding photo. What was the biggest surprise? The woman's face?

She realised then that she was no longer a frozen bystander on the edge of this drama. She was involved, and she had to try to make sense of it. Dietrich had been vain, vague and lazy, depending on her or Karen to make the necessary, boring adjustments and smooth things over.

But *this*?

She racked her usually logical lawyer's brain. His death was painfully puzzling. Could his bigamy, if that's what it was, make it worse?

Yes, she thought and felt. Much worse.

3

'LOVE THIS VIEW,' Basil James muttered, staring down at the khaki-coloured River Thames flowing slowly under Wandsworth Bridge. 'They say there are seals in it these days and you can swim in it,' he chuckled. 'It wasn't so long ago everyone thought the Thames was stinky, filthy, poisonous. It isn't. Still, I'll stick to the Med or the local swimming baths.' Not that he could remember the last time he'd swam in either.

He was talking to himself, as he often did.

Hands round a mug of hot tea, the short, round figure with a shiny bald head, still nut brown from last autumn's late sun, stood chortling and chattering in tracksuit bottoms and a decades-old pyjama top at one of the big windows of a fifth-floor living room late on a Saturday morning in early January.

Now, a weak sun shone through the gaps in the clouds and a cold wind swirled. Soon, the London skies would darken again, but he'd still be able to make out the river, with its compelling drama of changing colours, accessories to sunlight, moonlight, drizzle and cloud. From day to day, he enjoyed seeing the slivers of froth on small waves, the sporadic traffic of cargo boats, ferries, dinghies and the occasional aquatic police patrols. The river was why everyone had bought flats here in South Quay, horribly expensive though they were.

He hadn't bothered to get a survey done on his flat. There seemed no point in forking out hundreds of pounds to be told nothing he couldn't see for himself. The view was enough. His flat, in a tall riverside block built twenty or so years ago, curved at the top so that it resembled a bullet and had been 'lavishly refurbished' prior to him buying it, which was estate agents' speak for 'done up'. The boiler, all the kitchen appliances, the kitchen cupboards and the bathroom fittings were new and fashionable. The floors had been re-sanded and varnished, and the walls painted a putty grey. He'd bought the place from a firm called Premium Properties Six. They'd developed the whole block originally and had recently put three flats, whose short leases had expired, on the market. Basil chose the one on the highest available level with the best views from the living room and main bedroom widows.

It was meant to be just for himself, but soon, for a while, he'd be sharing with his son, Steve. The place was big enough and, in any case, the boy wasn't around that much. Young people always have somewhere else to be.

Steve had quizzed his dad about the place before he first went to look it over. Basil snapped back that he'd checked to make sure there was no cladding on the outside of the block, as there had been with Grenfell Tower, where that dreadful fire cost more than seventy people their lives. He'd known enough to look out for that. 'I'm not as stupid as I look!' he enjoyed saying to himself and to workmates who asked about it.

The bad news about the place, about the failings of the contractors to include fire doors and other safety precautions when the block was built, had only just started to trickle through. A few of the neighbours were getting aerated, arranging residents' protests against Premium Properties Six and the council and pinning up notices in the entry hall. Did they know anything for certain? Basil dismissed them as rumours.

He'd had a busy week delivering Johnson's Craft Beer in the small van the firm provided. Looking at the team of dopey blokes who 'crafted' it, Basil often smiled at the term. They could have been churning out toilet cleaner or soy sauce for all they knew.

Johnson's supplied a small group of pubs as well as a few cafés, restaurants and shops within a radius of about 30 miles. Recently, it had started selling directly to individual customers on a one-off basis.

Yesterday, a caterer had recommended the firm to someone who was arranging an event, and they ordered several crates. The venue, a sprawling, private house, turned out to be near Godalming in Surrey, a lot further afield than normal. Basil was a bit put-out by that, as he hadn't been warned, and he'd decided to mention it to his boss on Monday. It took him what seemed like hours to get there down the A3, past Guildford. Also, when he did finally arrive, a bossy little housekeeper kept changing her mind about where he should put the crates – in an outbuilding, no, in the hall, no, outside the kitchen under a shelf where rubbish bins were sometimes left. He'd felt like telling her to move the heavy crates herself but bit his tongue.

* * *

Michael Wilson-Green also looked at the river every day, viewing it as a silky loose ribbon winding between buildings. His flat in Disraeli Road was near the south side of Putney Bridge, just up the river from Wandsworth, and close to the kitchen design showroom where he worked.

Not long after lunchtime on Monday and Mike Green, as he called himself at work, had already had quite enough for the day. The thought of another four- or five-hour discussion about ovens and integrated dishwashers with time-wasting customers was too demoralising. He grabbed his old Harrod's overcoat from its hook on the door of the cubby hole at the back of the shop and strode out towards Fulham Palace Gardens. He didn't inform Beverley, his boss's PA. He disliked the woman, who was always drenched in cheap, sweet perfume, almost as much as he disliked Graham Frank, his young boss at Frank Kitchen Designs.

'Pompous little twat! He'll never have an original idea in his life. Never amount to anything,' he'd sneer as he walked around the gardens. 'If only I could tell him where to stick his job. If only I could ring him now and say I'm never coming back.'

But he couldn't. He'd done that in his last two miserable jobs and his CV was patchy enough. Anyone looking at it would think he'd been in jail for long stretches. If Frank asked where he'd disappeared to, he'd have to invent a headache and say he'd needed fresh air.

This coming weekend, he was due to see his sons, Rufus and George, for a pub lunch in King's Road, before each went back to university after the long Christmas break. They were great kids and, he liked to think, just like him: tall, skinny, bright. It hurt that he'd seen so little of them as they grew up and that they couldn't be proud of their dad. Perhaps that would change, eventually. After the weekend, he wouldn't get another chance to see them until the Easter holidays, and then only if Charlotte, his mean-spirited, resentful ex-wife, fixed it. Charlotte had filed for divorce, kicked him out of the family home and managed to separate him from the boys nearly twenty years ago. Fortunately for him, she'd remarried a successful accountant and moved with the children to his swanky house near Chichester. It meant that no alimony or child support payments from him were needed.

In the early days, they'd had a near-perfect marriage. The rising share price of FDA – First Domestic Appliances – the business he'd launched and developed with his old school friend was the envy of every other online retailer. Then it imploded and brought lasting shame on him. His career and his family life were ruined.

Since that happened, he'd lived alone in the top half of a Victorian house in Putney that he'd converted into two flats when he and his friend had the money and enthusiasm for such things. Luckily his name alone was on the deeds. The conversion hadn't been done on the cheap and the place was light and the interior thoughtfully modernised. Also, the tenant of the lower flat paid him in cash, which meant HMRC never knew to tax him. The regular cash came in handy now that he was earning peanuts.

That it *shouldn't* have been like that was engraved on his heart. But after the FDA debacle, Michael Wilson-Green's value to any business he tried to join had dwindled and was almost non-existent. So, he'd lowered his expectations, applied for less senior positions and dropped the double-barrelled name. But it wasn't enough. He needed money, other people's money, to launch a new enterprise and get back on his once well-shod feet.

In his own mind, he was still a man with clever ideas and drive. With his cut-glass accent and aged Savile Road suits, he was certainly personable, yet if you checked his background, you'd conclude he wasn't to be trusted.

What had happened was still puzzling to those who'd known him in his younger days. The Financial Conduct Authority discovered that FDA had over-stated its profits under his regime as chief executive by several hundred million pounds. The share price bombed, thousands of pension funds that had invested in FDA suffered, and an equal number of consumers were forced to pay more for their washing machines, cookers and fridges. One of the casualties was Michael Wilson-Green's career.

Lying in bed, staring at the ceiling night after night since then, he couldn't understand why it had happened. Had he been daydreaming of becoming a billionaire? Not exactly. Had he simply miscalculated the figures? He must have. He must have thought of it as a lark, a boasting game. His friend and co-founder, who'd resigned a few months before the crisis – and after awarding himself a bonus for good work – had been back in touch and had striven to keep many of the calamitous repercussions out of the media. So, thanks to those good connections, the company's disgrace was played down. But because Michael Wilson-Green had been CEO, he was the one whose face was in the papers, the man investigated for fraud. Similar treatment was meted out to five out of FDA's six directors, but no one remembered them.

They were fined under the Proceeds of Crime Act. Their savings accounts were emptied, second homes had to be sold, children pulled out of private schools and belts tightened.

They were banned from becoming directors of any other enterprise.

In the business world, everyone presumed the authorities had acted after a tip-off from a whistleblower – or a traitor, as some might see it. The sixth director was Wilson-Green's prime suspect. That man was his friend and co-founder, Dietrich Olson.

Anger gripped him each time he thought about the event. He fought it off, slid back his shirt cuff, looked at the Rolex Datejust, twin to one Dietrich had bought when their bank accounts were fat and they'd decided they needed a 'pat on the back', saw he'd been gone over an hour and walked back to his cubbyhole and his order books. He noticed on the way that Aris, Frank's best salesman, looked as though he were about to sign up a middle-aged Indian couple for a completely new kitchen. He liked Aris. If he ever started his own business again, and he still believed he could, Aris would be first on the hiring list.

All he needed was a few hundred thousand pounds and introductions to a couple of the right people to back him in his new enterprise. That was the main reason he'd been cultivating the traitor for the past year or so, claiming that he no longer bore grudges. If Sir Dietrich Olson didn't do the decent thing – and he'd spelled out exactly what sort of loan he needed and why – there was always blackmail. Or so he'd sometimes thought when sleep wouldn't come.

Would it have worked? The bloody man was dead, so, he'd never bloody know.

* * *

Late in the evening, Basil's phone buzzed. 'Whassup son?' he barked at it. 'Changed your mind about moving in?'

'Nah! Don't be daft, Dad! It's just that I had a couple of things to take care of today. All my stuff's together, waiting to be packed in the van. Kev says he can't wait to be shot of me! But he needs the van for a job he's got on early tomorrow morning. Doesn't know when he'll be back. So, I may go with him to help get the job done quicker. Anyway, I'll stick around, have a couple of beers with him tonight and be over at yours some time tomorrow. That OK?'

Basil said it was fine, and after he'd hung up, he decided he'd pop into the Sainsburys Local, which was among the small parade of shops and offices tucked into the bottom of the block and get some food in for them both. He'd also make up the bed in the second bedroom. Sort out some towels for him. Steve's mum, Dawn, once worked as a chambermaid in a four-star hotel in her native Antigua, and he knew she would have done that. God, he missed her. If only he could have behaved more reasonably. If only he'd had more control, hadn't lost it so often.

Basil was proud of Steve. He'd turned out all right, that one. He had steady work in IT, kept himself trim. Got around on a little Vespa scooter. One tank of petrol lasted weeks, apparently. He had no debts and no wife or family yet, but there was plenty of time for that, Basil was sure.

The thing that worried Basil, and had done for years, was Steve's school pal Kev – Kevin Miller. Basil had urged Steve to cut off all ties to the 'thieving little druggie'. He used to warn him, 'He may look harmless, like butter wouldn't melt, what with those ginger curls, but he's bad news, son, you know that. He's been stealing and taking drugs since he left school. Probably even before that. He's dealing the stuff too, I dare say. Hang around with him and you'll likely get a knife in the guts or end up in a police cell for being his accomplice.'

Basil wasn't exaggerating. Kevin's drug habit had needed to be funded, of course. That's why he was a part-time thief. And to give him his due, he was a good one too. He'd become famous as 'The Wandsworth Burglar' for evading the cops for years. Normally, the police didn't investigate burglaries, but this clever devil posed a challenge. He stuck to the areas he knew well in Wandsworth, Balham and parts of Tooting and Streatham and always went out in the early hours of the morning dressed in a dark hoodie, its top pulled down over his head to cover his distinctive hair and as much of his face as possible. And he walked down the centre of the street to evade the CCTV cameras that well-off owners installed near the front doors of their substantial houses.

Most cleverly, Basil reckoned, was that he studied the houses and their owners' routines carefully in advance and plotted the best ways to get inside their properties without causing much damage. He never left fingerprints, footprints or fibres from clothes, and he only took a few things each time, a watch or a laptop here, a smartphone and a pair of gold earrings there, but not the matching necklace. He pocketed only half the money he found lying around or in wallets and purses. That way, the victims often didn't realise they'd been burgled until several days, or even weeks, after the event.

Smart, eh?

Eventually, a determined woman detective constable, who'd been sitting in her car in the targeted area night after night, spotted Kevin as he left a stucco-fronted Wandsworth house, his pockets and money belt heavy with jewellery, mobile phones and cash.

Kev had told Steve he'd been gutted to have been nicked, especially by a girl. 'Only small stuff, weren't it?' he'd complained. 'From people who could afford it! It's not like it was the Hatton Garden heist or something.'

A spell inside with a drug rehabilitation requirement seemed to fix him. It worked because he wanted to be free of the drugs he knew controlled him. He was off heroin and could soon be off methadone. The scheme also fixed him up with a job in a wood mill in the depths of Surrey when he got out.

Basil knew Steve had visited his pal in Wandsworth Prison after the first few months of his incarceration. Breathing in the overpowering stench of bad food and disinfectant, submitting to the searches, hearing the clanging of umpteen gates being shut behind him and waiting with the wives, girlfriends and bewildered children in the visit hall as pale-faced inmates in their grey tracksuits filed in, made Steve determined to stay on the right side of the law, he'd said. That placated his dad.

Work at the wood mill when Kevin got out was a good fit for him, Steve said. He learned basic carpentry and cabinetmaking and then made furniture, mainly for kitchens, from the wood. He learned to love different grains and patterns. The countryside, after a lifetime on a council estate whose only claim to fame was that it was used in an episode of the '80s and '90s TV show *The Bill*, when the director needed to show the soul-destroying ugliness in which most petty criminals lived, suited him well too. He missed the pubs, clubs and noise of London. But he'd made a few pals.

The wood mill's owner found Kevin a cottage close by. He now had a room in which to display the hand-built oak table with two matching benches that he'd made when he first started.

It'd turned out handy for Steve too, Basil knew. The previous year he'd split with Sally, his girlfriend, and left the place they'd rented together. He planned to move back with mum and dad, only to find his parents about to divorce and the family home in Balham already in the process of being sold. He'd known about the split but not about the rapid house sale.

Kevin offered Steve the use of the big sofa that had come with the cottage and the shed at the back to store all his stuff.

'But there's only so long you can sleep on a sofa,' he'd told Basil. 'I've turned in my sleep and fallen on the floor too often.' He knew this was as amusing as it was true.

So, now Basil was to become Steve's landlord in the swanky high-rise flat he'd just bought with his share of the marital home money. Steve looked forward to getting back to the noise and busyness of a London suburb, where a mixed-race bloke like him wasn't regularly stared at. His work as a self-employed techie, which involved fixing clients' problems with computers, security systems, televisions, phones, cash registers – you name it – would improve too, just as soon as he could start advertising himself in the area.

It would be an adjustment for them both. Basil had come to like living alone; pottering around his flat in the evenings, opening a tin of soup now and then, but mainly eating bits and pieces picked at random in the supermarket, rarely a 'proper meal'; watching whatever television programmes he wanted, not having to negotiate everything with Dawn, the ex. He got a bit low sometimes, though. Very low once or twice. There was something in his head that sucked the enjoyment out of everything. He knew he'd been a wash-out as a husband because of it.

But all in all, Steve's moving in would be worth it, Basil had decided; worth the thumping reggae music, worth all the mess he knew the kid would make. He'd investigate the building's problems – if there actually were any – and sort things out.

A few nights earlier, Basil had tried to ignore a knock on his door, hoping that whoever it was would go away. No such luck. Janice, who lived in the flat below, had heard his TV, knew he was at home and persisted. She was determined to invite him into hers for a 'chat', as she called it, or a 'rant', as he would've called it. He begrudgingly went but soon lost interest and escaped after only ten minutes, saying he needed to get back for a television programme he couldn't miss.

She wanted to warn him about the dangers the South Quay residents apparently faced. They needed new fire and smoke alarms fitting in all communal areas, and for the smoke ventilation to be improved, fire escapes to be constructed and the roof to be made properly fire-resistant.

'It's just not safe, this block, Baz,' Janice kept saying, her eyes widening.

He hated being called Baz.

'We need to get the council in to do a full survey and advise us if we should have nightly fire patrols. Come to the meeting here next Monday night at seven and we'll decide how to tackle this. The work's got to be done and the developers have a duty to pay. Otherwise, no one will want to buy the flats off us. I think it's worth looking into, don't you?'

Basil smiled meekly and said he'd do his best to be there, depending on when he finished work. He agreed they should make the block as safe as possible, but he knew he wouldn't be able to manage the stress. The marriage break-up had made him suicidal. He couldn't risk a repeat.

'Perhaps my son Steve can come too,' he added, eager to put an end to the conversation. 'He's moving in with me for a bit. He works in IT and he's good at research and sorting things out.'

One thing Steve had been sorting out for years was his dad's mental health: dealing with his GP to have him referred, finally getting him to a mental health clinic. That had been a marathon task. A year ago, they'd agreed Basil needed help with what they thought was common or garden depression but what the GP said was his attention deficit hyperactivity disorder (ADHD). Then he lost his latest job, as overall manager at Johnson's, as he had lost several jobs before that, for 'unreliability'.

When Steve heard the news, he got angry, angrier than Basil had ever seen him. A few days later, after some online research, Steve marched into the brewery director's office and told him his dad should have been given a formal warning, that he'd acted illegally in firing him on the spot.

How Steve knew about those things, Basil couldn't imagine. The lad managed to get him a delivery driver's job with the same firm. A comedown, but a job that would give him a reason to get up and out in the mornings and provide a pay packet each month.

People, Basil included, used to think that only kids get ADHD, kids who mess around at school and can't seem to concentrate even when they're quite bright. But research showed that ADHD children become ADHD adults with similarly disorganised lives. Basil could give lectures on disorganised-ness, if only he could sit down long enough to write a few notes, then not become distracted.

Steve said he would put a stop to that. He knew what it was like when his dad's black moods descended and he lost the will to get out of bed, to work, eat, talk, live. It was as if it were a shameful condition that no one understood, least of all the sufferers.

Basil welcomed Steve into the flat on Sunday, after lunchtime. He explained to his dad that he'd promised to return the van 'as soon as' and collect his scooter.

Once inside the flat, Basil told him to help himself to a bottle of Johnson's from the fridge, something Steve needed no arm-twisting to do. He sat down in the kitchen, gathering his strength before bringing in his possessions.

'In the end, I went with Kev on the job he had yesterday,' he said, flopping on to the sofa, beer in hand. 'It was down in Surrey somewhere – a big house. Kev was delivering kitchen stuff from a hire company for guests coming to a party. They already had some but needed more, apparently. Loads of it. It was like a posh wedding do, only it was to celebrate some politician getting a knighthood. Then he needed help to get them returned to this firm in Tooting.'

Basil surveyed the messy mountain that Steve had brought up, thanks to Kevin's van. Computers, printers, routers, miles of wires and leads, laptops, iPads, books, three or four suitcases, bulging bags of trainers and exercise clothes – Steve planned to make good use of the residents' basement gym.

He'd pushed everything into the lift and dragged it out into the communal hall of the fifth floor. Basil's neat and sparsely furnished flat was about to undergo a tsunami.

On Monday, the evening television news included an item on the death of an MP, Dietrich Olson, at a party at his home to celebrate his getting a knighthood. It was, said the newsreader in an appropriately grave manner, 'from natural causes'.

Basil almost dropped his bowl of microwaved lasagne. He'd just realised that the house to which he'd taken the beer was where Kevin and Steve had delivered hired equipment and furniture, all for some big party. The one at which that famous bloke died. He told Steve.

'Who gives a flying fuck about a bloody Tory politician?' Steve scoffed, as he took off his crash helmet, sat down next to his dad and switched channels.

4

'You could just have clipped and saved the obituaries to read later, when you felt better,' Bella told her brother.

But Tom wanted to read them as soon as they appeared. He wanted to sort out in his muddled, inflamed mind who his father had really been. It might help him understand his own hopes and fears. So, for a week or so, he'd bought all the day's newspapers and spread them out on the dining table in the Victorian mansion block in Bloomsbury. One broadsheet's three-quarter page tribute was headlined, 'Dietrich Olson, the politician whose all-round affability finally cancelled the Conservatives' reputation as "the nasty party".'

'Bit of an exaggeration but not bad,' Tom reckoned.

Most of the others reported that Dietrich Olson was born Dominic Frederick Olson to parents who ran a hardware shop in Tring, Hertfordshire. An ancestor on his father's side had come from Sweden but an 's' had dropped out of the original Olsson name over the years. The Scandinavian heritage may have explained his father's fair hair and deep-set blue eyes.

Several of the obits praised him but few were effusive. According to a widely quoted ancient family friend, Dietrich's parents opened a second shop with accommodation above near Clapham Junction, so that their son could attend Emanuel School, a direct grant school that became a fee-paying 'independent' one, on an academic scholarship. He didn't shine at rugby or rowing but studied hard enough to win a place at Wadham College, Oxford, to read history. He worked in menial jobs during the holidays to help pay term-time living costs.

He joined the Oxford Conservative Club and, an unnamed politician told *The Times*, 'Did his best to ingratiate himself with students who seemed destined to become big hitters because he dreamed of becoming a politician.'

He befriended a few members of the famous Bullingdon Club but wasn't invited to join, almost certainly because Emanuel wasn't nearly a well-enough known school. It couldn't compete with, for example, Eton, or Westminster, or Fettes.

On graduating, he decided he'd rather be known as Dietrich than Dominic because, he'd said, it was unusual and memorable. He was a fan of the German baritone and conductor Dietrich Fischer-Dieskau and had discovered that Dietrich means 'Ruler of the People', which amused him. It also made him sound posher. Tom put his mug of now-cold coffee in the microwave to heat up. He thought his dad had been an idiot to switch from the perfectly acceptable Dominic.

Fellow Old Emanuellian, or OE as they liked to call themselves, Michael Wilson-Green confirmed in an interview they'd worked together to run an online retail business that flourished and then failed. Money continued to be a problem for Dietrich, several writers claimed, but he'd wisely kept in touch with Oxford contemporaries who'd gone 'into the city' – an investment banker and a hedge funder. He took a few low-level jobs these friends found for him while also dabbling in residential property ventures using money borrowed from his parents before setting up a small company.

Once installed in the city, he pushed his interest in estate planning. Considering that he'd no qualifications in tax matters, finance, or the law, this made no sense, the writer from *The Times* said. Yet he knew a lot of rich men by then and turned out to be good at giving them advice on tax matters by pointing out to them problems they didn't know existed, like a dentist who keeps finding new cavities to be filled, cavities the patient didn't know he had – and actually didn't.

In fact, Dominic was educating himself by reading everything he could find on tax law, and he made copious notes on patterns in financial and political markets.

'He was a fast learner,' commented Wilson-Green. 'He anticipated changes in government policy on everything from tax rates to stamp duty and rules on inheritance tax.'

He was also highly personable and a really nice bloke, a fellow MP said, so that rich people welcomed him into their homes and, in a few cases, appointed him to the boards of family foundations. He charged a lot for his advice and channelled it all into companies he'd set up, most of them shell companies registered overseas to evade UK tax.

Then a stroke of luck. He'd been keeping an eye on parliamentary vacancies and had spotted the Central London North constituency, which was always a safe Conservative seat and one of the smallest in the UK. When it became vacant and the intended Tory candidate had to pull out at the last minute through illness, Dietrich stepped smartly in and won it.

A few of the obit writers had consulted their city department colleagues to come up with an estimate of Dietrich's net worth. He'd died rich, very rich, they reported. The *Daily Mail's* writer couldn't resist remarking that Dietrich had more than enough money to support two families, one with Penny Bryant, the other with Jane Page-Smith.

Tom flinched at the mention of Jane, or, as he preferred, That Fucking Woman. He knew most of the background information about his dad but found the ways it was conveyed interesting. He thought about the techniques of the obit writers, how they found people in the know to provide information as quickly as they did. Did they begin drafting obits on celebrities and VIPs as soon as they reached fifty? As soon as they failed to attend annual events linked to their work? Or as soon as they were reported to have a medical condition more serious than flu?

The 'comment' articles were a different matter. Sometimes sanctimonious, often plain poor, they stretched Tom's tolerance to the limit. Once Jane Page-Smith had arrived on the scene and assorted columnists and agony aunts had got to work on the tragedy, the articles made for nauseating reading. Today's so-called analysis in a tabloid he never read was the worst yet.

Had he not been so tired, he'd have screamed obscenities, sworn and kicked the furniture. Being the rock of the family was a strain. He flung down the newspaper. Another article from another paper's award-winning columnist on the subject of bigamy was inspired by the imagined heartbreak of poor, unsuspecting Penny Bryant Olson. The writer, her picture by-line at the top of the page, showed a fat frump with a smug smile. She described Tom's mother as, 'She who'd faced the shock and misery of discovering that her husband had another wife, a legitimate one.' She then added, 'And don't forget the terrible irony of this news exploding at the man's memorial service.'

Aaarrrgh!

Similar drivel appeared in other papers, on radio 4's *Woman's Hour* or on television, with puerile comments from assorted psychotherapists and grief counsellors being churned out for days. The memorial service had taken place only last week. It felt like a year since Tom, Bella and his mother had started battling their real misery: Dietrich's death.

As light crept across the skyline, Tom stood in boxer shorts at the counter in the family's London kitchen to pour himself a glass of water. Then he looked again at the paper's illustrations, the familiar pictures of his mother with his late father alongside newer ones of a woman calling herself Jane Page-Smith but formerly Jane Olson, the gate crasher. Or, as he would have put it, the conniving, money-grabbing bloody liar. There were also photos of a young man who, she said, was Dietrich's son. From his hunched shoulders and bowed head, he seemed to be embarrassed by the whole situation. Poor bugger!

The woman had to be fantasising, didn't she? Tom wondered if the young bloke was *her* real son, let alone Dietrich's. Perhaps he was an actor she'd hired for the occasion. Lots of actors drifted around Bloomsbury, nearby Fitzrovia and Soho. The small hotel opposite Colt Court had recently stuck small tables and chairs around its doors to serve coffee and snacks, and Bella said it seemed like a hub for unemployed thespians. They lounged on the chairs, smoked and laughed loudly, seeming to be pretty pleased with themselves. Then there was the Oxfam second-hand bookshop up the road from Colt Court, which was usually packed with out-of-work actors, students from nearby University College and workers from the British Museum on their breaks.

Later, Bella put a cup of fresh coffee in front of Tom as he continued his spittle-sprayed rant about the latest 'think piece' he'd read in the *Daily Express*. 'I wanted to get on the phone right away to the editor and tell him or her that the article was disgraceful, insulting crap, that this Jane person is a fucking fantasist, and that the Olson family is considering suing her and the paper.

'We should demand to have the record set straight!'

Except they couldn't, Bella pointed out. These were just comment articles. Anyway, they didn't know anything. Not for certain. They'd need to know who this woman was and what'd made her come out of the woodwork after so long. Was it just to scoop up money? And why did she have to make it all so public? What was it she really wanted? To discredit Dietrich? And could she inflict yet more harm and embarrassment on them all?

There were so many unanswered questions. And perhaps the biggest one – the one that had been gnawing away at Tom since the party, since he'd walked around the suddenly empty farmhouse in a daze – was why and how his father had left them without warning, dying of a heart condition no one suspected he'd had.

He rubbed his eyes. Perhaps he needed spectacles, he thought glumly. Better get an eye test. What a faff! Still, he'd never become a surgeon if he couldn't see where he was sticking his scalpel. He was in his third student year at Guy's and St Thomas' hospitals and, thanks to the rotations in various departments, he understood a lot in general about the human body, diseases and symptoms, but only a little in detail about most of it.

He knew he wasn't a natural medic and felt ashamed that he'd had to look up sudden cardiac arrest – the official cause of Dietrich's death – on Google, then check it in his college's library. He'd found that it's usually an electrical malfunction of the heart linked to a toxic mix of constant high levels of stress, poor sleep, poor eating habits and insufficient exercise.

The fact was, he kept thinking, it didn't fucking fit!

Dietrich wasn't like that. He was relaxed, laid back. He didn't bottle things up because he didn't care that much about politics, and he was no longer a businessman. He didn't need to be. He had enough money. He didn't smoke or drink much, ate healthily, wasn't unfit. He rode his old push-bike to the House of Commons, for God's sake!

He must have had an undetected heart condition. That must have been it. Should Tom have nagged him to have annual checks? Should he have spotted small signs? Was he responsible in part for his father's death?

Guilty thoughts kept hammering away in his head.

He remembered his dad occasionally returning from his constituency office late, casually handing a thick file to his mother and asking her to assess and offer suggestions about settling 'the damn thing'. What he'd meant was, 'Make it go away.'

She never looked pleased and had gone on to work long hours on the matters. She often seemed as though she'd like to strangle his father for the mistakes... mistakes made because he was negligent and chronically lazy. Some of the complaints kept his mother awake at night. Not his father.

He'd always slept well and then had scrambled eggs for breakfast, usually humming and tapping his fingers to the music of whichever composer Radio 3 or Jazz FM were featuring at the time.

'So, this is the dilemma,' Tom told Bella over breakfast at the flat they shared in Bankside. 'Did the junior doctor who examined Dad's body at the Royal Surrey Hospital make a mistake because it was a Saturday afternoon and the A&E department was flooded with injured football players, victims of road crashes or dopey DIYers who'd fallen off ladders? Was he too rushed to thoroughly look at Dad's body?

'Or, was there another natural cause of death, a very rare heart condition, one that simply hadn't been picked up?'

Pen said nothing when Tom made a similar speech in Colt Court that evening. She had no way of telling and, anyway, she was still in a state of shock and barely speaking.

'Or,' Tom continued, talking to himself, hardly daring to think or say it, 'was there an *unnatural* cause? There's been no autopsy, no certainty. Now Dad's in a coffin in a churchyard in Godalming. And no one will ever know.'

He replayed in his mind his conversation with the junior doctor who'd examined Dietrich when the ambulance brought him into the hospital's A&E department. He'd had a faint Greek accent and was dressed in a thin plastic apron over baggy purple scrubs.

As soon as he'd heard sudden cardiac arrest, Tom had pointed out that his father didn't have heart trouble. 'He was in good nick and cycled around London, Godalming and other parts of Surrey. He was not out of breath when he arrived home or at any other time; he wasn't overweight; wasn't a boozer, and he didn't worry about things or enemies.'

He had to ask the doctor again.

'I see why you're still puzzled,' sighed Jonas Christos, when Tom had phoned and caught the doc at an unusually quiet moment. 'But high blood pressure and stress are very common among high-flyers of your father's age. Undetected problems such as ischaemic coronary heart disease are not uncommon. Young men, even teenagers, who seem to be perfectly fit, have been known to collapse and die on the football field or on the tennis court.

'And I promise you, although we were busy, I examined your father's body carefully with two experienced nurses and there was nothing to make us think an inquest would be merited for an unexplained death. There were no wounds or bruises, and we did the usual blood tests. He wasn't diabetic and nothing obvious showed up. He'd been drinking but not very much. If there had been signs of foul play, we'd have called the police. We're obliged to do that.

'Sadly, these things sometimes just happen.'

'Could there have been something else?'

'Only a full post-mortem and toxicology tests would have revealed if there were other factors...'

'Which could be what?'

'Well, an undiagnosed condition such as a congenital heart defect. Or he might have been taking prescribed medication at the wrong dosage. Or...'

'Or what?' Tom pressed.

'Or it was an unnatural cause. He'd been poisoned with something we wouldn't have known to run a test for.'

Tom lay awake night after night. *Was* it a mad notion?

Saturday morning back in Colt Court, he'd snapped back into the present, stacked mugs and plates in the dishwasher, checked with his mum that she didn't need anything, put on his coat and went out to walk to Regent's Park. Exercise, always a bore, but always a good idea. He passed the Lincoln's Inn Fields Tennis Courts, where he used to play tennis with his dad, usually beating him.

The following day, Tom read only the news sections of *The Sunday Times* with his coffee and toast. He took a cup to his mother, who had been self-isolating in her study room since the memorial service, gave her a hug and asked what he could buy for them to eat that evening.

Then he rang his sister. She'd chosen to stay in the flat on the Southbank that they'd shared for several years and into which she had invited piano-playing Ed, the boyfriend Tom wasn't quite sure was right for her. He thought about Ed, then stopped himself. Was he already taking over from his father, demanding no one less than a handsome prince with a country estate be allowed to woo beautiful Bella?

He smiled to himself at the thought. It was true that Ed had no money. He didn't even have parents – they'd died in a car crash in Romania about eight years ago – but as far as Tom was concerned, he was bright, funny, a diplomatic flat-mate and a good cook. And he clearly adored Bella.

Bella answered at the first ring.

'Bell, it's me,' Tom boomed, trying to sound upbeat because he knew she wasn't. 'How about we wake up old George Spicer? Can I arrange an appointment at his office with you and Mum? We can find out what damage, if any, the fucking Jane Page-Smith woman could do as far as Dad's estate is concerned. That's if she's telling the truth, of course. We should perhaps try to find out more about her, whether there's a real marriage certificate or not. What d'you reckon?'

He heard her say, 'Yeah, OK. Text me when.'

Two days later, Tom held his mother's Burberry-raincoated arm and guided her out of the taxi and up the couple of steps to the large, imposing doors in Bedford Street, Covent Garden, where George Spicer's office was based. She seemed nervous, afraid of journalists with their questions and cameras. Mercifully, the street was empty. Anyway, most of her face was obscured by a scarf and big sunglasses. Tom noticed that when she took them off there was an overall greyness to her that matched the cloudy late February sky. Bella arrived in a taxi shortly afterwards, looking similarly drained.

'As far as I'm aware, there's no will,' George announced, his Scottish accent faint. 'Over the years, I'd spoken and written to Dietrich several times suggesting he make one. I knew his business affairs were, shall we say, complicated. I tried to impress on him the importance of not leaving a huge tangle for you all to unravel. He told me he was fit as a flea, had no plans to conk out for at least another thirty years and promised he'd have meetings with Philip Coyne, his accountant, to set everything out on paper. I guess he just never got round to it.'

Pen nodded; it was as she'd thought. 'Typical!' she said. 'Dietrich always believed Karen or I would deal with boring things like that.

'I can't really remember my probate law, but the legal spouse gets the majority of the deceased's estate automatically, I think. No inheritance tax, no need to wait for probate to be granted. So, we need to work out what Dietrich's estate includes.'

She leaned back in her chair and sighed.

'The Colt Court flat is mine; I owned it before we married. No mortgage. Dietrich paid the bills, but the deeds will show I inherited it from my aunt Lillian, who died while I was at university.

'The Bankside flat is a leasehold in Tom and Bella's names. I made sure of that when Dietrich and I bought it. There's no mortgage and it's got a long lease too. So, that means that none of us will be homeless. Dietrich and I owned Batts Farm and the surrounding land fifty-fifty, as tenants in common. We paid off the mortgage years ago.

'So, if this woman was in fact still married to him and is the legal spouse – and we all hope she isn't – Batts Farm will have to be sold. She'd get half the value – Dietrich's half – and, if I can't buy the woman out, I should get the other half. Is that right?'

Tom watched unhappily as George slowly nodded.

Pen pulled a tissue from her handbag and dabbed her eyes. Bella put an arm around her mother's bony shoulders. Grief's a good way to lose weight, she noted.

'I have a reasonably well-paid job at the LSE,' Pen resumed, her voice still strained. 'Bella will have one once she's qualified in a few years' time and Tom will have one in three or four years, when he'll be a junior doctor. In any case, his student fees are paid from a special account that Dietrich set up for him, and one I hope this Page-Smith person won't know about and couldn't get her hands on anyway. I feel sure Dietrich had a pretty big pension pot, and with luck, he'll have been advised to nominate me to go on receiving the payments.

'So, I mean, whatever the bloody woman does, none of us will starve.'

Tom and Bella knew this, but it was reassuring to have it spelled out.

Bella asked George, 'Are there any legal consequences of bigamy, even when the guilty party has died?'

George screwed up his face as he thought. 'Bigamy doesn't often come up in court. There's a potential for one party to commit fraud to escape a marriage that is unsatisfactory in some way, but it's rare. So, I'd say it's the least of your worries.'

Tom sighed and asked, 'What about this Jane person, George? Can she really claim most of the rest of Dad's estate – presuming she's telling the truth about their alleged marriage?'

George sat back, looked up at the ceiling and pressed his lips together.

An uneasy silence filled the room.

'She won't get everything because Dietrich had children. If she produces a genuine marriage certificate, she'll inherit half the value of the farmhouse, or property to the value of about £270,000, and half of what remains. There are certainly other properties owned by companies he has a majority stake in. And a huge number of stocks and shares in other companies. Theoretically, she could get half of those.

'I've been in touch with Dietrich's accountant. He's doing his best to gather everything. It's a lot.

'Straight away, he sent me copies of deeds for a house Dietrich bought in Raynes Park, in South London, in the early 1970s. He seems to have bought it for a Jane Page-Smith and a Charles Olson. He also appears to have had two other accounts at Coutts bank. One of them made payments for Jane and the boy, payments you might describe as spousal and child support. The other shows that a life insurance policy was taken out on Dietrich, which he'd been making regular payments towards. It's worth between one and two million pounds. A Jane Page-Smith and a Charles Olson are the named beneficiaries.'

The temperature in the room plunged.

No one spoke in the taxi home. In the Colts Court kitchen, mother and children ate bowls of Waitrose tomato and basil soup, heated in the microwave, with toast. They discussed modernising the bathrooms and using a builder who'd been working on a flat on the same floor and who'd been keen to show them his transformative work. After that, Pen said she'd like to lie down in her bedroom.

Tom took out his phone and booked rail tickets for himself and Bella to travel to Oxford in a few days' time to look for evidence of Dietrich's marriage to Jane Page-Smith. He also rang the number he'd found for Ben Harding, his father's flatmate in Oxford. The line was dead. Damn!

They left their mother in bed, propped up on pillows and *The Guardian* and *The Times* on her bedside table. Earlier, Bella had checked that there were no articles about Dietrich in either.

5

It was a hot topic in the newspapers, but in the noisy Criminal Investigation Department at Holborn nick, no one was discussing who would replace Dietrich Olson as Member of Parliament in their constituency. No one gave a monkey's.

Candidates for the empty seat seemed to have been waiting to pounce. A by-election date was set for April and posters were suddenly plastered everywhere in EC1 and WC1; on walls, on lamp posts, in shop windows and in the windows of the flats and offices above them.

In Lambs Conduit Street, where the ugly police station building stretched 13 storeys into the sky, they appeared overnight at ground level, leaving bookshops, cafés, the Perseverance pub and NobleRot restaurant, clothes shops and even the Great Ormond Street Children's Hospital buildings were covered in headshots of smiling strangers urging people to vote for them.

If they weren't careful, coppers on their way to work from the Tube station, along busy Theobalds Road near the junction with Lambs Conduit Street, could be ambushed by canvassers for a candidate for the Conservative party, the Greens, the Liberal Democrats or the Labour party. There was an Independent 'Reverse Brexit' woman candidate too and a man from a far-right party no one seemed to have heard of.

Inside the building, however, in the bleak custody suite, with panic strips on its shiny grey walls and along the blue corridor to the cells, it was a politics-free zone that Monday morning. It was the same upstairs in the much messier CID offices.

Not that Detective Sergeant Mehmet Kharim, the department's funny man, didn't have strongly held political opinions he wanted to share, views almost as passionately held as those on Queens Park Rangers, the football team he supported obsessively and about which his boss, Detective Inspector Rob Howarth had, in exasperation, banned him from mentioning during working hours.

That was so entirely bloody typical of Rob Howarth, Mehmet thought. Weird in so many ways, that bloke. Didn't like football! Went to Cambridge University, apparently, though he never mentioned it himself, then fast-tracked by the Met. Few recruits made it to the rank of Detective Inspector *that* quickly. Loved cricket, rugby, even tennis. Just *not football*. Imagine that! And if you drove in a car with him, he picked classical music and played it loud. Would you believe it? Old codger's stuff. And Rob wasn't even forty!

The boss also snapped at anyone making remarks about women that he considered crude. Even referring to the team's newest recruit, DC Marley Brown as 'luv' elicited a frown from the boss. Marley, five feet ten tall and clearly comfortable in her size eight Doc Martens, was quite capable of fighting her own battles. One glance at her could tell you that. Yet Rob had made a point of plonking a cup of tea on Marley's desk on her first day. Probably to forestall any 'Make us a cuppa, there's a good girl!' remarks that might be forthcoming. As she walked, poker-faced, past him, Mehmet had almost said, 'Cheer up, Darlin!' Luckily his phone rang in time to stop him.

Still, Mehmet thought a few minutes later, as he flicked the switch on the kettle in the department kitchen and picked out a mug whose inside wasn't completely tannin-stained, he couldn't imagine a fairer or smarter boss than Rob Howarth.

He'd decided that soon after Rob had arrived at Holborn nick to be mocked for his toffs' accent and top-speed promotion. Mehmet had said as much to Elizabeth, Rob's wife, at the first Christmas party in the nick after he'd arrived. She was a pretty, friendly woman. No airs. She told him she was a university lecturer and had met Rob at Cambridge. She understood police work, he supposed. Brainy, obviously, like him. So, it made sense.

As he dropped a PG Tips teabag into the mug and poured boiling water over it, Mehmet wondered if he would ever find someone like that, a woman who'd understand if their social arrangements had to be dumped at the last moment or why he might not be in a good mood after a vital bit of evidence couldn't be found that day, meaning that it couldn't be disclosed to the defence solicitor and, according to some spineless CPS bloke, some bastard couldn't be charged with the crime he was certainly guilty of. In his opinion, most CPS prosecutors were spineless.

Mehmet's last girlfriend, Astrid, had taken almost a year to kick him out. He'd been expecting it. He just couldn't stick to their agreed plans. Ah, well. His love life had been more of a 'love death' for the six months since then, he reflected, as he sniffed what was left in the small milk carton next to the box of teabags, decided it wasn't off and poured some into the mug.

He took his tea to his desk and opened the file on an assault outside a pub in Red Lion Square on Friday night. Two stupid blokes who'd probably got to the end of a dreary work week, had too much to drink and needed to hit someone to prove it. Unusually, neither had been kept in the nick over the weekend. All the cells were full. From the photos of them, a dentist somewhere would be making a good few quid on repair jobs, Mehmet reckoned. But apart from knocked-out teeth, two sets of bloody lips and one black eye, it didn't look as though the punch-up had been a prolonged affair. Neither fighter had suffered what the law calls 'grievous bodily harm', whatever that actually was. Putting someone in a wheelchair? Or whacking them so hard they'd need a few stitches in A&E?

So, as he gulped his tea and finished off a packet of digestives that had been crumbling in a desk drawer for weeks, he reckoned their CPS people, Simon Guerrier-Belmont and his number two, Scott David, housed in their separate ugly building, this one in Petty France, St James's, would be happy with a Section 47, Actual Bodily Harm assault charge. One of the blokes, whose record showed he'd done this twice before, could possibly land himself in jail for up to six months. Or maybe he'd get a hundred hours of community service instead, which he'd almost certainly skive off doing. The other, whose first offence this would be, would probably escape with a suspended sentence or even a fine, especially if he could afford a decent defence barrister.

Mehmet knew the law. He'd read and taken tests on the PACE Code –The Police and Criminal Evidence Act of 1984 – the coppers' bible. He just didn't *like* it. Anyway, it wasn't a CID matter, he decided. He stood up and put the file in a basket of stuff to go downstairs to the 'uniforms'.

The sound of car keys clattering as they landed on a desk meant the boss had arrived. A stocky man with thick, close-cropped brown hair, Rob Howarth wore a waxed black jacket over an unironed shirt. Unpolished brown lace-ups peeped from the bottoms of dark jeans. As usual, he was holding a tall cup of what had been a Starbucks coffee, which he hurled into the empty rubbish bin outside his cubicle. He'd never been known to miss.

'Got a moment, Mehm? You still live on your own?' he asked his sergeant, who nodded, but warily.

'Fancy a secondment in the deep south?'

'Wha-a?' Mehmet was alarmed.

'For – I dunno – six months, maybe a year. It's not fixed yet.'

Mehmet's frown hadn't lifted. His guts were in knots.

'Don't look so worried. Secondment means it's temporary. And I'll be working with you.'

Mehmet sat down. Rob sat back.

'By Deep South, I mean Guildford not Alabama. About 30 miles away. And you won't need jabs.

'We'd be catching up with Izzy, late of this parish. Remember little Izzy? Course you do! She got married and was happy to move down to Guildford because she and the husband could buy a house there. They couldn't afford a one-bed flat in Holborn, or even a garden shed in Wandsworth, where they were living in his parents' spare room and apparently going quietly nuts.'

Mehmet was relieved that Izzy was now married. It had been obvious to everyone in Holborn CID that she'd had a serious crush on Rob, and he'd have hated to be piggy in the middle.

Shuffling papers on his desk, Rob went on, 'Well, after a few months in Guildford, our girl got herself in line for a commendation. Then a promotion to sergeant for nabbing the so-called Wandsworth Burglar. You might remember she started that job while she was with us, looking into burglaries in Bloomsbury that seemed to fit the same pattern. That brought her, in a roundabout way, to the attention of Surrey Police.'

Mehmet's face had still not completely uncrumpled. He'd liked Detective Constable Isobel – 'Izzy' – Wilmot, now Holland, but then so had everyone in Holborn CID. She'd been brilliant on the Louisa Mills rape case. Well, they all had, in his view.

'Izzy's husband got a job at the Royal Surrey Hospital as a manager of their paramedics' service. Izzy's boss, DCI Derek Villiers, was suffering from what he thought was just backache, but when he went for a scan, he was diagnosed with pancreatic cancer. And because he faced months of treatment, surgery and the rest, he decided to take early retirement, get his number two promoted and have a promising young detective transferred to Guildford to fill the empty desk. He'd met Izzy and liked her, and she was already earmarked for a move. He also decided to bring in some temporary help. Us.'

'Yeah, but why do they need a top detective inspector like you, boss? Guildford is not exactly a crime hotspot, is it?' Mehmet scoffed. 'What usually happens there? A couple of drink drivers and a few quid missing from the till in the golf club bar every now and then?'

Rob frowned. 'As it happens, the body of Esther Hall, an 18-year-old student, was found two months ago in a garage in Horsley. She'd been raped, beaten up and strangled.

'Horsley's a sleepy little village between Guildford and Leatherhead. Population about five thousand. The local cops have interviewed all the obvious people but turned up nothing, and the way Surrey Police explained it to me, they need new eyes on the crime. So,' he went on wearily, 'it's a bit of a challenge for us.'

Mehmet got that part. Rob added that he reckoned he would commute from home in New Malden on most days and stay in a cheap hotel in or near Guildford if he ever had to work too late to drive home.

'Thought you might like to come too?' Rob said. 'With Izzy there already, it could be Holborn's Three Musketeers back in business. I've been down there to have a look, and I can tell you that Surrey Police headquarters and custody suite are a lot cushier than in this place.'

Mehmet gave it five seconds' thought, before explaining how it would mean he'd be a bit further away from his mother, who hadn't been well recently.

'I don't know what's wrong with her but she's not her usual self,' he said.

'But you can easily drive up at the weekend or whenever. Use a squad car,' Rob argued.

Overall, it sounded OK, Mehmet reckoned. So, they were set to leave the city for the sticks. Within an hour, they were on their way upstairs to seal the deal with the big boss, Superintendent Roger Malden.

Later in the morning, Izzy emailed him to say a friend who was going abroad had a furnished studio flat in the city centre, five minutes' walk from the nick in Margaret Street. Mehmet could rent it on a rolling contract, giving only a month's notice to leave. What could be easier?

Then, with Mehmet driving a silver Vauxhall Insignia, the best squad car available, they set off for a preliminary nose around Guildford.

When she met them from the lift, Izzy looked great, Mehmet thought. New short, bouncy hairstyle, touch of eye shadow and the sort of well-fitting skirt, jumper and boots the female cop in TV's *Line of Duty* would wear. She was clearly thrilled to see her old muckers and quickly showed Rob the corner office she'd found for him and the desk for Mehmet just outside it. Then she introduced them to the other members of the CID squad sitting around in various states of busyness.

Pinned on a wall covered in blue felt in the main incident room were photos of Esther Hall, a baby-faced brunette in a student nurse's uniform; her parents, Patricia and Sean; their house on the other side of Horsley; the garage in an industrial park where Esther's body was found; a close-up of blood on the garage's concrete floor and, finally, a fellow student on the nursing degree course at Surrey University.

Annette Gould, described as Esther's best friend, was doing the same three-month clinical placement. Esther had been leaving the centre at around seven on a Friday evening, when it was thought she was somehow lured or dragged off by the perpetrator, probably in a car or van.

'CCTV outside the medical centre's front door gives us nothing,' sighed Izzy. 'The parents say she used her bike to travel from their house to the clinic, but we can't find an abandoned bike like it. It might have been taken away by the perpetrator, or it could just have been nicked later by someone else.

'We've interviewed the friend and the parents about boyfriends – apparently, she hadn't had one for months.

'We've also got a bit of forensic evidence. The perp used a condom but there's a spot of semen on her underwear. Presumably his. Forensics are testing it and obviously it's significant. Still, we can hardly get every male in the area to do a DNA test. And, of course, he may not have been a local.'

Rob stared at the photo display. 'We'll be back tomorrow after we've cleared our desks in Holborn,' he told Izzy. 'Meanwhile, it's worth checking out anyone on the Sex Offenders' Register in the area; we might start bringing them in next week. I know that Esther was 18 and legally not a child, but looking at her face in the photo, she could easily have passed for 15. Add a nurse's uniform and, well, you know what some of these creeps are like.'

As the unmarked police Vauxhall cruised back up the M3, Rob said, 'Let's go to the medical centre first tomorrow. We'll talk to the manager and whoever Esther was taking instructions from. Perhaps someone there had a special interest in her. One that had nothing to do with sprained ankles or backaches.'

The following morning, Mehmet was outside Holborn Station's front door in the Vauxhall at ten past nine. He'd already filled the boot with boxes of diaries, address books and some odds and ends from their desks. Strange how fond you can become of a particular pen pot or stapler, he thought.

Humming along to something on his earphones, Rob clambered in with his coffee and one for the DS. Mehmet looked at him, thinking about this whole event. He had the impression the boss was putting on an act of cheeriness for his benefit. He was probably right, but he could also tell Rob wasn't keen to talk.

They needed to use the sat nav, which Mehmet fiddled with, cursing when he tapped in the wrong postcode. To his surprise, they arrived at the West Horsley Medical Centre in less than forty minutes, probably due to light traffic on the A3.

Nigel Jones, the manager, looked at their police warrant cards and took off his reading glasses with the sort of sigh that said, 'I'm too busy for this'. As he begrudgingly pulled out plastic chairs for them to sit on, Mehmet wondered if Mr Cold Fish Jones was unhappy being quizzed by an Asian cop or if he was this unpleasant with everyone.

'Miss Hall had only been with us for about three weeks and hadn't formed any attachments to anyone on the staff here, as far as I know,' Fish said. 'She was here mainly to observe, check notes were in the right files and piles and tell patients where to wait. Later, she would have been allowed to do minor tasks, such as applying dressings, taking BPs and temperatures and checking medical histories. But she wasn't at that stage yet.

'Specialist doctors hold clinics on different days, and she was free to float around the centre. I'm not sure if any of them asked her to do anything. If you'd like, you could ask Mr Tait, the orthopaedic specialist, or Dr Wyn-Jones, the gynaecologist. They're both here today. I'll get my assistant to show you where to go.'

Celia, Wyn-Jones's assistant, a small, round woman of around forty, was altogether warmer and more willing to help. 'Esther's death has stunned us all,' she said. 'Such a lovely girl; bright and warm. She'd have made a wonderful nurse. I could tell.'

'Did she talk to you about her private life – boyfriends, girlfriends, the people around where she lived with her parents, others from the university?' Mehmet asked.

'She told me when we ate our packed lunch together once that she'd broken up with her boyfriend last summer. She said it was for the best because she'd be able to concentrate on her course, but I'm not sure I believed her. I don't know why.

'I got the impression she didn't get on brilliantly with her parents. There was something about the way she was never in a hurry to leave of an evening, not like the rest of us.'

Mehmet shot a knowing look at Rob.

They went through the motions of talking to the two specialists, neither of whom seemed even to have noticed a new student at the centre nor had anything of interest to add.

Later that day, the Vauxhall pulled up outside Esther's parents' house, a neat, 1960s pebble-dashed semi in a cul-de-sac with a double garage. Rob wondered who needed a double garage these days.

They were invited in and shakily handed tea in bone china cups and saucers by the mother, Patricia. Red-eyed, she was clearly as fragile as the crockery. Sean, the father, stayed in the kitchen, staring out of the window over the sink, with his back to them. Either he was overcome with grief or just a man fed-up with cops, but Rob thought his behaviour was strange.

When asked if her daughter had a boyfriend, Patricia thought for a few moments while nervously fingering the single row of pearls around her neck. 'As I told the other policeman who came here, there was Mark somebody, a boy in her class at school. I can't remember his surname. She used to go to parties and drinks at the wine bar with him and some other friends. But it wasn't anything serious. He went off to do maths at Manchester Uni – or was it Leeds? Esther didn't seem bothered. Anyway, when they met up at a Christmas party, it wasn't a big romantic reunion or anything like that. Was it, Sean?'

The father eventually came into the sitting room. 'Have they found her bike yet? It was new – a Christmas present from us – and I told her she had to be very careful with it and always lock it properly.'

It struck Mehmet that he sounded as concerned about finding the bike as he was about finding his daughter's killer. He made a mental note to look at his history and perhaps his bank details to see if there was any unusual traffic. He really hoped the father had nothing to do with the crime, but he knew he had to check.

'Did Esther ever say where she parked it at the medical centre?' he asked.

The father shrugged. 'I assumed there's a bike place near the parking area. Esther never said she'd had to search for somewhere.'

'Was she happy with the nursing course, do you think?' Rob asked, looking at Patricia and Sean in turn.

'I think so,' sighed Patricia, her face crumbling again. 'She'd have liked to move into a flat with Annette, but we didn't want her to have to take out a big student loan. It's a four-year course, so that would've been a lot of rent money. Now, of course, we'd find the money even if...'

Mehmet nodded and both coppers said thanks for the tea and headed for the front door.

'Phillips! Mark Phillips. That's it!' Patricia exclaimed as

they were about to pull the front door closed. 'I've just remembered. His parents live in Clandon, near the pub there, just up the road from here.'

Mr and Mrs Phillips could expect a knock on their door and a request for Mark's tooth or hairbrush for a DNA comparison test. But not that morning.

Half an hour later, in a not-too-bad Wetherspoons near Izzy's new nick, Mehmet asked her about her triumph with the Wandsworth Burglar. She blushed.

'Let's get the drinks in first, eh?'

When she'd come back with a half of bitter for Rob and soft drinks for herself and Mehmet, she was ready to tell them about her burglar.

'It wasn't anything really. I just got a break. You know how it is.'

Mehmet wanted the details.

'My husband's parents were among his victims. Half the cash in Alex's dad's wallet gone and a new laptop swiped from the kitchen counter. No damage to the house, no prints. Local coppers drew a blank. Then their friends in the next street were done over too. This time it was a similar amount of money – half of the notes in the wallet, so the bloke didn't notice they were gone for days – and an engagement ring left by the hand basin in the downstairs loo.

'I was intrigued and decided to do a bit of patrolling for myself. Alex was away on one of his courses – he was training to become a hospital manager. I used his little Skoda because it's dark grey and you don't notice Skodas. No one ever steals them. Isn't that true?' She smiled and Mehmet nodded.

'I sat with a coffee, fiddled on my phone and kept watch. Finally, I spotted a thin, young bloke in a hoodie walking quickly down the middle of the road. When he saw me, he seemed to understand why I was there and started to leg it. But I drove after him, blocked him in at the end of the road and arrested him on suspicion of theft.'

'Just like that. Easy peasy!' said Mehmet, mildly mocking her understatement but envying her success.

'Look, I knew I could have been making a complete prat of myself with no back-up or anything. But when I asked him to empty his pockets and his bumbag on the car seat, he had wads of cash and two or three mobiles. To my relief, he didn't fight me or make a run for it.

'We found a load of stolen jewellery and stuff at his council flat in Tooting. So, Kevin Miller, thief and drug dealer, pleaded guilty at the first hearing, got a discounted sentence of two years and nine months and went to HMP Wandsworth for it.'

Mehmet sighed. 'Who'd have thought it! Little Izzy Wilmot nabs London's boldest burglar in living memory!'

'Give over,' she said, smiling bashfully.

He hugged her, which was all the more significant because showing emotion was not something Mehmet did often. Rob was pleased to see it. It suggested his number two was at last loosening up.

Then Mehmet's phone rang. 'It's my mum,' he said, looking upset and embarrassed. 'She's not herself.'

He walked outside to take the call.

6

BELLA STIRRED, pushed back the duvet and looked at her watch, then at Ed, lying beside her, already thumbing his phone. 'Coffee?' she said meekly. Ed sprang out of the large bed in the front bedroom of the Bankside flat and pulled up the window blind. Her first proper boyfriend and, he said, his first real love.

Each often secretly wondered how long it would last.

She watched him shake back a clump of hair so that he could gaze out at the grey river four floors below, a mesmerising pleasure. Blackfriars Bridge to the left, with its fading pink and cream sculpted sides, and across on the North Bank, to the right, the huge, lead-coloured dome of St Paul's Cathedral towering over ugly modern City office buildings. In the distance were the towers of the Shard, with its jagged golden needle piercing the sky, and the Gherkin, the skyscraper architects were sniffy about, though Bella loved it for the swirling geometric patterns of its glass walls.

It was a panoramic view that none of the residents of the

far more expensive Bankside flats, situated in front of Bella's shabby block and with ceiling-to-floor windows, shared.

The balconies for Bella's block had to be built on the south side, looking at the Tate, rather than at the river. According to legend, this was because the company bosses in the offices next to St Paul's had lobbied Southwark Council back when the flats were being built. There was a danger, the businessmen apparently pointed out, of underwear belonging to the council tenants being hung out across balconies. Hardly what the staff of top accountancy or insurance firms would have chosen to look at. True or not, it meant that laundry left on the south-facing balconies always dried quickly in the sunlight.

Bella pulled the duvet back over her shoulders as she heard Ed's bare feet shuffling to the bathroom. When she wasn't thinking about her dad, she reflected that day-to-day life with Ed was comfortable enough. He'd lost both parents in a road accident and, recalling the shock it caused him and his brothers, had treated her sensitively since the awful Batts Farm party.

Before that, she'd often weighed up their relationship in her mind: the sex was pretty good, and most mornings, he got up to make coffee, which were two pretty big plusses. She often looked fondly at his slim, square shoulders and tight buttocks. There'd been no big arguments; he did his share of the boring things: the shopping, cooking something for supper and keeping a file of the service charges and utility bills.

Bella's student friend Claire thought Ed was really fit and joked that she'd take him off her hands any day. Bella knew it wasn't a great passion for her and probably wouldn't last. She hadn't spotted anyone else who was fanciable, and her legal practice course was horrendously hard work, even for the daughter of a law professor. So now wasn't the time to look around.

Anyway, her dad's death had pushed such minor matters aside.

After a quick shower, a naked Ed walked back into the open-plan kitchen-living room, leaving a tell-tale trail of footprints on the wooden floor. He flicked the switch on the kettle. She knew he'd spoon Colombian coffee, the good stuff bought from a place near the entrance to Blackfriars Station and kept in a special tin, into a cafetière and pour boiling water over it. The smell was even better than the taste. He warmed milk in the microwave, made two mugsful and took one to Bella. She sat up slowly and took a sip.

'Nice here when your brother's away, isn't it?' he said, smiling and picking up a towel from the floor to dry himself with. 'Peaceful.'

'Tom will stay in Colt Court with Mum for quite a while, I expect,' Bella mumbled. 'She's still in a state of shock. Doubt she'll go back to work for a while, certainly not this term.'

Then tears filled her eyes as the events of the past couple of weeks flooded back. Ed gently took her coffee from her, put it on the bedside table and wrapped her in his dry arms.

He was helping her through these awful weeks mainly by saying little and giving her tender hugs. It gave her the strength to help her mother. Tom didn't talk about his feelings, but she knew he was suffering too. She could tell by the way he sat and stared most evenings and was suddenly loudly angry at small things, such as a few drops of rain coming through a half-open window and puddling on the floor of the Colt Court kitchen.

'Let's have breakfast,' Ed said. 'Then I must get to college to see someone... I expect you have jobs to do?'

Bella sighed. She'd have preferred to hide in bed all day. But she worried about her mum, concerned she wasn't doing enough for her.

She sorted out clothes for herself, and while brushing her teeth in the bathroom, guessed that the someone who Eduard Gheorghe, to give him his actual Romanian name, had to see was his personal tutor at Imperial College – he'd promised to investigate the matter of his about-to-expire study visa.

He confirmed it as he handed her a plate of wholemeal toast spread with Marmite, then dashed for the door.

* * *

'I've lived in London for more than eight years and, before Brexit, qualified for settlement status under the Freedom of Movement provision in European Law,' Ed told the grey-bearded man in his book-lined study.

'My three years for the engineering degree and the two for a master's in aerospace at Imperial College are my proof of residence in the UK. I'm almost fluent in English, and I think I'll pass the Life in the UK test thanks to my friends here. So, I should be safe unless I stay out of the country for more than five years, which is something I have no plans to do, particularly since meeting my girlfriend.'

The tutor nodded.

'As you know, I finished my master's last summer, so now I want to apply for jobs in the UK, preferably in London. I must find work. My uncle in Romania can't go on supporting me. He's done it for over six years.

'I can't go back to live in a country village a hundred miles from Bucharest and nearly two thousand miles from the world I've been enjoying here,' he went on, suddenly miserable. 'My parents died six years ago, and my older brothers and their wives and children are happy in the family home. They don't want me living with them – it's cramped enough as it is.

'And there's no work for me there except building site stuff or farm labouring. I want to stay here and do interesting work.' He was now on the brink of tears.

'You're saying that gaining UK citizenship is essential?' asked the grey-bearded man. 'You do know, don't you, that even if you made the complicated application to the Home Office yourself, without instructing a lawyer, it will still cost you at least £1,500?'

'Not a problem. I've had an evening job playing the piano in West End hotels for a year now and I've been saving most of that money.'

The tutor nodded again. He was sympathetic and said he would write a letter on Ed's behalf. He'd heard similar stories from other overseas students in London.

'How soon will I know about UK Citizenship?' Ed pushed. The tutor hedged a little and they agreed to meet again in a month's time.

Back at Bankside, Bella offered him soup, a sandwich and sympathy.

'Look, you're not homeless and you're not penniless. You've saved quite a bit from the hotel work. You just need to work a bit on your language and stop saying he or she when they're just it. Learn a few more silly phrases and then you'll sound properly English.'

He nodded and agreed. Even though the piano playing

work meant he and Bella couldn't go out most evenings, it was very well-paid and not unpleasant. He'd politely turned down hotel managers' offers to accept cash in hand. He didn't need a law-student girlfriend to tell him that tax evasion was a bad idea for someone trying to show he could become an upright British citizen.

The piano money also meant he could contribute to the Bankside flat's kitty, from which the bills were paid. Bella had let him bring in a small Yamaha piano, which he'd bought on eBay and on which he practised a few hours a day. She was a tidy person who was constantly worried about germs, ants and mice, and she despaired over her brother's messiness. Ed had learned never to leave as much as a sheet of music or a pencil lying around, let alone a stray sock.

Tom, claiming to be speaking as a doctor, diagnosed her as having FussPotitis. 'It's a form of Obsessional Compulsive Disorder,' he said.

But, after long discussions about the need for a cleaner, which Bella won, a jolly Ukrainian girl came every Friday, changed the bedsheets and towels, ironed shirts and left the flat completely clean and shipshape.

Also, with Ed absent most evenings, Tom, Bella and their friends had no cause to complain that he was hogging the TV or eating them out of house and home.

As she sat one evening looking at the river, Bella remembered how she'd met Ed, in a queue outside the National Film Theatre. She often went to cinemas on her own. It meant she could walk out halfway through without a long explanation if she wasn't enjoying the film.

That afternoon, they happened to sit next to each other at a reshowing of an Almodóvar film and found themselves talking about it as they left. She'd liked it, he hadn't. Somehow, they were soon eating pizza together at Strada on the South Bank. When she pointed to a couple of blocks of stained, concrete-walled, former council flats behind the café, where she lived with her brother, and told him she was studying law at a college close by in Stamford Street, he said she was living a perfect life. He told her a few weeks later that he thought everything about her was perfect. He repeated it even after she'd confessed that her dad was a Tory MP who'd voted to leave the EU, making Ed's status in the UK annoyingly uncertain.

When she explained that her first name was Arabella so that her initials could be A O rather than the unfortunate B O, he'd laughed. As the weeks and months went by, he told her regularly how much he loved her. He was tempted to add that he wanted them to get married. But he didn't. He feared she might see it as a too-convenient solution to his citizenship quandary. Which, he knew, it would be. Anyway, aged only 20, they were both far too young.

Bella forced herself back into the present and went to bed early. In the chilly morning, she dressed in jeans, a t-shirt, two jumpers and a puffer-jacket, her hair scrunched up and away from her face, and walked from the flats, along Hopton Street and Stamford Street, before catching a bus over Waterloo Bridge. It carried on past Holborn Underground Station and up Southampton Row, turning left into Bloomsbury, where she got off. It was then a short walk to Colt Court.

'Good morning, Albert,' she called out to the concierge, who was sitting at his desk, nose deep in *The Sun*. He nodded without looking up. As she stepped into the clanking old bird cage lift, pulled the two wonky iron gates shut and pressed the button for the third floor, she decided that Albert probably wouldn't rouse himself if a gang of men wearing balaclavas and brandishing Kalashnikovs pushed through the revolving glass and bronze doors.

Too weary to search for keys in her bag, she pushed the bell and Tom opened the door. Inside, before she'd hung her coat on a hanger and put it in the closet, he handed her a to-do list.

'Your first task is to arrange a telephone chat with Tim Hadden, Dad's GP. Try to find out if Dad had shown signs of heart trouble. We know he'll give you the patient confidentiality bollocks, but you're sure to get something out of him.'

When the surgery put Dr Tim through, Bella put him on speaker.

'It's about my dad,' she began.

The GP jumped in to make the usual condolence speech. 'I can only say how puzzling it was. I saw your father so rarely. He certainly wasn't one of the worried well. He was always cheerful and full of life,' he sighed.

'The surgery manager sends texts to all patients as they approach sixty, inviting them to come in for a general check-up, including an ECG, but Dietrich never replied, so the practice nurse telephoned him. Dietrich twice made appointments but then got his secretary to cancel them. She said he was just too busy.

'I rang him myself and suggested a simple blood test, which the haematology nurse could do at breakfast time, but he never booked one. I knew an MP's life was likely to be stressful and wondered if he needed to be put on statins if his cholesterol was high. We never found out.'

Tom swore. Bella sighed. No one was surprised. Dietrich had been squeamish about needles and would run a mile from a flu jab, but Bella couldn't remember a day when he was ill with anything worse than a cold or a sprained ankle from running too quickly down a members' stone staircase in the House of Commons.

The next task required her to switch to Project Jane Page-Smith. Tom said he fantasised about tracking her down one dark evening, grabbing her by the neck, squeezing it hard until he'd crushed the hyoid bone and watching her eyes bulge out as she breathed her last.

'And land yourself in prison for murder? That would really help Mum and me,' Bella snapped. 'And do wonders for your career.'

She said she'd make searches for a marriage and birth certificate in Oxford, where Jane claimed she and Dietrich met and were together.

That afternoon, when she returned to Bankside from her lectures – God, how she hated business law and the Companies Act 2017 – she recharged her laptop and began an online search for contact details for Ben Harding, the one person from Dietrich's Oxford days whom he ever mentioned and occasionally met for a chat at a wine bar in Kingsway. Ben would or should have known about any serious girlfriends their father had at Oxford and could perhaps throw light on what had gone on.

Eventually, she found a telephone number for Dr Benjamin Harding. It was different from the scribbled one in one of their father's old diaries, and this time, it worked. Bella left a message and Dr Harding rang back an hour later. He was now a don in the history department at St Edmund Hall, he said, and he'd be happy to see them on Saturday, late morning, by which time he would be free of his students.

'I wonder what he's like,' Bella said, as she and Tom boarded an early train to Oxford, clutching paper carriers of coffees and muffins. 'Dad never really spoke about him. Sounded OK on the phone, though, not too crusty'.

'The main thing is finding out if Jane Lying Cow Page-Smith was lying about everything,' Tom spluttered, after taking too large a gulp of the scalding drink, which then prompted a coughing fit.

'We need to find out if they really *did* get married before we speak to Ben Harding. If there's no proof, meeting him will just be a social visit to learn what Dad was like as a student.'

Oxford's Registry of Births, Marriages and Deaths, a bleak Victorian building in one of the uglier parts of the city, was open in the morning. Tom had been calculating dates and thought that if their father had married this woman, it would have been in or around the summer of 1972, the year he'd graduated.

Thanks to a helpful assistant, it took only minutes to find a record of the marriage and get a copy of the certificate. Finding a record of the birth of Charles William Olson a few years later was similarly straightforward. Tom cursed, and then cursed some more, until the other customers in the registry turned to look at him, either puzzled or shocked by his swearing, or both.

Bella looked gloomily at her boots. How would they break this news to their mother?

She found Google Maps on her phone and checked the route to the café in Market Street where they were to meet their dad's old friend.

'Lovely to see you both. Take a seat,' Benjamin Harding boomed, almost dislocating Bella's arm when shaking her hand enthusiastically. He shook hands with Tom then pulled out chairs for them in a warm corner of a bistro around the corner from his college. Bella thought he seemed older than Dietrich, with his longish grey hair, oiled and combed back, curling behind the ears. In worn jeans and a navy pea coat, he looked more like an unsuccessful musician than an eminent don. The smiling waitress seemed to know him well and their order of white wine and fat baguette sandwiches arrived quickly.

He said he'd been stunned to read about Dietrich's death and commiserated with Tom and Bella about the untimely emergence of Jane Page-Smith. 'Must have been a colossal shock,' he said.

They nodded. Bella fought back tears, breathing deeply and exhaling slowly.

'Did you know her? What was she like?' she asked, getting quickly to the point as Tom never did.

'Yes, I knew Jane and liked her too. She was northern – from Leeds I think – and Dominic and I used to tease her about her accent. She used to hit back each time one of us said a word like bath, past or castle with a, "remind me where the r is in that word" type comment.' He paused, smiling at the memory.

'Jane had been Dom's girlfriend during his second and final years. They were intense, if you get my meaning. I think she was his first girlfriend. I have to say, she was great company; pretty and sexy too. So, I wasn't surprised when Dom told me they were getting married. He asked me to be his witness. I can't remember who Jane's witness was; a random student who happened to be passing the register office probably.'

Hearing this, Bella's heart sank. Clenching her fists, she managed to keep a blank face.

'It was the quietest and quickest wedding. No white dress,

no flowers, no fuss. Just the twenty-minute ceremony in the register office and a pub lunch with a few friends. Jane's mother came down for it, I seem to remember, and paid for the lunch, but I don't think Dom even told his parents. He was ashamed of them, in a way. They probably weren't as sophisticated as he'd have liked them to be. He was a bit of a snob, your dad, sorry to say.'

That wasn't news to Tom and Bella.

'Dom and Jane went off to France together as soon as they'd sat their finals. He phoned me from somewhere in the south, Toulon or maybe Toulouse, and asked me to look on the noticeboard for their exam results. Both got upper seconds. Dom was disappointed. He'd badly wanted a first. I had the impression he blamed Jane for distracting him!' Ben's shoulders went up and he laughed again.

'I asked him what his plans were when he got back and he was vague,' he continued. 'When they returned, they were different together. Cooler. I had the strong impression that he and Jane were already heading in separate directions. Dom wanted to get into the City, make money and then move into an environment where he could contest a parliamentary seat.

'Looking back, it would never have worked. Jane was basically a hippy. She was outspoken. She was chippy. She wouldn't do as an MP's wife, certainly not a Conservative MP's wife. I couldn't see her keeping a diplomatic silence in public, smiling on cue, opening fêtes, kissing babies and such like. She just wouldn't have—'

'Do you know what happened to her?' Bella butted in.

Ben shrugged and shook his head so that some of the grey curls bobbed up from behind his ears. 'I presumed they'd just split up, gone their separate ways. I knew nothing about them expecting a baby and I certainly never saw her back here, pushing a pram.

'When I read about Dom going into politics and marrying your mum, I presumed he and Jane had divorced as quickly and quietly as they'd got married.'

On the train home, Bella made notes of what Ben had said and put the pages in a file with the copies of the certificates.

'Nice bloke, wasn't he? Pity about what he had to tell us. Obviously, he quite liked the gold-digging bitch,' Tom said grumpily. What Ben had told them about Jane had made him put his plans to strangle her on hold. Bella gave him a weary smile and squeezed his arm.

As they were nearing Paddington Station, she said, 'I just can't stop thinking about the doctor's verdict that Dietrich died from cardiac arrest.'

'That's the thing,' Tom replied, 'it can't be right.'

Back at the family flat, Bella told her mother what they'd found and what Dr Harding remembered. Penny was silent. She'd expected the bad news, her daughter thought.

Tom spent the next few days at the hospital, returning late to the Bankside flat.

On Saturday, he was back at Colt Court. Bella had ordered a Chinese take away and they filled plates with portions of chicken with ginger, Singapore noodles and pancakes stuffed with slow-cooked duck. While Bella and Pen sat on the sofa watching a subtitled Scandinavian television series that they'd already seen but had mostly forgotten, Tom pulled out a chair and sat opposite them, his back blocking their view.

He took a deep breath and opened the topic of the riddle of Dietrich's death. 'I've been thinking about this for weeks,' he said. 'So, I talked to my friend Ludo at the hospital. He's two years ahead of me, specialising in genetics.

'Ludo knows an anatomical pathologist really well. Ludo's cousin is married to a cop or something and this pathologist, Stefan Kowak – I believe he's Polish – has worked for the police and given evidence at trials to help the cops.

'So, I went to see Mr Polish pathologist and told him about Dad and the diagnosis that makes no sense to us. It turns out that Kowak could perform a private autopsy and write a report for us within a week. Including the lab fee, it would cost us about £2,000 to £2,500, depending on the tests they'd need to do. Cash, of course. Obviously, we should try to get it done quietly and as quickly as possible before the body deteriorates further.'

'Gosh, you've actually gone into this, haven't you?' said Bella, feeling suddenly tearful.

Pen listened without saying a word, then she stood up and walked along the corridor to her bedroom.

What Tom had said made sense, but there was a lot to think through. After all, they'd effectively been talking about digging up her father's coffin and letting someone cut him up.

'We have to see what Mum thinks when she's processed it all,' Bella said. 'I've a feeling the news of the marriage and birth certificates has been enough as it is.'

It was. More than enough. But in a few days' time, it was Pen who asked over breakfast, 'What's next?'

Like Tom, she couldn't square the term sudden cardiac arrest with her healthy husband. Tom paused, then said the fearsome word – exhumation.

Silence followed, until Bella broke it. 'I've looked it up and we need to make an application to the coroners' court,' she said. 'We've got a good argument. The paramedics came and took Dad's body to the hospital, and that was that for us. We don't know what tests they did – if they even did *any*, apart from checking for a pulse and declaring him dead. I know you spoke again to the doctor, Tom, but did they really look for any signs that Dad might have been... killed?

'I've already spoken to George about this. He says if all members of the family give consent and agree to pay for the exhumation and autopsy, he thinks a court would allow the application. So, do we agree?'

Tom nodded immediately and Pen inhaled deeply. 'Yes, melodramatic though it sounds, we can't live with this doubt. Or at least, *I can't*. How did Dietrich end up on the floor in that wine store? Did he go there to fetch a particular wine, suffer a pain in his chest, fall and somehow gather the old dust sheets to break his fall?'

Their mother began to quietly cry. Bella patted her hand.

'And what explains the sudden appearance of Jane Page-Smith and her son?' Tom coldly added. 'They could have shown up at any time. Why didn't they? I'm not saying they were responsible for Dad's death, but if they aren't just bloody gold diggers, intent on inheriting his money, why didn't they show up earlier? If she wanted to damage him by revealing the bigamy, why didn't she do it when he was an MP? When he could have been taken to court for it? Can you imagine what the papers would have made of that?

'None of this makes sense.'

Pen stood up and began walking around the living room. She'd focused, as lawyers must do, and was thinking of the snags to making an application for exhumation.

'Given that Dietrich was legally married to Jane and that Charles was born two years after the marriage and is almost certainly Dietrich's son, wouldn't they also need to be asked for their consent to exhume?' she asked.

'What if they don't find anything out about the application until it's too late?' Tom said. 'And, presuming they *aren't* malicious, wouldn't they want to know the truth? Like we do?'

'I think a far greater danger is that the media will find out we've applied to dig up the body and make a big drama out of it before we've actually done anything,' said Pen.

Bella looked at her in silent agreement before adding, 'You can apply online for an exhumation licence from the Ministry of Justice,' she said, confident of her research. 'Licences are usually granted to move a body to a different grave, deepen an existing grave for a further burial or send a body for cremation, none of which applies to us, but that doesn't mean we won't get one. There's no hearing or even a charge for the licence. Obviously, you need to pay for the digging work and the autopsy itself.

'And remember that Dad's buried in a little churchyard tucked away near Godalming. I doubt *Mail Online* sends reporters to lurk around there on the off chance someone'll dig up a coffin. Even if someone found out and went to the papers, we could try for an injunction with the argument that it's a private matter. It would at least buy us time.'

Pen continued to look worried. Then she took a deep breath. 'I'm happy to see the vicar to let him know what we're hoping to do and why,' she said. 'Meanwhile, Tom can see this pathologist again and go into the details of how, where and when. It must all be kept low key.

'Let's think about it a bit more, talk again tomorrow and decide *if* we're going to do it,' she added.

But they all knew they *were* going to do it. And they did.

7

'Want a nuvver one?' Joe Jackson wrinkled his nose and looked in turn at his three mates. They were sitting around a sticky table in the backroom of The Bear in Clandon.

Somehow, talking did not dislodge the skinny roll up sticking to Joe's top lip.

As Surrey country pubs went, it wasn't a bad boozer, DC Tony Frowde decided, as he sat at a corner table, quietly sipping his half of bitter and watching them. At least it didn't have horse brasses on the walls, and the carpets looked as if they'd been cleaned within living memory. Jack, behind the bar, and Alison, the part-time barmaid and occasional caterer's assistant, were friendly enough and if you were prepared to wait for half an hour, you could get a decent burger or a beef and mushroom pie at lunchtime. Most importantly, the bitter was good.

Doug Elliot scratched his stubbly chin as if he really did have doubts on the beer question, then nodded at Joe. Kevin Miller shook his fiery curls. He'd never been a big boozer. Steve James held up his tankard, still half full.

It was a Saturday, so between the grunts and crude jokes, the friends had been talking at length for a good hour about work they'd done recently and the television shows and football they'd watched. Joe had piped up about a 'fit bird' he'd clocked in the newsagents and wanted to know better.

'Fancies 'imself, don't he?' said Doug, who was halfway through a bag of crisps. He parked a mouthful in one cheek while glugging the rest of his pint. Then he beamed and sniggered, 'If she's *that* fit, she won't be interested in a smelly old git like you. She'll 'ave a bloke already. Know what I mean?'

Kevin and Steve laughed.

'Fuck off, will yer!' Joe snarled, squirming in his elasticated tracksuit bottoms. He looked embarrassed. The Clandon Clan, as they liked to call themselves, may have looked out for each other, but they had to take the mickey whenever an opportunity arose. That's what blokes do.

From behind his copy of the *Surrey Advertiser*, DC Frowde had been listening carefully and making mental notes. He sighed, plonked his glass on the table and then folded the newspaper to the sports pages before resuming his fake reading.

Big, ugly Doug, 18 stone, most of it belly that strained the side seams of his stained blue T-shirt and poked out in a hairy bulge over a belt holding up baggy jeans, had long been suspected by Izzy of possessing drugs with intent to supply. But he didn't supply them as Kevin had done in his pre-prison days by selling little bags of weed, ecstasy, heroin and ketamine – or anything he could get his hands on – to kids and drug-addled men and women in clubs, on street corners or anywhere they thought the coppers or their informants wouldn't spot them.

Doug, the cops believed, was delivering top-grade cocaine

to people direct to their homes as if they were Amazon parcels. These were people who travelled widely, commuted to the city for work and lived in smart houses, people who liked to offer dinner party guests a line or two after an evening of elegant food, good wines and cultured conversation.

Such customers, women as well as men, thought of themselves as dabblers rather than drug takers and would telephone a contact such as Doug, who'd once done a bit of building work for them, as they might an emergency plumber or locksmith. It was a process so far removed from the County Lines gangs, who employed kids and wrecked families, that it was more like a community service for the well-off than drug dealing.

Doug, who was pushing fifty, was known by the police to specialise in this sort of drug supplying, but no solid evidence had been collected against him. He was also known to live with his disabled father in the family's council house in Guildford. Dad was a cantankerous old sod whose heavy drinking and refusal to look for any kind of legitimate work had driven his wife to run off with another man before their two children had finished primary school. Doug hadn't heard from her since he was thirteen.

These days, his dad, stricken with dementia, needed round-the-clock care, and Doug, with his ham-like arms that were blue with tattoos, was good at lifting the old man in and out of bed, into his wheelchair and on and off the lavatory. Those duties limited Doug's availability for scaffolding, building or delivery work to the weeks when his younger sister Pam came begrudgingly down from her North London home to stay with them and take over caring for their dad. Her trips weren't frequent, which was why the drug deliveries came in useful. He could also fit in small jobs, such as assembling hired tables and chairs for a caterer or helping a mate in the removals business.

His phone buzzed. After answering it, Doug grunted, 'Naah what?' with a pained expression, followed by versions of 'you'll have to wait'.

The unfortunate caller – his dad, most probably – got little more.

Joe, Doug's friend from school, now 46 and smaller by three or four stones, tried to be – or at least, to seem – as tough as Doug, and he occasionally made drops for him. In a much-repeated joke, Doug used to say how his friend was 'hard of thinking'. He was proud of the pun, and the Clandon Clan had found it hilarious when he first uttered it in Joe's absence. Doug also called him 'Slow Joe' behind his back.

But unfortunately, Joe wasn't slow when it came to fights and would thump anyone who gave him a wrong look or asked a wrong question.

Consequently, he had a list of convictions for assault that dated back to his school days. Tony knew this as he'd already looked up his four fellow drinkers on the national crime database.

Tony looked at his watch and realised he'd spent two hours inwardly cursing because he'd wanted to watch his eight-year-old son's rugby team play their rivals, then take his wife out for a curry while her mum babysat. Instead, damn it, he'd been stuck behind the *Advertiser* on a job to record anything drug-related and incriminating from Doug and his pals. But it was all for nothing. He admired Izzy Holland, his new boss, but had thought from the outset that this would be a waste of time.

He stood up slowly, leaving his half-full glass of bitter and newspaper on the table, rubbed his back and walked casually towards the gents, pausing by an exit to the pub gardens and car park to pull out his phone and check in.

'Nothing so far, Boss,' he sniffed, trying not to sound petulant. 'No cash or packages passed between them as far as I could see. Bloody football and some girl seem to be the only topics of conversation.'

'Listen out for any talk of future meetings and get snaps of their vehicles if you can,' came the reply.

As he heard that, he looked through the glass panel of the door to see Doug walking through the car park, his fat thighs chafing with every step. Joe was with him. The two men hitched up their trousers before clambering into a dirty Ford Transit, Joe taking the passenger seat. He heard Doug fire up the engine.

After taking photos of the van and the other cars near it in the car park and memorising the van's registration, Tony went back into the bar to jot down the numbers on the margin of the *Advertiser* and to carry on watching Kevin and Steve, who were still at the table. Kevin was gulping the last of his beer while Steve was loudly moaning about living with his dad. 'It's like being a fucking kid again,' he grumbled.

'No reason you couldn't kip at the cottage now and then, like before,' replied his pal. 'Hang on, mate, I'm going to Bristol this Friday for the weekend to see a bloke I was doubled up with in Wandsworth. Still got a key to the cottage, 'aven't yer? Praps you'd like to make yerself at home – and set up my new Sky TV system while you're there. I can't get it going but it'll probably take you five minutes.'

'You're on.'

'Another thing,' Kevin said. 'Be great if I could use your Vespa. Leave you the van. Whatcha think?'

'Bloody hell! What next?' sighed Steve. 'My leather jacket and best T-shirt?

'All right. But make sure you don't leave the Vespa somewhere it gets nicked. And there's gotta be petrol in the tank on Sunday night. I've got new clients to see early on Monday and I could do without the faff of queueing at a garage to fill the tank.'

When Tony passed that on, Izzy was more than a little interested.

'Let's find out who our boy Kevin shared cells in prison with,' she told him. 'And see if by any chance he's now living in Bristol.'

Because Kevin had received a relatively short sentence for the burglaries, he'd only had one 'cellie' in HMP Wandsworth. That was Jim Pugh, a thirty-eight-year-old career thief and stolen property handler. He also had a string of convictions for possession with intent to supply. And – hey ho! – he was thought to be living currently with his sister in a flat in the Knowle West district of Bristol, an area from which most people with an IQ in treble figures and a bit of money try hard to move away as soon as they can.

Avon and Somerset CID were asked nicely if they could watch Kevin Miller and Jim Pugh for a couple of days to see if they appeared to link up with known criminals.

* * *

As Izzy made her way home that evening, she was suddenly stricken with doubt. Why was she still pursuing Kevin? Drug dealing was everywhere, after all. Rehab centres were overflowing with cocaine addicts. Was she wasting her time and police resources? Was she getting ahead of herself and just too inexperienced at the job?

She blamed Mehmet and Rob. She'd swelled with pride when they'd congratulated her for catching the elusive 'Wandsworth Burglar' red handed, after his long reign. But that happened a few years ago. She'd decided she needed to be proactive if she wanted to keep and enhance her reputation. So, she'd been doing a bit of checking on Kevin's recent movements. She'd also looked to see if any burglaries from houses in posh parts of Guildford, mainly in the Onslow Village area, seemed to conform to his modus operandi of carefully picking locks and taking only a little from each household at a time. It turned out there had been reports of burglaries like that, and she suspected there'd been many more victims that hadn't gone to the police. Also, the chances were that Kevin's tactics, which were covered by the papers, had been copied by trainee burglars everywhere.

'I'll take a look at payments into the Clandon Clan members' bank accounts,' she mumbled to herself, nervous that she needed a warrant or at least a superior officer to sanction that. But when she found that Kevin and Stephen James, his pal from the wood mill, had been paid by the same party equipment hire company and had made deliveries to the same house near Godalming on a Saturday in early January, she felt her nosing around had been justified.

It got better: when she made online checks on Big Doug Elliot and Slow Joe Jackson, she found they were mentioned on caterer John Hardwick's website as part of his experienced team. The caterer had also advertised for waiters for an event in January. A little more research revealed that this was held at the house where the owner, Dietrich Olson MP, had ended up dead.

'Coincidence? Can't be, can it?' Izzy asked Alex over supper. 'And you know I don't believe in coincidences.'

Alex nodded and went back to his grilled salmon.

But once back at his desk the following day, he looked up which of the ambulance teams had been called out on that job.

'According to my guys, there's something a bit off about the way your bloke Olson was found,' Alex told Izzy that evening. 'It wasn't how they expected.'

In her previous job in Holborn, Izzy had been aware of the local MP. She'd considered him a bumptious buffoon, and he'd once almost cycled into her as she'd walked from Holborn Tube Station to work. But he seemed to have been popular with the locals and had increased his majority in the 2017 election.

She had a gut feeling there'd be more to the story of Dietrich's demise. She wondered if it was wise to mention it, casually, of course, to Rob Howarth. They were mates, after all. In fact, for a long time in Holborn, she'd fancied herself in love with him because he was clever, unassuming and handsome – if you didn't mind men who weren't that tall. Growing up, her heartthrobs were all short men. Tom Cruise, Brad Pitt, even 007 Daniel Craig could do with leg extensions. Being only five feet two herself, she didn't mind at all. But she reasoned he wouldn't be the least bit interested in her because she was uneducated and working-class. Yet he obviously thought she was good at her job. So why not tell him about this?

The thought gnawed away at her. She'd never been confident. Her parents, a primary school teacher and a librarian, both introverts, would have called it pushy and disapproved. It had taken her months to confess to them that she'd joined the police during the summer after A levels. They'd expected her to go to university to 'better herself', as they put it. As she had suspected, they were disappointed when she finally broke the news to them. They said they'd worry day and night about her putting herself in physical danger from violent criminals and in an environment, many believed was macho central.

Finally, Izzy convinced herself that she'd rather be laughed at by Rob and Mehmet than bollocked later for not passing on information.

She ambushed Rob a few days later, around midday on Thursday, in his tiny, airless office at Guildford Police Station. The whole office was quiet, and he was busy reading the files on local sex offenders.

'D'you believe in coincidences, Rob?' she asked, passing him a coffee in a takeaway cup.

'Nope.'

She offered him another cup containing milk and pulled a chair into his office so she could sit near him.

His dark eyebrows went up questioningly. 'Alright. Sometimes, yes.'

'And gut feelings?'

Same response, only with an additional look that asked, 'What *are* you on about?'

'Well,' she began, 'what I'm going to tell you amounts to nothing more than a load of circumstantial stuff. Complete rubbish, maybe. I've no actual evidence of anything like a criminal offence. So, you'll have to be patient for once and bear with me, OK?'

She was shaking inside, hoping it didn't show.

Rob nodded, still baffled.

'It's about our late MP, Dietrich Olson – or rather *your* late MP. I've been thinking about his death.'

Rob's eyebrows went up again.

'The cause of death was a heart attack. He literally dropped dead, apparently. There was no warning, and no one saw him clasping his chest and gasping for breath.'

Rob nodded.

'According to the paramedics, Olson's body was found halfway through a party at his house just down the road from here. No one had seen him or heard a thing. He'd just vanished.

'He was discovered in a storeroom off the back of the kitchen. So, two things: first, why had he abandoned his party to go down there? And second, how had he managed to fall on to a pile of coats and dustsheets and half shut the door *after* he'd collapsed and died?'

Rob sat up straight in his chair and frowned. 'How d'you know this?'

'The paramedics mentioned it to Alex, my husband. He's their co-ordinator at the Royal Surrey.

'On top of that, Kevin Miller, my champion burglar, and his mates, Steve James, Doug Elliot and Joe Jackson – they call themselves the Clandon Clan –visited Olson's house both prior and after the big event.'

'Why?' said Rob, wondering where she was going with this.

'They delivered chairs, tables and catering stuff both in the run up and after the party. They probably had a nosey round the place. It was a big celebration with lots of people and activity.

'When I thought about it, it occurred to me that they *may* also have popped in *during* the event. Who knows? They may have helped themselves to a few things from the house or from the coats and handbags of the well-off party guests, who haven't liked to complain to the grieving family.

'And if that *were* the case – who knows – they may, just possibly, have "*helped*" the host to land on the storeroom floor, especially if he'd noticed them hanging about and had challenged them.'

She waited.

After what seemed like an age, Rob said, 'That's a lot of supposition, Izz. Olson died of natural causes as far as I know. But write it all up. Get Mehmet to look into the files on Kevin Miller and Steve Whatshisname and the other two you mentioned. We need photos and potted biographies, plus everything about their backgrounds and recent movements. I'll do some research on Olson's death. And I'd like to speak to those two paramedics. Can Alex arrange that?'

Izzy nodded. 'Not sure when – it'll depend on their shifts – but of course it's possible.'

'Let's make it possible and get them together. Incident room, Monday, 10 o'clock?'

Rob rang Mehmet, who was on leave for the day.

'Look, I know we're in the middle of a rape and murder investigation,' he said, 'but something else has come up. Izzy may have turned up some information on the death of Dietrich Olson, our favourite MP, and we can't afford *not* to look into it, especially as we come from Holborn, bang slap in the middle of what was his constituency. We don't want the Met descending on us here and treating us like country bumpkins.'

He gave Mehmet a quick version of Izzy's discoveries and theories.

'Anyway, she and I are meeting here in the incident room

on Monday to try and weigh up if her uneasiness merits a proper investigation. I'd like you to be here too, pencil sharpened.

'It may mean you and I come off the Esther Hall murder enquiry for a few days or we brief another team to take over. I hope not, though. At any rate, we'll have to delay our surprise interview with Esther Hall's boyfriend for a day or so.

'Just marking your card, OK? Izzy could be on to something or nothing.'

He had a hunch that of the two, it was something. Though he didn't believe in hunches.

He cursed. One thing he knew for certain was that it wouldn't be the relaxed weekend at his new home with Elizabeth and Jacob, their four-year-old. He'd planned some decorating in the spare bedroom; rugby on TV on Saturday afternoon; off on Sunday to Dorking to look over the second-hand Alfa Romeo saloon he'd been thinking about treating himself to. He'd been looking forward to all that.

Now he'd be wrestling with his conscience for putting the investigation into the rape and murder of an innocent student nurse on hold to dabble into the death of a stinking rich, right-wing politician – one he'd already grown sick and tired of reading about.

8

It was an icy early Friday morning in the graveyard of St Mary's Church, one of the twenty or more cemeteries in the Godalming and Guildford area. Frost held tightly to the straggly grass that had escaped the lawnmower in the autumn, and weeds obscured the inscriptions on many of the older gravestones. Dirty plastic flowers were strewn here and there and only one gravestone, marking the life of a six-year-old boy, Bella noted with sadness, had a bunch of fresh daffodils in a vase by its side.

In warm coats and with scarves covering most of their faces in case a passing and curious dog walker took a picture on his mobile which then turned up in *The Sun*, Tom and Bella fidgeted on a wooden bench. The carved dedication on the back was mostly worn away and was half covered in moss. They watched as men laid wooden slats and a tarpaulin on the ground near the grave on which to heap soil. Their father's coffin was then dug up and carried from its plot by a small excavator, who transferred it to an anonymous grey van. From there it was to be taken to the North London

Pathology Laboratory, where Dr Stefan Nowak would perform his autopsy and write a report. Tom made sure the upturned gravestone's inscription was laid face down and mostly covered in earth and leaves. He was glad he'd insisted their mother stay home.

Short and wiry, Ludo was a med student, planning to specialise in genetics, who was two years ahead of Tom and two years more confident. They'd been friends since they'd met in the canteen and, as Tom panicked after missing a biochemistry lecture, Ludo gave him copies of his own notes. The fee was a couple of pints of bitter a few nights later. A good bargain for Tom.

Earlier that week, Ludo had taken Tom to meet Dr Nowak at what Ludo called his day job at St Thomas's Hospital. Tom reflected that the hospital was on the south side of the river directly opposite the Houses of Parliament, where his late father had worked his own day job. The friends walked down a flight of stairs and then along lino-floored corridor after corridor, mostly empty but with a trolley here and there stacked with dressings or bits of what looked like obsolete equipment, until they reached a cubby hole near the mortuary.

In a white coat only just fitting his broad shoulders and wearing Converse trainers and big, black-framed spectacles that were balanced on the end of his nose, Stefan Nowak greeted them enthusiastically, his Polish accent evident from the odd rolled r and the way he stressed every syllable. Tom had looked him up and knew that Nowak had qualified in forensic pathology both in Warsaw and in London and had served as an expert witness in many big trials. His work at a laboratory in Camden was his private sideline.

Nowak hugged the young geneticist. 'How are the classes going?' he asked.

'OK, I suppose. But I often wish I'd picked something easy, like pathology. Better still, astrology.'

Nowak laughed. 'How's your beautiful cousin, Elizabeth? Still married to that dull policeman?'

'Come on. That's not fair! Rob Howarth's not really dull. He's just got a bad dose of social conscience and wanted to do something worthwhile. So, he signed up to be a cop. He's OK, but he and Elizabeth have moved out to the sticks, so I hardly see them these days.'

Nowak turned to Tom. 'And what are you specialising in, young man?'

'Well, it was going to be general practice. I fancied myself as a GP, being presented with all sorts of medical problems and diagnosing them like a detective. But since Dad's death, I've been thinking that cardiology could be more interesting.'

Nowak nodded. 'Well, perhaps you'll learn something from this autopsy. I've booked a table in Camden for Saturday with my best assistant, Pawel. It'll be a top-rate job.'

He made it sound like a reservation for a meal at a Michelin-starred restaurant.

'I should be able to email you my report in a week to ten days, but a few tests may take longer.'

'Will the body have decomposed a lot since Dad was buried two months ago?' Tom asked nervously.

'No, no, don't worry about that. Burial slows down the rotting process. It would take about two years for all the soft tissue to disappear, probably longer in a good quality oak coffin, which keeps all moisture out. And it's cold down there in the grave. So, I expect your father will look quite fresh, strange as that might sound. Anyway, I'll look carefully at his blood, heart, lungs and liver, and see where that takes me.'

They shook hands. Tom walked slowly north over Waterloo Bridge, his favourite spanning the Thames, with its plain concrete walls and vistas of contrasting buildings both east and west. From the north side of the bridge, he strode back to the Bloomsbury flat, all the way trying to think like a scientist and be cool and objective.

Yet he knew the man he had just been talking to would, in a few days' time, line up his tools, including bone saws, scalpels and tweezers. He'd put on a thick rubber apron, a face guard and gloves. Then he'd begin cutting up his father. He'd slice into the thin tissue of the neck and run the blade of his scalpel all the way along the midline, down to his pubic bone, cutting through skin and fat and folding it sideways before clearing aside the muscles, like opening a book.

To gain access to the lungs and heart, he would probably break the fronts of several ribs with the surgical equivalent of bolt cutters. It would be necessary. As would removing the heart, weighing it and studying samples from the heart muscles for signs of cardiomyopathy, the disease that makes it harder for the heart to pump blood around the body and may have caused a cardiac arrest.

Because there were no signs of suffocation, at least Tom didn't torment himself with the thought of a drill piercing his dad's skull and removing a cap of bone to reveal a grey, wormlike loaf of brain. Things might be different if it turned out he'd been riddled with cancer that had spread to his brain, but there'd been no hint of that.

Nevertheless, Tom was an emotional mess at the thought of it all. He was surprised by his feelings of squeamishness. Three years at medical school and the knowledge of what surgeons did to the human body still affected him in a regrettably unscientific way.

He paused to sit on a bench in Montague Gardens to ground himself while watching the totally normal sight of small children shouting and laughing while having a kick about.

He couldn't possibly have loved Dietrich more had he been his biological father, a man he'd never had the slightest curiosity about. His mother had told him the truth when he was six, and they'd both told Bella a few years later. She'd shrugged. He was still her big brother. It was never important.

Often, Dietrich's political views had not chimed with Tom's. They'd had plenty of disagreements but never bitter ones. Dietrich considered himself a liberal Tory, a 'wet'. Margaret Thatcher would have disliked him. Too full of himself. Far too prone to make light of a serious subject. Way too genial and generous in his assessments. Too smiley and nice.

Tom always felt – no, *knew* – that whatever dubious deals Dietrich did as a businessman and politician, the man had loved his mother, sister and him deeply. He'd fought battles for Tom as a small boy, corrected his homework, cheered for him at sports day and argued with the headmaster at St Paul's who thought Tom should leave because he was messing about in lessons and wasn't keeping up.

'It shows you can't be teaching him properly,' Dietrich had pointed out. Tom stayed and thrived. So, they'd switched positions, and Tom was now his father's champion. He was determined to push to find answers about his death.

Would Nowak discover evidence of hidden heart disease? Tom knew that a heart attack occurs when blood flow to the heart is blocked, and sudden cardiac arrest happens when the heart malfunctions and unexpectedly stops beating. The two are sometimes connected, but not always. Sudden cardiac arrest can occur after a heart attack. But when sudden cardiac arrest occurs, heart attack is a common cause. He persisted with the idea that 'sudden malfunction', if there had been one, wasn't caused by his father's supposedly stressful life. It must have been caused by something else, though – a wound, poison, a shock? In other words, by some*one*.

Ten days after the autopsy, although it felt longer to Tom, Nowak's email pinged into his phone. He switched on his laptop in the smaller living room in Colt Court – they called it the library – that everyone in the family used as a workstation. He plugged in the printer and printed a copy, taking the wad of papers to his bedroom to read. His hands were shaking.

He read that his father's lungs had become waterlogged when his heart started to fail. Muscle at the front of the heart was scarred, indicating a myocardial infarction and the left ventricle was enlarged due to a blockage in the left anterior descending artery.

'In other words,' he told his mother and sister, who by then had grouped behind his chair, 'a blood clot led to a heart attack. The cardiac arrest meant the heart could not pump blood to the brain, lungs and other organs. Seconds later, he would have lost consciousness.

'Death occurred within minutes because, I suppose, no one saw him collapse so no one could have instantly given him CPR, the only thing that might possibly have saved him.'

'But where was he at that moment of collapse?' asked Bella. 'Already in the wine store?'

Tom was still reading, his breathing heavy.

'We don't know that. It's still unclear...'

He fell silent for several minutes. He tried to talk but it was as if the words stuck in his throat.

'Sit down on the sofa, Mum. You too, Bell,' he said finally, and almost in a whisper. Puzzled, the women did as they were told.

'Are you ready?'

They nodded.

'A blood test showed *why* the blood vessels were constricted, stopping enough oxygen reaching the heart muscle. Dad was injected...' his voice trailed off for a moment. Then he added, quietly and slowly, 'He was injected with a massive amount of cocaine. And if you mix cocaine with the alcohol from the glass of Champagne he'd drunk, the liver produces cocaethylene, a poisonous chemical that is many times more toxic than cocaine on its own.'

Silence followed for two or three minutes. Pen seemed frozen.

Eventually, Bella said, 'The doctor at the hospital told us they'd done blood tests. He must have been lying. How could they have missed it?

'Anyway, is Nowak sure of this? No, he can't be! It's crazy, like a bad crime thriller. Dad wasn't stupid! The idea's too far-fetched! He'd have realised that someone was trying to hurt him, and he'd have fought back'

Tom shook his head. 'It can take two seconds to inject a drug, especially with modern syringes. He probably didn't feel the needle going in. Some diabetics jab themselves several times a day and most say they don't feel a thing. So no, Dad probably wouldn't have been able to stop it.'

Bella calmed herself. 'Any signs on the outside of the body?'

'Nowak thinks he can see a faint puncture mark on his left thigh. There are no signs of a struggle or of him having been hit, just the small cut on his forehead, which is almost certainly from hitting his head on a shelf as he fell, and there is some dried blood from scratches on his left wrist where it looks as if someone might have swiped his watch.'

Pen gasped. 'The watch... yes, I'd forgotten about his watch!'

She added that it had been a valuable Rolex DateJust in stainless steel with a gold face and a gold rim around the glass. If she remembered correctly, Dietrich had bought it for himself when he thought he deserved it. That could have been when he'd talked his way into a job in a firm of City auditors and had, with little or no experience of auditing, outshone most of his colleagues to earn a large bonus. He wore the watch all the time, though it was usually hidden by shirt cuffs.

But the bloody watch wasn't important, she realised.

Bella asked, 'What about the syringe that must have been used? Was one found in the wine store?'

Tom thought back to his search after everyone else had left Batts Farm. He'd concentrated on all the kitchen cupboards, the downstairs loo and the wine store. For no special reason, he'd even picked over the stuff in one of the rubbish bins containing empty containers and half-eaten food. Surely, he'd have noticed a discarded syringe, wouldn't he? But he hadn't.

He shook his head.

'Lots of people are cocaine addicts,' Bella went on. She was struggling to make sense of all this. 'They drink at the same time. But they don't just collapse and die. It's a gradual process, surely?'

'If the stuff is pure, not bulked out with talcum powder or cornflour or any of the other stuff street dealers use, one huge dose can be enough to be fatal, apparently,' Tom said, returning to the relevant page in the report.

'This dose *was* huge. I'll have to go back and talk to Nowak. It's surreal. Whoever did this probably just brushed against Dad somewhere – in the back kitchen probably – without anyone noticing. And then they just walked away.'

Pen had moved round and was sitting on the sofa. 'But why? Why? What could have been the motive?' she said quietly. 'It was clearly a premeditated crime, not a robbery that went wrong.'

Bella shook her head slowly from side to side. 'No one could have thought there was a safe in the house containing bags of uncut diamonds or thousands of pounds and tried to make Dietrich hand over the key. It's absurd!'

Tom flopped into an armchair. He just wanted to find the killer and hit him. He doubted they could have been female. In his mind, not even Jane Page-Smith was a suspect.

A wave of fury swept over him. He wanted to leap on the killer before he'd plunged in the needle. He wanted to beat him with his fists. He wanted to smash up the room, break furniture against the walls. He wanted to weep and howl and bury himself in his dad's arms.

He opened a bottle of red wine and poured three glasses. Later, they went to bed, he and Bella in the small rooms they'd had as children and Pen in the main bedroom.

Tom couldn't sleep. He knew the implications of what they'd done. They'd have to do something quite drastic now and, if the autopsy result was leaked by someone at the lab, it could lead to a hell of a lot of news stories and 'think' pieces in the papers, articles far more disturbing than the bigamy ones already published. It would take the matter completely out of their control.

The three of them discussed it over an early breakfast. There was no alternative. They knew they'd have to go to the police and tell them that Dietrich Olson had been murdered. Then the police could do their job and find the killer.

Tom looked at Pen after he'd pointed this out. She seemed in a trance. It wasn't only grief. Now it was fear too. She believed she'd dealt with all Dietrich's enemies, his disgruntled constituents, councillors and civil servants, people he'd ignored or upset with a careless remark. She'd written the letters of apology, made sure Karen filed the correspondence and hoped that would be enough to resolve matters. Obviously, she hadn't succeeded. Would this unknown enemy now focus on her or the children? Were they all in danger?

She asked Tom. He had no answer. Nor had Bella.

Bella finished her coffee, then said, 'Look, instead of going into a police station and trying to explain the whole thing to the nearest detective, Tom, you should ask Ludo about his cousin's policeman husband. Then you and I should make an appointment and go together.'

Pen and Tom nodded.

'You realise what this means, don't you?' Bella went on. 'Once we've told the police, we'll have no expectation of privacy. None. We'll just have to hope no one from there speaks to the press.'

They knew it was a risk.

The following morning, brother and sister, Bella clutching a printout of Stefan Nowak's report, walked down

Southampton Row, crossed into Theobalds Road, turned left into Lambs Conduit Street and climbed the littered stairs to the front of the police station. The forbidding concrete building with its blue lamp, a relic of the older, traditional station, had been closed to the public for years, but CID and uniform still operated every day on most of the floors.

A notice outside informed citizens that telephoning 999 was the quickest way to report a crime, but a face-to-face interview was possible at a front desk if booked in advance using a non-emergency number. Tom had done this, and he pressed an entry button, hoping for a response so that he could explain all this. Eventually, a small metal gate swung open, and the pair walked into the building, where a uniformed police constable beckoned them over.

Tom asked if he could talk with Detective Inspector Robert Howarth, the name Ludo had passed on.

'Have you dealt with DI Howarth before on this matter?' asked the constable.

'No, but this is serious, very serious. It concerns the death of our late father, Sir Dietrich Olson MP,' said Bella, surprising her brother yet again with her sharp insistence.

They were asked to wait.

'Come in, come in,' Superintendent Roger Malden boomed at Tom and Bella, after Detective Constable Marley Brown had found them in the waiting room at Holborn CID. She'd smiled briefly at them before guiding them to the lift and to his pokey office, with its high, small window. Joining the meeting, she'd then quietly taken a seat and got out her notebook and Biro.

Malden gave the siblings an avuncular smile. 'I believe you asked to see DI Howarth, but I'm afraid he's not working in this station at present. Can you tell me what the problem is?'

Tom and Bella looked at each other, flummoxed.

'Oh! We'd been given DI Howarth's name by someone who has worked with him in the past. We thought he was based here. It's about the death of our father, Sir Dietrich Olson MP,' said Tom. 'Are you expecting DI Howarth to return?'

'Yes, but I'm not sure when exactly. He's on a secondment to Surrey Police headquarters in Guildford.'

Tom was surprised but quickly saw an advantage.

'That could actually be helpful, since our father died at a party on the fifth of January at the family's house near Guildford. Godalming, to be precise.'

Bella took over, adding, 'But the family's primary residence is still here in Bloomsbury, where his constituency is – I mean was. So, it's a matter in your jurisdiction.'

The policeman vaguely remembered meeting Dietrich at a local function and skim reading an obituary following his death. A warning voice sounded inside his head. They were talking about a well-known man with connections in high places and a lawyer wife.

The voice said, 'Do not fuck this up, Rog.'

Bella continued. 'We were puzzled, or rather dissatisfied, with the hospital doctor's decision that our father died from a sudden cardiac arrest,' she said. 'You see, he didn't fit the profile.

'He was a fit 60-year-old. He didn't have an underlying heart condition and he didn't suffer from stress. Tom—' she looked at her brother '—is a medical student and has investigated this. So, my mother, Tom and I, after taking advice from our solicitor, were granted an exhumation order last week.

We'd arranged for a private autopsy on his body to be undertaken. The pathologist who did it works at Guys and St Thomas's and has collaborated with DI Howarth on an investigation in the past. He now has our father's body in a laboratory in Camden, should a second opinion be needed.'

Tom patted Bella's tightly clenched hand and smiled at her. She'd been worried that cynical police officers would write her off as a neurotic nuisance.

'And why do you think a second opinion might be needed?' the superintendent asked, trying his best not to sound patronising.

'I have a copy of the pathologist's report here.' Bella pushed the stapled pages on to the superintendent's desk. 'If you look at the yellow highlighted paragraphs – highlighted by me – you'll see it provides clear evidence of an unnatural death; that our father's heart collapsed after he was injected with a massive amount of pure cocaine. He was murdered.'

Roger Malden swallowed hard but maintained his poker face. He and Marley, whose first murder case this looked like becoming, were as interested as they possibly could be. He called out to a young constable outside the room and ordered coffee and a plate of biscuits. It signalled that he wouldn't be rushing the rest of the interview.

Bella delivered a potted and unemotional account of the party at Batts Farm, the discovery of Dietrich's body, the hospital doctor's decision on the cause of death, her father's burial and the emergence at the memorial service of Jane Page-Smith, a woman who claimed to have been married to Dietrich. She explained how the family's bafflement led to the exhumation and autopsy. Marley furiously noted all this down.

'We can't point fingers at anyone,' Bella went on. 'As far as we know, nobody with a grudge against our father came to the party. We're pretty sure Jane Page-Smith wasn't there. But the fact is, our father was *not* a drug user. He founded and supported rehabilitation centres for addicts. That was the main reason he was given his knighthood. He didn't gamble, he rarely drank alcohol, and he hated smoking.'

Tom took over. 'A heavy cocaine addict would, on average, snort about one gram a day, but the pathologist estimated there'd been an injection of at least one hundred grams of unadulterated cocaine in his system. It would have made a heart attack inevitable.

'From an examination of his nasal passages, there were no signs that he regularly snorted the drug. But there was a faint puncture mark on his left thigh. Our father was right-handed. Had he injected himself – and he was a man who avoided flu jabs because he was horrified by even the *thought* of needles, so that's hardly worth considering – but if he *had* done it, he would have injected his right thigh.'

Marley dared to speak, 'And you say your father didn't have enemies, anyone who'd been causing him trouble recently?'

It was Bella who replied. 'He'd been in politics for over twenty years, so of course, he'd clashed with other politicians over policies, and over the years, there were local businessmen and constituents who thought he hadn't done enough for them. But he went out of his way to patch things up after arguments. Our mother, who's a lawyer, advised him on how to resolve these complaints effectively. As far as we know, he wasn't worried about anyone or anything. And no one had made threats against him.'

'Was anything stolen from your father before or during the alleged attack?'

'The autopsy also revealed signs of scratches on his left wrist,' said Tom, 'which suggest his watch was pulled off. We hadn't thought about it until then, but we quickly realised his valuable Rolex was missing. It was one with one of those fold-over straps, not a buckle. So, it was probably tugged off. But nothing else that we're aware of was taken. His wallet was upstairs in a drawer in the bedroom. The house contains a few valuable paintings, plus a Vienna wall clock, which a thief could have easily lifted off the wall. But everything was still there the morning after. I checked.'

Tom went on, 'There were about seventy guests, and many had left coats and handbags in the hall during the party. It's quite possible items were taken and the guests haven't wanted to tell us, given the drama of Dad's death. But you don't murder someone just to steal a watch, do you?'

The super glanced at Marley. 'You'd be surprised,' he mumbled.

Then Bella handed him a typed list of names and telephone numbers, including hers and Tom's, their mother's, Karen Peters's, Mrs Gibbs and John Hardwick's.

'Should we try to see DI Howarth in Guildford?' Bella pushed, staring hard at the DCI.

'Leave it with us for the moment. We'll be in touch in the next couple of days. This is a very serious matter, and I assure you we'll treat it as such. May I ask you not to speak to any journalists about this – at least for the moment?'

Tom nodded and put his arm around Bella as they walked out.

The superintendent was on the phone to Guildford as soon as the pair stepped into the lift. He had Marley scan the autopsy report and send it to DI Howarth within minutes.

9

'JESUS!'

Rob was stunned. He tried to keep his voice flat so as not to show it as he told his boss all that Izzy had found out.

When the autopsy report landed on his desk, he knew this was *the* evidence. Like DNA, which cops like to joke means 'Do Not Argue', the report dumped the earlier idea of natural causes firmly in the rubbish bin.

He called Malden back. 'On Monday, DS Holland – our Izzy – is bringing in the two paramedics who arrived on the scene when Olson's body was discovered by the wife, half-hidden under a pile of dust sheets and stuff. The door to the wine store hadn't been properly closed but it looked as though it had been pulled some of the way. Apparently, it's the sort of door that doesn't just slam shut on its own. Certainly, this doesn't fit with the idea that the deceased went into the wine store to look for something and then just quietly collapsed there, oblivious to his surroundings. Someone helped him to collapse.'

There was a short silence as the news percolated through their minds.

'Also, Izzy has some info about people of interest who delivered stuff to the house for the party. She's writing a report now.'

The super chuckled. 'Sounds like it'll be worth my making a foreign trip all the way down to Guildford. See you Monday.'

Rob considered if he should contact Tom Olson to reassure him that they were making this top priority. He decided it would be best once he had something solid to report.

Izzy had a late night on Sunday. She could hardly wait to get on the phone to Bristol's Central Police Station in Broadmead, known to most Bristolians as 'The Bridewell', at about 11pm. She needed to know about Kevin Miller's reunion with his Wandsworth prison cellmate.

Avon and Somerset Police Division easily trumped Surrey for incidents of serious crime. Izzy bore that in mind and treated her West Country cousins with as much deference as she could muster.

She introduced herself to DC Pete Hornsley, who'd been landed with the task of watching Miller and Pugh. Then she apologised for the call at so late an hour on a Sunday night.

'Any idea how my champion burglar got on with your Jim Pugh in Knowle West?' she asked.

'Well, up to an hour ago, they were laughing and joking in a pub near Pugh's sister's flat,' said the DC. 'I checked and they have good CCTV in the pub.

'From what we know, Pugh has been on benefits since he came out of jail and makes his living as a part-time fence for a few local thieves. He has a history of handling stolen goods but nothing recent. Your man left a small bag with him. We didn't get a look inside it, but my DC's recorder picked up talk about a couple of watches, including a man's Rolex, some diamond and ruby earrings that are probably quite valuable, and a couple of Mac Air laptops.

'Pugh had a good rummage inside the bag and then handed a thin wad of fifties to Miller. They agreed to be in touch to settle up properly in a few weeks, probably after Pugh sells the stuff on. He's bound to get a couple of thousand for the Rolex alone if he does. We're going to pay him a visit tomorrow, as soon as we get a search warrant.

'Your Mr Miller seems to have spent last night at a Premier Inn. He left on a scooter at around lunchtime, presumably to return to his cottage, or wherever he lives now. We have the reg of the scooter.'

'Great work!' Izzy said, and she meant it. 'Please text me the scooter's reg and I'll call you back tomorrow afternoon to see if you've got Kevin's stuff.'

Early the next day, she checked her notes on the computer. Kevin had been driving a scooter belonging to Steven James, one of the Clandon Clan.

When she'd spoken to Rob first thing on Monday, he'd given her an abridged version of the super's interview with the Dietrich children, mentioning a missing Rolex and the autopsy report. Now she felt an inner buzz.

On Monday morning, the car park next to Guildford's police station in Margaret Street had rarely been as full. Marley had driven Superintendent Malden from Holborn and had spotted Rob Howarth's dented black Mercedes B Class already there next to a Vauxhall Insignia, probably the Holborn squad car Mehmet used and should have returned, she noted. Izzy's husband's Skoda Citigo was tucked away at the back, rarely used. Izzy had parked it there but preferred to cycle to and from her home near the centre these days. How her poor husband got to work at the hospital was anyone's guess.

On the blue felt noticeboards in the CID war room were mugshots of Dietrich Olson, his wife Penelope Bryant Olson, and out-of-date photos of Tom and Bella blown up from the ones on their driving licences, produced by the DVLA.

On the other side of the board, grouped together, were photos of Kevin Miller, Douglas Elliot, Joseph Jackson and one of Steven James taken from his tech repairs website. Lower down were the names of other people known to have been at Batts Farm at the party on the fifth of January: Mrs Gibbs, housekeeper; Ed George, pianist; John Hardwick, caterer; plus the first names and phone numbers of four of the six waiters he'd hired for the event. A note pinned next to them said 'two more to come'.

The police officers sat on plastic chairs, the sort they had in sixth form and college, with small writing table flaps attached to one arm. The detectives sat or stood around, some with notebooks and pens. Rob was master of ceremonies.

When given the signal to speak, DC Tony Frowde reported that he'd spent an afternoon with John Hardwick gathering contact numbers. He didn't add that he'd also painlessly sampled canapés the caterer was preparing for the golden wedding party he was doing that evening. The copper said he'd looked into Hardwick's background and found there wasn't as much as a parking ticket on his record. He'd asked what Mr Hardwick had seen of his client, Sir Dietrich. The answer was that he'd seen him early on when the guests began to arrive. He'd been relaxed and in good spirits. That was it.

'By the time Mrs Olson was dashing around in a panic asking people where he was, it was as though he'd vanished into thin air,' Hardwick had said.

Geoff and Andy, the paramedics who took Dietrich to hospital, were the next to speak to the assembly of police officers.

'Our first concern was to see if we could get him breathing using a defibrillator,' Andy, the older one, said. 'But the patient hadn't been seen by anyone for at least twenty minutes, and his wife told us that when she found him, there was no pulse. Rigor mortis had set in, so we simply got him on to a stretcher as fast as we could and took him to Surrey General.'

Geoff added, 'I took a few quick photos of the body – he was lying on his left side, knees up, on and partly covered by what looked like a couple of dust sheets and an old coat. Mrs Olson said she'd pushed them aside with her foot to get into the wine store.'

'Tell us about the door to the wine store,' said Rob.

'Mrs Olson said it seemed to have been pushed or pulled back, but it wasn't completely closed. It was rough and unpainted but a proper door – I mean, a wooden one with a doorknob and catch. It didn't just swing open and close on to a magnetic strip like a kitchen cupboard door. Considering all the valuable wines and spirits inside, it's surprising really that it wasn't bolted.'

Geoff handed Izzy the prints of the photos he'd taken with his mobile phone. She and Rob looked at them for signs of footprints in the dust and – bearing in mind the autopsy report – a syringe. No such luck.

Rob went into chief-of-staff mode: Marley was to stay in Guildford for a couple of days to fix and attend meetings with

Mrs Gibbs and any of the waiters who could be pinned down. She would then return to Holborn and ask Mrs Bryant Olson or her daughter Bella for a list of all the guests who were invited and those who attended the party.

'Tony, please bring in Doug, Joe and Steven. I want them interviewed separately to see what comes out. If there's any hint they're involved in the killing, we can try and play them off one another.

Izzy was instructed to get the wine store door removed and brought in for forensic tests, though she could have told them that fingerprints were unlikely to be found on rough wood. She was to wait for the report from Pete Hornsley in Bristol. Presuming they were right about Kevin and the Rolex, she should arrange for him to be arrested so she could question him about the theft of it and other items.

She knew when that happened, he would recognise her as his Wandsworth nemesis.

And she looked forward to it.

10

Google said that Clandon was a village. If that were true, it wasn't much of one, Rob and Mehmet agreed. They'd seen only two other cars since they'd turned off the A3 on their way there, and they seemed to have driven for miles past large, detached houses with names like 'Windy Ridge' and 'The Cedars' half-hidden behind high hedges. No shops, no church, no school. There was supposed to be a pub in the area, but either they hadn't reached it yet or it had closed down.

Rob was listening to Bruch's Violin Concerto on his earphones while Mehmet drove with his phone in a cradle device above the dashboard, so that he could use sat nav. They were jolted as they drove over a hump in the road, and Rob realised it was a bridge over railway tracks. To the left, Rob spotted an unmanned country train station, with empty platforms. He'd have called it a ghost station had it not been for the cars parked on one side. About twenty of them. He pulled out his phone and looked it up. Clandon Station was two stops up from Guildford on a line with trains going fairly frequently to Waterloo. But at eight in the morning, no one was waiting on either platform. Perhaps they didn't have rush hour in this part of Surrey.

Mehmet knocked hard on the plain oak door of one of the large houses, wondering if the people inside may still be asleep. They hadn't phoned first to alert James and Madeleine Phillips of their visit. No point in giving the suspect, their son Mark, a chance to do a runner or fix himself an alibi. Anyway, if Esther Hall's mother was right, Mark may well be tucked up in bed in his hall of residence at Manchester or Leeds University.

'Mrs Phillips?' Mehmet flashed his warrant card at an alarmed woman in a dressing gown. 'I'm Detective Sergeant Mehmet Kharim and this is Detective Inspector Rob Howarth. We're here to speak to Mark.'

She gasped and then asked, 'What about?'

'It concerns his friendship with Esther Hall.'

'Oh! Oh dear, that poor girl! Yes. You'd better come in. Would you wait in here? Please, sit down.' She showed them into a room at the front of the house with a thick beige carpet and two sofas covered in a beige tweed fabric. On the walls were three amateurish paintings of birds.

'Not sure when he came in last night. Quite late, I think. He's upstairs. I'll get him.'

After a few minutes, they heard voices and the sound of someone lurching across the hallway above them into another room, then the sound of running water and a flushing lavatory. After four or five minutes, a tall, pleasant-looking youth in a mouldy-looking T-shirt, tracksuit bottoms and bare feet entered the room, making eye contact with his visitors for only a few seconds. Mehmet introduced himself and his boss again.

'We believe you knew Esther Hall and were boyfriend and girlfriend for a time. When did you last see her?'

'Yeah, course. I heard what happened to her. Awful! Still can't believe it.'

Mehmet thought he looked sad. But maybe he always looked like that...

'Yeah, we were going out in the first year sixth,' the boy continued. 'But we were doing different subjects for A Levels and didn't see much of each other, so it, like, tailed off last year.'

Mehmet waited. The boy started to sound distressed.

'I saw her this Christmas at a friend's house, then at New Year there was an evening in the Onslow Arms, when lots of us got together. She looked really nice but wasn't, you know, like, interested in me anymore. Said she'd met someone.'

'Did she mention his name?' asked Mehmet.

'Don't think so,' Mark said sullenly. He began to sniff. 'I thought he was probably a bloke at her uni who'd gone home to his parents for the holidays.'

'Did she give you any details about him?'

Mark sniffed again and shook his head. A tear may have been forming in one of his eyes, but he kept his head down.

'So, she wasn't interested in you anymore, then? How did that make you feel?' Mehmet pressed.

'Thought it was a bit shit, tell you the truth,' Mark stuttered. 'We'd been together a long time, and I thought, like, five minutes after she dumps me, she finds a new bloke... sort of thing.' He paused to inhale and, for the first time, looked truly upset.

'Inevitable, I s'pose, us being so far away and that.'

'You didn't suggest meeting for a drink – just the two of you – before you headed back up north?' Mehmet asked.

'No. I mean, yeah, would've been nice in some ways. But, like, it didn't make sense. She didn't want me anymore. Anyway, there's a new crowd of us in Manchester. I've moved on, sort a' thing. Couple of girls we go around with, and one of them, Liv, seems to like me.'

Rob sat up. 'Tell us a bit about Esther, Mark. We're trying to build up a picture of her. What sort of things did she like to do? What were her pet hates? Was she friendly with most people – you know the sort of thing.'

He really didn't. Or he wasn't trying. Mark rambled on for a few minutes, talking about the bands Esther liked, her clothes, favourite television programmes, and so on, but he didn't mention other boys or places she liked to visit. Or anything that would explain how she ended up on a cold concrete floor in an industrial park. It wasn't helping.

'Thanks very much,' said Mehmet, passing to Mark his notepad and a pencil, before standing up to leave. 'Could you write down your mobile number and the name and address of the friend who invited Esther and you at Christmas, please.'

Mark did as he was told.

'One last thing. We'd like a saliva sample for DNA purposes. That OK?'

Mehmet reached into the inside pocket of his coat and produced a couple of long cotton bud swabs alongside two tubes and sealable evidence envelopes.

At that point, the vague boy turned into a paranoid adult.

'I think I should speak to my parents and perhaps a solicitor before I agree to that.'

Mehmet took out a card with his name on it and the number of Guildford Police Station. He passed it gently to the now flustered possible suspect.

'Please ring us when you've done that. The test takes half a minute,' he said, noticing how Mark was now staring at the carpet. 'It means we can rule people out.'

Mark Phillips wasn't changing his mind.

The sky had become dark, and it was beginning to rain as they walked back to the Vauxhall. Inside the car, Rob said, 'Well, that was interesting. Esther had another boyfriend, but Mark couldn't or wouldn't remember his name or anything about him.

'And then he gets completely agitated over being swabbed for DNA.

'Esther wouldn't be the first girl to die because her boyfriend was insanely jealous, but raped and strangled? Doesn't seem right to me.'

Mehmet nodded. 'The thing that struck me was how little he seemed to care that his girlfriend had been murdered. I got the impression he'd have more sympathy if she'd dropped her mobile in a puddle on the pavement.'

'He was quite good looking and confident, though, wasn't he?' replied Rob. 'He didn't strike me as the sort who'd need to rape a girl in anger to prove he was capable.'

He paused, remembering his own shy and acne-plagued adolescence. 'But what the hell do I know about the attractiveness of 18-year-old boys?' he added.

Mehmet smiled. 'Anyway, you and I know that rape is about power, not sex.'

'Comparing his DNA with the semen trace on Esther's underwear would settle it,' Rob went on. 'We have the legal power to take a DNA sample and fingerprints but let's put that on hold. We're a long way from charging him. Markie-boy may change his mind and volunteer. In the meantime, we need to find out if this alleged new boyfriend exists.

'Let's start with Annette, the best friend, and see if she can lead us to other friends. Then we'll speak to the bloke who invited the gang over at Christmas.'

Mehmet nodded and turned his car round. Rob began to scroll through the notes on his phone to find Annette's contact numbers. He clicked on her mobile number, and she answered right away. They agreed to meet at a coffee shop in West Horsley not far from the medical centre during her lunch break in an hour's time.

'Don't know about you,' he said to Rob, 'but I could do with a coffee and a sandwich now. I left Guildford at dawn. It felt like it, anyway.'

He parked in a side street near the coffee shop, walked quickly while dodging puddles, and went inside. They were soon gulping hot, strong coffee and eating egg sandwiches.

Revived, Rob rang Izzy. She wanted to talk about Dietrich.

'We're collecting names of partygoers, loads of 'em. We can go through the list when you're in. But the good news is that my DC from Avon and Somerset found a pawnbroker who bought a man's Rolex watch matching the description of the one Dietrich Olson was apparently wearing at his party. Jim Pugh brought it in after my burglar handed him a bag of goodies. Kev's on his way here.'

'Good luck. Bet he'll get himself lawyered up fast. I'll be back at the station later this afternoon. Mehm and I are waiting to meet Esther Hall's friend, Annette.'

At that moment, a young woman in a padded jacket over a blue nylon nurse's tunic with a white-edged collar came through the door, prompting Mehmet to unfurl his long legs from under the table and get up to introduce himself. He towered over Annette as she smiled at the girl behind the counter and asked for a cappuccino. It sounded like a regular order from the young customer. Rob asked if she'd like a sandwich, putting his hand in his trouser pocket for change.

'They're kind to NHS workers here and let me eat my own sandwiches,' Annette said, pulling a plastic lunch box from her bag. 'Brilliant, isn't it?'

'Thanks so much for agreeing to meet us,' Mehmet said warmly. 'We need to find out as much as we can about Esther. Can you start by telling us how you knew her and what she was like?'

Annette's smile disappeared, and her eyes quickly filled with tears. 'I'm not really over the shock and don't think I ever will be,' she began, dabbing her face with a crumpled tissue from her pocket.

Mehmet wanted to comfort her by putting an arm around her shoulders, but he knew Rob would disapprove, considering it unprofessional.

'Yes, it must have been awful for you and her family,' he said gently.

There were no surprises in the picture Annette painted of the girl she'd first met at primary school. Esther was a regular, happy-go-lucky teenage girl, no hang-ups about boys, no dreams of starring in *Love Island* or starting her own fashion brand. The two had hoped to share a flat near the university but Esther's parents, unlike Annette's better off gym manager father and estate agent mother, put the kibosh on that. Still, they saw each other almost every weekday and often on Saturday nights too.

Mehmet asked when she'd last seen Esther.

'On the Friday she... she disappeared.' Annette struggled to fight back another wave of tears but kept herself in check. 'I saw her get on her bike outside the medical centre at around seven and head off. I assumed she was going home. We were going to see a film at the Odeon in Guildford early on Saturday evening, then have a pizza. I rang her on Saturday morning to check on the film screening time and where we'd meet up. But the number didn't ring out. So, I tried her parents' landline, and a family friend picked up and told me Esther was missing and to let them know as soon as I heard from her.'

'But you never did?'

Annette closed her sandwich box and began to weep again. Mehmet passed her a handful of the paper napkins from the table.

'We've been told Esther had broken up with Mark Phillips and had a new boyfriend...' Mehmet kept his tone light.

'She might have told Mark that. I didn't think she'd gone out with anyone else. There are four or five blokes on the nursing course. All nice but Esther never mentioned fancying any of them. She never mentioned them at all, really. Anyway, two of them are gay.'

'Did you go to the gathering of school friends at, er...' Mehmet looked at his notes from talking to Mark. 'Connor Jones's house or the Onslow Arms pub after Christmas?'

'Yes, me and Esther went together to both. She borrowed her mum's car and promised not to have more than one drink.'

'Mark Phillips was there, apparently. He said she mentioned a new boyfriend.'

Annette's nose wrinkled. She shook her head. 'Don't know anything about that. She might have said that just to get shot of him. They'd split up last summer, but he was a bit clingy, if you know what I mean.'

'No, I don't, actually,' said Mehmet. 'Do you mean he kept pestering her?'

'Don't know for sure. I got the impression he'd messaged a few times suggesting they meet. But she wanted to move on.'

'What do you think of Mark?'

'Not my type but quite good looking, I suppose. Got better A Levels than expected, so he's not thick. Not much of a sense of humour, though. I think that's one reason Esther wanted to end it.'

'Any other reasons?'

'I think she suspected he had other girlfriends. They'd had a few arguments.'

'Ever seen him lose his temper?' asked Rob.

Annette frowned and shook her head.

'What about Connor Jones. Were he and Esther close?'

Annette blew her nose and shook her head again. 'He's nice, not exactly a looker, and I've never seen him relax with a girl. Too awkward and shy. So, I don't think so, no.'

'Did Esther have any other girlfriends she might have confided in?'

'She was popular with other girls at school, but no one stands out. Most of them have gone off to uni now. I can look through the people in our WhatsApp group and forward their contact numbers.'

'Was Esther happy working at the medical centre?'

'She loved it!' Annette smiled but couldn't control yet another surge of tears.

'And did she get on well with her parents?'

'Her dad's a bit gruff sometimes but her mum's lovely. They used to go clothes shopping together and never fell out, which is more than I can say for my mum.'

Mehmet handed her his card with his mobile number and email address. 'The WhatsApp list would be great,' he said with a big smile.

In the car on the way back to Guildford, Rob was trying to decide if they'd learned anything significant.

'Let's review what the earlier lot discovered about the garage where the body was found and look at the known sex offenders around here.'

They hadn't gone far along the A3 before Rob signalled for them to stop in a layby. He started scrolling through a list on his phone. 'Hang on,' he said. 'Terry Thomson's mum lives just up the road. Let's pop in for a little chat.'

Thomson was one of the local sex offenders who Rob thought was worth looking at. Mehmet put the postcode into his sat nav and off they went. But it wasn't 'just up the road' and meant getting on to the slip road to Farnham and then looking out for signs to Puttenham, a tiny village without even a shop, just a pub, which was probably in danger of throwing in the beer-soaked towel.

After a period of staying out of trouble, Terry Thomson had been up before the Highbury Corner Magistrates' Court in North London, the area to which he'd been moved after short jail sentences for a string of offences of grooming and attempted grooming of young girls in the Clandon, Horsley and Leatherhead neighbourhoods. He had a long record of touching and other sexual offences. Taken 'into consideration' at the hearings were countless episodes of flashing and exposing himself in public.

Rob followed a link to read a report in the *Islington Gazette* of Thomson's recent court appearance, then he gave Mehmet a summary. The report said that Thomson pleaded guilty to voyeurism and sexual assault. In mitigation, he told the court that what caused his recent lapse, after eight years of good behaviour, was that he'd grown fond of the squirrels he saw playing in the communal gardens of the council flat that social services had found for him. He liked watching the creatures' frantic activity from his kitchen window with his breakfast cup of tea. Then, one morning, as three of them gobbled up crumbs he'd left out for them, he saw a fox spring out, sink his teeth into one and shake it to death, its bushy tail flapping helplessly.

'I was that upset, I started to feel different, like. That's probably why I went back to me offending behaviour,' he'd told the magistrates.

Their Worships heard how he'd travelled back to Surrey by bus, underground and train, to a co-ed state secondary school in Leatherhead. At one end of a field used for sports was a block of lavatories. Terry loitered until a group of year seven girls approached, chattering and laughing while also sending messages and swiping photos on their phones. Then he snuck inside the block and locked himself in the middle cubicle. As soon as someone entered one of the other cubicles, he bent down and held a mirror under the partition wall in a way that allowed him to see the genitals of the poor girl with her pants down. Two of the girls didn't notice it, but the third victim spotted the mirror and rang 999 before collapsing in tears. Two constables responded quickly, and Terry was rapidly escorted out of the park.

Rob and Mehmet laughed at Terry's pathetic idea of mitigation for his horrible behaviour. 'Couldn't make it up, could you?' Mehmet said.

That'd happened nearly two years ago, so Rob was certain Terry would have served whatever penalty was handed down.

He was likely to have visited his mother in her flat in Leatherhead on his release.

Maureen Thomson, still in her dressing gown, a cigarette in one hand, was alarmed to find Mehmet on her doorstep holding up his badge and warrant card. You didn't get many tall, whiskery Asian gentlemen in her part of Leatherhead. You didn't get many policemen of any description on your doorstep, come to think of it. She looked past Mehmet to Rob, who said, 'It's about Terry.'

'Woss 'e dun now?' she croaked, ushering them in, hoping her neighbours were busy watching *Homes Under the Hammer* or some such TV joy. At least the cops weren't in uniform and there were no blue lights on their car.

Rob ignored her question. 'When did you last see him, Mrs Thomson?'

'Comes 'ere for a Sunday dinner about once a month. S'pose the last time was about a fortnight ago. Yes, that's right. It *was*. He said the next time would be Easter and he'd bring me an Easter egg.'

'Does he still live in Islington?' asked Mehmet.

'Yes. Nice little place he's got there. Sticking to his job for the council, on the bins, too. He'd like to go on the vans, but they keep him in the loading bays for some reason. Hasn't got a girlfriend but you never know...'

'So, he didn't seem agitated or upset by anything? asked Rob again. 'I know he's quite sensitive.' He kept a straight face.

'No!' Barbara snapped, perhaps sensing a trap.

Rob thanked her, said she'd been very helpful.

In the car heading back to Guildford, Rob chuckled. 'She seemed surprised when I suggested her revolting son was "sensitive". Perhaps she hadn't heard about the fox and the squirrel.' They sniggered.

'Thinking about Terry's previous offences, maybe he's just a sad thicko. The man who raped and killed Esther probably has a history of more serious offences than flashing at schoolgirls.'

He paused then added, 'But on the other hand, every sex offender starts somewhere. It's worth getting a couple of uniforms to search the Islington place, see if it gives any clues about his hobbies. He might have a nurse's bike in the hall and a computer stuffed with child pornography.'

Mehmet nodded. 'I'll get on to the CPS about a warrant when we're back.'

Luckily, that was in less than 15 minutes.

11

'MR MILLER!' said Izzy sarcastically, flicking on the lights in the tiny, windowless interview room and glancing sternly at the thief, already seated on the other side of the metal table. She put down the items she was carrying. A green envelope folder. A new pad of lined paper. Two Biros. A few paperclips. A small packet of tissues.

She stretched to switch on the tape recorder at the side of the table, then spoke her own name and Kevin's. She looked purposefully at the pretty woman solicitor sitting next to him, bidding her to introduce herself for the recorder. It struck Izzy they looked like Beauty and the Beast.

'Vanessa Hallington, FTV Solicitors,' the lawyer said flatly for the tape, tossing and tidying her carefully streaked fair hair unnecessarily with both hands.

Izzy announced the date and time the interview was beginning and shuffled the pile of papers from the envelope folder aggressively. 'After our last encounter, I didn't expect to see you again, Kevin,' she said.

'Beats me why you *are* seeing me,' he grumbled, pulling

the sleeves of his sweatshirt over his knuckles, like a teenager rather than a thirty-two-year-old man, and not meeting her eyes.

'It seems that working in the wood mill isn't keeping you busy enough. Tell me about your other jobs.'

He looked at the lawyer and began the familiar mouth-to-ear communications.

'I got a van, yeah? Help me mate deliver stuff, sometimes house moves, sometimes for a hire company. That what you mean by *jobs*?'

Izzy nodded, looking at the government-grey walls to either side of the table.

'Sometimes the stuff needs to be collected and returned to the hire company, and I help him with that an' all.

'And I'll be, like, telling the taxman all about what I get paid, if that's what you're worried about.' He sniffed and sighed.

Vanessa flicked a long strand of hair from her face with the second, shiny, red-varnished finger of her left hand and threw it over her shoulder. Izzy had the impression she did that a lot. Kevin, meanwhile, had his head down. Izzy looked at his thick curls enviously.

He released one hand from a sleeve and concentrated on biting the cuticles of what remained of his nicotine-stained fingernails. She noticed that one of them was beginning to bleed. She also noticed his auburn eyebrows and lashes and wondered if he'd been teased about his colouring at school.

'Would you tell us the basis of your arrest of my client?' Vanessa asked imperiously.

Izzy pulled a clear plastic envelope from her pocket and put it on the table. 'For the record,' she said, 'I'm showing Mr Miller and his solicitor exhibit one.'

'This is the basis. Recognise it, Kevin?'

Vanessa whispered what must have been a caution into Kevin's ear. He shrugged and pulled a don't-give-a-shit expression.

'Yeah, so? It's a watch. It used to be mine, but I never wore it. Came across it when I was tidying up the cottage the other day. Asked me old friend Jim Pugh to sell it for me. Nuffin' wrong with that, is there?'

Izzy put her head to one side and gave him a pull-the-other-one face.

'Got a receipt for it?'

'Course not.'

'Tell you the truth, Kevin, I think you stole it.'

'Yeah? Got evidence of that, 'ave ya? Some bloke tell you it belongs to them?' A nerve in one of his pale, thin cheeks twitched.

Izzy decided not to mention the late Sir Dietrich Olson yet and, after offering her guests tea, which they both declined, she picked up the watch, adjourned the interview and left the room.

Mehmet, who'd been watching through the one-way glass window, walked out and towards her in the corridor.

'Shame the Rolex wasn't initialled,' he said.

'No, but there weren't that many of that design sold thirty years ago, and the Olsons are vague about when and where Dietrich bought it. He got it as a treat to himself when he was working in some job in the City, apparently making loads of dosh.'

'What about the other things he gave Jim Pugh to sell on for him?'

'Well, let me see.' She looked at the list she'd made. 'Two engagement rings, a gold bracelet, a pair of ruby and diamond earrings. Nice stuff but nothing unusual or of especially high value. I reckon those were from his old days as the Wandsworth Burglar, or maybe from some jobs he's done more recently in places like Onslow Village. The owners probably reported thefts, claimed on their insurance policies and that was the end of it. Kevin probably stored it away under the floorboards or at a mate's house.'

Izzy knocked on Rob's door.

'Not sure how much I should tell Kevin the Burglar about Dietrich. At the moment, the official line is that he simply dropped dead.'

Rob cottoned on quickly. 'Don't give any hint that we know Dietrich was murdered. The watch was pulled off his wrist after he collapsed, wasn't it? The information we need is how, when and why was Kevin in the house.'

'He'll probably stick to his story of having had the watch for years,' Izzy replied.'

'You never know. But Dietrich wore it often, and forensics are sure to find DNA evidence linking it to him. We needn't tell Kevin that quite yet though,' Rob smiled.

'Keep him stewing in his cell overnight?' Izzy asked, warming to the task ahead.

'Yes. There's sure to be a floating inspector who'll sign him up for a second night and then we'll find a tame magistrate for a third. We can stretch it out to ninety-six hours, remember, without charging him.'

Back in the interview room, Izzy switched the recorder on and announced the time.

'Kevin, would you tell me about the delivery job you did on Saturday the fifth of January. Where was it to?'

'Some big house in Godalming. They were having a party. Loads of people, caterers and all that.'

'And when exactly did you go there?'

'The Friday afternoon and then again on Saturday morning, about 10-ish.'

'Find out whose house it was?'

'Not at the time. But later, in the afternoon, I saw an ambulance pulling up and they took a body away. Then it was in the papers next day that some politician had died at his home, and I sort of put it all together. Somebody... was it Thomson? Johnson? Never heard of him, me.'

A hint of a smirk suggested Kevin was pleased with his answer and he leaned back in his chair.

'Did you go inside the house?'

'Well, yeah, 'ad to – to get signatures on the papers from the caterer bloke to say we'd brought in the right number of chairs and tables.'

'So, you had time to have a look around?'

'Door was open, people rushing around. Bit of a madhouse. Saw me mates Doug and Joe, the blokes who got me doing the delivery. They do a lot of jobs for that caterer. They were bringing in cooking equipment and food and stuff. We had a bit of a chat and that outside. Doug said I should come into the kitchen for a cup of coffee and somefin' to eat. So, I did, course.'

'How long did you stay?' asked Izzy.

Kevin and Vanessa had further ear-to-mouth communication, before Kevin cleared his throat and replied, 'I was going to 'ead off but then I thought, 'ang on, Kev, you'll have to go back later to collect the stuff and take it to the hire companies in Guildford and Tooting anyway. So, I changed me mind, yeah? I decided to sit in the van, parked in the garden with the other motors, eat a couple of bacon rolls, drink a few Cokes and listen to the football on Radio 5 Live till the guests left.'

'Did you see anyone at the party you knew – someone you might not have expected to see?' Izzy asked.

'Matter a fact, I did. Some posh bloke I met years ago. In a magistrates' court, would you believe?'

Izzy nodded for him to continue. She was intrigued.

'I forget which court – been in quite a few over the years – but I was sitting in the corridor next to this geezer in a classy suit and a shirt with cuffs and cufflinks. He was waiting to be called. We got talking. He was up for non-payment of fines – some driving offences, I fink. Told me his name but I've forgotten it. Anyway, I noticed his watch, a Rolex. *Very* nice indeed. He saw me looking and said in this la-de-da voice, "My business partner and I treated ourselves to Rolexes when our company was doing well." Okay for *some*, I thought!

'And, well, I saw this man at the party, knocking back the Champagne. I'd 'ave said 'ello, only he didn't look my way. Don't 'spect he'd have remembered me anyway.'

Izzy wasn't clear what this information amounted to, if anything. She'd noted the reference to a second watch. Could Kevin have known that Dietrich was the business partner who owned it? Unlikely.

She went back to the point of the interview. 'Do you know where Dietrich Olson's body was found, Kevin?'

'Some room off the kitchen, papers said.'

'Did you go into that room?'

Vanessa pulled Kevin to one side and Izzy heard her telling him to keep his trap shut from then on. Perhaps she's a real lawyer after all, Izzy thought.

'No,' said Kevin.

Izzy decided to stick it to him.

'The evidence shows that someone pulled a watch off Sir Dietrich Olson's left wrist. The scratch marks are clear. Furthermore, Sir Dietrich had been wearing a Rolex Datejust watch, just like the one you say was yours. *This* watch, in fact.'

She moved a file on the table that had been covering the evidence bag and nodded to the watch inside it.

Kevin's eyes flicked momentarily to the watch, then back to the bleeding cuticle on one of his thumbs.

'Turned up in Bristol, of all places. Your friend Jim Pugh took it to a pawnbroker.

'I'm handing it over to forensics. They'll examine it carefully. These sort of linked metal straps are devils to clean. What would you say are the odds that they find tiny skin flakes and other DNA evidence to prove this was Dietrich Olson's watch?'

Vanessa glowered at Kevin, possibly wondering why she'd ever thought the little creep she'd accepted as a client was quietly clever. He shrugged, said nothing. Izzy gathered her things and flicked the recorder off. Kevin was taken away by a couple of uniformed police officers and locked in a cell.

'Obviously, I'll be making a bail application,' Vanessa snapped before she flounced out, her high heels click-clacking on the hard floor.

When Izzy went back to see Rob, Mehmet was in the boss's office stroking his unshaven chin. He was considering growing a beard, he'd told her earlier when she'd asked him if he'd lost his razor. He smiled broadly at her and pointed to a tray on Rob's desk. He'd found three mugs, not too badly chipped, and made tea for them all.

'Been looking at your Kevin's file,' said Rob, clasping his mug and staring into the middle distance. 'Reading all the old probation reports and the pre-sentence reports from when you first nabbed him. Seems he was sexually abused for years as a kid by his mother's boyfriend. The boyfriend, Claude Pollard, was finally arrested for a whole raft of historic rapes and assaults of boys and girls.

'The victims reported having been drugged at the time, probably with Rohypnol. Some of them said that when they realised what had happened, that they'd been passed around a group of men, they felt so dirty they scrubbed themselves with bleach. Almost all of them went on to struggle with drugs and many turned to burglary or prostitution to pay for their habit.

'Pollard denied it, of course, but got twenty years after about ten of his victims agreed to testify.

'Kevin pulled out of going to court at the last minute. You can hardly blame him.'

Mehmet shot a baffled glance at Izzy.

'It doesn't change the fact that he's a menace, a very busy burglar and may, just possibly, be involved in a murder. But it makes a sort of sense, don't you think?'

Izzy and Mehmet weren't used to the boss empathising with people like Kevin. They walked out together silently, carrying their mugs of tea.

It had started to rain heavily, so Izzy abandoned her bike and used the Skoda.

Inside a dry car, she started to think of him as Kevin the Victim.

12

When Steven James got the call from Detective Sergeant Isobel Holland politely requesting he come talk to her at Guildford Police Station, he was halfway through setting up a Sky Q system of televisions linked to the wi-fi of a house in Sistova Road, one of the nicer streets of Balham, the area where his family had lived before his parents' divorce. He stalled, saying he was in the middle of a job he couldn't leave. This was true; it had already taken twice the time the client had been promised.

DS Holland suggested the Friday of that week and he agreed, but not before asking her if she was sure she had the right Steven James.

'It's a common name,' he tried.

'Are you the Steven James who is the owner of a grey Vespa scooter, registration LK65MYM?'

She had the right one.

'Tea?' she asked, as he took a seat in the interview room and rested his hands on the bolted-down table.

'Wondering what this is about?' Izzy said as she called out for two teas to be brought in.

Steve nodded.

'We believe you've recently helped your friend Kevin Miller out with a couple of things.'

A light went on inside Steve's head. Doug Elliot had told him Kevin had been arrested but no one knew why.

'That's what mates do. I slept on his sofa for months when I split up with my girlfriend. I lent him the scooter for a couple of days. So what? He got insurance for it.'

'Know why he went to Bristol?'

'See another mate, I think. Ask him.'

'Tell me about helping him deliver and collect hired furniture for an event in Godalming soon after Christmas.'

Another light went on in Steve's head. A dead MP. But still, what had that got to do with Kevin being nabbed? Kev was a thief who liked drugs, but he wasn't violent. He decided to tell the whole story and tried to make it clear and simple to get it over with.

'I was going to borrow Kev's transit van to take all my stuff from his cottage near Guildford to my dad's flat that weekend. My parents divorced a year or so back and my dad bought this flat with two bedrooms. He was all excited about me living with him, but he doesn't have a car to help me move.

'That weekend, Kev needed the van for the hired tables and chairs. I reckoned the sooner I helped him load and unload it, the sooner I could get my stuff in the van and take it to my dad's place.

Izzy finished her tea, then stared at him. 'What was happening in the house, Batts Farm, when you went in?'

'Went in? Well, hard to say. Not many people still there. A

short woman with grey hair was bossing people around, getting them to move crates of beer and other things near where the cars were parked outside, ready for them to be collected. Doug Elliot was putting the caterer's boxes in his van. The caterer he works for had been telling him which ones to take. Then the caterer drove off in his car with some students – or blokes who looked like students – hired for the job as waiters or washers-up. I got the impression he was giving them a lift home or to a station.

'Kev wanted me to come in and look around with him. He said I should see how the other half live. I wasn't that interested, tell you the truth. He had it rough growing up. You probably know?'

He looked at Izzy, who replied with a gentle nod.

'I didn't. My family was always comfortable. Not well off but OK. We didn't have the same lifestyle as those in the party house, though. That was obviously owned by people who'd had money for a long time. I think they call it old money.

'So, I told Kev to stop wasting time and get on and do what he came for. I just went into the house to collect the tables and those silly little gold chairs with red velvet seats they'd hired and take them out to the van.'

'See anyone else?'

'Yeah, a young bloke with dark hair. He stuffed some clothes into a rucksack, got on his bike and cycled away. He looked a bit – I dunno – upset. He'd been talking to another bloke. He was tall, about the same age. I'm pretty sure he was the son of the man who died because he was telling people what to do. He stayed and wandered about.

'I felt really sorry for him. I thought my dad had died last year and I remember how the shock hit me – like the proverbial ton of bricks.'

'Tell me about that, if you don't mind,' said Izzy, for no reason other than nosiness.

Steve thought for a moment then seemed to decide there'd be no harm in telling her.

'My dad suffers from bouts of depression, and he was going through his divorce from my mum. He was standing on a platform at Wandsworth Town station with a heavy rucksack on his back. For some reason, he turned around quickly, without thinking, and the weight of the bag pulled him over the platform edge and on to the tracks. A fast train to Waterloo was due any second. Two young blokes waiting for the train acted quickly and dragged him up. He was in shock and dazed. One of the men dug his phone out of his pocket while he was recovering on the platform and called the first number on it – mine. It'd looked like a suicide attempt. I hope it wasn't. That isn't to say dad wasn't badly shaken up. Anyway, I live with him now and keep an eye on him.'

'Glad to hear it,' said Izzy, meaning it. 'Let's get back to you and Kevin at Batts Farm.'

'Kev disappeared to use the loo. I stayed to look at some of the paintings. Traditional landscapes mostly. Not my taste. We weren't there long, really. I stayed over at Kev's cottage for another night, finally put my stuff in his van and took it to Dad's on the Sunday.'

Izzy stood up, asked him to excuse her for a moment and left.

Again, she sought out Rob for advice.

'I'm fairly sure Steve James isn't hiding anything, although he admits to going inside the Olson house with Kevin Miller,' she explained. 'This was sometime after Dietrich's body had been taken out. Any reason I shouldn't ask him about the watch?'

'Go for it. Show him it. Perhaps he remembers seeing Kevin wearing that model ages ago. When he was wearing his pin-striped, three-piece suit and bowler.'

Izzy laughed and Rob grinned, savouring the absurd image.

Back in the interview room, Izzy asked Steve for his recollections of any of the people at the party. After thinking for a few moments, he said, 'The missus in the green dress looked very posh and gracious, and she suited the house.'

Izzy, who didn't need lessons in class differences, guessed he was talking about Pen. Despite only seeing her in photographs, she nodded her agreement before closing her file and putting her pen in one of her pockets.

'One last thing, Steve,' she said, reaching into another pocket for the bag containing the Rolex. 'Seen this before?' she asked.

'Nope. Special, is it?'

'Your friend Kevin says it's his and he wore it a lot before he mislaid it somewhere in the cottage.'

Steve shook his head. 'Never mentioned that to me.'

'Would it surprise you to know that it's an extremely valuable Rolex that belonged to Dietrich Olson, and that Kevin took it to Bristol last weekend so that his friend Jim Pugh could fence it for him?'

Steve finally realised why he was there.

'Look, we both know that Kevin went to prison for breaking into people's houses and stealing money and stuff,' he said. 'As far as I know, he doesn't do that anymore... doesn't need to because he's off the drugs. He's got a job at the wood yard and a cottage to live in.'

Steve stood up and moved towards the door. 'I've never seen that watch and I have no idea what Kevin's connection with it is or was.'

'Did you see anyone else you know at the event?'

'Big Doug and Joe Jackson.'

Izzy thanked him and Steve left the station. The interviews weren't done with, but she decided to take a break.

Back in Rob's office she said, 'Steve James said he noticed a young bloke with dark hair talking to what sounded like the Olson son, then getting on a bike and cycling off after everyone left. Any idea who that could've been?'

Rob thought. 'Didn't someone mention a piano player? Ask the son and then talk to him, can you?

Izzy went back to her desk and typed up a short report on Kevin and a shorter one on Steve. Then she turned to the 'persons of interest' in her notes.

Joseph Victor Jackson, aged 46, as Izzy quickly found from tapping the name into the Police National Computer, had a record of common assaults and battery and assaults occasioning actual bodily harm, some of them aggravated by racial abuse. Over the years, three women had reported serious sexual abuse, but he'd never been charged with sex offences and wasn't on the Sex Offenders' Register. He'd served terms in both HMP High Down, in Sutton, and in HMP Coldingley in Bisley. He was now thought to be living between Bisley and Woking with his partner Jess Cummings. Izzy made a note to try to speak to his probation officer.

Doug Elliot was a 'person of interest' both for his presence at the knighthood party and his suspected cocaine dealing. He certainly wasn't an advertisement for it, Izzy thought, as she looked through the one-way window to view the ugly, fat man who'd plonked himself into a seat in the interview room to wait for her.

Izzy sent through a message that the interview was postponed so she could do more research on their mutual friend Kevin.

She knew the waiting would piss Doug off.

13

When she telephoned using the contact details Tom had passed on, Izzy caught Ed in the Bankside flat. He told her he was practising piano pieces before his session at the Strand Palace hotel later that evening. They agreed to meet at Holborn Police Station the next morning.

At the meeting, Ed gave her his full Romanian name, confirmed the Bankside flat address, the details of his tutor at Imperial College, and explained that he had 'settled status' and was in the process of naturalisation to become a British citizen.

He knew the results of the autopsy from his girlfriend Bella.

'Had you met Bella's father before the party?' asked the detective.

'Yes, on a couple of occasions at the Olson family's flat in Bloomsbury, and once we all went to the Albert Hall to hear the soprano Angela Gheorghiu sing. She's Romanian, like me, you see, and Mr – sorry – *Sir* Dietrich thought I'd like to join the group. It was a wonderful evening.

'I'd been to Batts Farm before too, one afternoon the previous summer. I'd wanted to try the piano there. It's a Chappell Boudoir Grand, built in about 1920, not nearly as good as a Steinway or a Bechstein, of course. Very nice tone, though.'

'Did you ask for Sir Dietrich's or Mrs Olson's help to get your citizenship?'

Ed was taken aback. 'No, of course not. I wouldn't try to take advantage in that way. Anyway, my tutor is helping me.'

'Whose idea was it for you to play the piano at the party?'

'Bella asked me, and of course, I agreed. It was an honour.'

'Were you paid?'

Ed bridled again. 'No, certainly not. Bella's my girlfriend. I cycled to Waterloo Station, took my bike on a train to Godalming and cycled to the house from there. I went back the same way. I'd offered to stay there with Bella after Tom told everyone about Sir Dietrich collapsing, but she wanted to concentrate on getting her mother back safely. I cancelled my job at a hotel in Covent Garden that evening and went back to Bankside in case she needed to talk.'

'What did you think when you heard about what happened to Sir Dietrich?'

'I was shocked. It was unbelievable. And I was very worried about Bella. And upset for Tom and their mother.'

He seemed quite agitated now. It was as though he felt Izzy was accusing him of not doing enough to help his girlfriend and her family.

Izzy paused to give him a moment to calm down.

'Did you see anyone behaving strangely at the party around the time Mrs Olson wanted to give a toast?' she asked.

'I'd stopped playing by the time this came around. Bella

had told me her father was going to make a speech and had been fussing over it, even though – she said it was a family joke – he always made it up as he went along.

'I didn't see anything strange really. A couple of guests had opened the big windows to the garden. It had become quite hot in the room with so many people and the log fires. I noticed some small children running around on the lawn and being pulled back by their parents. And one man, I think I'd seen him with Karen, the nice secretary, was outside too. Just walking, deep in thought, looking at the plants.

'I asked a waiter to pass me a glass of Champagne because I hadn't had a drink yet and thought I deserved one. I noticed how busy and noisy it was in the kitchen. Lots of waiters seemed to be going out to the back kitchen, and they were laughing and joking. And there was a young girl flirting with one of the waiters. I even saw them kissing. The caterer saw them too. He was very angry – with her, not the boy!'

Izzy thanked him and gave him her card, asking him to call if he remembered any other detail that could possibly be helpful.

Later that week, Kevin Miller, in his best blue zip-up jacket, his copper curls almost golden under the strong lights of Guildford Magistrates' Court, a building next door to the police station, pleaded not guilty to burglary, an offence – as the clerk announced sternly – under section 9 of the Theft Act, 1968. Izzy wondered what tone he used for murder.

Vanessa Hallington appeared at the side of the court in a grey shift dress, a matching blazer and black patent shoes with vertiginous high heels. She announced herself to be Mr Miller's defence solicitor and applied for bail. She said her client had 'strong ties in the community' and assured the chairman of the bench that an electronic tag would ensure that he attended his next hearing, which, considering the seriousness of the offence and Kevin's history, would be at Crown Court, where a judge could hand out longer sentences than magistrates.

Izzy took a train up to Holborn to brief Scott Davis, the young prosecutor she'd known during her time there. She told him that the theft of the Rolex was linked to what now seemed certain to have been the murder of Dietrich Olson. The forensic examination of the strap had come through to confirm the watch had belonged to the politician, which meant it was possible Kevin had been in contact with the man either before or after he died. Kevin's history of theft and his links to known drug dealers suggested he could have been the person with cocaine who jabbed Dietrich in the thigh.

Scott shot a dazzling smile at Izzy but shook his head. Izzy noticed his straight, white teeth. She wondered how he looked in his black robe and wig. A knockout, probably.

'It's an aggravating factor but not enough to indict him for murder or even conspiracy to murder, I'm afraid,' he said. 'But let's keep a close eye on him and see what corroborating evidence you and Rob can find.'

She'd expected as much.

Their Worships had clearly studied Kevin Miller's list of previous offences and, in keeping with the Ministry of Justice's orders to cut down on the number of defendants being sent to overcrowded prisons on remand before trial, granted him conditional bail: electronic ankle tag, reporting to the police station three times a week and a curfew of 7am to 7pm. He looked morosely at the solemn-faced woman chair, sitting with two male colleagues who seemed too scared even to whisper a word in her ear. Vanessa must have ordered her client to keep absolutely quiet, and he managed it.

He was facing a lengthy prison sentence for the theft alone. The fact that he'd almost certainly pulled the watch off a dead or dying man's wrist would certainly resonate with the judge and any jury. Izzy could tell from Kevin's face that the reality of what was happening hadn't yet sunk in.

Had Vanessa encouraged him to plead guilty to avoid a trial and earn a discount on his sentence? If she had, it probably hadn't worked.

Later that day, as he sat opposite her, Izzy studied Douglas Elliot's face with a sort of morbid curiosity. A nose like a blob of red broccoli, cracked red veins on his cheeks, uneven yellow teeth, the nicotine-stained fingers of a heavy smoker, wisps of hair sticking to his greasy scalp like seaweed to the post of a jetty.

He looked at his pocket-sized inquisitor and grinned. She pushed a paper cup and water jug across the table but then regretted it. Every time he moved one of his horribly tattooed arms, the stench of body odour seemed to intensify in the small, airless room.

He'd needed no one to tell him to keep quiet during his interview. He answered 'no comment' to all Izzy's questions. He couldn't resist regular smirks. She steeled herself to avoid showing her annoyance. Why give the smartarse the extra satisfaction? After nearly an hour, he waddled back to his cell in the police station. Izzy's team knew they must look for solid evidence of his drug dealing. Other drug peddlers had remarked that he was the 'king of coke dealers', but this was inadmissible hearsay, and anyway, it wouldn't convince a jury.

First, Izzy needed a warrant to search his home. Rob

agreed that a magistrate should be asked to sign one as soon as possible. This magistrate would need to know why the search was necessary, and the answer would be that caterer John Hardwick and Steve James had both confirmed that Doug Elliot had been among the catering team at the Batts Farm party, where a man had been murdered. The cops were aware of Doug's previous drug-related offences. They also knew how Doug lived with his frail dad and planned to contact Social Services for them to assess the situation and perhaps cart the demented old man off to a care home.

Any items found at the flat, such as little plastic 'deal bags', scales, lists of customers and cash would firmly nail Big Doug for supplying drugs. His mobile phone, especially any burner phone found, could provide vital evidence of ongoing dealing. It might reveal lists of customers, and the arrangements made for delivery. Digital experts could retrieve deleted texts and photos, as well as uncovering the recent places Doug had visited. Messages between him and Joe Jackson could help to prosecute him too.

At home in her bedroom that night, Izzy kicked off her shoes, took off the dark grey trouser suit and cream polyester shirt she'd been wearing and pulled on tracksuit bottoms and a baggy jumper. Tomorrow she'd wear her other suit, the navy one with a straight skirt and boxy blazer, which she'd pair with a grey, long-sleeved blouse. She'd never had confidence in her work clothes but made it a rule not to dither over her choices because no one would notice anyway.

She stared at herself in the mirrored door of the medicine cupboard above the bathroom sink. She still liked her relatively new bob hairstyle, but, pushing back each side, she spotted some grey hairs, which would need to be covered with a light-brown tint next time she visited the hairdressers.

How her mother would disapprove of hair dyes! Oddly, one side was worse than the other. She was beginning to realise what a funny thing ageing was, and she made a mental note to study Rob and Mehmet's grey hairs to see if the three of them were growing old in sync. Mehmet's nascent beard was definitely of the salt and pepper variety.

'Are we going to eat this lasagne or just watch it go cold and congeal?' Alex shouted from downstairs. Annoyingly, her husband's brown hair hadn't yet sprouted a single grey wire.

Izzy dried her hands, sat down at the small kitchen table and dished out the cheesy pasta dish whilst Alex plonked some salad leaves on each of their plates and poured Majestic Wines' Merlot of the Month into two glasses.

She summarised the Dietrich case so far.

He nodded, impressed. 'Sounds as though you're making headway.'

Izzy screwed up her face. 'I doubt either my favourite burglar or Disgusting Doug are killers, though,' she said. 'Neither has shown a tendency for violence and there is no real motive. You don't murder someone for a watch unless it's a priceless heirloom or something you think you're entitled to own.'

They moved on to a fruit salad – if you could call a few strawberries mixed with a carton of supermarket blueberries that – with scoops of ice cream from the family-sized carton in the freezer, before looking in the newspaper to see if there was anything on television that night worth watching. There wasn't. But as Alex put plates in the dishwasher, Izzy checked the stack of programmes she'd recorded over the last few months. She chose an episode of *Endeavour* she hadn't seen, hoping the hero wasn't sporting a dreadful 1960s moustache and that the plot wouldn't turn on ancient ceremonies of murderous monks that only young Morse understood.

Rob called her into his office the next afternoon. Mehmet was already there. 'This case is baffling,' he began. 'We've got Kevin Miller for the watch and with luck, we'll get Doug Elliot for cocaine dealing. But you don't need to be a genius to get your hands on a syringeful of Grade-A coke these days. It doesn't make him the one who jabbed it into Olson's leg. The big question is why would someone who wasn't a raving far-left agitator or a terrorist want a not-very-important Tory politician not just finished in government but finished altogether? Dead, deceased, bucket well-and truly kicked?

'To punish him for something he did in the past? To settle a score from a dispute that happened years ago? Did he shaft a rival at the elections in some sneaky way? Maybe it was to stop him from doing something he hadn't done yet but looked likely to do? If we can work that out, we've a good chance of finding the murderer.

'I've been reading up on the colourful life and times of Dietrich Olson and trying to get an overall picture – to see how he made his money, where it is now, the companies he ran or was a director of and who his friends were. It's a very big picture.

'Then of course, there's his family. Was something going on that we don't know about? Was he a womaniser, quietly bonking his secretary? It's certainly an unusual grieving widow who agrees with their children they should dig up her husband's body from the cemetery and get it autopsied.'

He stretched back and laced his fingers together behind his head.

'Come to think of it, it's amazing that the autopsy report hasn't made it on to the front pages yet. Can't be long.

'To cap it all, who should've turned up at the memorial service than a woman claiming to have been his real wife with a young bloke she says is Dietrich's son in tow. So, that makes him a bigamist. A dead bigamist. It makes his marriage to the grieving widow null and void. And the real wife is now due to inherit most of his phenomenal stack of dosh.'

'Yeah, when you put it that way,' said Mehmet, stroking his straggle.

'We need to go through all these aspects of his life with a fine-tooth comb. Then we'll have some idea of who would benefit from having Dietrich out of the picture and we can start finding the evidence to nail them.'

Rob had displeased his wife by taking his work home with him again – this time in the form of a fat file of papers and copies of photographs – in the hope that something new would jump out. It hadn't.

'I forgot to mention our progress in the hunt for Esther Hall's killer, Izzy. Mehmet and I have looked at Esther's last known boyfriend, Mark Phillips. For some reason, he refused to do a swab test for DNA, and we've held off on getting a warrant and bringing him in for that. I also read through the available details about the local known sex offenders.

'There are three on the register, one has been in hospital since before Esther disappeared, one has just died after a spell inside and the third is Terry Thomson. We're still looking at him. He's definitely a sexual deviant, but I don't see him as a rapist and murderer—'

'There's also Joe Jackson,' butted in Izzy. 'Some weird bloke we have on our list for Dietrich. He works for John Hardwick and is a big buddy of Disgusting Doug.

'He's not on the Sex Offenders' Register but he's known to

have sexually assaulted at least three women. One was his most recent partner. Maybe he also likes young female strangers. If so, he should be on the Esther list. He also knows Horsley well.

'I looked him up when Steve James said he was inside the house when Dietrich was killed. Joe's done time in HMP Coldingley for Actual Bodily Harm.'

'Better check him out,' said Rob with a sigh. 'Doesn't sound like our killer, but at the same time, I don't want anything coming back to bite us on the bum.'

14

'WHAT THE HELL's the matter with me?'

It was Pen's third attempt to visit Jane Page-Smith. In sunglasses and wearing her belted raincoat with a head scarf, standing on the opposite side of the street, rain pouring down, she looked like a private detective in a 1950s film noir, except that unlike the movie characters, she was half paralysed with uncertainty. Why was she there? What could she possibly achieve? She didn't know the answer. She'd been driven by a curiosity. It was irrational, foolish.

She – and Bella too – had taken several weeks to process the fact that a marriage and a birth certificate from Oxford Register Office proved Jane Page-Smith was not a fantasist. But just because facts are proved beyond reasonable doubt does not mean you can accept them in any real, emotional sense. Bella had made one more check: The National Archives in Kew, Surrey. No divorce application had been submitted by either party. Dietrich's marriage to Pen was bigamous and, had Dietrich been alive, she would have continued to be unaware, unsuspecting, duped. Jane was the widow. Not Penny. She hated Dietrich for not bothering to get a divorce and wished he were there so she could kick and slap him.

Perhaps the most painful thing was what it meant for Bella. She was now his *illegitimate* daughter. Dear, decent Daddy Dietrich. The truth was he was a first-rate fucking fraud.

Pen needed to understand. Perhaps a conversation with Jane would help. Perhaps not. She *had* to see. It would be cowardly not to. She'd tried to disguise herself so as not to alert Jane and give her time to ignore the knock on the door.

Jane would ask, 'How d'you find me?', but she must have guessed that her address was in Dietrich's accountant's files. She would also have discovered that Dietrich had paid a deposit to buy the house 30 years ago, arranged a mortgage and paid a generous monthly amount into an account in Jane's name to cover mortgage repayments as well as other household expenses. A separate account took care of Charles's school fees and enabled him to add his name to the list when the school proposed museum and theatre visits, climbing or ski trips, and to say yes to expensive holidays with friends and their parents – all the things Tom had enjoyed, and that Dietrich's own parents had never been able to afford.

Pen had been nervous on the first two visits and hadn't managed to step along the path to Jane's front door. It wasn't like her. On the first occasion, she'd simply frozen, turned and made her way back to Raynes Park Station the way she'd come. On the second, she'd meandered around the block, sat with a cappuccino in Starbucks and ended up in somewhere called Pepys Road, then passed a petrol station, saw the sign back to the train station and headed home.

Annoyed with herself, she decided to think of these first trips as rehearsals.

This time, the rain seemed to be telling her to get on with it. Or else she'd be getting wet for bloody nothing. So, she walked down the path of the pleasant Edwardian, brick-built semi with its square bay window and knocked forcefully on the door. By then, it was 6.15 and a silver Polo car was parked in what was once a front garden but had long been paved over. Through the window, you could see that lights were on. So, someone was home.

When she came to the door, Jane took a moment to recognise Pen under the headscarf. Jane looked calm, almost as though she'd been expecting this moment. Then she opened the door fully and, without a word, turned and walked through a narrow hall into the living room that led directly into a light, extended kitchen, beckoning her visitor to follow.

She held up an almost full bottle of Sancerre. Pen slipped off her raincoat and nodded as she sat down on a low armchair covered in brown velvet. The soft sound of Miles Davis's trumpet was coming from somewhere. Through the arch to the kitchen, she could see a ginger and white cat, its head in a bowl on the floor. It was munching on its food and intermittently lapping water from another bowl, like a good cat should.

After a short pause, Jane handed a wine glass to Pen and announced, 'Welcome to Château Page-Smith' with an ironic smile. 'Have you found out whether it was just the two of us or were there more wives?'

'Very funny,' said Pen, reluctantly cracking a smile, looking at some not-bad abstract canvasses on the walls.

'Why are you here?'

'To properly meet you. Find out who you are, what you want.'

Jane looked down at her glass and paused before answering. 'I'm just a woman who fell in love with a student called Dominic Olson in our second year at university. It was love – lust – at first sight. Like nothing I'd known before. Or since.' She turned her back on her visitor. Whether she was lost in the memory or gloating at the idea of making her feel uncomfortable, Pen couldn't tell. But a layer of sweat was forming on the back of her neck.

'Now? I really don't know what I want. Not yet, at least,' Jane said finally. Then she turned, blinked and smiled wanly. 'I was never going to grab all his money, buy a yacht and set up home in Monte Carlo with a 25-year-old lover, whatever you may have thought.'

'Why did you need to go public?'

Jane paused, breathed deeply and appeared to think hard. Pen watched her, intrigued.

'I hadn't planned it.' Jane shrugged. 'Dominic's death was on the news and all over the papers and I was really quite upset. It brought back some happy and some painful memories, memories I'd buried for a long time. Then I felt angry at myself for hiding away. It wasn't as though I was just some old, unsophisticated, northern girlfriend from his past, thrown aside when he went to London to become rich and famous. I was his lover and his wife, the mother of his son.'

Now that she'd mentioned it, Pen noticed a faint northern accent.

At this she looked up at a photograph on the mantle shelf of a group of young friends in gowns and mortarboards at a degree ceremony. In the middle of the group was the bespectacled young man who'd attended the memorial service with his mother. Jane stood up and disappeared up the stairs leading off the hall. A moment later, she reappeared holding a dog-eared blue envelope file.

She handed it to Pen. Inside were yellowing photos of Jane and Dominic taken when they must have been together at Oxford, clutching the other's arms, looking into the other's eyes with a sort of confidence for the future. One of them was a wedding photograph, taken outside a register office. Jane, beautiful, with long, dark hair and wearing a Laura Ashley-type flower-patterned, full-skirted dress and platform-heeled shoes, Dominic with hair over his collar, in a grey suit with a wide tie. An older woman, presumably Jane's mother, was standing to one side with a man in a corduroy jacket who might have been Ben Harding.

Pen managed to smile and say, 'You look very pretty.'

In fact, the truth that her devoted husband really had had a previous wife in a previous life but had concealed it was finally hitting her with the force of a ten-ton truck. She wanted to run and scream. And kill him.

Jane was still looking whimsically at her old photographs.

'I was happy. You can't look at those pictures and say I wasn't part of Dominic's life, his story. That's why I needed to attend the memorial service, hear what people said about him. I wanted to see you and your children – in the flesh. Then you and I started talking by your old photos. And, as I left, some journalists stopped me and started asking me questions.

'I spoke to them and wanted to make sure I didn't come over as bitter or jealous of you. Because I'm not, I never was. I never wanted your life.'

Pen continued drinking the wine and studying her predecessor.

'Look, I really don't think I have to apologise for anything. I'm not money grabbing, really. I didn't milk Dominic for cash. I didn't take money from the television people or the papers, although they offered me tens of thousands. I guessed all the bigamy stuff would blow over. And it has, hasn't it? More or less.'

Pen again noticed traces of Jane's Yorkshire accent. It wasn't Geoffrey Boycott broad. You couldn't mimic it as Tom liked to do whenever the famous old cricketer was heard on the radio or TV. It was rather attractive, she decided. She stood up, walked through the kitchen to the window and looked out to a small, well-tended garden, still fighting back the urge to shout and cry.

'So, what *do* you want, now you've had time to think?'

'I've got the recognition I wanted. You and your children know Charles and I exist, and that's important. I didn't want to upset you but it's better you know the truth. Don't you think?'

Pen supposed she was right. 'So, why didn't you divorce him?' she asked.

'No reason to. I had – and still have – no plans to marry again. So why bother?

'If he'd contacted me about a divorce, I'd probably have agreed. But he didn't.'

Pen knew he would have been too lazy to think about doing that.

'But what do you want from Dietrich's estate, from his property and his money?'

Jane inhaled, took her time again, then said, 'Not a fortune. Enough in the bank for a few good holidays. Travelling in comfort would be nice. India, South America perhaps. We'll get a wad of money from the life insurance policy, I think. I'd almost forgotten all about it, actually.' She paused, before adding bitterly, 'Just like the bastard forgot all about me and Charlie.

'When the insurance pays out, it should serve as a decent pension fund. I may need more to keep me from worrying about my old age. I think I deserve not to have to worry about money when I'm old and frail, don't you?

'And I'd like enough to help Charlie get a flat...' Her voice trailed off while she considered what to say next. 'I'm not trying to cadge money, really. As you can see, I live in a pretty nice house. The mortgage is paid off now. Dominic bought it for us. It suits me. I've got an OK job doing the IT and the artwork for an estate agents in Wimbledon Village. It's not as boring as it sounds. I work with nice people and there's no stress. It's even quite interesting at times.

'I've a live-in lover who doesn't annoy me – well not yet, at least. He does the cooking and shares the bills. He's an art teacher, out at a parents' session tonight. Or you could have met him.

'I've thought about moving, starting my own letting business. But really, I ask myself, do I need all the *bother*? I don't think so. And I'd *hate* to upset Malcolm,' she added, smiling and looking fondly at the cat who had silently jumped up next to her and seemed to be listening to the conversation. 'I've got nothing to prove.'

Pen was studying the woman – the competition – again. Good cheekbones, no wrinkles apart from a few lines on her top lip, possibly from smoking when she was younger. Good, thick hair, even though it could do with restyling by a decent hairdresser. Probably a slim, sexy body under her large jumper and wide-legged jeans.

'Tell me about your son,' she said.

Jane allowed herself to grin, maternal pride flooding in.

'You saw him. He's tall, fair and handsome. Clever and witty, like his dad was. Likes rugby, cricket and tennis, anything involving a ball really. I believe he's quite good at those sports too. He went to King's College School, got good A levels, went travelling to India and places, chose to go to City University, which disappointed me a bit. He could have gone to Oxford like his parents.

'He went there to look around. Came back and announced, "It's in a time warp, Mum!" I told him that that was the whole bloody point! But he didn't get it. He decided to do this journalism course, so City was his choice. Quite a bit of practical stuff, with exams at the end. He stayed on to do a master's there. He had to write a long dissertation, then there was a year of practical stuff, I think.

'He wants to be a television journalist – the next Jon Snow. You remember the news presenter with the look-at-me ties and socks? He retired a few years ago. It's probably a better job than one in politics – you don't have to get yourself re-elected every four years. He's a freelance. Says it's better paid. But it must be stressful. Then I wouldn't really know—'

'Does he live here?' Pen managed to interrupt the flow.

'Not now. Used to, until quite recently. He shares a flat in Bethnal Green with two blokes and, I think, a girlfriend. I miss him around the place. But it's my own fault; I should have had more children.'

'Bit late now!' Pen said, and they both laughed.

Then, as if guessing what the next question would be, Jane continued, 'I told him when he was quite young that Dominic – or Dietrich – was his father. He kept asking to meet him. I said he couldn't do that because his dad had a new family and a public profile, and it would cause problems. I also said that it might upset me because we'd parted after an argument. Bit of an understatement there!

'I reminded him that Dietrich had always taken care of us by finding us a nice house and paying the bills. I don't know if I did the right thing.'

Pen wondered too. She drained her glass but said 'no' to another.

'Well, you'll still have to decide what you'll do with the money you're entitled to. I'm afraid the Bloomsbury flat is mine. I had it before I met Dietrich. But half of our house in Godalming is now yours, legally. I've been told I must sell it because half of it was paid for by Dietrich.'

Jane laughed loudly. 'Don't bother. Take it off the market for God's sake! Godalming wouldn't suit me at all! I'm the type who likes the country only from the window of a fast train heading back to London.'

Pen smiled but felt sure she'd heard the same line from Dietrich.

'A friend of mine once worked for a charity whose offices were in Godalming. He called it God Awful Ming.' Jane laughed.

'I'll have to get a solicitor and he or she will sort things out with your man – somebody Spicer, is it? He keeps writing to me,' Jane went on. 'I'll be donating quite a bit to charities. Maybe I'll set up a foundation of some kind.'

'Hidden Wives' Aid?' Pen suggested, wryly.

She stood up, stroked handsome Malcolm, now poised to position himself on her lap, pulled on her wet coat and then left, feeling better than when she'd arrived.

Despite herself, she'd believed what this woman had said.

She realised as she pulled the front door closed behind her that she hadn't told Jane that Dietrich had not died of a heart condition but had been murdered. She didn't know if news of it had yet made it to the newspapers.

At any rate, by the time her train was pulling into Waterloo, Pen was convinced that Jane Page-Smith and her son could now be crossed off the suspects' list for his killing. She'd almost liked the woman. She asked herself whether, in other circumstances, they might be friends. Probably not, she decided. She thought Jane would have found her too 'straight', too conventional, and she'd have resented that.

There was also the stumbling block that Dietrich had once loved Jane passionately, according to Jane. Had she and Dietrich been passionate for each other, or had they just merged together well?

Well, it was passionate at the beginning. Obviously. All love affairs are or should be. And as the years went by, she'd supported him as a politician, turned up at the dinners, the election nights. But she'd always been independent and detached, never just the MP's wife. He'd been a good husband, affectionate, almost certainly faithful and a committed father. Wasn't that a recipe for a strong marriage?

As she sat on a bus from Waterloo going slowly towards Bloomsbury, she decided to lay that subject to rest. In any case, she thought, was it time for her to start the next phase? To find a lover? The idea both shocked and pleased her. If Jane could do it, surely so could she. Was it too soon? Where do you look? Would it upset the children? She couldn't guess. Tom might bridle, but he'd get over it, she decided. Bella would understand.

The fact was, she wanted to be wanted again and longed to touch a man's hard thighs and back. She wanted sex. There, she'd admitted it to herself.

She'd start by reassessing her male colleagues at the LSE.

15

Rob felt his anger rising through his chest. He wanted to thump someone, something, anything. His wastepaper basket had to do. He smashed it against the door of his office with his foot, sending bits of scrunched-up paper, Post-it notes and the peel of a clementine spilling onto the floor.

You never think that having a child will be difficult when both of you are healthy and there'd been no problem with the first pregnancy. Yet here he and his wife Elizabeth were, two rounds of IVF on and no sign of a second child. On Saturday, when Jacob was at a sleepover with a friend, they'd soberly discussed the question of whether to embark on a third round. The second course appeared to be working well until a test on the embryos before implantation showed that there were chromosomal abnormalities. Could he and Elizabeth cope with a disabled child? No, they agreed they couldn't.

There was little left of their savings, and he didn't want to ask his dad for a loan, and so the matter was on hold. Elizabeth wasn't yet 40, so she reckoned there was still a bit of time. He wasn't convinced. He felt cross that this was happening to them and guilty that his wife was the one suffering the endless check-ups, injections of hormones and God knows what. Not that she complained. She just seemed unhappy, even when she cuddled Jacob and looked around the unused and half-painted spare room, which had been earmarked as number two's nursery.

If that wasn't enough to make him mad, he'd learned that morning he'd been outbid on the second-hand Alfa Romeo he'd hoped to collect that evening. The owner had given his word yesterday morning but sold it for a measly hundred quid more before breakfast that day. The rotten swine!

He'd put on headphones and sang loudly in the car along with Jonas Kaufman and Dmitri Hvorostovsky as they gave their all to the Pearl Fishers' Duet. It helped a bit. He couldn't think of any cheery music he wanted to listen to, but the sad love triangle song calmed him. The moment he'd parked, he'd felt angry with the world again. Why was there no progress on his cases? What was he missing? At least his big headphones allowed him to avoid having to talk to people once he'd arrived at the station and barged his way to his office.

Mehmet had received far worse news over the weekend, and when he learned of it, Rob realised that his own problems paled by comparison.

His colleague was sitting at his desk, looking as though he hadn't slept in weeks. 'My mum was diagnosed with a brain tumour,' he said. 'Just about the worst kind, a glioblastoma multiforme, grade 4. She'd only just retired from her job as a pharmacist.

'I found out from a neighbour when I went to visit her on Saturday. She hadn't told me nor even Esme, my sister, who's a doctor and may have been able to suggest someone for a second opinion.

'She decided against chemotherapy after finding out that it could only buy her a few months longer to live. She was only sixty-five, for God's Sake!'

Mehmet was clearly broken that his mother had blocked him out of this awful process.

'They took her to hospital – St George's in Tooting – on Wednesday,' he went on. 'I arrived in the ward just as a nurse was pulling curtains round her bed, having pulled a sheet over her face.

'A doctor arrived at the bedside, picked up her notes from the end of her bed, looked me in the eye and said, "I saw your mother several times. I know you've had a shock, but if it's of any consolation, she didn't suffer much pain. A nurse had been visiting her at home for the past month to administer anti-convulsive pills, then morphine. Your mother had expressly forbidden the nurse to contact you or your sister because she didn't want to upset you."'

'She'd been so proud when Esme qualified as a consultant,' Mehmet went on.

'I bet she was proud of you too,' Rob said.

'Only when I scored fifty for the Met's cricket team.

'Unlike my dad, she was a Christian, so I've got time to think about a burial. Neither of my parents was particularly religious but I know she believed absolutely that she'd go to heaven, where they would be together again.' His voice was breaking up by now and Rob left him to search for Izzy.

Rob asked her to drive him home and then deliver some prepared food and other groceries. He pressed a couple of twenty-pound notes into her hand and smiled as he saw tears welling in her eyes.

'Ask him if he needs help to arrange the funeral,' Rob added. He was only just realising how deeply he liked and trusted his lanky lieutenant. 'No wait, I'll ask him that, but I bet he'll say no.'

And he did. 'Mum never converted to Islam – Dad didn't insist on it,' Mehmet explained. 'My parents became sick of religion after the fuss from both sides their marriage caused. So, there's no need to fix things in a mad rush. There'll probably be a short ceremony at the Lambeth Cemetery, which is right near St George's, for my sister and me and any relatives and friends who can make it.'

'Mind if I come?' asked Rob.

'What on earth for? You're too busy, and anyway, you'd be bored stiff!' Mehmet wanted to close the conversation. He wasn't used to expressing his feelings to anyone, least of all to his boss.

'Well, I'll come anyway.'

Rob meant it. And after ringing the cemetery manager a few days later to find out the date of the burial, he duly turned up one chilly morning two weeks later, to stand close to his friend as a coffin was lowered into a grave and earth shovelled on it. White flowers were laid around it.

Later, Mehmet thanked him. 'I might not have had the courage to turn up,' he said. 'But guessing you'd find out that I really was the pathetic wimp you'd always suspected I was made me get out of bed.'

Izzy had wanted to join them but realised that Guildford CID could not spare all three of them that morning. Instead, she got her local florist to send flowers, wrote Mehmet a letter of condolence and offered to help if or when he decided to empty and sell the family home. Marley sent a sympathy card and promised to buy him a throat-burning curry the next time he was in Holborn.

But even after Mehmet returned from compassionate leave, nothing was going right with the Esther Hall or Dietrich Olson murder cases. There was no progress, and Rob was running out of ideas.

He was staring at two big fat career failures, and his marriage was buckling under the strain.

He ordered a second forensics examination of the garage on whose floor Esther's body had been found. Like the Guildford team's first results, there were no tyre prints and no discernible footprints in the blood or the greasy patches around Esther's body. The garage owner's alibi for that weekend – that he'd been wintering in Spain – hadn't changed. This time, his wife produced some timed and dated photographs of them in their flat in Alicante to prove it. He'd thought that he was the only person to have keys to the place and said the padlock on the door must have been forced off.

Numerous fingerprints had been found on the garage door but none of them were in the police system. It was a similar story with the splodge of semen left on Esther's underwear. Whoever had left it hadn't been tested before by the police, it seemed.

Something had made Mark Phillips see sense, though. His father had called the station a few days after Rob and Mehmet's visit to say he would, after all, consent to a DNA test. Mehmet drove to the Phillips' house and returned with swabs to be tested. The result was that Mark wasn't a match.

A careful search of Terry Thomson's London flat had thrown up nothing to connect him with Esther. No child pornography, no collection of newspaper cuttings on missing girls, no 'trophies' of panties, trinkets or anything else he might have kept that would have reminded him of his victims. He was not their man either.

Bugger! Bugger! Bugger!

Rob thought about calling in a profiler. As a rule, he didn't rate them. Had there been anything similar about Esther's rape and murder to one or more unsolved relatively recent crimes, he could have seen a point in trying to get a profile of what could have been a serial killer. But no other unsolved violent rapes and murders of women in the Guildford area in the past few years fitted the pattern.

As he was doing nothing for Esther, he decided he'd better concentrate on Dietrich Olson's killer for a day or two at least. He called Mehmet and Izzy into his office.

'It occurred to me – just a wild thought,' he said, 'that someone we haven't yet brought in for questioning *might* have gone into the house early and hidden the syringe of cocaine for someone else to collect once the party was in full swing. And that someone got Dietrich to search for a special wine in the wine store. Then at the door they quickly and quietly jabbed him in the thigh.

'And, well, for Sir Dietrich MP, it was Goodnight Vienna.'

Rob sat back in his chair, stared at the ceiling and waited for reactions.

'Joe Jackson,' Izzy blurted out, her cheeks reddening.

Rob frowned.

'I'm not sure if it's of interest, but he works with Disgusting Doug, doing the heavy lifting for John Hardwick. Apparently, he's got a bit of a temper. Three convictions for ABH – none of them recent, though – and a restraining order from a former partner, if I remember correctly. He was recently seen drinking in the Clandon Arms with his pal Doug Elliott, along with Kevin Miller and Steve James. He seems to stay in Doug's shadow. Doesn't say much, especially not in Doug's company.

'Thing is, I suspect he also does some drug deliveries for Doug. There's no evidence, unfortunately, but he could have brought in the cocaine in a syringe and left it in one of the boxes of hire stuff – plates or glasses – or even in the wine store itself, taped under a shelf, for someone else to do the jabbing. I don't think fat Doug would be nimble enough to do it himself.'

Rob and Mehmet *were* interested. So, she went on.

'I'm not sure where Joe lives. I've got the registration for a van he drives. That should give us an address. Perhaps get forensics to check it for drugs? And we could track down the ex-partner.'

Rob perked up. 'Great! Yes, get a warrant to search the van and find out what the former partner's complaint was. Was he violent? A heavy drug habit? Could you do the interview yourself, Izzy? Girl talk and all that.'

'I don't think you're supposed to say that these days, boss. It's gender discrimination,' piped up Mehmet.

'Oh gawd, yes, sorry!' said Rob in tones of mock horror.

Izzy did a background search and was soon off to visit Joe's ex, Jess Cummings, at a busy nail bar in West Horsley. She worked with two Vietnamese women there.

Entering the shop, she noted the 'Cash Only' sign and looked at the rows of nail varnish bottles lined up on shelves on both sides. There were pinks, reds, greens, blues and greys. She decided she'd pick a pale pink if she were a customer. Two actual customers sat, hands flat on a counter, having long, false nails glued in place before they were clipped, filed and painted. Izzy wondered how these women managed to do up buttons, type a message on their phones or stick on their equally outrageous false eyelashes with those monstrous things on their fingers.

The Vietnamese women had their heads down and were hard at work. Had they been trafficked to the UK? They seemed happy enough, chattering away to each other, while not looking or smiling at their customers. Izzy thought how, when the Esther and Dietrich cases were done, dusted and filed away, she might do some research and investigate the nail bar business.

Jess was probably in her early forties, Izzy thought; a size sixteen squeezed into size twelve leggings and a T-shirt, she seemed by far the most ground-down of the women there. She ushered Izzy into the back room where the workers made tea, and where the clippers, cuticle pushers and other instruments were sterilised in a metal tank and small towels were left to be washed in an old, dusty washing machine. She found two stools for them.

'I put up with being bullied by Joe for two years,' Jess began, her voice ragged. She wore a sad face but when she continued, Izzy thought how she was beginning to relish the chance to vent her complaints about him.

'I was made to have sex when I didn't feel like it and had to put up with him leering at other women – even school-girls, some of them. He liked 'em young.

'When he bashed me in the face, that's when I *knew*! I packed up my stuff quick, left the flat and moved back with Mum. She'd always said, "Jess, if he hits you once, he'll hit you again." I knew she was right. So, I went to the county court in Guildford and they helped me to fill in the form for a Non-Molestation Order against him. When he got the letter, he went to the court and tried to object. He said he'd never laid a finger on me, even though I had photos of the cuts and bruises.

'I knew he'd deny it, the lying creep. Then he found out he could be arrested just for contacting me. So, he stayed away. Joe's not completely stupid, but I still live with Mum because I'm still afraid of him.'

'What about drugs? He likes a few lines of coke, I expect,' Izzy chanced.

'How d'you guess?' Jess smiled. 'Doug and him like nothing better when they get home from the pub. And Doug's always got gear on him.'

'We heard Joe often helps Doug do drop offs to customers in Onslow Village and other areas?'

'Couldn't say. Joe just disappeared of an evening. I'd be asking for another slap if I questioned where he'd been. Doug's never made a secret of supplying... to his mates, at least. He calls himself "The Wholesaler".'

Walking back to her car, Izzy sighed. If more women listened to wise mothers like Jess's, a hell of a lot of abusive men would be behind bars rather than bashing up their terrified partners and children time and time again. If that happened, police officers wouldn't need to go back repeatedly to try and persuade the same victims to stick to their stories and press charges.

When she reported Jess's information to Rob and Mehmet, they agreed to look more closely at Disgusting Doug's drug business. They'd also bring Joe in to assist the police with their inquiries in connection with the death of Dietrich Olson. Izzy wondered if Joe might be able to assist with their inquiries into the death of Esther Hall as well.

'Jess thought Joe could now be living in Ripley with his sister Maureen and her family,' Izzy explained. 'He didn't have a regular income to prove to a letting agent he could afford to rent, so it's unlikely he could live anywhere on his own. We could probably find Maureen. Meanwhile, forensics could take a good look at Joe's van.'

Joe Jackson was duly picked up at his sister's flat. It was mid-morning, but they found him sitting in front of the television, unshaven, wearing only underpants and a T-shirt. His bare feet revealed fungus-yellow toenails, and he was smoking a skinny roll-up. He grumbled and swore at the policemen before agreeing to put on some clothes and accompany them to Guildford nick.

Slouching in a chair in an interview room, sour faced, he said nothing when a uniform put a cup of tea in front of him, which he didn't touch. Izzy told him he wasn't being arrested. She'd have liked to have added '*yet*' but restrained herself and leant across the table to switch on the recorder.

'I don't need a lawyer then?' Joe grunted. Izzy detected a nervousness creeping in.

'You're here as a witness, so you don't need one. But it's up to you, Joe. I'm happy to wait until a solicitor arrives if you prefer.'

He shrugged reluctantly and shuffled on his hard chair.

'Today I want to talk to you about the party at Batts Farm on the fifth of January. I think you were working for the caterer John Hardwick alongside your friend Doug Elliot on that day?'

'Yeah, so?'

'So, can you tell me what you saw inside the house?'

'I weren't in there long. I just popped in to get the delivery note for the tablecloths and stuff signed so John could check it's what he'd asked for. He's dead fussy.'

'You and Doug must have stuck around for a few moments, having a coffee and a bite to eat?'

'Now you come to mention it, yeah, I think we did. Doug was chatting to a couple of the waiters. Dunno what about.'

Izzy forced herself to smile at the putty-faced man in his crumpled grey hoodie and once-white Polo shirt with brown stains down the front.

'See any sign of the family who own the house?'

'Saw the missus dressed up to the nines at breakfast,' he scoffed. 'And a middle-aged man in a dressing gown. Think that was the husband, the one who snuffed it.'

'Anyone else?'

'Nah! Well, there was the daft old girl in the car park telling us where to stop and where not to put down the boxes. Doug was swearing at 'er but I think she's deaf.' He thought that was funny. Izzy forced herself to smile.

'Did you need to use the toilet or go anywhere else in the house?'

'Yeah, I did need a piss. I'd have done it in the bushes outside, but the old dear was watching everyone. So, I asked her where the bog was, and she gave me directions.'

'There's one in what the family call the back kitchen, isn't there?' Izzy ventured.

'Yeah. Took me some time to find it.'

'Did you look around, notice anything else?'

'Nope.'

Izzy made a note of Joe's sister's address and his phone number and thanked him as she left the room.

She was still no closer to answering the big question. *Why* would Joe or Doug want to bump Dietrich off?

16

STEVE and his dad were by now well over the beginner's stage of flat-sharing and were learning how to co-exist peaceably. Steve was mastering the art of not turning a home into a hovel. It came partly from going into other people's tidy houses to fix their TVs and computers and partly from not wanting to upset his old man.

He'd worked out how to use the dishwasher and had found the quick wash setting on the washing machine for his gym clothes. He'd stopped hanging wet towels on the floor or over the corners of doors and started putting them on hooks and rails. His trainers ended up under his bed or in pairs in the hall cupboard rather than on the coffee table, the sofas or singly on the floor. Sally, the ex, would have been amazed. He also kept on his big headphones so that his dad didn't have to suffer his taste in reggae. It had been an effort but not really a hard one.

In turn, Basil remembered to put all the bills, doctors' letters and correspondence about his job and the flat in a large, red box file in a kitchen drawer so Steve could make sure bills were paid and appointments kept. He also forwarded any important looking emails to Steve.

The increasingly 'important' emails were news bulletins from Janice and other residents about their block's lack of fire safety provisions. It was making the properties unmortgage-able, some wrote. Others reported their worries about bank-ruptcy if they had to pay for all the recommended precautions or said the worst thing was their terror of going to bed at night, fearing a fire might break out as they slept.

Almost all the residents agreed to pay to install smoke detectors and alarms in the communal areas, but one of them, a surveyor, reported the bad news that his checks revealed there were no firebreaks in the wall cavities. Janice and her lieutenant, Keith Taylor, a retired physics teacher, proposed to hold a meeting with the flats' developers to try and shame them into fixing the faults. Two representatives from Premium Properties Six eventually agreed to attend a meeting in Janice's flat one Saturday afternoon in April. On the morning of the meeting, neighbours helped her to move furniture back or into bedrooms and brought in extra chairs for the worriers, who now included Basil and Steve.

Steve woke up that morning remembering that a friend, and recently one of his IT clients, Jerry Thorne, was an inves-tigative journalist for *The Sun*'s Sunday edition. He worked partly from home and had recently needed Steve to fix his elaborate computer system so that he could more easily hold Zoom meetings with colleagues. Steve rang him, mentioning the meeting and quoting Grenfell Tower, high rise and fire safety. Jerry arrived at Janice's flat before you could say Rupert Murdoch.

The meeting went off like a damp squib, which surprised no one. Premium Properties Six had clearly instructed their lawyers to investigate ways to duck all responsibilities and, while they were working on that, the two mealy-mouthed representatives who'd been forced to attend proposed that the angry leaseholders should send in succinct suggestions for improvements. When asked if PP6 would pay for fire wardens to patrol the building at night, one of the representatives said they'd put that forward to the directors as a suggestion too.

A stream of glum-faced neighbours filed out of Janice's flat. No one had expected the developers to admit there were failings or to offer much in the way of compensation. A few had hoped to be surprised, though. A woman gave Janice a bunch of Tesco lilies for her efforts, another gave her a bottle of New Zealand Sauvignon Blanc as they left. Janice smiled broadly.

Steve went back upstairs with Jerry for a beer. Months ago, before Basil had moved into the flat, he had searched on his computer for the names of the directors of the outfit he was buying from when South Quay was built.

He told Jerry, 'When dad told me about this flat, I looked up the original developers, Premium Properties Six. And guess whose name popped up among the directors? Dietrich Olson of 51, Colt Court, Bloomsbury Street, London W1, that's whose!

'If the man hadn't annoyingly checked out of this world already, I'd have been at the front of the queue to shove him into the Thames for the trouble he's causing my dad now.'

Jerry's face lit up. He now had a name to use to sell the story.

He didn't take long to take a few photos of the block and knock out a 500-word, page-lead article on his laptop, quoting and picturing terrified residents such as Steve James, and linking them with the dead MP Sir Dietrich Olson. Premium Properties Six's current directors would be choking over their muesli on Sunday morning. Steve would soon be receiving a decent tip-off fee from the paper's accounts' department, and Jerry would be able to bask in a brief glow of glory in the *The Sun's* newsroom after the BBC picked up the story for news bulletins later in the day and *Mail Online* put it at the top of its news list. If the BBC or a broadsheet followed up on a story, the paper's news desk gave it a gold star of importance.

Bella spotted the 'Death Trap Flats – Dodgy MP Dietrich Olson exposed' headline when she picked up a newspaper left by someone in the Bankside Starbucks. She was numb. She knew the paper's lawyers must have cleared it, yet it couldn't really be true, could it?

Rob Howarth also saw the headline when he went to the newsagents to buy batteries for Jacob's toy fire engine, the one with the annoying sound effects, on Sunday morning. He bought the paper. After reading the article, he began to wonder if they'd crossed Steven James off the Dietrich murder suspects' list too soon. The man clearly had a grudge to hold.

He did his own bit of computer digging on Monday morning. It turned out that Premium Properties Six had, over the years, been involved in several lawsuits and complaints about shoddy work and cost-cutting measures. Dietrich was quoted in an old *Daily Telegraph* article. He'd expressed surprise at the claims but pointed out that he had resigned from the company before he became an MP. It showed his complete lack of empathy for other people's problems. That and what a sneakily clever bloke he was.

Another name among the early PP6 directors, Michael

Wilson-Green, rang a bell in Rob's mind. He scrolled through his file on guests at the Batts Farm party and there he was. When he researched a little more, he found that Wilson-Green was also linked to Dietrich through First Domestic Appliances. The difference between them was that, after a whistle-blower's tip-off, Wilson-Green had been investigated by the Serious Fraud Office and the Financial Conduct Authority. He'd lost everything after First Domestic Appliances had massively inflated the company's value. Dietrich, meanwhile, had jumped ship months earlier, evading responsibility. He'd lost nothing.

Rob badly wanted to quiz Michael Wilson-Green about the knighthood party. But what would be the pretext, he wondered? That the police were talking to all of Dietrich's friends who came to Batts Farm on the fateful day, perhaps? That might work. What did they hope to find out?

A pow-wow with Izzy and Mehmet was convened for 11 o'clock.

Over strong coffee, Rob told them about Steve James, the faulty flats of South Quay and Premium Properties Six. Most important was the coincidence that both Dietrich and Michael Wilson-Green were once PP6 directors. He also told them what he knew about First Domestic Appliances. The pair listened, rapt, then scratched their heads.

Izzy said, 'Might it be a good idea for me to call in on Mr Michael Wilson-Green and invite him to assist us with our inquiries while Mehmet does some in depth research on his background? We have an address from the guest list that the Olson daughter gave us, and we could probably find out where he works these days through his tax returns.'

'On it,' said Mehmet. 'Great idea.' He wasn't brilliant at research and had to concentrate hard, but at least it allowed him to stop thinking about his mother. He also wanted to read a couple of online reports on Queens Park Rangers' triumph in the match against West Bromwich the previous Saturday.

Izzy popped into Rob's office later to say she'd call on Wilson-Green the following morning at his job at Frank Kitchen Designs in Putney, South West London. It sounded a bit of a comedown for a former CEO of a big company, she added.

Inside the shop, she knew immediately she was in the right place. A voice like Jacob Rees Mogg's came from a man explaining to a customer the differences between vented and condenser tumble dryers.

A thin, greying but still handsome Michael Wilson-Green studied Izzy's warrant card while she explained why she was there. She told him she hoped he'd have time to come down to the station in Guildford for a talk. He was hesitant.

'Dietrich died of a heart thing, didn't he? What could I possibly tell you? I'm not a doctor.'

'Well, it now seems he was quietly and cleverly murdered,' Izzy replied. 'That's why we're trying to talk to everyone who knew him well and who attended the party.'

He was either deeply shocked or doing a brilliant impression of being so. 'No? Really? That's appalling. Poor Dominic – I mean, Dietrich – poor darling Penny. Of course, I'll tell you what I remember of the party, if it's of any use. But I said a few words to Dietrich when I arrived and that was it. I'd hoped to have a proper catch-up with him later, but it didn't happen.' He sank into his chair and looked serious and upset. Izzy was surprised.

Then he looked her in the eye. 'Taking a morning off to go to Guildford is a bit awkward for me. Can we chat during my lunch break – at about twelve thirty? I usually take a walk in Fulham Palace Gardens, just over the road.'

Izzy had been prepared for this and agreed to a preliminary chat, deciding she'd get him down to the station if she thought he had important information to impart. She killed an hour in a Caffè Nero in Putney High Street until 12.30.

As they walked in the drizzle under his large black gentleman's umbrella, Izzy asked if he minded her recording their conversation as she couldn't take notes in the rain. She held up her recorder under the umbrella.

He nodded. 'Fine. Well, at the party, I had a long talk with Penny about her work. Brilliant woman – she lectures in family law at the London School of Economics, you know?'

Izzy nodded.

'We talked about the children. Bella had grown so pretty since I'd last seen her. She's the same age as Rufus, one of my sons. We joked about a spot of matchmaking.

'She told me that Dietrich was thrilled to get the knighthood because, deep down, he'd always felt socially inadequate, and with this he could effectively stick it to his critics in the Party. I think she was right.'

Izzy knew she had to get him to the point in his own way and wondered how long it was going to take. She chanced it. 'Didn't you and Dietrich fall out over the First Domestic Appliances fraud investigation? He left before it all happened, I believe. But you had to face the music. You're still paying the price, I'd guess.'

Michael looked down at her, as if surprised that an ordinary plod – and a young female one at that – could have worked it out.

'Very good, Isobel.'

Izzy decided that being patronised by him was worth it if what he said was illuminating.

'Yes, it was a very difficult time. I don't deny that. But that was years ago now. Dietrich and I were school friends, and we've stayed friends, apart from a few times when we've had a bit of a spat and there's been radio silence for a while. I've been to a couple of Penny's parties and was delighted to be invited to Batts Farm to celebrate the knighthood.

'When Bella came into the sitting room, looking like she'd seen a ghost and telling all the guests there'd been an accident and asking them to leave, I guessed something dreadful had happened. But heart attack is one thing – murder is quite another.'

Izzy reminded herself to stay low key. 'I believe Mrs Olson was getting ready to call for a toast and then couldn't find Dietrich. He was due to make a speech. Did you spot anyone behaving strangely at that point?'

'No. I've thought about this… how Dietrich could have suffered and died without anyone seeing anything. I'd had a few glasses of Champagne, and the guests and waiters were milling about the place. There was lots of activity in the kitchen, I think. We could hear it. I saw the piano player chap talking to one of the waiters but I've no idea what they were talking about. There were no sudden arrivals or dashes for the doors.

'Then Bella began asking guests to leave. I was alarmed but I didn't try to question her – I just grabbed my coat from the hall. Then I spotted a couple of people I'd been chatting to – forget their names, Rodgers, Richards, something beginning with an r – who offered me a lift to Godalming station. I was grateful and caught a train to Waterloo and then home, to Putney.'

Izzy nervously broached the main reason for her visit. 'FDA wasn't the only company that you and Dietrich shared an interest in, I believe,' she said. 'I'm talking about Premium Properties Six.'

'Oh that,' replied Michael dismissively. 'Dietrich fancied himself as a property developer when he left Oxford and didn't have a job to go to. He needed money, though. He started buying up run-down houses in a few locations in South London, borrowing a bit from his parents. He got a gang of Polish or Bulgarian builders in, had them put in new kitchens and bathrooms, update the electrics and plumbing, repaint the walls and stick some plants in the front gardens. Then he sold them on, for much higher prices, of course. He'd soon repaid his parents and was building up a nice little pile. Wasn't hard.

'I didn't have a job either, so I was happy to be his project manager, meaning I kept tabs on the builders, checked the bills for materials, dealt with estate agents and took a fee for it – about a quarter share of the profits. Eventually, Dietrich formed this company and called it Premium Properties Six – the six was because his first few houses were in Fulham with the SW6 postcode. The company had a range of projects on its books, mostly residential, a few commercial. He pulled me in with him and we both became directors. On pretty good salaries, I seem to recall.'

'So, what happened to it?' Izzy asked gently.

'Well, he talked about teaming up with a developer who'd got planning permission for a big block of flats by the river. I told him he was getting in over his head. After all, he wasn't an engineer or a surveyor. Never studied an architect's drawing in his life!' He made a strange noise that Izzy took for laughter. 'I doubt he'd ever used a screwdriver, let alone gone over a planning application.'

He was warming to the subject.

'I tried to tell him that the developers could be cowboys, and he shouldn't touch the project with a barge pole. Dietrich wouldn't listen, said they had experts on board who knew all about the legal requirements for foundations, water supplies and such matters.'

Izzy nodded. 'What went wrong?'

'Blasted First Domestic Appliances, that's what! Dietrich had quit in time, so I took the heat. Once you've been investigated and sanctioned by the Financial Conduct Authority, you're not allowed to hold directorships in any company. Anyway, he lost interest in property development when he managed to land a job with some tax auditors in the City. He saw it as a route to a career in politics, and so it proved.

'Meanwhile, I was floundering – out of work, out of everything. My marriage imploded, I lost our home, our weekend cottage in Dorset and, worst of all, I lost custody of my boys.

'All I had was the Premium Properties Six's salary, and I had to resign from that directorship the following year. Luckily, I managed to keep hold of the house in Disraeli Road, near the Putney Library. Dietrich and I had bought the house and converted it into two flats years earlier. It was a stroke of luck for me – I expect it was part of Dietrich's plan to avoid tax – that my name alone was on the deeds. I still live there.'

Izzy nodded and checked that her tape recorder was still working. 'Don't know if you read about it in the papers or saw it on the TV news, but that big block of flats has serious flaws, and the leaseholders are demanding Premium Properties Six install fire safety measures and nightly fire patrols. They say the flats are now worthless.'

'Oh God, no. I've seen items about cladding and fire risks with tower blocks, but I never made a connection to those flats. Guess I was right after all about not trusting the developers. I feel sorry for the people who bought the flats.

'There was another project, now I come to recall. It showed how Dietrich was clever enough to sail into a place at Oxford while I struggled to be accepted by York!'

A bitter laugh followed.

'Another school friend we both knew, a chap called Guy Watford, owned the freeholds of six shops in the Tooting and Mitcham areas. What were they now? Oh yes, chemist shops. His dad had been a pharmacist, and he set them up.

'Guy wanted to escape to the country, or rather, as we later learned, escape the hefty gambling debts he'd accrued. He wanted to relocate with his family to Devon, where property was cheap. New start sort of thing. But he died a few years ago, so it was a short escape, you could say.'

He was starting to waffle again. Mercifully, he got back to the point.

'None of these chemist shops were making money because they were the old-fashioned type. They stocked aspirin and cough syrup but didn't sell the things that draw customers in and make money, like sunglasses, make-up and perfume. None of the shops' managers had forged links with local GPs to dispense prescriptions directly to patients, so the pharmacists sat twiddling their thumbs most of the time.'

Izzy nodded.

'It'd been my plan that I should take over the management of the shops and the rented flats above them. But Dietrich, who'd funded the purchase, of course, wanted to buy and then quickly sell them off individually. And sell off the flats.'

'Is that what they call asset stripping?'

'Exactly that,' Michael replied, looking down at her, again impressed by the little detective sergeant.

'That way, he made three or four times the purchase price for the group. He didn't care about the shops' employees being sacked or that the tenants of the flats would be made homeless because their rents had suddenly trebled.'

'Did he share his profits with you?' Izzy asked, guessing the answer.

'Ha! He offered me a sum equivalent to the profit on one of the six shops. Told me to consider it a finder's fee. We haggled and I got a bit more, but only a bit. I let him cheat me again.'

His focus seemed to drift away.

'Anyway, it was all a long time ago.'

He sighed and looked at the daffodils and other early flowers, folding his umbrella now that the rain had stopped.

Despite herself, Izzy felt a bit sorry for him. 'No other projects? More recent ones, perhaps?' she prodded gently.

'I had a few ideas, but you need start-up funds. The bank won't lend to me. Dietrich had Penny's banker father to open doors for him at the beginning. No one would trust me after FDA. So, I've had to take beastly, rubbish jobs like the one I have at the moment, just to pay the bills. I'm thinking of advertising for a rich widow.'

Izzy thought he was joking but wasn't sure. 'Got one in mind?'

'Oh yes,' he said with a pantomime wink and a light laugh.

'You must have felt bitter towards Dietrich, surely? Yet you were still on his guest list?'

'I don't hold grudges, Isobel. As I told you, Dietrich and I were at school together. In the same house. We rowed together, played cricket for the same team. We went back a long way. I knew Penny well too. I'm tremendously fond of her.'

It struck Izzy that she and Mehmet should have found all this out a lot earlier. Was this frightfully nice chap Dietrich's frightfully nice friend or his foe?

'You didn't have ideas for new projects for Dietrich to consider?'

'Funnily enough, I had lots. But nothing I suggested appealed to him.'

Izzy decided she quite liked him, though she wouldn't trust him to recommend a brand of toaster to her. She thanked him and walked back over Putney Bridge to Disraeli Road, where her interviewee lived in a tall, cream-painted Victorian house near where she'd parked her car earlier. It was an elegant place and one that suited him, she decided.

She was relieved that there was no parking penalty ticket under one of the Skoda's windscreen wipers.

She was in Rob's office for afternoon tea.

17

MEHMET LOOKED into the backgrounds of the directors of First Domestic Appliances and was eager to talk about his findings with Izzy. None of the other directors sparked his interest because none had placed all their eggs in that one particular basket. None of them appeared to have suffered catastrophically after its closure. He realised that Michael Wilson-Green had good reason back then to suspect Dietrich of having tipped off the Financial Conduct Authority about the fake profits forecast and inflated share price before he himself resigned. The firm ended up being fined more than one million pounds. No wonder it put a bomb under Wilson-Green's promising career and blitzed his family life.

Rob's conclusion was that despite his assurances to the contrary, despite Izzy's view that he was simply too dim to have succeeded, Wilson-Green *must* have been bitterly jealous of his old schoolfriend and *must* have hated his guts. Was Dietrich's knighthood the last straw?

Rob went on Google and found a photo of a young

Wilson-Green from a newspaper article about the First Domestic Appliances' case. He printed it out and pinned it to the blue felt line-up, writing *Jealous? Betrayed?* next to it.

Later that morning, Izzy reported on the Esther Hall case. Digital checks on Esther's mobile phone showed no activity apart from Annette's calls soon after she disappeared. Annette supplied the details from their WhatsApp group of school friends. Mehmet spoke to them all. None knew of any new boyfriends following Esther's split with Mark Phillips.

The trio looked glumly at each other.

On Friday, their luck changed. At the start of the investigation, Esther's father supplied details of her missing bicycle. A keen-eyed police support officer had spotted a wheel of a bike with similar pink mudguards almost completely submerged in sludge on the banks of the River Wey between Godalming and Guildford. She also spotted the corner of what turned out to be a silt-covered wallet a few yards away. It had probably fallen from the rider's pocket or the bike's pannier. When it was cleaned up by the forensics lot, it was found to be a student's photo identity card belonging to Esther Hall. There was also a Visa card in her name, deep inside one of the wallet's pockets, and a sad, single five-pound note. They found one decent fingerprint on the identity card, which, thanks to the thick leather of the wallet, the river hadn't washed off.

It belonged to Joe Jackson.

The creep was picked up within the hour at his sister's flat. Again, he was wearing only underwear as he sat in front of the television with a skinny roll-up stuck to his bottom lip. This time, he was told he was being arrested on suspicion of the murder of Esther Hall and that he need not say anything but that it may harm his defence if he did not mention when questioned something he later relied on in court. Did he understand this caution, he was asked. Probably not. Very few suspects did. But he'd heard it several times and nodded robotically.

He got up from his armchair, found some crumpled clothes on the floor behind the sofa, cursed, but said nothing else as he was handcuffed by one of the two arresting officers.

In the main interview room at the station, he sat in a dung-coloured anorak that matched his dusty brown hair and sallow complexion. He was allowed to wait for a solicitor. Arnold Kowalski, one of Guildford's most experienced criminal defence lawyers and almost certainly the oldest, arrived twenty minutes later and demanded private time with his new client. Joe must have given him a full summary of his previous encounters with the justice system because Arnold came out of the interview room looking down at the floor and frowning. He'd obviously advised Joe to stay schtoom and to let him answer the questions unless he nodded in his direction. He must have guessed that the evidence was damning.

Rob accompanied Izzy into the windowless room and sat next to her as she switched on the tape recorder on the metal-topped table. Mehmet watched through the one-way glass on the wall behind where his colleagues sat, as they gave their names and ranks for the benefit of the tape. Izzy then announced the time and Joseph Jackson and his lawyer did the same.

Izzy studied the ageing heap in front of them and remembered how Jess had bitterly remarked how he "liked them young".

She put a photograph of Esther on the table.

'Do you recognise this young woman?' asked Rob.

Joe slowly shook his head.

'My client does not believe he knows this person,' Arnold Kowalski snapped. 'Please explain why you think he might know her. Is it in connection with the matter about which you interviewed him only a week ago?'

'No, it is not,' Rob replied. 'This is a separate case, and the young woman in this photograph was Esther Hall, a student nurse.'

He let the information hang in the air.

'Where were you on the second of January this year, Mr Jackson?'

'Nowhere,' Joe grunted.

'Please answer the question. Were you at the home of your former partner, Jess Cummings?'

'Can't remember. Might have been. Might have been at me sister's.'

'It might help you to remember that this was just after Christmas,' said Izzy, 'three days before you and your friend Doug Elliot were working with John Hardwick, delivering items to Batts Farm where there was a big party on Saturday the fifth of January.'

'Still don't remember,' Joe persisted, the corners of his mouth turning downwards.

'You don't remember pulling this young woman, a student nurse, off her bicycle after she left the health centre in Horsley? Dragging her to a garage you knew had only a small, old padlock on it, one you could easily break, throwing her on the floor and raping her? And then strangling her?'

Joe's breathing quickened. Arnold Kowalski grabbed his client's right arm and glared at him, signalling that he should shut right up.

Rob nodded at Izzy, as if to say, "I'll go for it!"

'A bicycle matching Esther's was found a few days ago, along with a wallet that probably fell out of the bike's pannier. Tucked deep in a pocket was an identity card with a fingerprint on it that matches one of yours taken before your last arrival at our custody suite. There is also a semen stain on the underwear Esther was wearing when her body was found in the garage.

'An officer in the custody suite took a saliva swab from your mouth,' Rob said. 'This was a DNA test.'

Joe became agitated. 'I didn't fucking consent to that – you'll fit me up. I know my rights.'

Rob sat back, wedging one foot against the tabletop with his fingers interlaced around his knee. He kept his voice calm. 'Perhaps you should also know, and your lawyer can confirm, that under the Criminal Justice Act of 2003, the police have the power to take and retain a DNA sample of any person arrested for any recordable offence, regardless of whether they have yet been charged.'

Kowalski whispered in his client's ear. Three days later, the DNA test showed a match to the semen in the stain found on Esther's knickers. It was extraordinary that it had not been made as soon as the forensic report on the stain came through, given that Joe had a list of previous convictions, and his DNA would have been collected each time. Perhaps Joseph Jackson was too common a name. Or perhaps the truth was that a database is only ever as reliable as the people who input the information. Anyone can make a mistake or just forget to do it.

Rob knew they had ample evidence to convict Joe Jackson for Esther's rape and murder. The defendant was looking at a long spell in grey pyjamas in a Category A prison such as

Belmarsh in Thamesmead or Woodhill in Milton Keynes. Nevertheless, the policeman booked a meeting with the head CPS prosecutor in Guildford to talk it through.

There'd be no celebratory drinks in the pub yet, though. Rob knew from bitter experience that however strong the evidence against a defendant, the harder the police had to work to stop the case collapsing because of a stupid little error in procedure, which a good barrister could turn into a whopping great one.

For instance, did the suspect receive all his entitlements when first brought into custody? Was he offered a phone call by the custody sergeant before his fingerprints were taken and the swab test done? Was he offered food? Did a nurse or a mental health professional check him over to make sure he was fit for interview?

He checked the file and read the custody report. In Joe's case, all those criteria could be ticked and the green light for prosecution was soon flashing. Joe Jackson was charged with rape and murder. Two days later, he appeared in Guildford Magistrates' Court, where he chose not to enter a plea to the charges. He was committed to crown court for trial in four months' time and was remanded to Wandsworth Prison, a Category B institution, in the meantime.

Rob felt a rush of relief. *So, we haven't been entirely useless in Esther's case*, he thought, as he drove home that evening. He'd told Izzy to visit Esther's parents and update them. It wasn't that he deliberately ducked the difficult, emotionally messy jobs, or even that he knew Izzy would always be sympathetic and tactful with bereaved people. It was that he could never understand why the family of dead victims tended to be so pleased and relieved when perpetrators were charged. It didn't lessen their grief, surely? Their loved ones had still suffered and died. It was still unfair and devastating.

An arrest didn't change anything. Justice was a big concept. He'd have liked to debate it with some grieving families of victims, but of course, that wouldn't be fitting. He often debated whether he should study for a law degree in his free time, but then he remembered. He didn't have any free time.

True to pattern, Sean and Patricia Hall were clearly relieved to receive Izzy's news, even though Patricia's tears streamed immediately. In her car before driving home, Izzy herself shed a few.

Back in his miserable office above a shoe repair shop in the centre of Guildford, Kowalski thought hard about which defence barrister to instruct for Joe's trial. Even though his legal aid fees would not pay for the new sofa his wife wanted, it had turned out to be a couple of interesting weeks for him.

* * *

Pen felt a bleakness she'd never known before. Eventually, she took the initiative and telephoned Rob to demand a meeting. She told him she was concerned about the lack of progress in their case. Rob agreed to see her, with Tom and Bella, in his office in Lambs Conduit Street. He'd have to tell them that they were no further forward, a prospect that wiped out his satisfaction at cracking Esther's murder.

Despite a cold wind, the sun was shining on one side of Pen's face as she left Colt Court and walked towards and then down Southampton Row the next morning. Bella and Tom strode up from Bankside and caught a bus over Waterloo Bridge to Holborn Underground Station. They met outside the police station.

Pen hugged them. 'Let's give him a hard time, eh? He's had the autopsy report on his desk for weeks and what's the result? Nothing!'

Once inside his office, she repeated this to Rob's face. Perhaps her talk with Jane had emboldened her.

Rob wasn't surprised. He too was frustrated that the inquiry seemed to be floundering.

'Look, it may not seem like it to you, but we've been working hard on this case,' he said. 'We're prosecuting a career burglar called Kevin Miller for the theft of Sir Dietrich's Rolex. He'd taken it to Bristol and sold it to a handler. He may have been the killer. But we don't think so.

'It's more likely he happened to spot a man wearing a valuable watch, followed him and took it from him as he lay on the ground in the back kitchen. Alternatively, he could have jabbed Sir Dietrich and then pulled off the watch. The CPS say there isn't evidence enough yet to charge him with the murder, though. So, we're still working on it.

'Yesterday, we charged a man, Joseph Jackson, with the rape and murder of an 18-year-old student nurse in West Horsley, the case which my sergeant Mehmet and I transferred to Guildford to investigate. Interestingly, he worked for John Hardwick and came into Batts Farm before and during the party. When DS Holland interviewed him, he was foolish enough to admit that he'd gone into the back kitchen to use the lavatory there. That way he put himself on our suspects' list for Sir Dietrich's murder.

'I don't see him as the perpetrator, though. He's a violent sex offender with low intelligence, but would he have a motive where Sir Dietrich was concerned? I don't think so. Unless he'd been paid to kill him by a third party. We can't find any sign of money from a pay-off where he was living. He doesn't have a bank account, and his ex-girlfriend says he wasn't suddenly flush. She doesn't think there's a link.

'We've looked hard at a third local man, Doug Elliot, who also works with John Hardwick assembling tables and carrying boxes of hired equipment and food. You may have noticed him – dishevelled, fat, always looking as though his clothes are about to split. We believe he deals in high-grade cocaine and may have supplied the lethal dose that killed Sir Dietrich.

'I'm telling you this to show you that we haven't been sitting on our hands. Doug Elliot is not the killer, in my view. He's just too big and clumsy to have sidled up to Sir Dietrich and injected him without anyone noticing and without leaving any trace of himself. Also, there's the question of motive again.

'In my view, the killer was a psychopath. Or Sir Dietrich had an enemy no one else knew about. Or – and this is my best guess – the motive was historic, perhaps relating to one of the business enterprises Sir Dietrich was involved in before he became a politician. It comes down to finding out who resented your husband badly enough to want him dead.

'I've taken it upon myself to go through Sir Dietrich's former business interests to search for possible reasons a person might have had to want to do this.'

Bella and Tom looked at their mother with concern. She seemed far too calm. It was a performance. She was as tense as she'd ever been because, like everyone else who knew him, she'd believed that Dietrich had been Mr Nice Guy and hadn't bothered to quiz him about his dealings in the financial and business world before they met.

'We've talked to Michael Wilson-Green, because he attended the party,' Rob went on. 'As you know, he was involved in a couple of business ventures with Sir Dietrich many years ago.

'There were difficulties between them when the Serious Fraud Office investigated their company, First Domestic Appliances. What do you remember about those difficulties, Mrs Olson?'

Pen replied, 'I remember that Dietrich denied tipping off the SFO or the FCA, whichever it was, after he resigned from FDA. He did everything he could to keep the details out of the papers. Back then he knew a few journalists with influence. But the company was fined heavily and just couldn't survive. Michael had been the CEO. He couldn't blame Dietrich for the collapse. Anyway, whether Michael bore a grudge or not, he's a gentle person who wouldn't conspire to kill anyone.'

Rob asked, 'Do you remember that Sir Dietrich set up Premium Properties Six? And that Michael Wilson-Green was also a director?'

'I know Dietrich did a bit of property development before I met him. I didn't know he'd set up a company and that name isn't familiar to me.'

'More recently, Mr Wilson-Green asked Dietrich to back him in one or two new ventures. Dietrich declined. What did your late husband tell you about those?'

Pen screwed up her face. She hadn't expected this inquisition. 'Nothing. I don't think he gave them much thought. Michael is the sort of person who has ten ideas before breakfast. Nine are complete non-starters and occasionally one is just about worth investigating. Michael told me at the party that he was thinking about new businesses but needed to improve his online skills, and that one of his sons was going to help him set up a website. He absolutely was not seething with resentment. As I said, he's not the type. Anyway, deep down, he and Dietrich were like brothers.'

Pen looked down at her hands, stifling any sign that a tiny doubt could be forming in her mind.

Rob decided to turn the tables. 'Have you come to suspect anyone else?' he asked.

It was Pen's chance to report a development. 'After Tom and Bella found a wedding certificate confirming that Dietrich and Jane Page-Smith were indeed married in 1972, and we discovered that neither party filed for divorce, I went to see her.'

Rob puffed out his cheeks in surprise. Bella and Tom, who hadn't known this either, were shocked but managed to keep looking straight ahead.

'Jane says she doesn't want or need much of Dietrich's money, and the pay out from a life insurance policy he took out will probably be more than enough as a pension.

'She's happy in the Wimbledon house he found for her all those years ago, and she has a job and a partner. Her reasons for turning up at the memorial service were complicated. She hadn't planned to talk to journalists, but she didn't accept any offers of money from newspapers and television companies to elaborate on her marriage. I believed her when she said she just wants to get on with her life now.'

'So, you don't think she should be on the suspects' list?' Rob asked, leaning back in his chair. 'Or her son for that matter?'

'Charles continues to receive a monthly amount from one of Dietrich's accounts. He'd have had no reason to want to rock the boat. And anyway, he has a good independent life now as a master's student and a freelance journalist.'

Bella looked at Tom, blinking with surprise. Rob moved

on. 'We're going to interview the Batts Farm housekeeper about anyone else who had access to the house before the party.'

Pen nodded.

The meeting broke up with everyone feeling irritable and irritated. Each would have liked to punch a large hole in a wall.

18

INDEPENDENT, as his mother believed, or not, Charles William Olson was content to continue to receive monthly payments of £3,000 from the 'Bank of Dad', Dietrich. It didn't help him make decisions, though. He wasn't sure he wanted to go to university, for instance, despite his mother's assumption that he would want to have a proper education. What she meant was that he should go to Oxford or Cambridge and leave with a degree in anything – except perhaps golf-club management or cake decorating. He should consider classics, politics, philosophy, history or modern languages – the sort of subjects that would provide him with the invisible key to open so many doors later on.

Nah, he thought, as he lay in bed late most mornings. He didn't like the sound of that. Too much hard work. So, along with a couple of former school mates who also had trust funds of one sort or another, he took off on a gap year. He told his mother it would help him find himself. They both laughed at the ridiculousness of the expression.

Bangkok was his first stop. Then to Nepal, where he

emailed his mother about the temples and palaces, although he'd looked at them only from seats in assorted cafés.

The thought of going back to suburbia depressed him so he concentrated on the moment, the girl he was with and the spliff he was sharing with her.

After six or seven months he began to miss his mum. He knew she had a partner but worried that the relationship wouldn't last. The art teacher was a drip, even the cat knew it.

In the end he decided that a degree in journalism wouldn't be too taxing. Ella, a girl in their dope-smoking group, was going to do something called media studies. From an internet café in Islamabad, he applied to City University in East London for a place on their undergraduate course. Thinking about his future career that night, he plumped for Will Page as his byline. It was short, memorable. He was accepted.

Jane was thrilled to open her front door to her boy, to share his preparations for the start of term, to persuade him to cut off his baby dreadlocks and buy clothes to replace those left in rucksacks somewhere in the Himalayas. Dietrich's money bought him a Brompton fold-up bike, which he could take on District Line trains to Liverpool Street Station and the university. Or wherever.

Charles himself thought more about how well he would blend in with the other students. From primary school he'd realised that lots of kids are brought up by a single parent. They say that what you've never had, you don't miss. A load of crap.

On his travels, he'd found he was cool enough, clued-up enough, smart enough. Girls liked him and he liked them. He was obviously not a shit shag. And if they thought of him as a posh boy, so what? His public school was cool too.

When, after the first term at City, he left the house in Wimbledon to live with Gabriel and Jay in a Bethnal Green flat, he found the squalor and untidiness difficult to take. The lavatory was permanently smelly and stained and he joked it could have been twinned with one in the Congo.

Why didn't a cleaner arrive every week, as one did at his mum's house? After a month or so, he took an executive decision and hired a young Polish woman who blitzed the place, took their dirty laundry away and returned it to them a few days later. Dietrich paid for her, too. Should he move to a place on his own? He weighed the pros and cons but couldn't decide. Despite this, he felt his freedom was almost complete.

More to his surprise, he'd found the undergraduate journalism degree interesting and challenging. He'd half hoped the course would have involved little more than reading tabloids and watching television. But no. Annoyingly, it entailed actual reading, analysing and working. Such as learning what news is, how to write concisely so that even the dullest reader could stick with a five-paragraph story to the end. It turned out to be harder than he'd guessed. Mastering how to quickly write a breaking news story was surprisingly tricky, he found.

He was taught how to use basic interviewing techniques, to ask questions clearly and to shut up rather than rushing to fill a silence. Sitting through lectures on Public Affairs, which turned out to be about who runs what in Britain, had also seemed worthwhile, if dry. Even learning the basics of law, defamation and contempt, copyright and privacy had its moments. A raddled old journalist from *The Guardian* taught that part of the course, giving colourful examples of past libel trials and their unexpected outcomes, as well as talking about his own triumphs.

Part of the course involved turning up at Magistrates Courts to watch the justice system in practice, then writing up what he'd seen and heard, sticking to the same deadlines as an actual reporter on a daily paper. This was a challenge.

He chose Lavender Hill Magistrates' Court, which was a few stops on the train from his mother's home in Raynes Park and a short walk from Clapham Junction Station. It held sessions on Saturdays, when people arrested all over London and held in police stations overnight were bussed to this one court to have their first hearing. The idea was to sentence or transfer newly arrested suspects and to empty police custody cells as quickly as possible.

Will liked to hang around outside the court before and after the sessions, observing the usually anxious-looking defendants, the lawyers weighed down with bundles of case files, the probation officers looking overworked and cross.

On one Saturday, Vincent Billen, a sad-looking gardener, who'd been arrested the day before in Guildford, appeared at the court as a defendant. He pleaded guilty to possession of two small packets of cannabis and a small amount of cocaine. Will had watched as the magistrates dispensed with him quickly after learning from the duty solicitor that he was of "previous good character" and used the cannabis to help him cope with painful arthritis and the stress of caring for a son with Down syndrome. His stay the previous night in a cell at Guildford Police Station was deemed to be "time served". Vincent sighed with relief as he was released.

Later, outside the court, Will saw him staring at passing cars seemingly waiting for a friend to drive him home. He smiled broadly and introduced himself to the older man as a student journalist.

'I'm hoping to write an article headed Cannabis City as

part of my course,' he explained. 'I'd like to quote people with experience of the court system, to see if they thought it fair or not, and if they believe cannabis should be legalised. All anonymous, of course.'

'I'll have to think about that,' Vincent replied nervously. 'I don't want anything to go public and embarrass my boy.'

'Oh, don't worry about that. It's just a college exercise. I won't be sending it to a newspaper.' Big smile. 'Why don't I ring you and put some questions to you? You think about it for a couple of days, and I'll ring you again to see if you want to help me out or not. I could pay you a bit...'

Vincent scribbled his telephone number on Will's notebook and, spotting a friend beckoning from a car poking out from the end of Lavender Hill Gardens opposite the court, dashed across the road.

When Will rang a few days later, Vincent answered a few questions about his life and described a few of the places where he worked. They agreed on a fee of fifty pounds. Will sent the cash wrapped in several sheets of blank paper by registered post. The article earned Will a merit from his lecturer.

Will took Ella to Pizza Express that evening to celebrate. He ordered the best Chianti on the menu and the chocolate cake for dessert.

19

'Ed, quick, give me a big hug and a big glass of wine and tell me what happened today has been a bad dream.'

Bella had returned from the showdown in Holborn Police Station to the Bankside flat, her head spinning. Exhausted, she flopped on the sofa. Ed managed the first two demands and suggested that, as he'd played piano at a hotel at lunchtime for some special guests and wouldn't be needed that evening, they go out to eat. Better still, to La Barca, an old-fashioned Italian restaurant at the back of Waterloo Station. First, she should rest, Ed suggested, but she was already out cold. Ed put the untouched glass of wine in the fridge.

Later, over antipasti at the restaurant, Bella told him about the meeting in Lambs Conduit Street and the various suspects the police had investigated. She told him about the burglar and the watch and Joe Jackson, the caterer's helper who'd used the loo near the wine store. He turned out to be the rapist and murderer of a teenage student who'd lived not far from Batts Farm.

'A student nurse, only 18! Rape and murder! You hear about these terrible crimes but somehow you always think they're happening in a world far away from you. Imagine, this monster was in and out of Batts Farm bringing in trays of food!'

Ed ordered the house red.

'There's more,' said Bella. 'My mother... you won't believe this. Tom and I didn't when she came out with it to the police. I still don't. Can't.'

She paused then told him how Pen had talked about visiting Jane Page-Smith, the woman who'd revealed her father's bigamy. The woman they'd agreed was a money-snatching bitch.

'But Jane's not a conniving gold digger after all, according to Mum. An hour's chat and she's putty in this woman's hands!'

Ed was intrigued.

'I'd love to have been a fly on that wall,' said Bella. 'I bet they sized each other up and were super careful in what they said. Mum said after they talked, she accepted that Jane doesn't want all the money she's entitled to as the legal spouse. She doesn't need Batts Farm to be sold because she doesn't like the country or country houses. She hasn't even seen the place – at least I don't think she has – so I'm not sure I believe it. Not sure I believe any of it. I'm still suspicious of her.'

Ed gently put his hand on Bella's arm. 'Your Mum's a clever woman. I don't think she'd have been fooled or taken in by—'

'And Jane's clever too,' Bella butted in. 'Remember, she met my dad when they were students at Oxford. But if she wasn't after his money, why did she suddenly show up at the funeral and speak to journalists?'

The La Barca food was good. Ed chose calves liver pan-fried with sage, and side portions of green beans and new potatoes. Bella picked at a mushroom risotto and a green salad.

She looked at Ed's plate with a frown, then filled both their wine glasses to the brim.

'In Romania people like to eat liver and kidneys. Here people seem to like it only when it's on a restaurant menu in Italian!' he said.

Over tiramisu and coffee, Ed ventured, a little nervously, 'I've been thinking a lot about the party... about what I saw. You and the family were so upset over your dad's death that I didn't dare say anything before. It's probably nothing anyway...'

'Go on, go on.'

'At the party, I gave myself a break from playing after about an hour. I was tired after the cycle ride there. I got up from the piano and went into the kitchen to grab some of the nice food I'd watched the guests eating and I took a glass of the champagne, ready for the toast. I was telling one of the waiters how they hadn't offered me anything while I was hard at work and how unfair it was.'

Bella nodded.

'Then I spotted a different waiter doing something a bit odd. He was laughing and joking, and I saw him throw what looked like a Biro into one of the rubbish bins. I stared at it and realised it could have been anything. It was like he was throwing a dart.'

Ed held up his hand, holding an imaginary dart between his thumb and first finger.

'He saw me looking and said, "Don't worry, it's only a little disposable syringe. Insulin for my diabetes." I made some silly remark about being terrified of needles and that I was glad he hadn't thrown it in my direction. Which is true. It's pathetic of me.

'Then this waiter said, "I'm terrified of needles too. Bit of a bummer when you're a diabetic! After I was diagnosed, just before my GCSEs, I had to practise jabbing oranges for weeks before I could bear to do it to myself."'

Ed added, 'I didn't think anything of it because, until you told me about the autopsy report, I accepted your father died of a heart problem. I didn't make any connection with an injection in his leg.'

Now he was the one who was upset, and he wished he'd never mentioned it. Bella had to soothe him. She was intrigued, though. 'Did you get this waiter's name?'

Ed shook his head.

'What did he look like?'

'Like the rest of them there. In his twenties, probably. White shirt, black trousers.'

'This was some time before Mum found Dad's body, yes?'

Ed nodded. He was beginning to feel sorry he'd burdened Bella with more pieces of a jigsaw no one could put together.

'Why didn't you mention this when you went to Holborn Police Station to talk to the woman detective?'

'It didn't occur to me. Didn't seem important. Maybe I'll send her an email; I have her card somewhere. Now,' he said, trying to sound upbeat, 'drink up and let's take a walk and look at the river.' He paid the bill using the card from his hotel earnings' account and they set off along the river walk back to Bankside.

In the morning, Bella went to Colt Court to see her mum

and found that Tom had stayed the night after dosing off in front of the TV. Pen had left for a meeting at the LSE and Tom was now having a late breakfast before scooting off to the hospital. She quickly summarised Ed's account and his eyebrows shot up. An insulin syringe in one of the rubbish bins!

'I'm not sure now if the bins had been taken away immediately by John Hardwick. He prides himself on leaving the house cleaner and tidier than it was when he arrived. But I think there was one bin there, outside the kitchen waiting for the rubbish collection. I had a quick look in it. I didn't poke around, though. All I saw was food waste.'

He cursed his prissiness and wondered how he would ever make it as a doctor.

Bella had been mulling it over, though, imagining how the story might play out in a criminal trial. She'd be assisting the counsel for the defence in that scenario, of course.

'Don't get excited, Tom. Think carefully. Ed was beating himself up for not telling me sooner. But it's just a coincidence if it's anything at all. And I'm not sure it is.

'Whoever injected Dad planned it carefully. He or she wouldn't have risked a syringe with traces of cocaine still inside it being found in a rubbish bin. Even if it was covered with bits of cream cheese or other food it would probably have been carrying an incriminating fingerprint or two. It's far more likely they'd have slipped the syringe into a pocket or a rucksack and then dumped it in a hedge or down a drain, miles from Batts Farm. Or taken it home with them. And they wouldn't have blurted out a story to a stranger like Ed, a story that might be checked out.

'There weren't more than about six or seven waiters, after all. My guess is that if a waiter had diabetes and there was a possibility he'd have to inject himself during his shift, he would have told John Hardwick when he applied for the job. And John Hardwick, being a total control freak, wouldn't have hired him.'

Tom pulled a face. He was confused. 'So, you think this waiter's conversation with Ed was some kind of boys' joke?'

Bella nodded. 'Yes, exactly. It was probably the sort of silly thing people say when they've had a glass or two of champagne and everyone's a bit excited. What Ed saw probably *was* a Biro, as he first thought, or a wooden stirrer stick, you know the sort of thing you get in coffee shops?'

Tom nodded. He wasn't convinced but had decided not to argue with his sister until this nightmarish puzzle was solved.

'Ed should probably tell the cops about it anyway,' he said as he headed out, running down the stairs and towards Southampton Row, looking for a bus with Waterloo on the front, so that he could leg it to St Thomas's from the stop near the station. He feared he'd be late for a lecture on managing the impact of advanced liver disease.

* * *

Basil was also in danger of being late that morning.

'Got your deliveries' schedule?' Steve had started to ask his dad each day before he set off for the brewery. He had persuaded Johnsons' manager to email a list as early as possible each morning so that Steve could print it out and warn Basil of any road works or other possible problems he might encounter. It lessened his anxiety.

Steve's IT client numbers were building up steadily and he was considering upgrading the Vespa. He'd added the fixing of shop security cameras to his list of specialities. After messaging everyone on his contacts list about his new services, he'd even heard from Sally, his former girlfriend, via Facebook, suggesting they have a friendly catch-up drink. He was suspicious of her motives – had she just been dumped by the replacement boyfriend? He was curious to see her, nonetheless. They made a date for the following Saturday night.

Meanwhile, he continued to wonder if his neighbour Janice and her gang were exaggerating the fire risks at South Quay. But he couldn't ignore his dad's mounting anxiety about bills for new fire precautions and night patrols. It wasn't as if Basil needed something else to distract him and keep him from sleeping at night. The special amphetamines he'd been prescribed weren't working as well and the old ADHD symptoms of forgetfulness and disorientation were returning. After all they'd been through to control his mental illness, Premium Properties Six was pushing Basil back down into the abyss. Steve didn't know if he could be pulled out again. He sent an email to his dad's GP asking for an appointment so that Basil could change medication and perhaps talk about a suitable form of exercise that could help. So far, Basil had laughed at Steve's attempts to take him down to the gym in the basement.

Again, Steve cursed the cheapskate builders of Premium Properties Six. Dietrich Olson, Michael Wilson-Green and the other directors deserved a new ring of hell entirely to themselves, he decided.

* * *

Michael Wilson-Green had no sense of guilt, of course. It wasn't his fault. Nothing was, not after all this time, after all the punishment he'd suffered. He often thought about it on his 'nothing to do' days. On his days off, he'd spend hours in the public library at the end of Disraeli Road, thumbing through historical fiction or the section on crime thrillers. Usually, he borrowed a few books and read only bits of them.

Occasionally he'd be spotted by people who'd come into the kitchen appliances shop with queries. It made him nervous so, eyes down, he tried to blend in with the other people like him in the computer section with nowhere else to be. Taking a cup of coffee from the library's new drinks and snacks counter and grabbing a newspaper from the stand helped to pass the time. Then a voice in his head would ask why he'd paid £3 he couldn't afford for a mediocre Americano nowhere near as good as the coffee he made at home.

20

THE POLICE SEARCH of Douglas Elliott's van and his father's flat had turned up a burner mobile phone, which was being examined by digital forensics officers. They also found several traces of cocaine in the kitchen and bathroom and a small quantity of loose ecstasy tablets.

Disappointed, Rob knew it wasn't nearly enough to charge the slob with intent to supply. He felt sure the stock of drugs they were looking for was stowed somewhere else.

'Any suggestions where we should look next?' he asked Izzy and Mehmet.

'What about the sister who comes occasionally to look after the disabled father?' Izzy suggested. 'Perhaps she goes back to her own place after each visit with a heavy handbag containing something to keep safe for big brother?'

'Hmmm. Worth looking at her circumstances,' the boss agreed.

Mehmet, who seemed to have brightened a little in the past few days, had the background checking job again.

Pam Elliott lived with her teenage daughter Tracy in a flat on a Peabody housing association estate in Islington. Ten years earlier, the Peabody Trust had employed clever architects to dismantle the outside lavatories and construct half-decent bathrooms inside the flats. They couldn't, of course, stretch the walls or install lifts. The flats remained small, cramped walk-ups.

Mehmet decided to take a stroll around the block. It was raining so he had an excuse to weave in and out of blocks and the areas reserved for rubbish bins, staying in dry spaces. He saw Pam walking up to the entrance carrying Tesco bags bulging with food shopping.

On his return to his parking place, with a view of the entrance to Pam's flat, he spotted her coming out and getting into a shiny red Mazda MX30 in the parking area, which, as he soon discovered from a Google check, wouldn't leave you much change from £50,000 if you'd bought it new with leather seats and all the other extras.

As she drove off, windscreen wipers thrashing, Mehmet jotted down the registration number and decided to drop into a nearby Mazda car dealership to see if he could find out anything about who might have bought the vehicle and when.

A salesman, with Bob on a badge on his lapel, looked at the tall man who'd parked his Insignia in the forecourt and was now examining the gleaming new and second-hand cars in the showroom.

'Looking to upgrade the Vauxhall, sir?' Bob asked hopefully, as he rushed to Mehmet's side.

'No, sorry. But I noticed a red MX30 in the neighbourhood and wondered if you were the one who sold it?' said Mehmet, taking out his warrant card when the salesman seemed hesitant. Deflated, Bob said he'd indeed sold a red MX30 a few months ago.

'Why d'you ask?' he asked nervously. 'The customer went for a trial run in her and liked her. We negotiated a fair price on the car being exchanged and everything was done properly. You can check our accounts if you want.'

'Please don't worry. I'm not suggesting there was anything at all irregular about the sale, but would you please check your records for the details of the owner?'

The customer had been a Mr Douglas Elliott, who'd given Pam's address. Mehmet asked for a photocopy of the sales receipt and left feeling pleased with himself.

Back driving the Vauxhall, heading south, he relayed this information to Rob. 'It means we can ask for an extension to the search warrant, doesn't it? To Pam's flat and the car?'

Rob put Izzy on that job and a search warrant was signed the following day by an obliging magistrate at the court next to Guildford Station. Off to Islington went a couple of Guildford's brightest uniforms.

At Pam Elliott's flat, a large quantity of Class A drugs together with fat rolls of £20 and £50 notes were duly recovered from a kitchen cupboard, parked behind tins of beans and soup. Mehmet was happy to receive Rob's slap on the back for his lateral thinking and good work. It produced probably his first smile since his mother's funeral.

Usually, it was Izzy who did the clever stuff and took chances, acted on her hunches and sometimes achieved results. Mehmet thought of himself as the plodder who was good at basic research. But this time, he'd had the wild idea, and it'd produced a result, a good one.

Meanwhile, forensics produced a list of recurring telephone numbers on Doug's mobile phone. Rob emailed them to his two sergeants.

'These are some of Doug's regulars. Do the background checks. Let's see if any of them has links to Dietrich Olson.'

Douglas Elliott was arrested in his father's Guildford flat, charged with possession of drugs with intent to supply and remanded by other magistrates two days later. Like Joe, he was sent to HMP Wandsworth.

Elliott senior was collected and taken into a care home from which he'd never return.

21

DEEP DOWN, Rob had known that connecting Doug's customers with Dietrich and his party guests was a long shot. Too long. And he was right.

'Not all murder cases end up with a suspect tightly trussed with ties of irrefutable evidence,' he told himself as he drove in from New Malden in unusually heavy traffic. He was trying to convince himself that making little – no, *sod all* – progress on the Olson case was not unusual. One of Bach's English French suites played by Murray Perahia was flowing softly into his ears. Yet for once, listening to the music he loved wasn't helping.

He'd caught a good few murderers in his time as a copper. Catching the stupid ones, who thought they've left no traces of evidence until the forensic scientists got to work, was usually satisfying. Catching the clever ones, who'd meticulously planned everything, made his life more difficult. His only hope in those cases was that something unexpected would happen; an alibi witness discovered to have been lying or a fluke uncovering the murderer's cleverly hidden past.

Those cases were the *really* satisfying ones. He could count the ones like that he'd been involved in on the fingers of one hand.

At the station, he called Izzy and Mehmet into his office.

'Can either of you think of any bit of information Doug Elliot or Joe Jackson might have that could help us with the Olson case? They're each banged up on remand facing long sentences, so I thought we might visit them, go through their stories again and see if there are any discrepancies.'

Izzy thought it sounded mad. 'Why would they tell us anything now?'

'Well, we could make it sound as though we could influence the sentencing court in return for a tip-off.' Rob was struggling.

The detective sergeants looked at each other, straight faces, sinking stomachs.

'You mean, ask them if they know if anyone brought cocaine to the Batts Farm party?' Izzy asked.

'Well, maybe not as blatantly as that,' said Rob, fiddling with a couple of paper clips. 'Something vague like, "Did you see anyone using drugs at the party?" One or other of the guests could have been a friend of one of Doug's customers. He or she could be a regular user.

'Or one of the waiters? They were students still on their Christmas holidays, weren't they? And students take drugs – or at least they did in my day.' Rob smiled but the blank faces in front of him didn't change. 'No harm in visiting them, being polite, making them think that perhaps their luck might have changed, when of course it hasn't.'

'OK,' said Mehmet. 'I'll take Slow Joe, rapist and murderer. Izzy, you can have Disgusting Doug, the drug baron.'

Izzy nodded lamely. 'Lovely, thanks. I'll take a peg for my nose.'

'Anyone had a chance to speak to the housekeeper yet?' Heads shook. Rob decided he'd take that job and would drive alone to Batts Farm. He felt ashamed that he hadn't once visited the crime scene.

He'd found a boxset of La Traviata CDs, the early '90s Covent Garden production with Georg Solti conducting, in a box in the room he was supposed to be redecorating at home. Without Mehmet in the passenger seat, he could turn up the volume.

Mrs Gibbs was surprised to open her bungalow door to a detective inspector, and she ushered him inside enthusiastically. She missed the visits by members of the Olson family every couple of weeks.

'What a nice surprise!' she said, stepping back into her kitchen and switching on the kettle to make tea, before putting a biscuit tin on the table then opening it.

'Yes and no,' Rob replied, wondering how much, if anything, she knew about the autopsy report. 'I may have some bad news for you. I take it you haven't been told yet that a post-mortem examination came up with some startling evidence about Sir Dietrich's death?'

She looked blank. 'No, Mrs Olson hasn't been here, so no, I haven't had any information about that.'

Rob realised he'd have to break the news gently. 'The family decided to have an autopsy done because they couldn't accept that Sir Dietrich had a bad heart. It showed that the cause of death wasn't his heart after all. It seems that someone injected him with a high amount of the drug cocaine, and that's what killed him. We don't yet know who injected it.'

'Oh dear!' said the widow, alarmed by the news. Her face crumpled and she rummaged around in the pocket of her cardigan, pulling out a handkerchief to wipe away her tears. She slid down on to a chair. Rob took over the tea making while she composed herself. He put a couple of teabags from a box near the hob into a large brown teapot on the counter and poured in boiling water.

'Are you sure?'

Rob nodded.

'Such a nice man. I can't think who would have wanted to harm him.'

'Can you tell me who else came to the house in the weeks before the party? Did anyone apart from you know the layout of Batts Farm?'

'Let me see,' she replied, pouring the tea into large mugs and adding milk from a jug in the fridge. 'There's Vince the gardener. He does odd jobs too, such as clearing the gutters. He's been coming here for ages, but he hadn't been around since September, when he dead headed some roses and pruned some of the other perennials. I think he was going to have some surgery on his knee. He told me he might need to use crutches and rest for a while.'

'What's his last name? And have you got a phone number?'

She stood up, opened a kitchen cupboard drawer and took out a crumpled piece of paper with Vincent Billen written on it and a Guildford landline number. Rob copied both.

'Anyone else? A plumber, electrician? Burglar alarm person?'

'No. There *is* a burglar alarm, but it hasn't been set for about ten years. When we did use it, it kept going off when tree branches swayed outside the windows in front of one of the sensors. One time, a bat flew around the top bedroom and set it off. It must have got into the loft somehow and then flew down when someone went up to get a suitcase or something. Mrs Olson decided the alarm system was more trouble than it was worth.

'Hang on. I'm forgetting we had the windows cleaned. A lovely young man did them.'

'Tell me about him,' said Rob, between gulps of strong tea.

'Well, this young chap knocked on the door of the big house when I was doing my usual dusting there of a Monday morning. Said he'd cycled past and thought the windows looked as though they could do with a clean. He offered to do them, inside and out, for £100. That may sound a bit high but there are a lot of big windows that I certainly can't reach even with a cloth on my broom. Anyway, the job takes about four or five hours. So, I agreed. Mrs Olson makes sure there's always cash in the kitty – in one of the drawers in the kitchen – for these things and other household bills.

'That was about 18 months ago, and he's been back a couple of times since then. As I said, nice young chap. Said to call him Oliver or Ol.'

'And you left him in the house on his own – you didn't follow him around?'

She frowned and scratched the back of her head with the handle of a teaspoon. The grey curls wobbled. 'I did the first time. I showed him where to find the sink to refill his bucket and where the toilet was in the back kitchen. And I removed everything from the windowsills, just in case of accidents. And, of course, I brought him a cup of tea and a few biscuits.'

'What does Oliver look like?'

'Tall. Fairish hair. Jeans and those tops they all wear, with a hood. Seemed nicely brought up. Know what I mean? Nice speaking voice. Like Tom.'

'Age?'

'Mid-twenties, maybe, or a bit older. Came with his extendable wiper thing strapped along the side of his bike. I showed him where the ladders are kept.'

'Did he give you his phone number?' Rob asked hopefully.

'No. He told me he'd lost his mobile and was saving to get a new one. So, he took down my number. He said he'd come back in a few months but would give me a call at the bungalow the day before to make sure it was convenient.'

'When was his last visit?'

'Just after Christmas. It was good timing for the party, as it happened.'

'And did he call you beforehand?'

'Yes, pretty sure he did.'

Back at the station, Rob ordered the phone records for Mrs Gibbs at her bungalow. Izzy rang all the mobile numbers of any callers in late December. One of them was a discontinued line. There was no record of an owner.

As he drove back to the station, Angela Gheorghiu as the dying Violetta was singing at full throttle, the gorgeous sounds filling the car and startling other drivers at two sets of traffic lights. Rob pondered the Oliver question.

'How do people find window cleaners these days?' he asked Izzy, after relating what Mrs G had said.

'We found ours when we spotted him cleaning the windows of a house down the road. He handed us a contact number on a little slip of paper.'

'And if you hadn't seen one in action, where might you have looked?'

'At the cards in the newsagent's window or on the Nextdoor app. You'd just post a message on it asking for recommendations for a window cleaner.'

'Could you try that? Join the Godalming Nextdoor and see if anyone recommends an Oliver,' Rob instructed.

'Of course. But most window cleaners are middle-aged men. This well-spoken young bloke sounds a little odd, don't you think?'

'Yeah, but he could be a student doing odd jobs during his term breaks.'

The following morning, Izzy had arranged a visit to Wandsworth Prison with Mehmet to see Douglas Elliott and Joe Jackson in separate interviewing rooms. Mehmet was ready for the searches, the series of gates noisily opening and closing and the unfriendly stares of inmates.

To Izzy, what struck her the most was the atmosphere of what she could only think of as unhappiness; the stench of disinfectant and body odour were difficult to tolerate. She'd squirted on some of the Jo Malone scent Alex always gave her for Christmas before leaving home, put the bottle in her handbag and sploshed on more before getting out of the car.

She smiled at the notice at the front gates of the grim, grey stone fortress of a building, 'Welcome to HMP Wandsworth'. As if anyone would *choose* to go there!

After the checks and walks along seemingly endless corridors, she sat at another table opposite Doug Elliott, who was wearing his own tramp's clothes, a so-called privilege afforded to remand prisoners.

'How's it going?' she asked. 'Sorry I couldn't bring you any cigarettes. Not allowed. But here are today's *Daily Star* and *The Sun* if you're interested.'

'You 'ere to tell me it's all a mistake and I'm gonna be released?' he smirked, crossing his big arms over his chest.

'Can't do that, I'm afraid,' Izzy came back, managing a little smile. 'But you may be able to help us, and the police can make sentencing recommendations. I'm not saying we could definitely get the sentence reduced but we could perhaps help the court decide which prison you are sent to and fix it for you to visit your father at the care home... things like that.'

'Don't see how I can 'elp yer,' he grunted.

'Doug', Izzy said, trying to sound authoritative but reasonable. 'Now you know that Dietrich Olson was murdered during the party in the house near Godalming just after the New Year. Yes?'

Doug gave a minimal nod.

'Well, someone injected a full syringe of cocaine into him when he was in or near the wine store.'

'Fuck! If you think you can pin that on me...' His face reddened in anger.

'We don't. Calm down.'

He seemed to manage it.

'We know you delivered some of the food and furniture for John Hardwick and weren't inside the house that long. But we wonder if you heard anything strange? Spotted anyone acting oddly? Was anyone fiddling with something that might have been a syringe and getting close to Mr Olson in the lower kitchen? One of the guests, perhaps?'

'I 'spect a few of the guests went to the toilets for a line or two. But they'd have used a toilet upstairs. Anyway, I didn't see 'em and I certainly didn't supply 'em.'

'Did you recognise any of the guests, spot if they were customers of yours?'

'Naah. Anyroad, who said I 'ad customers?' he growled.

Izzy gave him her best 'come off it!' look.

'So, you didn't see anything really apart from the waiters going in and out of the kitchen carrying trays of drinks and food?'

Doug shrugged and shook his head. 'I saw a couple of waiters going into and coming out of the bog downstairs after Joe went down there. And I noticed the young bloke who was playing the piano talking to a few people. Could've been them asking him if he knew bits of music they liked.'

Izzy was not surprised by his answers.

'Well, if something occurs to you, here is my phone number at the station.' Izzy passed her card to him. 'Thanks for your time.'

Mehmet was already waiting for her in the car outside the prison.

'Fat lot of use that was!' Izzy said. 'Could have told Rob as much! What was he thinking? I had to endure his horrible bad breath. Got any peppermints in there?' She rifled through the Vauxhall's glovebox without success.

'Joe Jackson was worse than useless,' Mehmet said. 'I got a torrent of abuse. When I suggested we may be able to increase the number of visits he got, he said he never wants to see any of his family or his ex-girlfriend again.

'Probably good news for her.'

They laughed. Then drove back to the Guildford nick.

22

'ARTHRITIS, IT'S A REAL BUGGER,' Vincent Billen said as he lowered himself carefully into a worn, winged armchair after opening the front door to Izzy. 'Only advantage is I get a blue disability badge for my car so I can drop the wife off and wait for her right outside Sainsburys without worrying about the wardens.

'Anyway, what can I do for you, love?'

'It's kind of you to see me, Mr Billen,' Izzy began, sitting down in a scruffy armchair close to his.

'Call me Vince, dear, everyone does.'

Izzy had easily found Batts Farm's former gardener in a housing association flat in South Guildford. He was probably younger than he looked, which was old and ill. He lived with his wife and his middle-aged son, who had Down syndrome. They were out that morning, but there were several photos of the family on the mantle shelf.

'I'm just making routine checks on people who know or knew Batts Farm.'

'Yes, the Olson house. I used to look after the garden.'

'That's right, Mrs Gibbs gave me your phone number. Did you know that Sir Dietrich Olson died there at a party just after Christmas?'

'Yes, I remember, it was on the local TV news. Heart attack, wasn't it?'

'Well, no, actually,' Izzy said. 'That's why I'm here. We now know he was murdered. Someone injected him with a drug.'

Vincent looked shocked. 'No, whaaat?' he gasped. 'I'll be damned!'

Izzy nodded and reached out to pat his hands. She noticed how swollen his knuckles were. Her own father suffered from arthritis, and she knew that painkillers could never properly ease it.

'You don't expect things like that in posh people's houses.' He shook his head from side to side.

'Can you recall when you last went there?'

'I did a bit of work there in late September, I think. Did some rose bush pruning and mowed the grass. I used to go every couple of weeks, but I had to stop going there – and to all my other gardens – because my back and knees got so bad. But I returned to Batts Farm in December because I'd left some tools and a thick jacket I wanted in the shed.'

The word shed was immediately neon lit in Izzy's mind. 'Did you by any chance spot anyone at either of those times, anyone you'd not seen before, in or around the house?' she asked.

'Can't really say. My memory's not so good these days. Don't think so. I'd probably have asked Mrs G about it if I had.'

'Did you ever spot a window cleaner or a bike or a van you hadn't seen before parked outside?'

Vince screwed up his eyes, then shook his head again.

'If anyone had been there when I was, Mrs G would have invited them in for morning tea with us. She always likes a bit of company. No, no one. Place is deserted most of the time. Lovely house, lovely garden. It's a shame.'

Izzy thanked him and left. Vince was biting his lip. His memory wasn't so bad that he'd forgotten he'd been back to the Batts Farm shed after Christmas, on the day before the party. His knees may be knackered, but his brain was doing just fine, he thought.

Instead of going straight back to the station, Izzy drove to Batts Farm and knocked on the door of Mrs Gibbs' bungalow. It was opened by a woman she hardly recognised: the formerly dumpy, frumpy housekeeper was wearing smart trousers, a plain light-grey jumper and ankle boots with small heels, which elongated her short legs. She had also been to a hairdresser, who'd tinted, trimmed and tamed her wild hair.

Blimey! Izzy thought. Her face must have shown it.

'Jim, my son, and my daughter-in-law took me out yesterday,' said the new glamour puss, proudly. 'What do you think? It's going to be a surprise for Jeff, my boyfriend.'

'You look very nice,' Izzy managed, suppressing her surprise at *that* word. She could hear the voices of a man and a woman in the background. 'I just called to ask if I could look in the shed?'

'Yes, of course, dear. It's tucked behind the bungalow. Near the hen house. Not locked.'

Izzy passed two noisy hens and opened the shed door.

Several hundred spiders and woodlice scuttled amongst the dust and dirt. A lawn mower, a can for petrol, rakes, spades, secateurs, half-full bags of compost, trowels, balls of string and canes of differing lengths, packets of slug pellets and a selection of old gardening gloves confronted her. No syringes or wraps of white powder. Izzy poked around behind some paint tins and rags. Nothing. Only more dust. Then she took photos of each shelf in case she'd missed something.

Back at the station, she washed her dusty hands in the basin in the loo then flopped into a chair opposite Rob and Mehmet.

'I went back to Batts Farm after Vince the gardener mentioned that he'd popped into a shed there in December. I thought it merited a quick look.

'I had to knock on Mrs Gibbs' door to ask where it was located and if it was locked. And I was shocked. First of all, she has a son, Jim, and a daughter-in-law. I could hear two people there in the background. Secondly, Mrs G had undergone a makeover thanks to them, which made her look 20 years younger. And – wait for it – she said it was going to be a surprise for Jeff, her *boyfriend!*'

Mehmet's eyebrows shot up. 'A few other people worth checking out, you're saying?'

Izzy nodded. 'It's crazy that I never asked her before about her own family. I could kick myself.'

Rob pulled himself out of deeper thoughts and got back to the facts. 'Anything in the shed?'

'I took some snaps in case I missed anything. It looked exactly as you'd expect. Lots of spiders and beetles. No syringes or packets of cocaine, unfortunately,' Izzy replied with a smile. 'I'll study the pictures to make sure.'

Mehmet perked up. 'We have Mrs Gibbs' phone records from trying to find the window cleaner. Let's see if there's regular traffic to and from a phone registered to a Jim or James Gibbs, and if so, pay him a visit. He may know this Jeff, his mum's boyfriend.'

They found the son. Next morning, Mehmet walked up the garden path of a neat-looking terraced house in East Horsley. When the front door was opened by a slim woman in her thirties, holding a wriggling toddler, Mehmet showed her his warrant card. 'I'm looking for Mr Gibbs.'

'He's at work at the garage at the other end of the village,' she said pleasantly. 'There's only the one, you'll probably find him underneath a car, covered in grease.'

As predicted, a greasy Jim Gibbs in blue overalls wheeled himself out on his back from under a Range Rover. Again, Mehmet introduced himself and showed his police credentials.

'Are you due a break soon, I'd like a quick chat?'

'Funny you should mention it,' the mechanic replied, getting up. 'I'm just about ready for a cuppa. Join me?'

Mehmet felt he couldn't refuse, especially after Jim (as everyone called him, he insisted) was spending an age scrubbing his hands clean at a sink near the kettle.

'It's about the death of your mum's former employer, Sir Dietrich Olson,' Mehmet began. 'Yes, it's unbelievable. Mum told us yesterday. She said a policeman had been round, asking her who else came to the house and might have been involved in the killing in some way.'

'Yes, that's it. My guvnor DI Howarth was the officer. We need to talk to everyone who knew Batts Farm and may have seen someone or something that, looking back, may be significant. That's why I'm here. By the way, I'm not getting you into trouble with your boss, am I?'

'No, you're all right,' said Jim, smiling broadly. 'I *am* the boss.'

'Well then, when you visited your mother before Christmas and in the weeks following it, when the family wasn't there, did you happen to see anyone hanging around, peering through windows, that sort of thing?'

As the kettle boiled, Jim looked thoughtful but shook his head. 'Nope. It's pretty quiet there normally, so I would have noticed. I'd have seen a car. But I didn't.'

He made two mugs of tea and passed one to Mehmet.

'How often do you pop in on Mrs Gibbs?'

Jim looked surprised. 'Not that often, really. Mum comes to us on Fridays to mind Kelly, our two-year-old. It gives Hazel, the wife, a break, a chance to do the shopping, go to the hairdresser or look in on a mate. She usually brings us a box of eggs from her hens, and she cycles over here if the weather's good. If it's not, Hazel collects her in the car. If we take Kelly to Mum's and leave her there, the bungalow gets left in a right old mess. Kelly isn't the sort of kid who's happy playing with one toy at a time. Everything has to come out on the floor with our kid. She likes pulling things out of drawers and cupboards. That doesn't go down too well with Mum. She likes everything nice and tidy.'

Mehmet asked, 'Do any other family members or friends call in on your mum, as far as you know?'

'I'm her only child, and my dad's family are all up north.' Then he grinned. 'You referring to Jeff O'Byrne, Mum's friend? She calls him her boyfriend, but I don't think it's a great passion for him, if you get my meaning.' He began to chuckle.

'What's he like, then?' Mehmet asked, as nonchalantly as he could.

'Jeff? Harmless, easy-going sort of bloke. Works in a big hardware place, near Guildford, on one of those industrial estates. There's a chain of the places. Bit like B&Q or Wickes but smaller. Forget the name.

'He did up Mum's kitchen for her last month. Painted all the doors on the units, put down new floor tiles and fitted a new worktop. Charged her not much more than the cost of the materials. Transformed it.'

'Good for him,' said Mehmet as he put down his mug. 'Why do you think he likes spending time with your mum?'

'Lonely, probably. Got no family. His wife kicked him out – not sure why, but he's not over it, apparently. Mum's easy going. And I don't think he's after her pension book, her post office savings or her hens' eggs!'

Mehmet smiled, thanked Jim and left.

He rang Izzy from the car and summarised what he'd just found out. She agreed to check out a Jeffrey or Geoffrey O'Byrne on the police computer. She was able to call him back 15 minutes later.

'If it's Jeffrey with a J, he came out of Wandsworth last summer after a six-year stretch. For dealing Class A drugs!'

Jeff O'Byrne was picked up at a branch of Hardiman's in a business park near Guildford and asked to come into the Margaret Street Station to assist the police with their inquiries. When asked for his address, Jeff said he lived in a rented flat over a newsagent in Woodbridge Hill, a 10-minute walk to work.

Izzy thanked him for coming, as though he'd really had a choice, and assured him he was not under arrest but just 'helping the police with their enquiries'. He spoke briefly to his boss, a younger man with an extraordinary stick-up hairdo, then said nothing as he followed her to her car.

In the station, she looked carefully at the ordinary-looking man in his ill-fitting salesman's suit. He had Bryl-creemed-flat hair and darting grey eyes, making him seem younger than the 48 years on his record.

'We're trying to interview everyone who has a connection of any sort with Batts Farm to try to untangle the mystery of Sir Dietrich Olson's death there just after New Year,' she said.

'Oh, yeah. I heard about it. Never met the bloke myself,' Jeff blurted out before Izzy had a chance to explain further. She nodded and smiled.

'We understand that you're friendly with Saiorse Gibbs,' she said. She was glad she'd asked a mate at Holborn, Irish custody sergeant Pat Fry, how to pronounce it. Sur-sha worked.

'Yeah, that's right. Jim, her son, brought her into the store last autumn asking about new kitchen units. He'd measured and drawn a plan. When I gave them an estimated price, they were a bit shocked, even though they wouldn't have got the units cheaper anywhere else. I suppose you're thinking, he works for Hardiman's, so he would say that, but it's true. Anyway, they decided to stick with the old cupboard units they had. Jim asked me if I knew anyone who could do a good painting and tiling job. Jim seemed like a nice bloke, down to earth, and it led to me offering to do the work for Saoirse in my spare time. I'm saving up for a new car, so a bit of extra money came in handy.'

Izzy made a bold move. 'Mrs Gibbs referred to you as her *boyfriend* last week. You and she have obviously formed a romantic relationship.'

Jeff shuffled in his uncomfortable chair. 'Well, I wouldn't

put it that way. She's quite a bit older than me. But we get on, so it doesn't seem important. She's a nice woman and she's good company. There's no one in my life at present, either. Me and the wife broke up years ago. So, sometimes I bring a pizza or a takeaway to hers and we eat it watching telly or a DVD. Sometimes we go out for a drink.'

'So, it's not a sexual relationship yet?'

'None of your fucking business!' he snapped with a force Izzy hadn't expected. *So, that's a no*, she thought. She was beginning to wonder if Mr Helpful here was one of those predators who zone in on lonely, older people and gradually take control of their finances or persuade them to sign new wills or even marry them to inherit their property.

'And how are you with the Class A drugs? Still like to dabble now and then?' she asked in the interview room.

Jeff shook his head and said nothing. Izzy would have put any money on a bet that his pulse rate had just spiked dramatically.

'Where do you live at the moment?' she asked, even though he'd already given her his address.

'I've told you. It's a flat over the newsagent near Hardiman's. I rent it. Can't afford to buy.'

'Lived there long?' Izzy asked idly, knowing that HMP Wandsworth had been his address for quite a while.

'Best rented place I had was over a chemist in Tooting. Big windows, light and airy. Janice, my ex, loved it. But some cowboy company – weird name – bought it and some others, tarted them up a bit and then sold them at a fat profit. All the chemist's staff got shafted and tenants like us got new leases at rents none of us could afford. Criminal, it was.'

'Premium Properties Six?'

'Yeah, that was it.'

'Back to Sir Dietrich, then,' Izzy said brightly. Jeff looked puzzled.

'Were you visiting Saoirse around the time of the party at the big house? The fifth of January?'

He shook his head. 'No,' he said finally. 'We had a sale on at work and it was all hands to the pump.'

'Before then, did you notice anyone hanging around, behaving oddly?'

'No. I wasn't around much then. I did a good few extra shifts at work around that time. As I said, we had a January sale on. It started before Christmas and went on until mid-January. Lots of customers.'

'Did you ever have reason to go into the shed behind the bungalow, perhaps to look for a screwdriver or something Saoirse needed?'

'No.'

'Not even when you were doing the painting and tiling?'

'I said no', he snapped, unpleasant again. 'I have a toolbox in my car, anyway.'

'So, if we were to do a fingerprint check on the shed door and the things inside, we wouldn't find any of yours?' Izzy said. Jeff looked uncomfortable.

'Same goes for places inside Batts Farm. Places near where Sir Dietrich's body was found. We've got your prints on record, you know. They don't change over the years,' she added.

'No,' he snapped again as he leaned forward, elbows on knees.

After a few minutes of cold silence, he said, 'If you're not going to arrest me, I'm free to end this conversation and leave, right?'

Izzy nodded. Jeff O'Byrne stood up to his full five-foot six height and stomped out of the interview room.

Izzy went to her desk and typed up her report. What she needed, she knew, was to find a link between Jeff and one of the other suspects. Find a time and a place where paths had crossed. Jeff hadn't been in Wandsworth at the same time as Kevin Miller. There was no obvious link between him and Steve James. He could have been a cocaine middleman or even a customer of Doug Elliott's. Was it worth a second visit to see Doug?

Izzy reckoned the chances of Doug admitting he'd had dealings with this man were infinitesimal. But it was worth making sure that Jeff's phone number wasn't on Doug's burner phone. Would there be any value in tracking down Janice, the ex-wife? Izzy couldn't think of a good enough reason to. But then she couldn't think of a good enough reason not to.

As for haughty Michael Wilson-Green, he and Jeff inhabited different worlds, even if they now did similar work, she decided.

It occurred to her that, as a first step, she should check with Jeff's boss that he was working on the afternoon of the party. If he'd been at work, she'd have no grounds to suspect him. Her phone rang. It was Mehmet, telling her that John Hardwick had agreed to go through his records to find which waiters he'd hired for the Olson party and forward their photos and any contact details.

'You never know,' Mehmet said dolefully. 'He was a bit vague when Tony Frowde grilled him a few months back. We might get lucky this time.'

'We certainly deserve a break,' sighed Izzy. There'd been

no replies to the search for an Oliver the window cleaner on the Nextdoor website.

Finally, too tired to cycle home, she walked out to find her husband's car at the back of the police station car park. She felt sure that her grey hairs had multiplied and hoped against hope that Alex had put the chicken she'd bought yesterday in the oven.

She was starving.

23

Ed was sitting at his Yamaha in the Bankside flat, thinking about his hotel job that evening. He got up and checked he had a clean shirt. An email pinged and he looked at his phone.

His tutor emailed to say that his British citizenship was 'on its way' and that he should start applying for jobs. Unmanly tears ran down his face. His Romanian brothers would have mocked him. Luckily, Tom and Bella were out, and he was alone. He flopped on the bed, Bella's bed. Handing over all his savings from his hotel work to an immigration lawyer had been worth it. When he got a proper job, he thought, he'd find a place of his own. He felt sure it would impress Bella and her family.

At the same time, Mehmet was on his way to meet John Hardwick in a branch of Costa on Esher High Street. John had been in the neat little town to see a client and had agreed to meet the DS for coffee before he headed off on to the wholesaler.

'It's about waiters,' Mehmet said as he sat down at John's table holding his flat white and a large sticky pastry.

'*My* waiters? Excellent boys, all of them,' John replied with a big smile that quickly vanished as he remembered he was talking to a policeman and not a client. 'What about them?'

'I know you've already told a colleague a bit about them. But now we're trying to talk to as many people as we can find who were at Batts Farm at the event where Sir Dietrich Olson died and see if any links between them show up.

'Sir Dietrich was quietly murdered. There was an autopsy, and it seems that someone injected him with a massive dose of cocaine. Obviously, we have to treat it seriously. Your waiters were moving around the guests and were in and out of the kitchen and in the back kitchen where the body was found.'

Shock flushed across John's face. 'Murdered? No! He just collapsed, didn't he? A heart attack?'

Mehmet was nodding. 'But the injection caused the heart attack.'

There was silence. Then John Hardwick seemed to wake up. 'I don't like what you're implying,' he said angrily. 'It couldn't have been... I mean, I interview these boys. I talk to them for at least half an hour so I can get a real impression of them. I quiz them about their health because I don't want them having an asthma attack or something like it during the event. That would kill my reputation stone dead! I check that they haven't been in trouble with the police... I realise they can lie but, even if I say it myself, I'm a good judge of character.'

Mehmet let the man calm down. 'As I said, John, we're talking to everyone, not just your team. You've kindly spoken to Tony Frowde about this once. But we're going over everything again. So, could you give me the contact details of the waiters for that party? Photographs would be really helpful too.'

John Hardwick looked affronted, as though his judgment was being questioned. Then after a little sigh and a check of his buffed fingernails, he reached inside his tailored blue tweed jacket for a zipped pocket, retrieved his phone and fiddled with it for a few moments. He asked Mehmet for an email address and then forwarded several files to it.

'That's great,' said the detective, hearing pings as the messages reached his own phone. 'Will I find photos here?'

'Some,' replied John, his composure regained. 'There were a couple of boys I hadn't used before. I'll have their details and photos at my office at home. I remember I had them in for an interview. You can't always trust everything they say in their applications, can you? If they've provided references, I call those numbers. Like I said, I'm a good judge when they're sitting a few feet away from me.'

Mehmet nodded vigorously to please him. 'And they'd have known about the event how exactly?' he asked, wiping crumbs from his chin with a napkin.

'I put it on the local Nextdoor. Anyone in the area who is on the app can contact me and send references.'

'I'd be most grateful for all the information you can dig out,' Mehmet said, standing up to leave, while clutching his cup of untouched coffee.

John looked up at him and forced a smile. 'One other thing,' he said, feeling guiltily unprofessional. 'My niece Alison, that's Alison Hardwick, my sister uses her maiden name. Alison wanted to work as a waitress. I said no because she's a bit young and really not suitable. Nice kid but not the brightest, if you get my meaning.'

Mehmet wondered where the hell he was going with this.

'But because she told me she needed to earn some cash, I let her help in the kitchen with the washing up and tidying, as that was where I could keep an eye on her. She's at that age – you know, hormones raging – and I didn't want one of the waiters coming on to her.'

He paused and looked a bit confused. Mehmet wondered if he realised he'd probably said too much.

'I have her number if you want it,' John Hardwick said.

'Yes, please, add it to the list.'

Back at the station, Mehmet read and printed out the caterer's full, quirky notes on the waiters and Alison. He looked Alison Hardwick up on the PCN and immediately saw why her uncle had been beating around the bush.

Alison had a record in the Youth Court for assaulting both her mother and a sibling. She'd received a referral order for these offences. Mehmet was about to quit the search but then saw there was a social worker's report. There was a reference to something that had apparently emerged during sessions with the Referral Panel, a process that aims to bring young offenders and their victims together for some restorative justice. Alison had seen a psychologist during these sessions and had claimed to have been sexually abused by a stranger, in a house where her uncle was catering for a party. The stranger was a delivery man. This allegation, which had not been reported to the police at the time, accounted for what seemed to be her irrational outbursts and assaults of third parties who associated with him. That's what the psychologist told the social worker and what got Mehmet puzzling.

Could Alison have seen this delivery man at the knighthood party? And could she have presumed that Uncle John and the man who owned the house – Dietrich – knew how dangerous he was? Or was she a teenage fantasist? And did it help them find the murderer?

Mehmet forwarded John's notes and his own comments on Alison to Rob and Izzy. Izzy thought she should interview the girl, and the others agreed.

Were they all thinking of the same man?

Joe Jackson?

They were.

Izzy was to interview young Alison the next day, though she knew to tread carefully because legally she was still a child.

Izzy invited her to the local coffee place. It was a difficult exchange. Her mother came too. Alison thought she was in trouble for snogging one of the waiters in the back kitchen. They'd agreed to meet the following evening outside a pub in East Horsley, but he hadn't turned up.

'Bloody students!' was Alison's conclusion, as she eyed a couple of what looked like sixth-form boys walking past.

Alison had not seen Dietrich at the party, nor at any time in the past.

Izzy decided the girl was a flirt but not a suspect.

Back at the nick, Mehmet told Izzy and Rob that three of John's young men seemed to fit Ed George's description of the waiter he'd chatted with. He said he'd ring the people named as referees to make sure they were genuine. Izzy also sent Rob a report on her interview with Jeff O'Byrne. He thought the cocaine-supplying conviction was interesting and said he was beginning to think they were making progress. The Three Musketeers were due to go to dinner at a pizza place that evening and agreed there'd be no shop talk. They almost managed it. Rob was the culprit. He compared a woman at the table next to them as looking like Penny Bryant Olson.

Izzy nearly choked on a slice of margherita. 'Are you mad? Penny's far prettier! And a hell of a lot posher!'

If she'd been telepathic, Izzy's endorsement should have been good for Pen's digestion as she ate dinner at the small vegetarian restaurant at the bottom of Kingsway, near the university. But she wasn't and her digestion wasn't the problem. The problem was the bloke sitting opposite her.

Pen had invited Francis, a long-term colleague in her department at the LSE. He taught Equity and Trusts law. She knew little about him except that he was single and not gay. It was a sort of rehearsal for a real date. God, how old-fashioned that word seemed, she thought.

Conversation was easy at first and the plant food was less boring than she'd expected. She enjoyed hearing gossip about people they worked with. Yet she could tell within minutes that Francis would never be more than a work mate.

Not only was he long-winded – Pen had to bite her tongue to stop herself finishing his sentences – but he also expressed views she found outdated and in language her own father would have used in the seventies. He described some red wine a waiter brought for him to taste as 'filthy', leaving the poor bloke to scuttle off to return with a different bottle, which Pen tasted and accepted with a gracious smile. The waiter flung a tea towel over his shoulder and walked tall back to the kitchen.

Whatever the word chemistry meant in terms of personal relationships, there was none of it between them, she realised.

Pen described the evening to Eleanor Jones, a friend who

lectured in employment law at University College. She prescribed a few blind dates and announced that she would arrange them.

'Oh no, no, no!' Pen shook her head, panicking. But a few glasses of wine later, she said she'd consider a few introductions so long as there were ground rules. She required basic information about the person, so they would need to be partially sighted rather than blind dates.

The week after the Francis event, the friends met for dinner in an unpretentious Greek restaurant near the British Museum. Eleanor said how sorry she was about Dietrich's death. Pen was guarded. She guessed that Eleanor had never much liked Dietrich and when she referred to the 'other woman', Pen realised where her friend's interest really lay.

'Don't call her that,' Pen said, quietly but firmly. 'She and I never overlapped. Dietrich and Jane split up almost immediately after they got back from their honeymoon in the summer, when they came down from Oxford. I met Dietrich a few years later. Actually, I went to see her and quite liked her.'

Eleanor's eyes widened with intrigue. 'What? You found out where she lived and just turned up and *assessed her?*'

'Yes, more or less. I asked her to fill in some of the blanks, to tell me why she'd turned up at the memorial service and what she'd wanted.'

'Apart from Dietrich's cash, you mean?' Eleanor scoffed, putting Pen on the defensive again.

'Look, everyone jumped to that conclusion. I certainly did, so did the children and our solicitor. We quickly decided she must be a fraud. Then it turned out that Jane Page-Smith *was* the first wife, and her son *was* Dietrich's child. That changed everything.

'Dietrich left no will, dammit, so I presumed, just about remembering the provisions of the 1837 Wills Act – not my field, as you know – that I'd get the first £270,000 and I'd share the rest with Bella and Tom. I was getting ready to put Batts Farm up for sale because Dietrich and I owned it as fifty-fifty Tenants in Common, and I thought I'd have to give her half of its value. And she'd automatically get half of the rest of his estate, which is considerable.'

'Got it. Then what?'

'Jane told me she didn't want or need much more than the payout from a life insurance policy Dietrich had set up. He'd already bought her and her son the house she still lives in and paid what amounted to generous alimony and child support. And she doesn't want Batts Farm. She says she just wants enough to supplement her pension if and when the insurance money runs out, some holidays and a flat for the son. She's got a partner, a job and a cat, and it all seems cosy.'

'Wow!' said Eleanor. 'This sounds like the finale you'd expect in one of those early evening television dramas where everyone ends up smiling at the camera. Can't stand 'em myself.'

Pen was silent, sipping her wine. 'I came away from Jane's house feeling a bit jealous, to tell you the truth,' she confessed. A waitress reappeared by their table, and they ordered hummus, followed by souvlaki with Greek salad.

'So? What?'

Eleanor slapped the palm of one hand on the table. 'What you need is a solvent, fifty or sixty-something bloke, who doesn't need Viagra, has his own teeth, preferably but not essentially, all his hair, a good brain and an interesting life. Yes?'

Pen smiled and added. 'And with no wife or partner still in the picture.'

Before they parted, Eleanor said, 'I can think of a couple of men you may like. I'll check them out if I can, make sure they're single before I send you their details, and if you're interested or curious, I'll think of ways to casually introduce them to you. It could turn out that none of them seem worth even talking to again.'

Pen looked sceptical.

'Better than signing up to Tinder and ending up with someone twenty years older than his photograph or getting lumbered with Mr Octopus Arms fighting to get up your jumper after five minutes,' Eleanor laughed.

They shared a taxi to their respective flats.

As promised, Pen soon found herself included in group emails inviting her to University College law faculty seminars for people who used to be thought of as high achievers. She turned up on two occasions and found herself chatting easily to a man called Nathan Harris.

According to Eleanor, Nathan was a possible fit for Pen. Now 62, he'd retired from the army with a colonel's pension a few years ago and had split from his wife fifteen years before that. He had two daughters, one still at university, the other a teacher in Zambia.

'He's lived all over the world, so he's got plenty of stories,' Eleanor assured Pen. 'Doesn't suffer fools, likes bright women. You're right up his street.'

Pen waited a few weeks then, on a Saturday afternoon, grasped the nettle and rang the number Eleanor had given her. Nathan was expecting her call. Even so, when she put the phone down, she was too disorientated to take her hand off the receiver.

They'd agreed to meet at the Colbert restaurant near Sloane Square on the following Wednesday evening.

* * *

Pen shook out her white napkin, ready to enjoy the food, if not the chat. Nathan had arrived early and had been waiting for her, wine ordered. She cut to the quick. How ex was his ex-wife?

'She found army life difficult,' he said. 'She's an artist and felt she was never taken seriously outside the UK. And she couldn't make many friends among the other wives. Only a few of them had ever worked. It was a miserable time for both of us. Divorce was inevitable.'

He studied his hands, then took a piece of bread from the small basket on the table.

'Now I'm back in London – for good – living in the little house in Finsbury Park I bought after the divorce and before I was deployed to Cyprus. You wouldn't believe it, but having it freshened up after the tenants left and getting furniture, paintings and things out of storage after so long is damn hard work,' he sighed.

Pen gave him a brief outline of her life, omitting Dietrich's name and the fact he'd been murdered and posthumously found to have been a bigamist. The sudden cardiac arrest diagnosis was useful.

The day before, thinking ahead to the 'date', she'd decided on a lawyer's plain navy dress, cheered up with a large, cream-coloured silk scarf. She searched her jewellery box for her favourite earrings, small rubies ringed with tiny diamonds. They weren't there. The last time she wore them was at Christmas. She hadn't chosen them for the knighthood party because her dress was green. She'd worn pearl studs instead.

Must have left them in Batts Farm! she thought and resolved to go there one weekend soon to collect them as well as clothes, shoes and a few other items. It would be the first time since the party. It occurred to her that selling the property and buying a new, smaller weekend home would be a good idea. She'd ask the children.

She and Nathan had arranged to meet when he returned from seeing the younger daughter in Edinburgh. He'd telephone her, he'd said. She wondered if she would in fact hear from him and decided she'd survive the snub if he didn't call.

A barn owl was hooting as she parked her Volvo in the Batts Farm parking area. Or she thought it was a barn owl. She was glad she'd asked Mrs G to put on the heating the day before, although the house was hardly warm.

Upstairs, she looked at the bed, unused since the eve of the party. Mrs G had changed the sheets, of course. Still, getting into it was another test. She must have passed it because she had a good night's sleep, until the twitter of a thousand birds roused her. They squawked, chirped and flapped on the branches of the garden's dozen or so trees. Few birds sang in Bloomsbury. There it was just the chatter of busy people and the hum of angry traffic. As a comedian once observed, city birds didn't sing, they coughed.

Fresh milk, butter and bread, and eggs from Mrs G's hens were in the kitchen, and there was a new pack of Colombian coffee waiting to be opened. She switched on the radio.

At ten o'clock, she began the search for her forgotten jewellery. The earrings, a matching ring, a gold chain and a couple of other items that had belonged to her mother were not in the old toilet bag kept tucked to the side of the top shelf of a linen cupboard behind piles of towels. She searched drawers, shoe boxes and a large wardrobe cupboard in the main bedroom, plus a small desk Dietrich sometimes used. No luck.

She rang Tom and explained the disappearances. 'Is it worth reporting this to DI Howarth?' she asked. Tom said he'd have a word with Bella and call back.

Bella made the return call. 'Yes, Mum, it certainly *is* worth reporting. I remember those lovely earrings. You let me borrow them a few times. You can claim on insurance and try to replace them, of course, but it's important you tell the police because it suggests someone nipped upstairs while the party was going on. Perhaps it was the man who stole Dad's watch. Or the rapist. It shows that one of them did more than spend a few minutes eating bacon rolls in the kitchen before leaving, as they said they had. Perhaps Dad saw them and... well, who knows?'

Pen wandered around chilly Batts farm, deciding that selling it and buying somewhere smaller and warmer would definitely be the way forward.

On Monday, she emailed an account of the lost property and the possible implications to Rob. She also attached photographs of the missing pieces, taken years earlier for insurance purposes. She asked if they had an inventory of the items Kevin took to his fence. If so, perhaps they could check if anything matched them.

Rob forwarded the emails to Mehmet and Izzy and suggested they meet at the end of the day to discuss next steps.

24

AT THE TOP of Izzy's jobs' list for the day was to finish off her checks into Jeff O'Byrne. She rang his manager at Hardiman's asking to see him confidentially. Usefully, Jeff was due to be measuring a client's kitchen the next morning and so wouldn't spot her coming into the showroom.

When she took a seat opposite Phil Cullum, alias Mr Sticky-Up Hair, he had Jeff's file on his desk and was ready to summarise what it showed.

'Jeff had worked in a branch of Hardiman's in South Wimbledon near Tooting, near where he'd lived with his wife,' he explained. 'Apparently, she was furious when he decided to move out of Tooting – said she didn't want to leave her friends and give up her job to go to what she called the middle of nowhere – and she started divorce proceedings the following year.

'After that, because he didn't have a wife and kiddies to think about, he was a very useful member of my team. Didn't need time off in school holidays and was always willing to cover when we were short staffed.'

Izzy noted it down. 'You wouldn't have a record of whether he was working on Saturday the fifth of January this year?' she asked, as casually as she could.

Phil turned to his computer, and a few moments later said, 'No, he was due to work but called in sick. That wasn't like him. Luckily, he'd recovered by the Monday because we were very busy with our winter sale and everything.'

Izzy went back to the office and reread the notes of her interview with Jeff. He'd spoken of a flat over a chemist shop. She began ringing pharmacists in Tooting and asking about former tenants of the flats above them. By a stroke of luck, a pharmacist at a chemist in Tooting Broadway, near the tube station, remembered they had kept a yellowing pile of bills and other letters addressed to a Mr Jeff O'Byrne and a Mrs Janice O'Byrne in their back room. He presumed they'd been the previous occupants of the flat.

Tooting Police Station had just closed for the evening, so Izzy told the pharmacist that she or a colleague would call in the following day to collect Mr O'Byrne's post, hopeful that it might give a clue to Janice's current whereabouts. Later that day, she spotted a clearly bored constable reading a newspaper. She gave him the chemist's address and explained what he had to collect. The next morning, a bag containing yellowing letters held together by an elastic band was on her desk.

Usefully, a letter from a gym where Mrs O'Byrne was a member was among them. Izzy rang them and discovered that Janice had transferred to a different branch of the chain in Balham.

Izzy thought about visiting the Balham gym but decided her chances of finding Janice or getting her address at the reception weren't good. She picked up a phone, called the gym and asked to be put through to the secretary. She explained who she was and politely requested that the secretary contact this member and ask her to telephone DS Holland of Guildford Police.

Within the hour, Janice rang. Izzy explained calmly that nothing awful had happened. They agreed to meet at six that evening outside Balham underground station.

'Jeff was furious when we received notice to quit the flat,' Janice said, as she sipped a cappuccino at the station's AMT coffee shop. Izzy noted how much younger than Jeff she looked.

'He rang up the company that was buying the chemist and gave them what for. Did him no good, of course. Our tenancy agreement was out of date, and they were giving us three months' notice, which is all they needed to do. If we'd stayed, they said they'd modernise the place, but we found out the rent would be about three times what we'd been paying. Even though we were both working, me as a secretary for a firm of accountants, Jeff at Hardiman's, we couldn't have afforded it. All the chemist's staff were out on their ears. Dreadful it was. Bloody unfair. Jeff kept ringing the directors of the company and making stupid threats.

'In the end, he went to their offices, in somewhere like Holborn or Camden, and waited for this director, a man called Olson, to arrive. When he did, he just told Jeff that he'd been given three months to find other accommodation, to go to the council or move out of London. Said he'd call the police if Jeff didn't stop complaining. Wasn't a bit sympathetic, apparently. Mind you, Jeff was threatening to do him over, so it wasn't surprising.'

Izzy agreed with her. But did she think Jeff had murdered Dietrich Olson all those years later?

No, she didn't.

25

DURING HIS TIME as a journalism student, Will had a yellow Post-it note taped to his computer that repeated the maxim of a former deputy editor of *The Times*: 'Ask yourself why is this lying bastard lying to me?' He was sure Jon Snow took that approach.

He'd survived two periods of work experience, even though each time the prospect had depressed him for weeks beforehand. The thought of a fortnight in the newsroom of the awful *Daily Mail* had kept him awake at night. To his relief, it'd turned out the journalists weren't *all* scary right-wingers; they were just under daily pressure from their news desk colleagues to produce copy to fit the headlines someone dreamed up at that morning's conference. Not filing the words before the deadline meant being sworn at and threatened with the sack, or, at the very least, the punishment of having to doorstep hostile people for comments they'd not want to give. Reporters needed to grow hard shells.

Will had come to admire several of the reporters he shadowed, for their quick thinking and good research and writing skills.

One female features writer told him, 'You just need to read your notes or listen to the tape recording and write it up. Don't think about time, just do it. If you get a couple of sub editors to fall in love with you, they'll polish up your words so they read like poetry.'

'Sounds like the title of a romcom – The Sub Who Loved Me,' he'd replied.

His two weeks at Radio London doing background research for presenters and watching them juggle phone-in interviews with idiot listeners was lighter work. Again, he realised that several of the well-known voices belonged to people who were a great deal smarter than they seemed on air. It was a shock, akin to discovering that Noel Edmonds was not just a vain, annoying little prick with a child's sense of humour, but a grown-up who totally understood the medium and the audience.

After sitting his finals, Will had to make another decision about what to do.

He wasn't ready – or rather couldn't be bothered – to start sending his CV to the BBC or Sky News. His new girlfriend had told him she wanted to improve her Italian and fancied a spell in Rome. Off she went, leaving him in an empty flat in Bethnal Green to do what? A bit of research?

The easiest thing was just to stay put and do a master's degree at City University. Not at all hard. No stack of books to read in advance. All he had to do was to think of a title, waffle away for about 15,000 words and ... ta-da! It wasn't as if he had to worry about paying the rent or the tuition fees. The Bank of Dietrich would take care of that.

A master's wouldn't tax his strength, he reckoned. He'd

learned investigative techniques as an undergrad and there was a chance that after he wrote the dissertation, stuck on some headlines, sub heads, photographs and captions, he could get it published in a paper or magazine. He also visualised the book that would follow, and he really liked the thought of putting 'author' on his Linked-In profile.

So, what would the thing be about?

Unlike the journalists he'd shadowed, he wasted time. Days, weeks and months were spent thinking and over-thinking, drinking coffee or beer and nattering with pals. Suddenly, the deadline for producing the damn thing was looming. He felt as if a large foot was pushing down on him.

* * *

Rob also felt a large foot squashing the joy from his life. He was late arriving in CID at Margaret Street. Mehmet was about to crack his usual 'and what time do you call this?' joke as the boss appeared just after nine-thirty. Then he spotted the thunder face.

Mehmet wasn't to know that the boss had had another argument with Elizabeth about a second baby. She wanted to take on more work at King's College, where she taught history. With a higher salary, she believed the bank would allow a £10,000 overdraft for another round of IVF treatment. Rob thought she – they – were under enough pressure without her taking on more work.

On top of that, there was the aggro Rob was getting from his boss.

'Malden thinks we're skiving, that we're sitting around drinking tea, looking at Facebook or discussing what we watched on telly.' Rob almost spat out the words. The bitterness in his voice alarmed Izzy and Mehmet. Mehmet noted that Rob wasn't blaming them, his subordinates, as other gaffers might. It was 'we' who were in trouble.

'He says we've failed to make any progress in finding Dietrich Olson's killer – and he's right, we bloody *have* failed – so he says we should get our arses back to Holborn and earn our wages.'

Mehmet, who had to buy most of his clothes online from brands catering for tall men with long arms and legs, studied his shirt cuffs, which pleasingly reached to his wrists.

Izzy twiddled a strand of hair and pulled at a loose thread in her jacket. Long minutes passed.

'My money's on Michael Wilson-Green. I think we should think about charging him.

'We can cross off Disgusting Doug and rapist Joe – even if he did assault or try to assault little Alison Hardwick – and Steve and Jeff O'Byrne. At least I can.'

Her colleagues agreed with her. More or less.

'Kevin's a thief, not a murderer,' Izzy resumed. 'Wilson-Green had by far the strongest motive, the best opportunity and more sense than the others...' Her words trailed off. She hadn't planned to make a choice.

Mehmet muttered 'this is crap' under his breath and looked at Izzy as if she were an idiot. A girl idiot.

'Look, we know that no one is more dangerous than someone with nothing more to lose,' Izzy muttered. 'And Wilson-Green lost it all years ago.'

Finally, Rob spoke. 'Explain. You changed your mind. Why?'

Izzy stayed silent.

'Why? Come on. Spit it out!'

'Yes, OK. I took him for an upper-class twit who was

jealous of what his friend had achieved in life. Then I thought of him flogging kitchen cupboards in Fulham, a bit like Jeff O'Byrne does in Hardiman's. It's a colossal come-down for him.

'His motive wasn't *just* jealousy. Dietrich Olson wrecked Wilson-Green's whole life when he tipped off the Financial Conduct Authority about the First Domestic Appliances fraud. They'd been friends since school. It was a massive betrayal. And for all his suave performance of shrugging this off when I talked to him, I sensed a deep wound.

'Yeah, I know he's got a nice enough flat and a steady job, even if he thinks it's beneath him, but compared with what he had before and, more importantly, compared with what Dietrich had – wealth, status, celebrity, a lovely wife and kids – Wilson-Green's been socially down and out and slumming it for years.'

'But that's not enough to plan a murder,' Mehmet scoffed.

'He wanted his revenge, don't you see?' Izzy said. 'Because he thinks Dietrich blew the whistle to save his own neck. Wilson-Green tried hard to work on ways to relaunch himself. He had to ask for money to get started. Beg, almost. But Dietrich kept turning a deaf ear to Michael and rejecting his ideas.'

'But I thought you were on to something with the house-keeper's boyfriend,' said Mehmet. 'Didn't you find out he lied about working on the day of the party? Didn't his ex-wife add something?'

Izzy shook her head.

'And the bloke whose father bought a worthless flat from the property company Dietrich Olson started...' Mehmet continued.

Izzy shifted in her seat. 'Jeff O'Byrne and Steven James,

you mean? Both of them were and probably still are mightily pissed off about Dietrich's dirty dealings all those years ago, that's true. Neither would vote for him. But kill him? No. What Dietrich did to them wasn't personal, so their possible motives don't seem strong enough to me. Not compared with Wilson-Green's.'

Rob was a long way from being convinced. 'I still don't buy it, Izz. Because Wilson-Green had lost so much and blamed it on someone he thought of as his best friend, you're saying he somehow acquired a syringe of cocaine and jabbed Dietrich at the party without anyone noticing?'

Sarcastic now. Didn't suit him. But Izzy had expected something like it.

'Kevin was stupid enough to tell us he'd met Wilson-Green at a court. What if they'd been in touch and Wilson-Green had asked Kevin to inject Dietrich?

'Kevin's certainly quick enough on his feet to do it. The Rolex watch, which Michael knew Dietrich always wore, was probably Kevin's fee.'

Mehmet spoke now, condescension dripping from every word. 'Izzy, what ifs aren't evidence. It's just theory, and a far-fetched one at that. If you think that's enough to charge him, you're barmy. Scott David and Simon Guerrier-Belmont will fall about laughing.'

Izzy paused then took a deep breath. 'Thanks for mansplaining, Mehmet. I didn't say it *was* evidence. I'm not an idiot! We should start looking for evidence to arrest him. Search Wilson-Green's place in Disraeli Road for any trace of drugs paraphernalia. Get forensics on to his phone records to see if he's been talking to Kevin.'

The men nodded. Rob picked up the phone.

They got a search warrant easily enough but didn't tell

Wilson-Green they'd be searching his home, which would give him time to hide things. The two constables who'd been despatched to Disraeli Road quickly reported they'd found nothing in any of the flat's kitchen cupboards, and the chest of drawers in the bedroom held only clothes. His shoes weren't home to packets of cocaine and the medicine cabinet in the bathroom contained just shaving foam, razor blades, Elastoplast, TCP and packets of paracetamol.

'Damn, damn, damn,' Izzy muttered.

She spoke to one of the constables, mainly to be reassured that they'd left the flat exactly as they found it. She planned to persuade Mehmet to go back with her for a second visit. The search warrant hadn't got 'one use only' printed on it. It would be a legal second search, she explained.

To her surprise, Mehmet agreed. He liked picking front door locks.

Off they went the next morning and, after checking that the suspect was at work by driving past the kitchen design shop and spotting him in his cubbyhole, proceeded through Putney High Street then left into Werter Road, then Disraeli Road, parking much farther down from Wilson-Green's flat.

Inside, Izzy checked behind books on shelves and under lampshades. They felt under drawers and behind pictures for small packages attached with tape. Lastly, they tackled the bathroom. Nothing was hidden in the lavatory cistern, as it so often is in crime films, but when Mehmet unscrewed the bath panel and rummaged around at the back with his long arms, he located a cashbox whose lock could easily be broken. Inside were small trays containing plastic bags of white powder, almost certainly cocaine, three brown plastic bottles and syringes with needles of different sizes, probably bought at Boots or through the internet. There was also a burner mobile phone, some women's jewellery, including a pair of diamond and ruby earrings, and a couple of old photographs of Dietrich and his family.

'Persistence pays!' Mehmet gave Izzy a hug.

A digital search of the burner phone later revealed calls to Kevin. A full, detailed report would soon be on its way.

Rob didn't wait but called in to Roger Malden's office the next morning with the news. It went down well. Then he took his Dietrich Death File to the CPS office of Simon Guerrier-Belmont.

They greeted each other as the old friends they were. Simon Guerrier-Belmont, mocked by the cops for his habit of sniffing and struggling to pull his black robe back over his shoulder in court because, voluminous though the robe was, it hardly covered his Rumpolian tum, was genuinely pleased to share coffee again with the copper he considered the brightest of the bunch.

Before Rob began, Simon summoned Scott David, his number two, to join them. The young and (according to several female lawyers) most sexy barrister in London – a sort of English Sidney Poitier – his hair now cropped stylishly short, pulled up a chair, took out a notebook and unscrewed a fountain pen. Barristers don't *do* Biros.

Rob gave them a potted version of the story: rich politician, philanthropist, joker, everyone's idea of Mr Nice Guy, holds big party in his weekend house to celebrate being awarded a knighthood in the New Year's Honours. He's found in a heap in his wine store, quite dead, before his wife can call for the toast.

The official cause of death is 'sudden cardiac arrest'. The family is certain that there was more to it and arranges for the body to be exhumed and a private autopsy. It reveals the presence of a massive dose of cocaine, the sign of a jab on one thigh. The only conclusion: unnatural death.

'We looked at possible suspects, people who were guests and others at the house for one reason or another,' Rob explained. 'This man, Michael Wilson-Green, who was a guest, is our favourite because of his long history with the dead man.'

'Motive?'

'Historical. Revenge. They were schoolfriends, set up a couple of companies, earned a lot of money from them. The future looked rosy. But apparently Dietrich double-crossed Wilson-Green, who was investigated for fraud. Olson watched him bankrupt himself to pay the heavy fine. Wilson-Green was also banned from taking on any new directorships, was promptly divorced, kicked out of the family home, hardly ever saw his kids and had to work humble jobs as a salesman just to survive. So, he became bitter, especially when he put up new business ideas to Dietrich, which were turned down flat. More humiliation. Dietrich's knighthood was probably the last straw.'

Rob then explained the link with Kevin Miller, a persistent thief and former drug dealer, who was already charged and almost certain to be convicted of stealing a Rolex watch from Dietrich's corpse. The phone calls between the two were evidence of conspiracy. Then he explained Izzy and Mehmet's treasure hunt and the box under the bath.

The well-nourished senior barrister listened, sipped the last of his coffee, sniffed, pulled the waistcoat down over his pin-striped paunch and looked at Scott, who nodded.

'Charge him then, Rob.'

26

In the showroom, Izzy quietly recited the caution: 'Michael Wilson-Green, I am arresting you on suspicion of the murder of Dietrich Olson on the fifth of January this year at Batts Farm, Godalming. You do not have to say anything, but it may harm your defence if you do not mention something when questioned that you later rely on in court. Do you understand?'

She and the detective constable she'd pulled from his desk in CID allowed their startled arrestee to grab his raincoat but spared him the indignity of having handcuffs clicked on in front of customers as they marched him to their car outside.

In the interview room, Michael Wilson-Green's heart was thumping. He was in the middle of a nightmare. That must be it. Not real life. He'd wake up from it, soon.

A white-bearded Indian duty solicitor sat by his side on the metal chairs as DI Robert Howarth and DS Isobel Holland sat opposite, each tidying a few papers in front of them. It was a well-rehearsed choreography to help unnerve a suspect.

Mehmet watched from the adjourning room, behind the one-way glass window. The suspect had been advised by the solicitor to answer 'no comment' to all the questions. 'We have to find out what their case is based on,' the duty solicitor had said.

'We've conducted a search of your flat in Disraeli Road,' Rob announced.

Wilson-Green struggled not to show his fear. He thought miserably about the photographs, the ruby and diamond earrings and the gold necklace he liked to take out and hold to his cheek, sure he could still smell the scent she wore.

The following day, at Wimbledon Magistrate's Court, an unremarkable two-storey red brick building backing onto train tracks, Michael Wilson-Green pleaded not guilty to the murder charge. Because of the gravity of the offence, the case was sent to Kingston Crown Court and a hearing was arranged for two days later. From there, he was sent to HMP Wandsworth. He'd thought the FCA's investigation into First Domestic Appliances was pure hell. But this was the beginning of what were to be the worst weeks of his life.

An agency reporter slumped on the bench at Kingston Crown Court had woken from his reverie to the importance of what he was supposed to be noting down in shorthand.

Murder. Dietrich Olson.

He was out in the corridor in minutes and on his mobile to the news desks of several daily papers.

Guessing this would happen, Rob got Izzy to bring Pen, Tom and Bella Olson to the Holborn nick that evening to fill them in.

'We've charged Michael Wilson-Green with the murder

of Sir Dietrich,' Rob said flatly. 'He's being held on remand at Wandsworth Prison. A reporter was in the court, so the story is likely to break in the papers.'

Pen, who'd been clenching every muscle to avoid showing a reaction, managed a small nod. She sat still and kept her gaze fixed high on the wall above Rob's head. Tom and Bella were silent.

'I can't believe it,' Tom said finally. 'You've made a big mistake. How could it benefit Michael to kill our father? They were school friends, practically brothers. He'd been to dinner with us loads of times. We knew he'd been through a rough patch and was broke, but he was muddling through. He was continually suggesting new schemes to Dad that Dad didn't want to be associated with. We felt sure Michael would eventually think up something Dad *would* agree to.

'With Dad dead, Michael would never get any backing from anyone. So, the idea that he killed his only hope of getting going again doesn't make sense.'

Rob said quietly but firmly, 'We've gone into this carefully and, as you know, the CPS doesn't go ahead with a case unless it's in the public interest to do so, and they believe they have more than a fifty per cent chance of winning. That's what they believe is the situation here. The evidence is conclusive.'

Back at the Bankside flat, Tom and Bella ate a Thai takeaway at the small, round table. Tom sipped a bottle of lager. He and Bella had agreed not to discuss Michael's arrest until they'd each had a chance to digest its implications.

Eventually, Tom thought of another topic of conversation. 'So, now that Ladyship Jane Page-Smith has said she isn't interested in Batts Farm, does Mum go ahead and sell it?' he asked.

'Do *we* still want to go there?' Bella replied. 'Mum wouldn't let it go if we objected. I've so many happy memories of birthday parties there. And all those winter weekends with log fires – the living room filling with smoke until we found a chimney sweep. Do you remember?

'Then there were the summers in the garden, the rickety tree house Vince made us, me splashing you in that big plastic swimming pool that took so long to fill. Chasing the hens—'

'Then Dad was murdered there,' Tom said, totally wiping away any nostalgia. They fell silent again.

Tom moved from the table to look at the river in the late spring twilight while resting his elbows on the windowsill.

'I doubt she'll sell Batts Farm before the case is closed,' Bella said. 'None of us believes Michael killed Dad, and that means the police will have to continue the investigation after the jury acquits him, which I bet they will. Effectively, it's still a crime scene. We could be having this same discussion in five years' time.'

At the hospital the next morning, students in Tom's year group received their timetable for their forthcoming exams. After three years, Tom should have been used to the relentless series of tests and assessments medical students endure. He wasn't, though. Thank God for resits.

He decided to collect a few files and books from Bankside, pack his laptop along with some underwear, socks and a couple of T-shirts, leave a note for Bella and head off to Batts Farm in Dietrich's old Volvo. His little Ford Fiesta had failed its MOT and had been towed to a scrapyard two months earlier, so the Volvo was now resident in one of the narrow garages by the side of the Bankside flats. He managed somehow to squeeze his legs into the driving seat without scratching the door on the garage wall. The car started with one turn of the key, and it even had petrol in its tank.

'Thanks, Dad', he muttered.

He headed off for the A3, telephoning Mrs Gibbs on the way to tell her to expect him.

He woke the next morning, in the bedroom he'd occupied since before he went to prep school, to the sound of cupboard doors downstairs being opened and shut. He shuffled down in an old dressing gown of his dad's.

Mrs G had arrived with eggs, milk and a pot of home-made marmalade. She'd also defrosted a loaf of bread from the freezer.

'You're looking well, Tom. How's Bella and your poor mum? She seemed all right when I saw her the other week, but...'

Tom rubbed his eyes, yawned and did his best to reassure her that they were all getting over the shocking news of their father's killing. He told her that a trial was coming up, but that in his and Bella's opinion, it wouldn't be the end of the matter.

'It's still a mystery. Dad didn't have enemies as far as any of us knew. But he had such a full life.

'I suppose the police have grilled you, asked about who comes to the house when we're in London?'

'Oh yes,' Mrs G replied. 'They're being ever so thorough! I told them that Jim, my son, visits here occasionally, when he brings little Kelly of a Friday. Vince, the gardener, used to come regularly, as you'll remember. Got terrible bad knees now, poor chap. I haven't found a replacement so the garden's not going to look too tidy this summer.

'There's my pal, Jeff, who pops in here once or twice a week to keep me company. That young detective girl has been along to see him at his work; she even had him go to the police station in Guildford for questioning. Really embarrassing for him. Lot of nonsense, he said.'

Tom nodded, feigning sympathy.

'There's the nice window cleaner who'd been here a few times. Wish he'd phone to make another appointment. The windows could do with a good clean.'

She went on to repeat what she'd told the DI, about how she'd once left the young stranger on his own while she went to the back kitchen for fresh water for his bucket.

'Helpful young chap! Told me to call him Ol, like his friends do.'

Tom nodded, curious, so she continued.

'When Mrs Olson ordered a new fridge freezer, John Lewis delivered one the next week. But would they take away the old one? No, they bloomin' well would not. Ooh, I was *so* cross! So, when Ol was here the next day, I told him about it. Straight away he started moving the old fridge up from the back kitchen and putting it outside for the council to collect. Ever so strong, he is.'

Tom thanked her for the food, and she hurried away. He thought about this young knight with a shining bucket and sponge. He wasn't sure why, but figured it was an excuse not to think about biochemistry or pharmacology.

After breakfast, he tried to knuckle down to his revision. He was reasonably confident as far as the biochemistry papers were concerned. The three-hour pharmacology exam, on the other hand, kept him awake at night. He'd paid little attention in the lectures, concentrating instead on Danielle, a girl in his group who'd been to the pub with him a few times. And he hadn't learned enough about the interactions between some of the most important drugs. Today, he could find nothing helpful on the internet. He'd not brought the right textbooks and realised he'd need to go back to London and study in the King's College library. Shit! The one upside was that he could nobble Ludo for tips on those exams – that's if Ludo could remember taking them two years earlier.

Meanwhile, Bella had asked her friend at law school to grab her copies of any course material from the lectures she was going to miss. She'd also told her personal tutor she'd be absent to attend the trial of someone charged with her father's murder. The experience would enlarge her understanding of criminal law litigation, the tutor said. But that was just one of her three elective subjects. She'd have to bone up on the lectures she'd be missing in the other two.

The roads were empty on Tom's way back and he parked the Volvo in Bankside and dashed up to the fourth floor with less than an hour to search for the textbooks and notes he needed. He raided the fridge for leftovers, began reading on the sofa and must have dozed off as the skies darkened.

The jingle of keys in the flat's front door and the clomp of his rucksack hitting the hall floor signalled Ed's arrival and jolted Tom back to life. Bella's boyfriend had been playing piano in the American Bar at the Savoy, where a group of Yanks had asked him to play the 'Frank Sinatra Songbook' as they leaned on the piano and crooned along.

'Good songs, I suppose,' Ed admitted. 'A lot by Cole Porter and Burt Bacharach. But they couldn't sing, so not that exciting for me. Big relief when they decided to go in search of a late dinner, which meant I could leave. They left a £50 note tip on the piano, so I shouldn't grumble, I suppose.

'Hey, now that I'm a British citizen, grumbling is normal, isn't that right?'

'It's obligatory,' said Tom, while collecting his files and

books before his sister discovered the mess. By now it was getting late, so he decided not to drive back to Batts Farm.

Bella had decided to work on her latest assignment in the college library, and she arrived at the flat ready for a glass of wine and whatever she could find to eat. It was late as the three headed for their beds. Bella paused and grabbed Tom's arm.

'You asked Rob Howarth what Michael could possibly gain from killing Dad, but you know what that was, don't you?'

Tom stared at her.

'He'd get Mum. Or at least he thought he would. He's always loved her. You only had to look at his face when he was near her.'

Tom nodded.

27

THE FIFTH OF June was set to be the first day of Michael Wilson-Green's trial at Guildford Crown Court in Bedford Road, around the corner from the police station and a short walk from the train station. Because the witness list was short, the trial was estimated to last only two weeks. Bella knew nothing much would happen on the first day but went to size up the counsel, judge and jurors.

Oh dear! she thought, looking at a court building that would have made an architect's heart sink. It was as unlike the Old Bailey as you could get. No vaulted ceilings in the hall, no marbled walls, no gold-painted statue of Lady Justice on its roof, no notorious old prison in the basement. No drama to it at all. Instead, a redbrick construction, perfect for a 1980s supermarket.

The inside of Court One was a pleasant surprise, though. Its unchipped wooden benches were better and brighter than the Bailey's scratched mahogany ones.

A notice outside told her that the judge was to be Her Honour Lady Beatrix Delauney, a 'red robe judge' who dealt with serious criminal matters. That meant she could wear a short bench wig rather than the longer droopy ones that make judges look like superannuated spaniels.

Counsel for the prosecution was Simon Guerrier-Belmont, as DI Howarth had warned Tom and Bella. Not the old duffer he might appear to be but a man who thought of a trial as a game of chess; an 'excellent operator'. He described junior counsel Scott David as 'sharp'.

What Rob hadn't told them was that Simon had confided that he wasn't confident they'd win. For technical reasons.

Michael's defence barrister was Jacqueline Guy, QC. Bella looked her up and discovered she was 49 and had successfully defended a whole raft of crooks. Consequently, she charged over £1,000 an hour for her services.

'Wow!' said Tom when Bella told him over the phone. 'Michael must somehow have got a mortgage on his flat, robbed a bank or sold a kidney. No, both kidneys.'

Inside the court, nothing. Silence. No jurors, no legal clerks, no one in the public gallery, no reporters on the press benches. Puzzled, Bella went outside and found an usher, who told her that the trial had been cancelled. Or rather that there was a 'continuance', but with no sign of its duration.

She was soon back on a train to Waterloo, heading for Holborn Police Station where Rob had agreed to meet her.

'What happened?' she asked angrily.

Rob had been planning to explain to Bella, Tom and Penny, but the decision to postpone had been made only at eight that morning, when Simon Guerrier-Belmont and Scott David had presented a motion to the judge in her chambers. They had decided that the prosecution had insufficient evidence at this stage and the case had to be dismissed.

On the previous Friday, in their Petty France offices,

Simon Guerrier-Belmont had been reading Scott's notes on Michael Wilson-Green and his reversal of fortune. Scott had been to Kingston Crown Court for his committal hearing to watch him in the dock.

'He's tall, elegant, receding hair. Think of actors like Charles Dance or that Scottish one who used to be in the James Bond films,' Scott reported, forgetting that his boss didn't go to the cinema or watch TV. 'Plummy voice, good shirts. The jury will consider him a proper gent and probably like him. Jacqueline Guy will make sure of that.'

'And, in a nutshell, why didn't he succeed like his friend Olson?' Simon asked.

'Three reasons. Not as clever. Scraped a lower second at York. Nor as forward thinking. Nor as brazen in puffing up his talents to rich businessmen as Dietrich Olson apparently was – convincing them they should pay him generously to advise them on estate planning or something when he knew bugger all about it.'

Simon smiled.

'And Wilson-Green was greedy as well as foolish. The First Domestic Appliances fiasco, for example. Bigging up the value of the company with a whole pack of lies! He was the CEO, and it seems it was entirely his idea, as far as I can make out. The truth would have surfaced soon enough with or without the whistleblowing that he apparently thinks was down to Dietrich.'

'What's this about a property company he and Dietrich Olson ran?' Simon asked.

'I had a long conversation with DS Holland about that,' Scott replied. 'Look under tab six in the bundle.

'Izzy Holland interviewed Steven James because he was

at the Olson party and had shared a cottage with Kevin Miller, the burglar slash drug dealer Wilson-Green had phoned. James's father had bought one of those expensive riverside flats in Wandsworth a few years ago. Premium Properties Six, Dietrich's and Wilson-Green's company, was the original developer and they've refurbished a few of the flats as some short leases expired. It was the Grenfell Tower story again. No cladding this time but no fire insulation nor other safety measures such as fire detectors or fire escapes. So, the flat owners are facing huge costs to make them safe. More than the flats are probably now worth.

'Wilson-Green resigned from the company some years ago and is apparently bitter that Dietrich Olson made millions from it when he didn't. He even had to resign as a director because of the FDA sanctions. But he could have done a bit of low-grade property development on his own, had he chosen to, and worked it up to make himself a decent living. He had plenty of experience but not a scrap of initiative.'

Simon nodded, sniffed, sat back, then slowly put one foot then the other up on the desk. 'So, the strongest physical evidence against him is the drugs stuff found at his Putney flat and the record of phone conversations with Kevin Miller?' he asked.

'Our theory is that he got Kevin to source and sell him the cocaine. Wilson-Green may have been doing a little dealing on the side – possibly with Kevin as his supplier and the person who passed on clients' details. Kevin's remanded on bail and is likely to be found guilty of snatching a Rolex from Dietrich Olson's corpse. That could have been his fee for being Wilson-Green's accomplice.

'Snatching a watch from a dead or dying man is a serious matter, of course. So, I think we should concentrate on the syringe of cocaine intended to kill Sir Dietrich at the party.

'We'll issue a summons for Kevin Miller, hoping he'll be stupid enough to come to court and say things that implicate him in a murder,' Scott continued.

'Surely his solicitor would warn him of the dangers?' Simon was having serious doubts.

Scott shrugged. 'He's not the sharpest, but still...'

'So, our story will be that Wilson-Green arrived at this house – Batts Farm, which he knew well – used a bathroom upstairs ostensibly to change his shirt and left the syringe in, for argument's sake, a cupboard under the washbasin,' said Simon. 'Later, Kevin, who helped deliver some hired furniture for the party, nipped up there, collected it, waited for the opportunity to jab it in Dietrich's leg then shoved him in the wine store after pulling off his watch.'

'Yep.'

'Hmmm.'

The men looked at each other, knowing it would be a lot for a jury to accept. Especially as they had no actual evidence apart from the syringes and small packets of coke under Wilson-Green's bath. On top of that, there were serious legal problems concerning Kevin's trial for the theft of the watch.

They talked long into that Friday night. Putting his doubts aside, Simon read through his opening, bade goodnight to his junior, grabbed his ancient green Loden overcoat, and went out and looked for the minicab he'd ordered to take him to his Hampstead home. On Sunday morning, he was on the phone to both Rob and Scott with his decision.

Early on Monday, Simon stood in a book-lined room in

front of a surprised judge and alongside a slightly flustered Jacqueline Guy.

'Your Honour, I regret to say that the prosecution has come to the conclusion that, despite our earlier decisions, our evidence is not strong enough to support the murder charge. We would therefore like to adjourn the trial for six months. The defendant's counsel does not oppose this motion.'

Jacqueline Guy nodded.

Beatrice Delauney frowned.

'Our main witness, Kevin Miller,' Simon continued, 'is currently on remand awaiting trial for aggravated theft, for stealing a valuable watch from the wrist of the victim here, Sir Dietrich Olson.

'He is alleged to have snatched it when Sir Dietrich collapsed and was probably in the process of dying. Whatever the outcome of that matter, it is an active case and, of course, under the law of contempt, Miller cannot be properly questioned or cross-examined here without me or Ms Guy creating a substantial risk of serious prejudice to the course of justice in Miller's case.

'The prosecution's second witness is Brian Dunne, a former director of the company of which the defendant was one of the bosses. He'd been a director of First Domestic Appliances, one of the six suspended by the Serious Fraud Office after Michael Wilson-Green issued a public warning that the company had overstated its profits by about £400 million. It caused sales to drop and the company's share price to plummet. These facts are central to the prosecution's case.

'Dunn's testimony, it turns out, would be that he and the other directors firmly *believed* that Dietrich Olson, a former director, had tipped off the SFO because he'd disapproved of

Wilson-Green's profits overstatement. He hadn't personally witnessed Olson expressing this view or seen the two arguing about it. So, it's meagre. And there's no other evidence that the two men *had* argued over the profits statement. We need time for the police to help us research this historical event.

'As the jurors have not yet been sworn in, I felt it better to serve this motion as soon as possible. Obviously, if the situation changes and stronger witness testimony can be obtained against this defendant, we will be ready to prosecute.'

Judge Beatrice Delauney sighed, looked at Jacqueline Guy for comment but received none. 'Motion accepted. Continuance of six months.'

When she heard the news from Rob, Bella knew there was a precedent, the case of R v Galbraith. It concerned a man who, in 1981, was convicted of affray at a bar near Putney Bridge. He'd joined in a fight in which three men were stabbed, one fatally. The argument of insufficient evidence worked for Mr Galbraith. As Simon and Scott predicted, it also worked for Michael Wilson-Green, the man they both still believed had murdered Dietrich Olson.

If Kevin Miller hadn't been on remand awaiting his trial, Simon could have grilled him about dragging a watch from the wrist of the dying man he'd just killed or helped to kill. He'd have suggested that, as implied by the many phone exchanges shown on Michael Wilson-Green's mobile, he had been working as an accomplice. Then the story would have been different.

A completely dazed kitchen appliances salesman left court and was soon walking from Putney station to his flat carrying a plastic bag of his possessions. It would be several weeks before the taste of prison left his mouth, and he realised that he would no longer have to endure the misery of incarceration. All he needed to do was shower, sleep, try to forget and then find another job.

As he was walking along Putney High Street in driving rain, a minicab was taking a grumpy old buffer from Guildford Crown Court back home to Hampstead.

28

In Rob's office in Guildford CID, the dejected detective told Izzy and Mehmet that the case against Michael Wilson-Green had collapsed before it'd begun.

'Yeah... a fucking nuisance. You'd have thought the drugs in his flat and the phone calls with Kevin Miller would have counted for more. What had they been talking about if it wasn't killing Olson? Whether Arsenal was going to beat Chelsea on Saturday? What they were having for dinner that night?

'Malden's not going to like it,' he went on wearily. 'He's probably already worked out how much money we've wasted. We'll get it thrown in our faces for years to come.'

As charging Wilson-Green with murder had been her idea, Izzy wondered if she should apologise to Rob and Simon and then prostrate herself at Malden's feet.

Should she suggest charging Wilson-Green with possession of Class A drugs? Common sense made her decide against doing either.

Instead, she asked, 'More digging on Jeff O'Byrne, the

housekeeper's boyfriend with a record for drug dealing and assault, then?'

Rob asked wearily, 'What've we got so far?'

'He lied about being at work on the day of the party. Not sure if or why he was at Batts Farm, but I could certainly do some research. Maybe the housekeeper got him to help her with parking the cars and he nipped into the house after that.

'Something's not right about his relationship with mumsy Mrs Gibbs. It's weird. Perhaps he's softening her up to make her leave him something in her will – if she has anything to leave, that is. I think her cottage belongs to the Olsons. And she looks hale and healthy to me. Not about to peg out.

'As for a motive for killing Olson, we've got his anger over losing his Tooting flat when Premium Properties Six asset-stripped the chemist. Apparently, he went to Olson's office in Holborn and threatened him. And there's the fact his wife left him because she didn't want to move out of London with him.

'Not enough, though, is it? Why would he wait all these years to get his revenge?' Rob asked.

'I get that. But what if he was paid to do it by someone else, someone we haven't found yet, a person with a stronger motive and enough money? That rules out penniless Wilson-Green, of course.'

Rob put Izzy out of her misery. 'Let's all go back to the files and look again into Olson's background and into the backgrounds of our original suspects. Maybe we missed a link.

'We can't blame the collapse of the trial on Simon. He did as well as anyone could with what we had. That reminds me – I need to see him.'

With that, Rob grabbed his jacket and ran off before his sergeants could say another word. From his car, he rang the CPS office to confirm that Simon and Scott were available for a short meeting. Happily, neither was the sort to head off for the golf course on a free afternoon.

When he got to their office, Rob didn't beat about the bush. 'Our failure to find Dietrich Olson's killer looks bad, makes the Chief Constable look bad. He's probably already got the leader of the Tory party giving him an earbashing.

'Until Wilson-Green's trial, there'd been very little in the papers about Olson having been murdered. Now everyone knows about it, and we look like incompetent fools for not finding the culprit, but all is not lost. I've had another idea.'

The lawyers looked at each other, showing surprise.

'It's a longshot but I'll spell it out anyway. Of our original suspects, I liked Kevin Miller, the burglar, who pulled the Rolex off dying Olson's wrist. Mouthy little shit, a proper criminal but not stupid.

'Today, I remembered that he'd been abused as a child by his stepfather Claude Pollard, a vile creature who got sent down for about 20 years after several of his child victims accused him of abusing them. It came to light at about the time Jimmy Savile, Rolf Harris and others were being exposed as paedophiles. As a kid, Kevin was definitely one of Pollard's victims, but I don't think he gave evidence.

'A couple of the witnesses – all anonymised, of course – said they were taken to a house and passed around a group of what they thought were posh men – bankers, businessmen and politicians. They took their turns to rape or abuse them physically. Horrible, horrible.'

Simon sniffed and folded his arms.

'I can't request those old files to read the victims' accounts,' Rob continued. 'But *you* can.'

A long silence followed.

'What do you want them to show?' said Simon. 'You're not implying that Dietrich Olson was one of those paedophiles, are you?'

'No. Nothing I've read about him made me think he was creepy in that way. But there could be something in one of the victim statements, something that Kevin found out and was the basis of a grievance he *might* have had against Olson. Could be something as vague as a perpetrator saying he was a friend of Olson's, or even just a fellow Tory MP.'

Simon closed his eyes and grunted. Eventually, he opened them, sat up and said, 'No. I'd need a lot more than your desperation to pull a culprit out of a hat. These files are sealed for a reason. They can't be opened on a whim. And I'm too busy to attend hearing after hearing trying to persuade a judge.'

Rob drove home to New Malden in time for a walk in Beverley Park with Jacob and Monty, the family's new Jack Russell. The boy's delight in the badly-behaved puppy made him feel slightly less of a deadbeat dad and a clueless cop.

* * *

Pen had been thinking about her lost jewellery. She hadn't yet heard from the police after asking if the stolen earrings and necklace were among the items Kevin Miller took to sell in Bristol. She thought perhaps she should cut her losses and just claim on her insurance policy. But she decided to dither a bit longer.

What she *had* decided was that she'd see the colonel

again. When she rang Nathan on Saturday morning, he suggested a trip to the Royal Horticultural Society Garden Park at Wisley, off the A3. He wanted to find a few hardy shrubs for his garden in Finsbury Park and would pick her up. Within the hour, she was stepping swiftly into the passenger seat of his Peugeot hybrid. She didn't lean over to kiss but felt that perhaps she should have.

Soon they were walking around the gardens, Pen explaining that she knew little about plants except the way certain flowers looked in vases. Luckily there were knowledgeable gardeners weeding and pruning to provide answers. They then walked towards the site's small restaurant. A table booked for Mr Harris for lunch was waiting for them.

Four shrubs for a windy garden in the car's boot, they headed back to Finsbury Park.

'It's so much bigger inside than you'd expect,' Pen said, walking into Nathan's living room.

'That's because it's really a Tardis. A dilapidated one. I hired an electrician and a plumber, but some things, like the painting, I tackled myself. And discovered I'm rubbish at it!'

Later they ate M&S smoked salmon with salad and drank Muscadet Sur Lie. Nathan said he hoped to find a job and was seeing an army consultant the following week.

'Teaching or lecturing work of some kind, perhaps. You'll have to give me tips,' he said.

'Don't wear high heels,' Pen deadpanned as she took out her phone and ordered an Uber. As the Prius pulled up, she said, 'Let's meet next week for dinner – my treat this time.' Then she kissed him lightly. And liked it. Perhaps the next kiss would be in Colt Court. And be a proper one.

29

TOM SAT the last of his exams on Friday morning.

The on-off trial of Michael Wilson-Green had been an emotional rollercoaster for him as well as for Bella and his mum, and he'd hardly dared think about his studies. When he did, he thought he'd probably scraped through pharmacology after using Ludo's old notes. So, obviously, they'd have to meet for a drink afterwards. Ludo chose a traditional pub in the Seven Sisters Road, near to Finsbury Park tube station and his flat.

Tom walked from Colts Court to Holborn Station to catch a Piccadilly Line train north to Finsbury Park. Standing outside the station was a man whose face was familiar. But he couldn't immediately place him. A tall, bulky bloke. He was smoking and reading a folded copy of *Metro*. Then he looked up and smiled.

'Hello, Tom. Sorry about your dad. Karen told me what happened after we left the party. Terrible.'

The penny dropped. Of course! He was Don Peters, the husband of his father's secretary, Karen. 'Dreary Don' as he was known to the Olsons. His dad once said Karen deserved better than a morose car insurance salesman.

'Thank you,' Tom said, reaching out to shake his hand. 'It's been tough for us all, especially as the police seem at a loss over how to solve the crime. How are you and Karen? Will she stay working in the constituency office for the new bloke?'

Don breathed in and dropped his cigarette on the pavement, before swishing his foot from side to side to stub it out. 'Dunno. You'll have to ask her. We're not together. Been brewing for a while but it's a permanent split now.'

Tom couldn't think of anything to say apart from how sorry he was to hear that. Then he pretended to be in a hurry to get his train. Emerging at Finsbury Park he rang Bella with the news. Bella told Pen, who'd mentioned a few days earlier that she felt duty bound to ring Karen to check if she needed to unload more of Dietrich's papers from the constituency office before the new incumbent – another Tory, unsurprisingly – settled in.

Pen agreed to see Karen for coffee in Kingsway the following Wednesday.

Karen looked tired. 'I've been meaning to meet you for a couple of weeks, since I received this letter,' she said, passing over an envelope sent to the constituency office and addressed, 'Please forward to Mrs Olson.' On the back it said, 'From Mrs David J. Cohen.'

'I opened it and read it because I remembered Mr Cohen and the problem he brought to the office for Dietrich to try to fix. There'd been a fire at his bookshop off Theobald's Road due to faulty wiring or something. They lived in a flat above the shop.

'The insurance company wouldn't pay up because the

direct debit from Mr Cohen's bank account the previous month hadn't been paid. He'd simply run out of money after exceeding his overdraft, and because of this the insurers cancelled the policy. Mr Cohen thought Dietrich could try to change their minds, or at least give him time to get back on his feet.

'I'm sorry to say, Dietrich had an aversion to helping people he considered had caused their problems themselves and he just threw the letter in the wastepaper bin.' Karen looked sad.

Pen read the letter from the man's wife. The woman was angry. It turned out she was now a widow. She said her husband had suffered a stroke, probably brought on by the worry of losing his livelihood and their home. They'd had next-to-no savings but one of their daughters had let them live with her.

'Oh dear,' Pen said. 'She wanted to let me know what sort of an MP he was; that he didn't care about a constituent in trouble. The thing is, even if Dietrich had tried, I doubt he'd have got anywhere with a big insurance company. Nevertheless, he could have asked for some compensation for the poor man, especially if he'd been insured with them for a long time.

'But enough of that, tell me about you and Don.'

'Ignore Don,' Karen said as she stirred a third sachet of sugar into her cappuccino. 'He's always been convinced I had an affair with Dietrich. I'm pretty sure he suspected we'd been having it off over the desk in the office for ages. Nothing I could say would convince him that was nonsense. It *was* nonsense. You believe that, don't you, Pen?'

Pen nodded and patted the younger woman's hand.

'Then Don and I went to the office one evening on our

way to the cinema. I'd left a blouse in my desk that I needed to take home to wash. He came in with me and I collected my bag. I had to dig around in it – there were trousers, a top, a pair of tights, a few bits of jewellery, a hairbrush and some make-up in it as well as the blouse—'

'Why did you need them?' asked Pen.

'In case I had to go somewhere formal that I hadn't expected. You know how Dietrich could never be bothered to write things in a diary or even tell me to do it. At first, I thought it was absentmindedness, but really it was a sort of vanity. He thought that if someone wanted him to attend something badly enough, they'd remind him.

'Sometimes he forgot to tell me about evening drinks at the council's offices or something like that until we were packing up for the day. I hadn't put it in the diary, so I'd find out at the last minute. We *had* to put in an appearance. I had to go so I could take note of anything important being announced. I needed to look fresh. I'd always make sure Dietrich had a clean shirt for the same reason.

'After poking around in the emergency bag, Don said it was evidence we'd been doing it. He was going to leave me, and Dietrich was going to regret it. He kept saying rubbish like that. We didn't get to the cinema, needless to say!

'After a few weeks of not speaking, we tried to paper over the cracks... again. I worked hard at being nice to him, but the peace never lasted.'

Pen's expression showed sympathy. 'Jealousy is a dreadful disease,' she said. 'I know that from family court!'

'So, about six months ago, I told him we'd reached the end of the line, and we had to split up. I went to a solicitor to talk about the marriage having irretrievably broken down due to his unreasonable behaviour! I think I now know more about divorce law than you do, Pen.' Karen laughed, before adding, 'I've already moved out of our house and I'm sharing with my sister in her council flat in Archway. She's thinking of moving out of London, so I'll try to take over the tenancy of her place.'

Pen saw how deeply shaken Karen was and offered to help in any way if she had a legal query. She went home to think about her opinion of Don. And of Dietrich. Karen was right. He *was* vain and incapable of empathy for strangers.

When she arrived at Colt Court, Tom was unexpectedly there, wandering from room to room. His exam results were due the next day and he awaited them with the sort of trepidation he hadn't experienced since he was six and anticipating his mum's reaction to the news he'd kicked a ball in the living room and smashed two windowpanes. The carpet had been covered with glass splinters, and for weeks no one could walk around with bare feet.

Now aged 26, he told Pen he was too nervous to stay in the Bankside flat.

He was already a mature student having taken two gap years after dropping out of Durham University where he'd gone to read classics. His parents had been disappointed with the way he'd failed to apply himself to his studies. Girlfriends, films and music were clearly more engaging than the ancient Greek and Roman worlds.

So, when he announced his intention to begin the endless years of study required to become a doctor, his mother feared it might be another five-minute wonder. The sort of students who choose medicine tend to be self-controlled and with a strong sense of social responsibility. You couldn't accuse Tom of having either of those qualities, but he had good A-level chemistry and physics passes. To his and the family's surprise, Guys and St Thomas's accepted him.

After finishing his first year, he told his family he'd found his metier. He was cut out to learn about bodies and how to treat them when something went wrong. Though Pen still worried his newfound enthusiasm for exploring and curing illness and disease would evaporate as fast as his love of Virgil's poems.

Tom knew that if he flunked these exams, this year, after all its shocks and sorrows, he could be adding to his mother's pain, and in a way that might not be easy to cure.

30

THE EMAIL about Tom's exam results arrived on the allotted day. He tapped in his student log-in details and up they came. He'd passed commendably, even in pharmacology, largely thanks to Ludo's notes and the old exam papers he'd found and saved with sample answers stapled onto them.

Later that day, as the two walked from St Thomas's to the Bankside flat together, Tom slapped his saviour on the back. 'Thank goodness you're such a compulsive swot,' he said. 'I could kiss you!'

Ludo gasped, '*Please* don't,' he said as three other med students, one of them a Danielle, whom Tom ardently and secretly admired, joined them on the trek. En route to the flat, they collected bottles of wine and beer from a small supermarket in Stamford Street. Pen had passed on the good news to Bella and Bella and Ed had set out glasses and bowls of crisps, nuts and sandwiches grabbed from the Starbucks' shelves just before the branch locked its doors.

Ed was seated at the Yamaha and, as the heroes burst through the door of the flat, he struck up what he thought of as triumphant music, including 'Jupiter' from Holst's Planets and 'Largo al factotum' from *The Barber of Seville*. After opening a few bottles, they added a selection of pop songs speeded up, with Tom, Ludo and the other med students singing patchy versions of the words.

Tom could hardly believe how relieved and happy his mother still sounded on the telephone the next morning.

Bella had been an ideal student, studying for her first degree in modern languages without doubts or dramas. But Tom had given Pen and Dietrich a succession of headaches. Finally, it looked as if they were over!

So, Pen suggested that Bella, Tom and she go to dinner on Saturday evening to discuss Tom's brilliance and the selling of Batts Farm. She was also thinking about bringing Nathan Harris into the conversation. Was it too soon? Probably.

Tom wished his dad had been there to hear that his son wasn't the timewaster he'd often seemed to be at prep school and at St Paul's. Tom knew that had it not been for Dietrich's protection, encouragement and support, he'd have nothing to celebrate.

He wouldn't have been the lucky beggar he was.

31

Will was supposed to have been conducting research for his dissertation. It had been slow and sporadic. He'd dithered and had decided to choose a different topic, something safe – the way the reporting of news or of the arts had changed since Rupert Murdoch left Australia and became a British media mogul. He stuck with this idea for a full week. Then he switched to the rise and fall of Robert Maxwell, the so-called 'bouncing Czech'. He laboured over the internet and bought biographies of both men and made notes. Perhaps he could explore the interaction between them – if there was any?

His girlfriend suggested he research what she called the femininization of the media – the phasing out of photos of topless so-called glamour models and the growth of newspapers devoting large sections to feature articles about women's health, relationships, emotional problems, ambitions and achievements.

He wrote synopsis after synopsis, trying out different angles when approaching each subject. His heart was never in them, though. It slowly dawned on him that those books had already been written, the fanfares blown, the reviews published. Other people, who cared, would write more.

He always drifted back to Dietrich Olson. No one knew more about that man than he, he was sure. But was he any more interested in a dead politician than the demise of Murdoch's greatest gift to British media – Page Three Stunnas? He couldn't be sure. Finally, he decided that a biographical dissertation would be easier than having to think up clever arguments and draw conclusions.

So, he pored over the obituaries of the man and decided to write a chronological account of his life. He borrowed his mum's car and travelled to Tring in Hertfordshire to see what had become of the hardware shop Dietrich's parents had run.

The place had been expanded and modernised and seemed to be thriving under a different name. He took a photo. The town's library had photographs of the original shop, which looked as though it specialised in garden forks, rat poison and metal dustbins. He checked who held the copyright of the photographs so he could ask for copies.

On another occasion, he persuaded the headmaster of Emanuel School in Clapham, South London, to let him look through the old scrapbooks. He copied a blurred photograph of a house cricket match in which a skinny Dietrich and Michael Wilson-Green had played.

He read about First Domestic Appliances and learned about the price his father's partner – the same Michael Wilson-Green – had paid for lying about its profits. He also researched the property developments that made Dietrich rich enough to attend receptions thrown by banks, accountancy firms and political groups.

He'd wavered about digging into the background of Penelope Bryant, knowing from his media law classes how there was only so much private information he could include in print without her consent. Nevertheless, he was curious and wanted to investigate her early life and her banker father's career.

Borrowing Jane's car, he took a trip to Woodstock to see Justin Grieg, Penelope Bryant's now retired tutor at law school. Will told him about his project and said he wanted to know what sort of student she'd been to add colour to his book.

Pleased to have an excuse to stop rearranging the books on a wall of shelves, Grieg remembered Penny as a bright and vivacious member of her year. There were several of those, he pointed out, naming two who'd become judges. Will noted down their names.

'Penny Bryant was remarkable,' Grieg said after a pause. 'Not only clever but the only student I ever had who sat her exams while six months pregnant. And she passed with top marks!'

Will submitted the dissertation before the start of City University's Christmas vacation. He delivered it on a memory stick to his course leader's secretary, who ticked his name off her list and put it in what looked like a shoe box, all within the deadline. Will knew it was good enough. He would get his master's degree but not necessarily with the distinction he half hoped for.

But the man he'd been hoping to impress with it, the man he'd been hoping to impress all his life, was already dead. That would be a postscript of the dissertation and the book, which he now felt sure would follow.

Dietrich's death and Jane's revelation of his bigamy had made the publishing world very keen on a biography. And a biography written by the man's secret son would be a sure-fire hit. Will didn't need an agent to play one publisher off against another. On his own, he negotiated and landed a good deal. There followed a few spats with the publisher's editor and later, a couple of interviews to promote the thing. Then it was all over. He was free to lounge around for months thinking of himself grandly as an author.

One Monday morning in early autumn, Tom was leaving Colts Court just as the man who polished the brass of the revolving door's handles was putting his cloths back into a small wooden box. Tom smiled at him, noting for the first time that he was enormously fat.

Tom was wearing the new spectacles he'd collected from the optician only the previous day and, as he stepped out into the street, he glanced at the people lolling on chairs at the café opposite. He paused to stare and then to recognise one face among them – a fair-haired man in a sweatshirt with a Paul Smith logo on one side. The wearer stared back at Tom and looked bizarrely pleased with himself.

Tom walked across the road. 'Charles?'

'I prefer to be called Will these days, Tom. How are you? Sit down. Have some coffee.'

Tom shook his head. 'No thanks. No time. Why're you here?'

'Oh, I've been coming here a lot. Just hoping to bump into members of my other family, making up for lost time. That OK?'

'Sounds a bit creepy and sad to me. Perhaps I can recommend a therapist?'

Will laughed. Then he bent down to fish out a book from a gym bag on the floor. 'Have one of these review copies. It'll be hitting the shops in a few weeks' time, but this will save you sixteen pounds and ninety-nine pence. Would you like me to autograph it?'

Tom grasped the hardback copy of *My Secret Father, Sir Dietrich Olson.* He looked at the photo of his dad cycling to the House of Commons on the front and the flattering photo of the author on the back of the dust jacket. He was about to say something and then stopped.

Nodding his thanks, he hurried off to catch a bus to Waterloo and then run for St Thomas's, where he was on a list to begin a rotation in the cardiology department the following week. This was to be a preparation and revision day, and he was late.

During his lunch break, Tom pulled the book from his rucksack and flipped through the chapter headings. The photographs of Dietrich's parents and their hardware shop were interesting – although he and Bella had been shown them by their dad years earlier. The ones of Dietrich and Jane as students and on their wedding and honeymoon were new to him, of course.

A chapter dealt with what Will called Dietrich's abandonment of his wife and baby son so he could be free to fulfil his ambitions to become rich and famous. Dietrich's early years as a businessman and tax advisor seemed to have been collated from his obituaries and padded out with a few quotes from contemporary colleagues.

It seemed Will had googled and copied details about his father's early life, followed by the disaster of First Domestic Appliances. The chapter entitled 'Dietrich in the House' centred on the backbencher's infrequent contributions to parliamentary debates, with comments from fellow politicians. He'd served on only two committees and then, it seemed, without ever making a useful suggestion. As regards his father as a politician, Will was generally disparaging. He quoted other MPs who'd derided and disliked him. One said he treated parliament as a gentlemen's club.

Will had also found a trio of retired Camden Council members who said their local MP was reluctant to listen to their or their constituents' concerns. He'd interviewed Karen Peters, Dietrich's number one fan, she claimed. And her former husband, who was no fan and was happy to explain why. Will had assured him that anything he said about the break-up of his marriage would be off the record. He'd lied. Would Karen complain that Don had libelled her by saying she worshipped her boss? It wasn't actually defamatory, so he doubted it.

He covered the charity Dietrich had established to support centres for those who needed rehabilitation for alcoholism and drug use. Photographs of him with young people – graduates of the centres – were easy to find and Dietrich had been clever at dragging in a celebrity from sport, television or the music world to pose with them.

So far, so dull.

Then it changed.

Tom was alarmed to read a short chapter about Penelope Bryant and the way she had continued her studies throughout her pregnancy. Bloody nerve! Wasn't this a serious breach of his mother's privacy? And his? Was it a reason to have the book pulped?

He rang Bella and she thought it through. Her conclusion was that births, marriages and deaths weren't considered private. They were registered and any member of the public could consult these registers, as she and Tom had done in Oxford.

Back in Bankside that evening, Tom speed read Will's

account of how his mother met and quickly married, or thought she married, the already-betrothed Dietrich. Before that, Pen's wealthy parents paid for a full-time nanny to look after the baby while she lived in the Colt Court flat and completed the two years of her lawyers' training contract. In the meantime, the unnamed nanny had apparently stayed while Pen continued to work as a solicitor for one of the city's so-called 'Magic Circle' law firms. Will had tracked down the nanny, though she wasn't named.

The book's final chapter dealt with Dietrich's death. The author's account of the knighthood party, which included Pen's green dress, the food that had been served and the tunes played on the piano by a Romanian friend of the family, was puzzling, especially as the chapter also featured a detailed description of Batts Farm. It suggested that Will had carried out a lot of research. But how? Had he bluffed his way into the house or pumped someone for information? Or both? Tom pulled out his phone and asked DI Rob Howarth if he could spare him ten minutes.

At the police station, he handed the DI the book, drawing his attention to the photo of Will Page on the dust cover. He said the author seemed to have a detailed knowledge of Batts Farm and the events at the party, which made him suspect Will had attended it himself. Added to that was the fact that Will had been stalking the family by sitting in the café opposite their Bloomsbury flat for months, even though his home was in Bethnal Green, or so his mother apparently believed.

He suggested that a detective take the book's dust cover with its photograph of Will to interview John Hardwick and speak to Mrs Gibbs.

The sun was starting to set as Tom drove back to Bankside and flopped on the sofa clutching the book. By the door,

Ed was tucking his tracksuit bottoms into his socks and folding a bagged tuxedo into a panier.

'Cycling to work rather than walking it tonight?' Tom asked.

'Yep, the Strand Palace and I'm likely to be late as it is. Biking it is better than walking over Waterloo Bridge. Will you tell Bella I'll ring her in my break? I think she's gone shopping.'

Ed was halfway down the stairs carrying his bike on his shoulder when Tom remembered the curious incident of the waiter and the flying syringe. He sped after him, almost twisting an ankle on the stairs while waving the book's dust cover.

'Is this the waiter who said he had diabetes at the Batts Farm party?' he asked breathlessly.

Ed paused, put down the bike and studied the photo. 'Could be. Yes, I think so. He's got different hair but something about his deep-set eyes looks familiar. They're a bit like your dad's.'

Tom sprinted back up to their flat's front door, went inside and took a long shower. Meanwhile, Bella had returned and had begun taking out packages from her bag and from the fridge to put a chicken salad together for them. Tom pulled her away from the fridge.

'Supper can wait. Sit down and have a glass of wine. I've found out who murdered Dad.'

32

Rob was happy to go to the Bankside flat with Izzy to see Tom and Bella the following morning. He'd recovered from Simon Guerrier-Belmont's slap down of his request to open juvenile witness statements. Simon called it flimsy. Tom's news didn't sound flimsy. If he'd understood it correctly, it sounded sensational.

Bella met them at the front entrance and asked if they'd like to come up or sit around a table with coffees in the almost empty Starbucks next door. Izzy opted for coffee and Bella passed this over to Tom through the flat's intercom.

Tom brought down Will's book and its dustcover. He'd done some photocopies of it in the newsagent near the flats, which he passed on to Izzy. He'd also made photocopies of pages from the book that showed Will's familiarity with the events at the party and the layout of Batts Farm.

After Bella brought the coffees to their table, Tom explained how he'd often seen a youngish man sitting outside the café opposite the entrance to the family's Bloomsbury flat. He'd stared intensely at him as he left to go to the hospital. It was only when he was wearing new glasses that he recognised the man as the one with Jane Page-Smith at his father's memorial service. On that occasion, Will had been wearing horn-rimmed specs and staring at the floor.

'The book revealed Will's resentment at never having been acknowledged as Dietrich's legitimate biological son,' Tom explained. 'This resentment had obviously become weapons-grade when he found out that our mother had been pregnant with me before she married Dad. He didn't say who told him. It could have been a fellow student, Mum's nanny or just guesswork, because I don't look anything like Dietrich.

'And he didn't know who my father was – it could have been anyone Mum had known when she was a student. I don't know either and I don't care. But he'd guessed right that Dietrich had adopted me. This drove him nuts because he felt that he'd effectively been ignored. It was a sort of aggressive sibling rivalry.'

Bella chipped in that Will had hardly been forgotten. He'd had a comfortable life with his mother, been privately educated and continued to have what amounted to a trust fund, all thanks to Dietrich. So, Will's bitterness must, in part, have been learned from his mother, who considered herself to have been abandoned.

Tom took over. 'Dietrich had provided Will with a trust fund and cared for him in his own way. The problem was it wasn't in the way Will wanted. Will was his legitimate child. He was clever at school and a rugby and cricket captain; and he was polite, well-spoken and good-looking. A model son. Not one to be ashamed of. Yet for all those years, as Will saw it, Dietrich Olson had treated him like a dirty little secret.'

'Quite why they'd never met, I don't know,' said Bella. 'Dad wasn't hard to find – what with all the charity things and constituency events he had to attend. Will could just have turned up at the House of Commons. And I doubt Dad would've chased him away.'

Rob and Izzy exchanged puzzled glances.

'All this is very interesting as background for his book,' Rob said finally. 'And it shows what a twisted mind Will Page has. But what the hell's it got to do with the murder?'

'Well, until we saw this book, we'd been fairly certain that neither Will nor his mother had attended the party in January. We now think Will *did* attend. He was one of the waiters. Before that, he was the window cleaner. He won Mrs Gibbs round, and she let him go around the house and refill his bucket in the back kitchen, where Dad died. No doubt he had a good look around down there to familiarise himself with the layout.

'We think he could also have been the waiter who threw a syringe into a food bin in front of Ed George, when Ed took a break from playing the piano.'

Rob and Izzy looked at each other again and sighed. They were even more baffled.

'I remember Ed George telling me that tale,' Izzy admitted. 'I thought it was nonsense, that he'd had too much to drink and imagined it, to be honest.'

Tom kept calm. 'I've spoken to the caterer, John Hardwick. He says he recognises Will Page's striking blue eyes even if the hairstyle was different. Bella's boyfriend Ed, who was there too, says the same thing.

'Will's a journalist. It wouldn't have been hard for him to find out how to buy cocaine. He had plenty of money, thanks to the father he hated. Perhaps he hid the coke somewhere while he was there cleaning the windows.

'At the party, in his guise as a waiter, all he'd have needed was a quick conversation with Dietrich, a suggestion that a bottle of something special would be good for the toast after his speech. Dietrich didn't recognise him, of course, because he and his mother Jane had kept in the background for nearly thirty years. Perhaps Jane thought if they came out of the woodwork, the payments would stop. Like it was hush money...'

The cops drank up, thanked Tom and Bella and said they'd look into it. Neither shared Tom's enthusiasm. Izzy feared his theory was another blind alley.

That weekend, for reasons he hadn't quite worked out, Rob drove to Batts Farm to have tea with Mrs Gibbs. She was, she said, grateful for the company and for an excuse to open a packet of Walker's shortbread biscuits, her favourites, which she'd been keeping since Christmas.

Rob put Will's book on the table and explained who the author was. Mrs G was flustered. When he took off the book's dustcover and pointed to a photograph of Will Page, she almost dropped one of her best bone china cups. He didn't need to ask another question.

'That's Oliver!' she gasped.

33

Normally, getting the ever-cautious Simon Guerrier-Belmont to agree to prosecute someone for murder was hard. After the Wilson-Green debacle, it was harder still. But handing him a report from Guildford Police's forensic scientists showing evidence of an object having been taped on the back of a lefthand shelf in the Batts Farm wine store and both DNA traces and fingerprints on the light switch, which were different from the victim's wife's, sparked the old barrister's enthusiasm.

He became even more amenable when he read the full witness statements identifying Will Page as the window cleaner who'd craftily visited the house only days before the party, one of the waiters John Hardwick had hired and the one who'd allegedly thrown a syringe across the kitchen like a dart and had joked with Ed George that he'd just given himself an insulin jab. One of Will's flatmates had laughed when a police officer tracked him down and asked about Will giving himself insulin injections.

If a DNA test on the light switch prints produced a match for Will's, it would amount to strong evidence that he had been at the party.

Mehmet and Izzy were happy to waste half a morning sitting with Tom in Colts Court, looking down from the kitchen window and waiting for Will to take his seat in the café. As soon as he arrived with a couple of pals, the detectives pounced and arrested him to help them with their inquiries.

'What am I supposed to have done?' an indignant Will asked. 'Dropped a cigarette end? Slurped my coffee too loudly? I know this is a posh street, but...'

'Surely as a journalist you know that stalking is an offence under the Protection from Harassment Act 1997,' sneered Izzy. 'It carries a penalty of six months.'

Will had started laughing sarcastically and turned to one of his pals. 'I don't believe this!' he said. 'Take a photo of Little Miss Plod here and put it on Twitter, will you? I'll be complaining to the head of the Met!'

At Holborn Police Station, the custody sergeant took Will Page's name and address, swabbed him for DNA and fingerprinted him. He was then led to an interview room, where Rob and Izzy were waiting. Izzy switched on the tape recorder, told him he'd be given a copy of the interview tape, and said their names, the date and the time.

'Good morning, Mr Page – or do you prefer Mr Olson? I suppose either name will help you plug your book,' said Rob.

'Why am I here? Do I need a lawyer?'

'It's up to you. We can wait until one arrives or you could just answer our questions, to assist us with our inquiries.' Izzy poured water from a plastic jug into a paper cup for him.

Pennies were dropping in Will's mind. This wasn't about stalking. 'What's this really about?' he asked.

'It's about a party at Batts Farm, near Godalming, a house you know, I believe. And the party was the one at which Sir Dietrich Olson, your father, died.'

Will could have sworn the contents of his bowels were turning to water. He managed to retain a neutral face but felt panicky and sick.

'I want a lawyer. Not one of your worn-out old ambulance chasers. I'll find my own, if I can use my phone to find her number.'

'Go ahead. Tell your lawyer not to keep us waiting too long, though.'

Rob and Izzy left Will pecking at his mobile. He was ringing the chambers of Jacqueline Guy KC to ask for the solicitor who was ready to act for Michael Wilson-Green before the trial was delayed. Like Bella, he'd attended the court before the case was supposed to start and had seen who was due to appear. He reckoned this would be someone who already knew about the knighthood party and Dietrich's death.

An hour later, Ms Nikolina Drakos wafted in, trailing Chanel Coco Mademoiselle eau de toilette and wearing a navy trouser suit that was definitely not from Next.

Izzy looked at Rob and whispered, 'He's obviously spending his book royalties in advance.'

Twenty minutes later, the interview continued.

Nikolina gave her name, her Greek accent soft. 'Why are you questioning my client?' she then asked, smiling sweetly.

'We believe he has been harassing Mrs Penny Bryant Olson, Mr Thomas Olson and Ms Arabella Olson by stationing himself opposite the entrance to the block of flats where they live in Bloomsbury. The manager of the café confirmed that your client visited the café three or four times a week at around breakfast time and has been doing this regularly for well over a year,' Rob said.

Will sniggered.

Nikolina continued to smile. 'Is that why he's here?' she asked.

Rob smiled back. 'It's one reason.'

'And the other reason?'

'He also attended a party on the fifth of January in the Godalming home of the man he claims in his new book was his father. The book is entitled, *Dietrich Olson, My Secret Father*. Sir Dietrich died at the party. He was murdered.'

'There were almost one hundred people at the party, I believe,' Nikolina said quickly.

'Your client was not invited as a guest, but we believe he attended, disguised as a waiter, having visited the house previously on several occasions pretending to be a window cleaner in order to familiarise himself with the layout, and in particular, with the back kitchen where we believe the murder of Sir Dietrich took place.'

Will's nervousness had changed to belligerence. He looked Rob steadily in the eye. 'No comment'.

'Two people who were at the party saw you there. One witnessed you throw what appeared to be a syringe across the kitchen into a food waste bin. A third person recognises you as the fake window cleaner.'

'Absurd.' Will sat back and looked at the ceiling.

'The victim, Sir Dietrich OIson, was your father. But you didn't like him, did you?'

Will shrugged. 'Never met him.'

'But you went to the party at Batts Farm to observe and meet him. Then to kill him. Isn't that correct?'

'No.'

Rob gathered his papers and stood up. 'Let's adjourn this interview and recommence tomorrow at 10,' he said.

When they were back in the CID room, he asked Izzy, 'Will we have the forensic stuff tomorrow?'

'I'll chase them up.'

The following day, Rob again sat at the bolted-down table and laid out photographs of the underside of the left-hand top shelf in the Batts Farm wine store. A piece of twisted masking tape had stuck to the back of the wooden baton of the shelf and an area of about twenty centimetres was free of the thick dust that lay everywhere else. The photographs were clear.

A partial thumb print was found on the tape.

Other photographs showed the grimy light switch on the right-hand wall inside the wine store, from which two sets of fingerprints, a forefinger and middle finger of each set, had been taken. One set matched Penny Bryant's. The other matched the prints taken by the custody sergeant when Will had arrived at Holborn Police Station. The thumb print on the masking tape was also his.

Rob had summoned Scott David to Lambs Conduit Street, summarised their case, the forensic evidence and the passages from Will's book that showed his familiarity with Batts Farm.

'Looks a pretty strong case to me,' Scott said. 'But today, I'd prefer to watch and get an idea of the man rather than sit in, if that's OK with you?'

Rob nodded.

Marley Brown appeared with a mug of tea for the boss

and one for the junior prosecutor. She assessed him quickly to be the most shockingly attractive man she'd ever seen and almost dropped both mugs of tea.

Will was brought up from his cell and then Nikolina arrived, this time wearing a light grey shift dress with a matching blazer. Her high-heeled black patent shoes clacked on the hard floors. She requested a short time to speak to her client in private.

'I don't want to be sandbagged by them,' she whispered. 'So, tell me what sort of evidence they could produce?'

Will shrugged. 'Can't say. Just because some old dear says I look a bit like some window cleaner and I *could* have been a waiter if my hair was pulled back, they think they've snared me. It's crap, all crap!'

Nikolina looked serious and unconvinced as she moved to the door to summon the detectives. Then she took her seat next to Will. 'You have some real evidence today, Inspector?'

Rob was not going to discuss the photo identifications. Instead, he put on the table photographs from the wine store of a small twist of masking tape and the light switch. Nikolina put on glasses to look at the images, then removed them and raised her eyebrows. Will also studied the photographs but showed no emotion.

'And these suggest *what* to you?' Nikolina asked.

'We say this is a fragment of masking tape that your client forgot or failed to pull off and hide after he'd removed a syringe of a cocaine solution that he'd earlier attached to a shelf in the wine store. That's the place where the victim's body was discovered. The second photograph is of the wine store's light switch, which is not far from where the tape was found. Fingerprints were found on both the tape and the switch. Your client's fingerprints.'

Nikolina looked quickly at Will and then at Rob. 'And this is all you have? A bit of tape? A smudged print that could have been left there months, even years earlier. It doesn't amount to a smoking gun exactly, does it?'

Rob ignored her and left the room.

Outside, he met Scott, who nodded and said, 'Go ahead.'

Rob returned to the interview room. 'Charles William Olson, I am charging you with the murder of Sir Dietrich Olson on the fifth of January 2019, at Batts Farm, near Godalming, Surrey. You do not have to say anything, but it may harm your defence if you do not mention when questioned something which you later rely on in court. Anything you do say may be given in evidence.

'Do you understand? It means that if you say nothing now a jury could – and is likely to – draw adverse inferences. In other words, they may think you kept quiet because you needed time to concoct a story to explain the evidence.'

Will was silent, feigning boredom and alternating between staring at the ceiling and examining his fingernails. Mehmet entered and snapped handcuffs on his wrists.

'There will be a bail hearing at the City of London Magistrates Court tomorrow,' Rob said as he stood up to leave.

Rob and Izzy left the room, allowing Nikolina time enough to tell Will that she would represent him there but that she wasn't hopeful he would receive bail because of the seriousness of the murder charge. He would more likely be remanded to custody. She asked if he wanted her to instruct Jacqueline Guy QC and a small nod signalled that he would. She would be paid from money he'd saved from the regular payments from his father, the man he was accused of murdering.

Will stared at her back as she left the room, then two uniformed police officers arrived to take him to his cell.

Nikolina had been right. Will was remanded to custody by Their Worships at the City of London Magistrates Court. Led away through a back door, he boarded a white Serco van shortly afterwards that drove to the A Wing of Wormwood Scrubs prison in Hammersmith. He felt as though this was all a very bad dream. And when he glanced through the bars on the van's windows as it drove through the Scrubs Gateway, through the famous buff-coloured brick pillars with their bright white quoin stones, he was sure of it.

Inside the building, built by convicts in 1874, and in which – he was to learn from googling the prison on the phone that would soon be taken from him – forty to fifty violent incidents occurred every month, warders examined and confiscated Will's shoulder bag. His newly published book, phone, flat keys and watch were also taken. He was frisked for drugs and weapons, told he could continue to wear his own clothes – an ensemble of designer jeans, T-shirt, sweatshirt and trainers that cost more than the average person might receive in Universal Credit welfare payments for a couple of months – and was provided with four pairs of boxer shorts and socks, a grey sweatshirt and tracksuit bottoms, a towel, a toothbrush, a tube of toothpaste, a bar of soap and a rough grey blanket.

A short-haired female warder whose head seemed to have grown directly from her shoulders led him through a series of gates and corridors to a cell, where a man of about fifty lolled on the lower of two bunks.

'This is Clive,' announced the bullfrog. A sour-faced old man glanced at him then returned to flipping the pages of a dog-eared magazine. Will surveyed the furnishings: a stainless-steel lavatory, unshielded, without a seat and apparently blocked, and a small washbasin stained with Clive's spat-out toothpaste. A thick metal door thudded as it shut behind him.

Staying here, he decided, would be hell. He was wrong. It wouldn't even be purgatory.

During those mornings observing the wheels of justice at Lavender Hill Magistrates Court, no one had told him that.

34

Simon Guerrier-Belmont had rarely been surprised when he learned of a defence counsel's tactics. That Monday morning was an exception. On the top of the files handed to him by his secretary Dawn as he sat at his desk was one marked R v Olson. Inside it was a letter from Jaqueline Guy disclosing that her client, Charles William Olson, would be pleading guilty to the murder of his father, Sir Dietrich Olson, but he would be raising the defence that he was suffering from diminished responsibility within the meaning of section two of the Homicide Act, 1957. Will had decided on this strategy after long conversations with Nikolina and his barrister, Jacqueline Guy.

Effectively, Simon's learned friend Ms Guy would be attempting to persuade the jury that Will was guilty of the lesser offence of manslaughter because he suffered from 'an abnormality of mind' at the time of the crime. In other words, he was partially insane when he jabbed Dietrich to death with a large syringe full of liquid cocaine.

'Get Scott in here and bring us coffee, extra strong, please,' he barked at Dawn.

When Scott arrived, Simon outlined the dilemma they faced. 'They're using this as a platform to nullify the crime. We'll have to prove to the jury that his defence is a load of piddle. It might be *unusual* for a son who's been supported financially all his life by an absent father to hate the man so much that he plots to kill him, but he certainly wasn't mad during the months when he was planning the crime and carrying it out. He knew exactly what he was doing, and he knew it was wrong.

'Jacqueline must come up with a recognised medical condition and convince the jury it explains the killing. Wonder what she'll choose?'

'A quick urine test will show he doesn't have Type 1 diabetes, which he told the pianist he had,' Scott said. 'He's obviously not schizophrenic or autistic, so I'd guess she'll come up with depression and anxiety. I'd be surprised if she has any proof – a prescription for anti-depressants, for example.

'Interesting that this medical condition didn't stop him from researching and completing his master's dissertation and then work on turning it into a book.'

Simon drank his strong coffee and said, 'We'll just have to chip away at everything she says.

'I know it's not relevant to the defence, but to make sure no one on the jury feels a surge of sympathy for the poor, unloved boy' – he broke off to smile at his sarcasm – 'let's get the police to find out what he and his mother actually received from Dietrich. I seem to recall Rob telling me it was a lot – they had a decent house we must get a photograph of. They were also given regular support payments for about 30 years. Private school and university fees were taken care of and there was a tidy payout from a life insurance policy. Perhaps the dead man's accountant or solicitor will provide a list.'

* * *

In her decent house, Jane was left reeling after a phone conversation with Nikolina. It couldn't be true, could it? She googled Nikolina Drakos to check that she was a real solicitor. Satisfied, she rang Wormwood Scrubs to find out the procedure for a relative's visit and learned that Will would need to request it. Nikolina promised she'd tell him to do that on her next visit.

At about the same time, Tom was contacting Rob for an update. He was surprised to hear that Will would be pleading guilty but would argue he was suffering from a mental illness of some kind. He wondered how his lawyer would convince a jury of it.

'I wondered if he might try something like guilty but with diminished responsibility,' said Bella when he passed on the news. 'That's the defence battered women use after they've killed their abusers. They usually wait until the abusers are asleep.'

She wished she could remember more from her criminal law lectures. 'If it works, he'll get a much shorter sentence for manslaughter not intentional murder.'

Pen was disappointed but not surprised by the news. A guilty plea could have meant the family might at last lay Dietrich to rest in peace. Any other defence meant that his bigamy, his whole life, would be forced back into the public arena. The twisted mind of Dietrich's biological son was truly terrifying.

A call from Jane caught her off guard. For Jane, the news from Nikolina had left her scared and heartbroken. Pen knew that she was not the appropriate person to console or advise her. She had to listen, though.

'I had no idea he held this grudge against his father,' Jane said. 'He didn't even tell me he was researching Dietrich's biography.'

She broke off and Pen could hear her crying.

'It was my fault. I should have let him contact Dietrich when he was a child. He may have stayed bitter and resentful, but it would have been nothing like... this, this terrible *crime*.

'He may think he's tough, but he isn't strong enough to survive prison with sadistic warders and...'

Pen knew she was going to say 'common criminals' but couldn't.

'I'm so sorry, Jane. I'm sure it wasn't your fault. None of us suspected it. If Tom hadn't suddenly recognised Will as the person who seemed to always be drinking coffee in the café opposite our flat, the way he felt about Dietrich would never have come out.'

* * *

Nikolina met her client in an interview room at the prison, both to check on his health and to try to prepare him for the trial. 'There'll be at least one plea and trial preparation hearing. You won't need to say anything,' she said.

She then confirmed the judge would be the Recorder of London, Sir Marcus Greene. 'He'll be wearing a purple silk robe with a black sash. You must address him as "Your Honour" – always. The general view is that he's fair-minded. He's never been successfully appealed, which says a lot.

'The clerk will read the charge and will ask you to state your plea, which is guilty. The prosecutor is Simon Guerrier-Belmont, who may strike you as a doddery old fool. Beware, he's still got all his marbles. At trial, he will try to unsettle you, craftily provoke you, make you sound callous.

'Don't let him succeed. Don't rush to answer questions. Answer them calmly after you've had a moment to think of the implications, ideally with yes or no. And don't elaborate. Just look straight ahead.

'Most of the jurors won't understand a word of the legal argument. They never do. They'll decide matters entirely on whether they like you or not.

'This is the most important piece of advice I can give you. You must make a good impression on them, strike them as an honest young man who was deeply hurt by the way your father treated you. And you regret that he died.'

Will nodded.

'But I'm not sorry he died,' he said petulantly.

'Well, you are an idiot, then!' she snapped. 'So, *pretend* that you are.'

The case management hearing took place in a meeting room at the Old Bailey three months later, a few weeks before the trial was due to begin.

Nikolina accompanied Jacqueline and carried a plastic clothes bag on a hanger. It contained a man's grey suit, four plain cotton shirts and ties in shades of blue. Jane had bought them, unaware that Will had lost a great deal of weight due to his predictable dislike of prison food. The lawyer explained to Will that the prison would allow him to keep the bag in his cell ready for his court appearances.

As the Serco van drove into the side road through a secure gateway to the Old Bailey, lights flashed through the window and Will suddenly realised the press were swarming for the event. Cameras were pointed at the vehicle's windows. Guided by a warden, Will walked out in his too-big suit to a holding cell.

In Court 1, the clerk boomed 'all rise' and the lawyers and the spectators, who had packed into the public gallery, including Tom and Bella Olson, plus the journalists on the press benches, all got to their feet noisily until Sir Marcus Greene had taken his seat opposite the jury's benches.

The twelve jurors filed in, six men and six women, all middle-aged and white except for two Asian men. Several of the women looked nervous, as if they'd turned up expecting to have to judge a case of shoplifting and not a *proper* crime.

They stared in concentration as they received the judge's thanks and his instructions to consider only the evidence to be presented during the trial, to resist reports in the media or on the internet and to tell no one about the jury's deliberations in the retiring room. Not even their families. He also instructed them to elect a foreperson. The nervous-looking ones looked even more alarmed.

When the clerk, a thin-faced young man, ordered that everyone be seated and the court was quiet, a stern-faced Judge Greene looked down to his right, awaiting the prosecutor's opening statement.

'Your Honour, I am Simon Guerrier-Belmont, and I appear for the Crown in this matter.'

Scott David sat with Detective Inspector Rob Howarth

just behind him. The judge then looked across to the defence bench. Jacqueline Guy QC stood up to her full five feet four inches, at least three of them due to her high heels, in her black silk robe. Her horsehair wig was now as yellowed from use as her experienced learned friend's, but her jabot collar and its pair of white bands gleamed whiter than his.

'Your Honour, my name is Jacqueline Guy, and I appear on behalf of the defendant.' She took her seat with her junior, a pallid young man under a beginner's bright white wig.

'Are you ready to proceed?'

On receiving positive nods, the clerk called for the defendant to be brought into the dock.

The clerk stood up to face Charles William Olson, and he asked him to raise his right hand. Then he asked Will if he wanted to swear or affirm the oath to tell the truth. He affirmed, and the clerk read out the charge along with the place, date and time of Sir Dietrich's death, and instructed him to state his plea.

Will stood straight and in his clear, public-school voice said, 'Not guilty.'

The barristers on both sides of the court were puzzled. What had happened to the guilty but with diminished responsibility defence?

Simon stood up slowly and faced the jury. He coughed and almost growled.

'Ladies and Gentlemen, the defendant is a son of the victim's early marriage to Ms Jane Page-Smith.

'Most of you will have heard of the victim, the late Dietrich Olson, MP. Perhaps you saw him on television, asking a question in the House of Commons or making jokes on television programmes such as *Have I Got News For You*. He'd been the Conservative member for an inner London constituency since 1994 and was due to stand again for that seat in the next election.

'He became *Sir* Dietrich in the New Year's Honours list last year, an honour awarded for his work with the several charities he'd set up to help young people with addiction problems. He'd also been a successful businessman and was consequently a rich man.

'He was murdered by poisoning with cocaine in his home near Godalming on the fifth of January last year at a party to celebrate his knighthood.'

In the dock, Will tried to remain calm while his heart was pumping what felt like hot lead. He looked at the jury then turned his attention to the dark oak panelling and the white walls. Very nineteenth century, he decided. Court rooms in television dramas always looked brighter, better, he thought. The judge reminded him of someone's reclusive uncle.

Simon adjusted his billowing robe and continued. 'You have the job not only of deciding whether or not the defendant actually killed his father, but also of whether he intended to kill him by ambushing him at the party and injecting him with a solution of a massive amount of cocaine, causing his almost instantaneous death.'

He paused, hoping that the jurors were following him.

'My job is easy. It's to show you that Charles William Olson knew *exactly* what he was doing on the fifth of January in the wine store of Sir Dietrich's house because he'd made an elaborate and complicated plan to kill him weeks, if not months beforehand.

'His motive? Simply put, it was hatred of his father. He'd never met the man but had been writing a thick biography of Sir Dietrich for months before. Doing that requires energy to carry out the research and write. His research told him something he hadn't known, which incensed him and led to him making the plan to kill him at the party to celebrate his knighthood. This new knowledge made him angry and mad.'

Simon held up a copy of the book. An usher took it and passed it to the jury to look at in turn.

'Please note the photograph of the defendant, the book's author. It led to his downfall.

'As the trial progresses, we will present witnesses who will attest to the fact that this same young man went to the house in Godalming, Surrey, before the event pretending to be a window cleaner so he could familiarise himself with the layout of the place.

'And at the time of the killing, at the victim's party, when he'd managed to get hired by the caterer as one of the team of waiters, Charles William Olson could not only control exactly what he was doing but he also *knew* that what he was doing was wicked and *wrong*.

'The prosecution can prove that the defendant had cleverly hidden a syringe of cocaine inside the wine store where Sir Dietrich's lifeless body was found.'

Jacqueline Guy announced that she was appearing for the defence. 'I will show,' she said, 'that my client was not in fact guilty of the charge of murder. Despite his disappointment at the fact his father refused to acknowledge or even meet him, he is an honest and intelligent person.'

Will seemed not to hear this. His jacket was bunching around his waist as he leaned back against the bar.

Simon rose, coughed, tugged at his gown, fiddled with the buttons on his waistcoat and addressed the defendant. 'Mr Olson, what were you doing on January the fifth this year?'

'I was working as a waiter at my father's party in Godalming.'

'Working as a waiter? Why would you do that? You don't need the money. Your late father has always paid you a generous allowance and continues to do so,' said Simon.

'I thought it would be an interesting way to observe my father among his friends.'

Simon nodded and then asked, 'Do you suffer from insulin-dependent diabetes?'

'No.'

'That's odd,' Simon continued. 'Because at the party you told Ed George, the pianist for the occasion, when he took a break and saw you fling a syringe into a bin in the kitchen, that you'd needed the syringe for your diabetes.'

'I don't recall the conversation but if it took place I must have been joking.'

Will shrugged and looked at his feet.

'Do you acknowledge the pain this murder inflicted on your mother Jane, on Sir Dietrich's second wife, Mrs Penelope Bryant Olson, on your half-sister Arabella and her brother Tom?'

'I care about my mother.'

'Not the others?'

'No.'

Simon looked up at the judge. 'At this point, I have no more questions for this witness.'

Jacqueline was quickly on her feet. 'Your Honour, may I request that we adjourn for today at this point?'

Sir Marcus looked at his watch. 'So ordered,' he said.

'I am grateful, Your Honour.'

Nikolina sat opposite Will in a tiny room behind the court. 'I sensed you were becoming irritated with old Simon, and it would be a good place to stop,' she said.

Will breathed deeply. 'I was going to kill him, my dad, then I changed my mind. Should I say that?'

Nikolina was alarmed. Was this young bloke *really* mad?

'I don't think so,' she said.

'Don't you see, it explains the window cleaning and the waiter business. And they might bring in Vincent Billen, the gardener who got me the cocaine.'

Nikolina gasped. She felt panicked, confused and a little annoyed. 'How are we going to convince the jury that you really did have a change of mind?'

'You've already said I'm intelligent. That's the point. At the party, seeing my father in the flesh – in his dressing gown and ~~old~~ slippers – I realised he was just a silly old buffer. And I suddenly woke up to the fact that what I'd been planning to do was just fucking stupid!

'Up until then, I'd been driven entirely by my emotions. Then my brain took over. I came to my senses, guessed I'd be found out. Of course I would. The cops probably found out I'd been phoning Vince and got the old sod to spill the beans. And at that moment, at the start of the party, I suddenly guessed I'd be killing myself as well as my father.

'Also, I imagined what life in prison would be like if they got me. Now that I've had a few months of it, I know it's a million times worse than I thought – than anyone thinks. The media loves to paint a picture of luxury hotel comfort – televisions in every cell, decent food, mobile phones in everyone's back pocket – but that's all rubbish. It's indescribably awful. I thought I was going to be attacked every time I went in the shower. And the food – I was sure everything on my tray had been spat on. I knew I'd never survive.'

Nikolina sat back. 'So, you're now saying that someone else came along with their own syringe of cocaine or found the one you'd taped to the shelf in the wine store and managed to inject Dietrich without anyone seeing him – or her? Who the hell could it be?'

Will pushed back a clump of hair from his eyes and looked the stupid little boy he said he wasn't. 'It would've had to be another syringe. When I arrived at the house and lots of people were busy with the preparations, I rushed to the wine cellar, tugged off the syringe I'd left and put it in my coat pocket. When I left, John Hardwick took a group of us to the station in Godalming and I dropped it in a drain in a side street. No one saw me. There, that's what really happened.'

The lawyer seemed on the brink of tears. 'I'll speak to Jacqueline,' she said. 'Let's all think about it. We'll all talk early tomorrow before ~~the trial~~ court resumes.'

In the morning, the two met again, this time with Jacqueline Guy.

The barrister said calmly and coldly, 'Will, you're going to tell it as you told it to Nikolina yesterday. After researching your dissertation when you were a student, you were angry at your father and planned to kill him. But then, seeing him in the flesh – or rather in his dressing gown at the party – you realised he was just a man. You also realised what a monstrous plan it was. What you'd be risking. You swiftly removed the weapon – the cocaine – and carried on working as a waiter.'

Will nodded.

In court, he was moved from the dock into the witness box.

Simon Guerrier-Belmont wished the jury good morning and said, 'Mr Olson, did you kill your father?'

'No, I did not—'

Simon cut Will off before he could say he'd planned to do

it. 'Is it not the case that you had found out while doing your research that Sir Dietrich was not the biological father of Tom Olson, the man you'd believed was your half-brother, because he had in fact been adopted?

'Is it not true that this news effectively plunged a dagger into your heart and led you in a jealous fury to plunge a syringe with a lethal amount of cocaine into Sir Dietrich at the party in Batts Farm?'

Will kept calm. 'Yes, it is true that I was upset and angry when I made this discovery. Tom wasn't his real son, yet he was the apple of Dietrich's eye while I was the opposite, a dirty little secret!

'I wanted to kill my father – I planned to do so over a period of months. Everything was ready. But then I changed my mind. Thank goodness!'

Simon and Scott were floored.

Rob Howarth was stunned. His mind was racing. This isn't just a bit of bother, he thought, we're in the shit. Christ! if *he* didn't do it, who the hell did? What did we miss?

Scott whispered to his boss, 'What happened to his syringe in the wine cellar? Is he saying someone else conveniently came along and used it? The only other person who could have known about it was the person who supplied the stuff. We don't know who that was. Was it Kevin, the burglar who grabbed the watch?'

'Worth getting him into court to grill him on that,' grunted Simon. Then he turned back to the defendant.

'Mr Olson,' he began. 'Your fingerprints were found on masking tape on a shelf in the wine cellar, tape that had almost certainly been used on a syringe filled with cocaine ready for you to grab and use to murder Sir Dietrich. Are you seriously telling this court that while you put it there, someone else came along, knew where to look and did the job for you?'

'I'm saying someone else did it – for *their own* reasons. Not for me! I don't know who it was.

'When I arrived at the house, I went down to the wine cellar and removed the syringe. I put it in my pocket and got rid of it later.'

Simon let the preposterous answer hang in the air.

'Where did you get the cocaine?'

'It's not hard to get drugs if you live in London. Surely you know that? If you must know, I got the cocaine from a person I'd met years earlier. When I was a student.'

It had suddenly occurred to Will that Vincent Billen had access to Batts Farm in the days before the party. But why cast suspicion on the old bloke? It wasn't as if he was flogging stuff to kids to supplement his pension!

'Tell us more about why you hated your father.'

'I've told you. His refusal to acknowledge me. It was making me depressed.'

'I see. In all the years between your learning about his relationship to you – I believe you were about six when your mother told you – and your father's death, did you not consider confronting him to explain how his behaviour was affecting you?'

'No. Unthinkable.'

'We know that your father always provided generously for you and your mother, provided a comfortable home – this is a photograph of it.' He gave the usher a picture of the handsome Edwardian house, with its front garden edged in trimmed box hedges, to pass to the witness box, and produced a copy for the jurors. Will looked at it and nodded. The jurors seemed impressed.

Simon continued. 'He also paid your fees at a top private school, covered the cost of skiing and other holidays and provided an allowance of about fifty thousand a year for you alone – an allowance you are still receiving. You are also entitled to a half share of the proceeds of a life insurance policy worth one point five million. Is that not correct?'

'That's correct.'

'So, he *was* acknowledging your existence by his actions,' Simon said, still gently.

'Money didn't matter to him. He had loads of it.' Will's composure was crumbling. 'Don't you see that?'

'Why did you decide to kill him after so long?'

Will took a couple of deep breaths, but he couldn't stop himself. 'Dietrich spent his married life to Penny Bryant doting on an adopted son while refusing to acknowledge my existence. I did everything at school to make him proud, but when it came to it, he must have considered himself little more than a sperm donor.

'Yet Dietrich and my mother had been in love, had married for love and conceived a child for love. Then the bastard dropped us like old clothes.'

Simon waited until Will appeared to be breathing normally. 'You're a grown man, Mr Olson. Is your reaction not a little childish?'

'No.'

'You say that your depressive state made you lethargic and often unable to leave your bed.'

'Yes.'

'Yet you devised this intricate plan to pose as a window cleaner, to familiarise yourself with the layout of Batts Farm, to hide a syringe full of a massively strong solution of cocaine, which you could retrieve at the party and use as the murder weapon. You also had the strength to manoeuvre a large fridge out of Batts Farm's kitchen to the road, to help the housekeeper. Then you were smart enough to get signed up as a waiter for the occasion there. All at a time when you now say you were lethargic and depressed.'

Will stared straight ahead, breathing fast.

Simon looked at him, then at the jurors. He could see the bafflement on their faces. 'You're lying about your depression, aren't you?'

Will shook his head. 'No.'

'Your responsibility for committing this murder is not diminished by a fit of pique that Tom Olson may have got more attention than you. Not diminished at all. Isn't *that* right?'

Will shook his head. 'But in the end, I did *not* do it!' He was shouting now, ignoring everything Nikolina had told him. 'I was going to, but I changed my mind. I realised what the consequence would be if I were to be caught. Also, there was the sight of my father in a dressing down and slippers – he looked pathetic, like a silly old man.'

He could no longer care if the jurors liked him. He hated them, hated everything about this trial.

Simon was on his feet, frowning. He retrieved his gown just before it fell down his right arm and shot Scott Davis a worried look.

In her closing speech, Jacqueline Guy reminded the jury that Will had pleaded not guilty and then explained in detail how he had planned the murder but later changed his mind.

It was irrelevant to him, in an emotional sense, she said, that this father had supported him financially throughout his life, paid for everything he needed at school and university and was now, effectively, paying his legal costs. Her fees.

Then she reminded them that there was no evidence, forensic or otherwise, that the defendant was the person who injected the victim.

'It was not up to the defendant to provide the police with the name of the real killer. They must do their job – properly this time!'

35

THE JURY TOOK two days to come to a ten-to-two majority decision that Charles William Olson had in fact jabbed his father with enough cocaine to kill him instantly. The 'change of mind' argument hadn't washed with them.

Simon and Scott were surprised and relieved.

At the 'post-mortem' back in Simon's office, Rob said, 'I think it shows that the jury were disappointed in Dietrich Olson. They'd thought he was a good bloke, not a bigamist, not a bloke who shafted his old friend, built flats on the cheap, flats that weren't safe, and threw the tenants of some of his other flats out on the street. Everyone thought he was Mr Nice Guy, a bloke only a nutter would want to kill. Will was that nutter.'

Scott nodded. 'It struck me that Olson must have been heartlessly cold. No normal father would have failed to be curious about their son. But he was ambitious; he simply couldn't risk the public knowing he'd been two women's husband at the same time.'

'Hmmm,' said Simon. 'I've a feeling that bigamy is far more common than we realise.'

Rob wondered if that were true. Surely few men had the energy for more than one marriage at a time, he thought.

A week later, His Honour Sir Marcus Greene handed down a sentence of fifteen years imprisonment for the murder of Sir Dietrich Olson. Will would probably serve ten before being released on licence.

Jane had been in court. She knew she should have been relieved by what was a relatively short term of imprisonment, yet she remained in the same state of shock that had hit her when Will had been arrested. She felt responsible, as though she ought to have predicted all those years ago that Dietrich would abandon them. Was it her fault that her son never met his father during his childhood and adolescence? Probably, yes. Things could have been different. Yet there was never the right time.

Now the two of them just had to get through this ordeal, she thought. She must visit him as often as possible, take him newspapers and books, encourage him to write about his experiences in prison.

She wondered if she should encourage his lawyers to push for an appeal or a parole hearing and the earliest release. But she knew there was no new evidence to present.

* * *

Over those years of his incarceration, Will's biography of his father remained a bestseller and was republished several times.

In his cell at Wormwood Scrubs, he was working on a

sequel, a novel about a race to kill a seemingly decent man. It wasn't easy, he was discovering.

Pen had also been at the Old Bailey, sometimes accompanied by Bella, who was starting her training contract in the litigation department of a large city firm.

Pen watched and admired the barrister's skills. Perhaps it was time, she thought, about combining practice with teaching. She might even study for 'higher rights' to become a solicitor advocate and argue for her clients in front of judges in family court. Secretly, she hoped Bella would one day decide to work with her now that Ed George was leading a separate life in Manchester as an aerospace engineer and seemed to be permanently out of hers.

Sometimes, Tom came to court when he felt he could skip lectures for a few hours. These days, Danielle photocopied her notes and made sure he slotted them in the right file. She had slotted into his life with ease, to his delight, and that of his mother~~'s~~ and sister~~'s~~.

Was Pen relieved that the riddle of Dietrich's death had been solved? No. But she couldn't explain why that was.

A few years later, when a new branch of Frank's Kitchen Appliances opened in the King's Road, Chelsea, and Michael Wilson-Green's despised boss was promoted to run it, he became the manager of the Fulham branch. It meant a higher salary, fewer hours and a secretary of his choosing, someone quite unlike Beverley. Michael could afford to buy himself a few new shirts to replace those with the fraying cuffs.

He still paused now and then on Putney Bridge to look at the river and reflect on how his old, good life had been washed away. At least his skies were brightening. He paid an odd job man he knew from work to redecorate his flat. He ordered new curtains and blinds from John Lewis. His sons began to ring him, visit him, introduce him to their girlfriends and discuss his new ideas for business ventures. Occasionally he'd telephone Pen and very occasionally she'd agree to go to the cinema with him.

Steve James and journalist Jerry Thorne eventually succeeded in pushing the directors of Premium Properties Six to install fire safety precautions at South Quay and Steve kept a beady eye on his father's mental state. He was reunited with his former girlfriend, Sally, and they began searching for their own flat.

Thanks to the closure of the Olson murder case, and its heavy coverage in the newspapers, Rob Howarth was promoted to Detective Chief Inspector. The increased salary that came with it helped him afford a second-hand Alfa Romeo. Two years into Will's sentence, Rob's wife underwent another round of IVF and a healthy second son was the result the following year.

Batts Farm was sold in the week it went on the market for the asking price. The furniture, including the huge bed, went to auction. Pen arranged for Mrs Gibbs to become the legal owner of her bungalow, which Jeff O'Byrne refurbished.

The Olson children remained frequent visitors to Colt Court, which Pen modernised and refurnished without dithering or arguments from a spouse. No photographs of the former MP remained on the shelves. Several of his pictures, along with his books, were packed off to Oxfam.

Bella and Tom met and liked Nathan Harris from the first time they met him when he stayed overnight in Colt Court.

The irony had been slow to hit Pen: Dietrich's admirable qualities and achievements celebrated in speeches at the memorial service and in the obituaries were not just false, they were irrelevant. No one had properly known him, known that he wasn't the nicest man you could ever meet. He wasn't parliament's answer to Michael Palin. That was just a part he *played*. They hadn't been paying attention.

Pen had thought she knew her husband, but he wasn't her husband and everything she thought she knew about him was wrong.

* * *

Ten years later, the burglaries started again. That's if they'd ever stopped. Most victims thought it hardly worth reporting break-ins to the overworked police. But the numbers were on the up and Izzy wondered if a chat with her favourite watch-snatcher Kevin Miller was worth the effort of tracking him down.

Not much effort, it turned out. His old boss at the wood mill had given him back his job when he got out of jail.

Oddly, she thought, he seemed pleased to see her walking up the path to the wood store. He lowered his face mask and pulled off his protective glasses and ear defenders.

'Well, well! Busy Izzy! Detective Sergeant Holland! Come to order a dining table and chairs, have we?'

'Come to ask your advice, actually,' she replied with a smile. 'Won't take long, fifteen minutes, tops.'

They sat at a dusty table and Kevin swigged water from a plastic bottle. She asked if he'd heard anything about a spate of burglaries in the Guildford area by someone who seemed to be copying his old techniques.

'Nope, sorry. Can't help yer. Cost of living's so high now, more people are nicking stuff, I 'spect.'

'Amateurs would be taking wallets, not just lifting a few tens and twenties out of them like you used to do,' Izzy said.

'Well, it ain't me. Ask my probation officer and my girlfriend.'

Izzy was intrigued. '*Girlfriend*, eh? Well done *you*.' She was genuinely pleased for him. 'Well, keep your ears open. You know where to find me,' she added as she got up and left.

Back in her car, she checked for missed messages on her phone. Then suddenly Kevin was knocking on the driver's window.

'If you're interested, I've an idea who done it.'

'Done what?'

'Jabbed Dietrich what's his name in Godalming. At that party where I got his watch.'

Izzy wondered if she were being played. Might he not have read in the papers back then that a jury had found Will Page guilty? Then she remembered that his reading level had, at some time or other, been assessed by an expert as that of an eight-year-old.

'Yes?'

'This bloke. Big, old, dark hair. Quite a few men like that there, I get that. But I think he was the husband of the woman with the big knockers.'

'Kevin, this event was nearly ten years ago. You were there. I wasn't. What did you see?'

'I saw him standing in the garden. Someone had opened the big windows for fresh air or somefin' and he was just, like, there, looking a bit rough. It was just after 'er ladyship tried to make a speech, and all the guests were looking the other way.

'A few little kids had followed him and were running around getting muddy and their parents were rushing out to grab them back.

'So, I went through the kitchen door into the garden. Thought the bloke was ill or somefin'.

'"Alright mate?" I asked. He didn't answer so I went back into the kitchen where they were packing up all the hired stuff and helped myself to some leftovers. But when I looked back in the garden half an hour later, the bloke was still out there, wiping his eyes with a handkerchief and pushing about the earth under a bush with his foot. I didn't realise what he was doing at first, but I think he was trying to bury something.

'Later, when it came out that the MP had been injected with a massive amount of blow, it dawned on me. This bloke could have dropped the dog end of his fag. But why try to bury it? Then something else dawned on me.'

He paused, lifted his head and gave Izzy a knowing look. 'He was burying a big needle.'

Izzy gulped, confused. 'You obviously didn't hear that someone got fifteen years for Dietrich Olson's murder,' she said. 'But give me your phone number, Kevin. I'll pass on what you've told me. Any idea what the man's name is?'

'Don. Someone called out to him when he was in the garden. Don't know his last name.'

Izzy started the engine. 'Thanks. Keep an ear out for any news about the break-ins for me.'

She rang Holborn CID. Finally, Rob came to the phone, and she had his attention.

'Mind if I come up to see you? Kevin Miller, my favourite burglar, has told me something new about the Dietrich Olson murder. It's about a guest called Don something. You need to hear it, even if it's a load of old cobblers.'

Rob sighed. He thought they'd finished with bloody

Olson an age ago. But he also knew better than to shut his ears to inconvenient theories.

Izzy came early and repeated Kevin's account.

Mehmet cursed under his breath. He too had thought the Olson file was closed. He had an interesting GBH case on his desk. Nevertheless, he busied himself going through the papers on the Batts Farm partygoers looking for this Don person. He soon found the name of Don Peters, the husband of the victim's secretary. He asked a uniform to track the man's current whereabouts. Getting a warrant to search the flowerbeds of Batts Farm took a bit of arguing with Scott at the CPS. Finally, it came through. Izzy spoke to Kevin, who readily agreed to go there in a few days to point out where he thought a needle, syringe, dog end – or whatever it was – had been thrown.

At the Holborn Central constituency offices the following day, Karen Peters told Izzy about her separation from Don and his belief that she and her former boss Dietrich Olson had been lovers. She also passed on the addresses of Don's motor insurance office and the flat where he was living at the time of the divorce. When she found her, Karen was, of course, curious about the reason for Izzy's interest.

'How would you describe Don's temperament?' Izzy asked.

'Well, until he got the idea that I was having a passionate fling with Dietrich, I'd have said he was a mild man. Pretty boring, really.'

'And after that?'

'He went off on one almost every day. He used to sneer about how everyone thought Dietrich was so clever, so generous to these charities, such a nice guy and a good MP.

He said he'd like to give him a good hiding. I'd never seen him so angry.'

'Off the record, were you and Dietrich... you know, having sex?'

Karen blushed and studied her hands.

Izzy took that as a yes.

* * *

A team of forensic experts from Guildford spent two days the following week searching for a discarded syringe in the earth around the flowerbeds near the French windows of Batts Farm. The current owners asked that the men and women in white paper suits avoid the interior of the house as much as possible and restore the flowerbeds after any digging.

Mrs Gibbs made herself available to guide, advise and distribute mugs of tea.

On the third day of the search, several metal objects, including large screws, half a door bracket and a syringe were unearthed from the roots of an overgrown rhododendron bush twenty yards from the main reception room of the house. In the laboratory it was decided that garden soil was too porous for any fingerprints on the syringe to have survived, even if the user hadn't wiped it before discarding it.

Rob was flabbergasted when Simon Guerrier-Belmont agreed there were grounds for charging Don Peters with the murder of Dietrich Olson.

When questioned, Don said he believed his wife had been in a sexual relationship with Dietrich for many years and that his marriage had broken down because of it. He loved and had been proud of Karen and felt belittled by the

MP. The man's knighthood had made him even more jealous and angry.

'She thought the sun shone out of his arse!' Don spat out the words bitterly.

To Rob's further surprise, at the trial, Don pleaded guilty to poisoning Dietrich Olson with a large syringe of insulin stolen from his mother, who suffered with Type 1 diabetes. He'd done the research and learned that insulin is absorbed by the body and wouldn't have been detectable in an autopsy after a couple of days. It explained why no insulin was detected in the autopsy while the cocaine was.

He told the court he hadn't known that someone else had injected him with another poison at the party.

'That rotten bastard had loads of enemies,' he said lamely.

His defence said he was guilty of attempted murder and used the controversial partial defence of loss of control. It was triggered, the young and nervous barrister claimed, by anger at Dietrich's secret affair with his wife and exacerbated by the news of Dietrich's knighthood.

Simon did his best to shoot the argument down, claiming that anger at his wife's adultery could not be accepted as a genuine trigger for a 'loss of control' killing.

He reminded the jury that Don had gone to Batts Farm intending to poison the victim. He'd been prepared for it, with a syringe of stolen insulin in his pocket. He had planned the crime and had gone to the party ready to carry it out.

Don's defence lawyer argued strenuously and sarcastically that Will Page had already served nearly ten years in prison for the same crime and was due to serve a further five. He told the jury that his client was a sad and simple man, guilty only of loving his wife too much.

'Dietrich Olson did not die twice,' he sneered.

The jury nevertheless decided that insulin, rather than cocaine killed the MP and found Don guilty of murder.

* * *

Will, still in Wormwood Scrubs and counting the days until he could apply for parole, was totally confused when he was told by a senior warder that he was to be released then and there. He thought it must be a joke.

Yet Nikolina met him at the prison rear gates, gave him a summary of Don Peters' trial and drove him to Jane's house in Raynes Park.

'Will, you are not only a free man, but your conviction may well be expunged altogether. Sir Marcus Greene, the judge at your trial is re-considering all the evidence,' she explained. 'If he decides to set aside your conviction, you will be entitled to compensation from the government. What you get is at the compensation panel's discretion, but judging by other similar cases, you can expect a six-figure sum.

'Do you want me to apply on your behalf and push for the maximum?'

Will said he had to think it over and would contact her for a meeting in a week or so.

He didn't really care about the money. A nice big pile of it was gathering interest in the bank and there was no threat to Dietrich's monthly payments.

First a long bath, then a thick steak. A clean one.

Tomorrow, he'd start to draft the plot of his next book, a crime thriller. The title would be *A Race to Murder*.

ABOUT THE AUTHOR

Hilary Kingsley was a national newspaper television critic and features writer before switching to the law. She trained as a solicitor and worked for 10 years in the legal department of Associated Newspapers. She's written more than a dozen non-fiction books but her experience as a magistrate stoked her interest in crime and the ordinariness of most criminals. An avid reader, she searched for a contemporary thriller in which the characters were successful yet sympathetic and the plot is not relentlessly grim. Not finding one, she decided to write her debut novel, The Wrong Husband.

Central to the story are three coppers – quiet, Cambridge-educated DI Rob Howarth, football fan DS Mehmet Karim and diminutive DS Izzy Holland. They're the 'Three Musketeers' of Holborn nick. Look out for them in Hilary's next books.